THE CHAPERONE

Comment — Excellent!

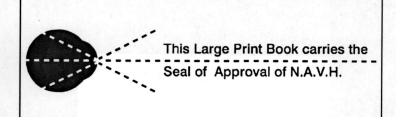

This Large Print Book carries the
Seal of Approval of N.A.V.H.

THE CHAPERONE

LAURA MORIARTY

LARGE PRINT PRESS
A part of Gale, Cengage Learning

GALE
CENGAGE Learning

Detroit • New York • San Francisco • New Haven, Conn • Waterville, Maine • London

GALE
CENGAGE Learning®

Copyright © 2012 by Laura Moriarty.
Large Print Press, a part of Gale, Cengage Learning.

ALL RIGHTS RESERVED
This is a work of fiction.
While the author has made every effort to provide accurate telephone numbers and Internet addresses at the time of publication, neither the publisher nor the author assumes any responsibility for errors, or for changes that occur after publication. Further, the publisher does not have any control over and does not assume any responsibility for author or third-party websites or their content.
The text of this Large Print edition is unabridged.
Other aspects of the book may vary from the original edition.
Set in 16 pt. Plantin.

LIBRARY OF CONGRESS CATALOGING-IN-PUBLICATION DATA

Moriarty, Laura, 1970–
   The chaperone / by Laura Moriarty.
     pages ; cm. — (Thorndike Press large print core)
     ISBN 978-1-4104-4848-4 (hardcover) — ISBN 1-4104-4848-7 (hardcover)
     1. Brooks, Louise, 1906– —Fiction. 2. Motion picture actors and
actresses—Fiction. 3. Middle-aged women—Fiction. 4. New York
(N.Y.)—History—1898–1951—Fiction. 5. New York (N.Y.)—Social life and
customs—Fiction. 6. Large type books. I. Title.
   PS3613.O75C47 2012b
   813'.6—dc23   2012010510

ISBN 13: 978-1-59413-642-9 (pbk. : alk. paper)
ISBN 10: 1-59413-642-4 (pbk. : alk. paper)

Published in 2013 by arrangement with Riverhead Books, a member of Penguin Group (USA), Inc.

LT

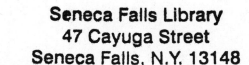
Printed in the United States of America
2 3 4 5 6   17 16 15 14 13

THE CHAPERONE

■ ■ ■ ■

Part One

■ ■ ■ ■

When lovely woman stoops to folly, she can always find someone to stoop with her but not always someone to lift her up again to the level where she belongs.

> — "MR. GRUNDY" FOR
> *Atlantic Monthly,* 1920

It excited him, too, that many men had already loved Daisy — it increased her value in his eyes.

> — F. SCOTT FITZGERALD,
> *The Great Gatsby,* 1925

There is no Garbo! There is no Dietrich! There is only Louise Brooks!

— HENRI LANGLOIS, 1955

ONE

The first time Cora heard the name Louise Brooks, she was parked outside the Wichita Library in a Model-T Ford, waiting for the rain to stop. If Cora had been alone, unencumbered, she might have made a dash across the lawn and up the library's stone steps, but she and her friend Viola Hammond had spent the morning going door-to-door in their neighborhood, collecting books for the new children's room, and the considerable fruits of their efforts were safe and dry in four crates in the backseat. The storm, they decided, would be a short one, and they couldn't risk the books getting wet.

And really, Cora thought, staring out into the rain, it wasn't as if she had anything else to do. Her boys were already gone for the summer, both of them working on a farm outside Winfield. In the fall, they would leave for college. Cora was still getting used to the quiet, and also the freedom, of this new era of her life. Now, long after Della left for the day, the house stayed clean, with no muddy footprints on the floor, and no records scattered around the phonograph. There were no squabbles over the car to mediate, no tennis matches at the club to cheer on, and no assigned essays to proofread and commend. The pantry and icebox actually stayed stocked with food without daily trips to the store. Today, with Alan at work, she had no reason to rush home at all.

"I'm glad we took your car and not ours," Viola said, adjusting her hat, which was pretty, a puffed turban with an ostrich feather curling down from the crown. "People say closed cars are a luxury, but not on a day like this."

Cora gave her what she hoped was a modest smile. Not only was the car covered, it had come with an electric starter. *Cranking cars, no business for a lady,* was how the ad went, though Alan had admitted he didn't miss cranking, either.

Viola turned, eyeing the books in the backseat. "People were generous," she allowed. Viola was a decade older than Cora, her hair already gray at the temples, and she spoke with the authority of her added years. "Mostly. You notice Myra Brooks didn't even open her door."

Cora hadn't noticed. She'd been working the other side of the street. "Maybe she wasn't home."

"I heard the piano." Viola's eyes slid toward Cora. "She didn't bother to stop playing when I knocked. I have to say, she's very good."

Lightning shot across the western sky, and though both women flinched, Cora, without thinking, smiled. She'd always loved these late-spring storms. They came on so fast, rolling in from the prairie on expanding columns of clouds, a welcome release from the day's building heat. An hour before, when Cora and Viola were canvassing, the sun was hot in a blue sky. Now rain fell fast enough to slice green leaves from the big oak outside the library. The lilacs trembled and tossed.

"Don't you think she's a tiresome snob?"

Cora hesitated. She didn't like to gossip, but she could hardly count Myra Brooks as a friend. And they'd been to how many suffrage meetings together? Had marched together in the street? Yet if she passed Myra today on Douglas Avenue, Cora wouldn't get so much as a hello. Still, she never got the feeling that it was snobbery as much as Myra simply not registering her existence, and there was a chance it was nothing personal. Myra Brooks didn't seem to look at anyone, Cora had noticed, not unless she was the one speaking, watching for the impression she made. And yet, of course, everyone looked at her. She was, perhaps, the most beautiful woman Cora had ever seen in person: she had pale skin, flawless, and large, dark eyes, and then all that thick, dark hair. She was certainly a talented speaker — her voice was never shrill, and her enunciations were clear. But everyone knew it was Myra's looks that had made her a particularly good spokeswoman for the Movement, a nice antidote to the newspapers' idea of what a suffragist looked like. And you could tell she was intelligent, cultured. She was supposed to know everything about music, the works of all the famous composers. She certainly knew how to charm. Once, when she was at the podium, she had looked down at Cora, right into her eyes, and smiled as if they were friends.

"I don't really know her," Cora said. She looked back out through the blurred windshield, at people ducking out from a streetcar, running for cover. Alan had taken a streetcar to work, so she could have the Ford.

"Then I'll inform you. Myra Brooks is a tiresome snob." Viola turned to Cora with a little smile, the ostrich plume grazing her chin. "I'll give you the latest example: she just sent a note to the secretary of our club. Apparently, Madame Brooks is looking for someone to accompany one of her daughters to New York this summer. The older one, Louise, got into some prestigious dance school there, but she's only fifteen. Myra actually wants one of *us* to go with her. For over a month!" Viola seemed pleasantly outraged, her cheeks rosy, her eyes bright. "I mean, really! I don't know what she's thinking. That we're the help? That one of us will be her Irish nanny?" She frowned and shook her head. "Most of us have progressive husbands, but I can't imagine any one of them would spare a wife for over a month so she could go to New York City, of all places. Myra herself is too busy to go. She has to lie around the house and play the piano."

Cora pursed her lips. *New York.* She felt the old ache right away. "Well. I suppose she has other children to look after."

"Oh, she does, but that's not it. She doesn't take care of them. They're mother-less, those children. Poor Louise goes to Sunday school by herself. The instructor is

13

Edward Vincent, and he picks her up and takes her home every Sunday. I heard that right from his wife. Myra and Leonard are alleged Presbyterians, but you never see them at church, do you? They're too sophisticated, you see. They don't make the other children go, either."

"That speaks well of the daughter, that she makes the effort to go on her own." Cora cocked her head. "I wonder if I've ever seen her."

"Louise? Oh, you would remember. She doesn't look like anyone else. Her hair is black like Myra's, but perfectly straight like an Oriental's, and she wears it in a Buster Brown." Viola gestured just below her ears. "She didn't bob it. She had it cut like that when they moved here years ago. It's too short and severe, a horrible look, in my opinion, not feminine at all. But even so, I have to say, she's a very pretty girl. Prettier than her mother." She smiled, leaning back in her seat. "There's some justice in that, I think."

Cora tried to picture this black-haired girl, more beautiful than her beautiful mother. Her gloved hand moved to the back of her own hair, which was dark, but not remarkably so. It certainly wasn't perfectly straight, though it looked presentable, she hoped,

14

pinned up under her straw hat. Cora had been told she had a kind, pleasant face, and that she was lucky to have good teeth. But that had never added up to striking beauty. And now she was thirty-six.

"My own girls are threatening to cut their hair," Viola said with a sigh. "Foolish. This bobbing business is just a craze. When it's over, everyone who followed the lemmings over the cliff will need years to grow their hair out. A lot of people won't hire girls with bobbed hair. I try to warn them, but they won't listen. They just laugh at me. And they have their own language, their own secret code for them and their friends. Do you know what Ethel called me the other day? She called me a *wurp.* That's not a real word. But when I tell them that, they laugh."

"They're just trying to rattle you," Cora said with a smile. "And I'm sure they won't really bob their hair." Really, it seemed unlikely. The magazines were full of short-haired girls, but in Wichita, bobs were still a rarity. "I do think it looks good on some girls," Cora said shyly. "Short hair, I mean. And it must feel cooler, and lighter. Just think — you could throw all your hairpins away."

Viola looked at her, eyebrows raised.

"Don't worry. I won't do it." Cora again

15

touched the back of her neck. "I might if I were younger."

The rain was coming down faster, rapping hard on the roof of the car.

Viola crossed her arms. "Well, if my girls do cut their hair, I can tell you now, it won't be so they can throw away hairpins. They'll do it to be provocative. To *look* provocative. That's what passes for fashion these days. That's what young people are all about now." She sounded suddenly stricken, more confused than indignant. "I don't understand it, Cora. I raised them to have propriety. But both of them are suddenly obsessed with showing the world their knees. They roll their skirts up after they leave the house. I can tell by the waistbands. I know they defy me. They roll their stockings down, too." She gazed out into the rain, lines branching beneath her eyes. "What I don't know is why, what's going on in their little heads, why they don't care about the message they're sending. When I was young, I never felt the need to show the general public my knees." She shook her head. "Those two cause me more grief than all four of my boys. I envy you, Cora. You're lucky to only have sons."

Maybe, Cora thought. She did love the very maleness of the twins, their robust health and confidence, their practical taste in clothing, their easy reconciliations after heated quarrels. Earle was smaller and quieter than Howard, but even he seemed capable of forgetting all worries when he held a racquet or a bat. She loved that they had both wanted to work on a farm, seeing it as an adventure in country living and physical labor, though she also worried they had no idea how much labor they'd signed on for. And she knew she *had* been lucky with her sons, and not just in the way that Viola meant. The Hendersons next door had a son just four years older than the twins, but those few years had made all the difference — Stuart Henderson had been killed in early 1918, fighting in France. Four years later, Cora was still stunned. For her, Stuart Henderson would always be a gangly adolescent, smiling and waving from his bike at her own boys, who were small then, still in short pants. Really, being lucky with sons seemed a matter of timing.

But whatever Viola said, Cora thought she might have fared just as well with daughters. She would have been good with girls, perhaps, using the right combination of instruction and understanding. Maybe Viola was just going about it the wrong way.

"I'm telling you, Cora. Something is

wrong with this new generation. They don't care about anything important. When we were young, we wanted the vote. We wanted social reform. Girls today just want to . . . walk around practically naked so they can be stared at. It's as if they have no other calling."

Cora could hardly disagree. It really was shocking, how much skin girls were showing these days. And she wasn't some old prude or Mrs. Grundy; she was fairly sure she wasn't a *wurp*, though she didn't know what that meant, either. Cora had been pleased when the hemlines moved up to nine inches from the ankle. Some leg showed, true, but that change seemed sensible: no more skirts trailing in the mud and bringing typhoid or who knows what into the house. And calf length was far preferable to the ridiculous hobble skirts that she herself had stumbled around in, all for the sake of fashion, not so long ago. Still, girls were now sporting skirts so short that their knees showed every time the wind blew, and there was no practical reason for that. Viola was right: a girl who wore a skirt that short just wanted to be looked at, and looked at *in that way.* Cora had even seen a few women her own age showing their knees, right here in Wichita, and really, in her opinion, these half-naked matrons looked especially vulgar.

Viola looked at her brightly. "That's one of the reasons I'm joining the Klan."

Cora turned. "What?"

"The Klan. Ku Klux. They sent a representative to the club last week. I wish you would have been there, Cora. They're very interested in women joining up, holding positions."

"I'm sure they are," Cora murmured. "We vote."

"Don't be a cynic. They were much more specific than that. They know that there are serious women's issues at hand, and that women need to be in the fight." The ostrich feather bobbed as she spoke. "They're against all this modernization, all these outside influences on our youth. They're interested in racial purity, of course, but they're just as interested in teaching personal purity for young women. We do need to keep our race pure, and Good Lord, we need to keep it going. My brother-in-law says a veritable takeover is coming, and it's all being planned in the basement of the Vatican. That's the real reason Catholics have so many children, you know, and meanwhile, our people have one or two or none at . . ."

Viola trailed off. She rolled her lips in. It took Cora a moment to understand.

"I'm sorry," Viola said. "I didn't mean you. Your situation is different."

Cora waved her off. The twins were what she had. But both she and Viola were silent for a while, and there was only the tapping rain.

"In any case," Viola said finally, "I think it would be good for the girls. Good, moral people to mix with."

Cora swallowed, feeling short of breath. She had been wearing a corset day in, day out, for so many years that she rarely registered it as a discomfort. It seemed a part of her body. But in moments of distress, such as now, she was aware of her constricted rib cage. She would have to choose her words carefully. She could not come across as personally concerned.

"I don't know," she said, her voice breezy, not betraying her in any way. "Oh, Viola. The Klan? They wear those white gowns, those hoods with the spooky eyeholes." She fluttered her gloved hands. "And they have wizards and grand wizards, and bonfires." Even as she smiled, she glanced into Viola's small blue eyes, analyzing what she saw there. She had to consider her options, her best route to success. Viola was older, but

Cora was richer. She would capitalize on that.

"It just seems a little . . . common." She shrugged, apologetic.

Viola cocked her head. "But lots of people are —"

"Exactly." Cora smiled again. She had chosen the right word, precisely. It was as if they were shopping at the Innes Department Store together, and Cora had shown disdain for an ugly china pattern. She already knew, with certainty, Viola would reconsider.

When the rain let up, they slid out and carried the crates in, sidestepping puddles, each woman making two trips. Inside, waiting for the librarian, they chatted about other things. They flipped through a pristine copy of *Alice's Adventures in Wonderland,* and smiled at the illustrations. They stopped at the Lassen Hotel for tea, and then Cora drove Viola home.

So many years later, this easy ride home with Viola would be the part of the story where Cora, in the telling, would momentarily lose the regard of a grandniece she adored. This grandniece, who at seventeen, incidentally, wore her hair much longer than her mother preferred, would be frustrated to the point of tears that in 1961 she was not yet old enough to join the freedom riders in the South. She often admonished Cora for using the word "colored," but she generally showed her more patience than she did her own parents, understanding that her aunt Cora was not a hateful person, just an old woman with tainted language.

But that patience was tested when she heard about Viola. Cora's grandniece couldn't comprehend why her great-aunt would remain friends with a woman who even *considered* being part of the Klan. Did she not know what they did to people? Her grandniece would look at Cora with scorn, and with forsaken, teary eyes. Had she been unaware of their cowardly crimes? Their murders of innocent people?

Yes, Cora would say, but in the end, Viola never joined. Only because she was a snob, her grandniece would counter. Not because the Klan was repugnant. It was a different time, was all Cora could say, defending her old friend, who would be long since dead by then. (Cancer. She'd started smoking after her daughters picked it up.) Consider the numbers, Cora would try. That rainy day with Viola was in the summer of 1922, when the Klan was six thousand strong in the city limits — and Wichita only held maybe eighty thousand souls in total. That wasn't unusual for the time. The Klan was growing in many towns, in many states. Were people just stupider then? Meaner? Maybe, Cora allowed. But it was foolish to assume that had you lived in that time, you wouldn't be guilty of the same ignorance, unable to reason your way out. Cora herself had only escaped that particular stupidity because of her special circumstance. Other confusions had held her longer.

There's plenty of stupidity now, the grand-niece said, and I know it for what it is. True, Cora conceded, and I'm proud of you for that. But maybe there's some more, and you don't know it's there. Do you know what I'm saying? Honey? To someone who grows up by the stockyards, that smell just smells like air. You don't know what a younger person might someday think of you, and whatever stench we still breathe in without noticing. Listen to me, honey. Please. I'm old now, and this is something I've learned.

After she dropped Viola off, Cora drove back downtown and parked on Douglas, just outside Alan's office. No one looked twice at her as she climbed down from the car. Just two years earlier, one of the most discussed events of the annual Wheat Show was the Parade of Lady Drivers. Even then, the organizers had no trouble finding almost twenty women anxious to display their competence behind the wheels of various cars. Cora had driven the fifth car in the line, Alan sitting proudly beside her.

She had to push hard on the big door to his office, and when she finally managed to open it, she saw and felt why. The big window in the front room was open to the rain-cooled breeze, and a huge electric fan was pointed right at her. On her left, two girls she didn't know sat typing. Alan's secretary stood behind another desk, using both hands to turn the crank on a rotary duplicating machine. When she noticed Cora, she stopped.

"Oh, Mrs. Carlisle! It's nice to see you!"

Cora was aware of a pause in the typing, the typists looking up, taking her in. She was not surprised by their scrutiny. Her husband was a handsome man. Cora smiled at the girls. Both were young, and one was pretty. Neither posed any threat.

"Let me tell him you're here," his secretary said. She wore an ink-stained apron over her dress.

"Oh no," Cora said, glancing at her watch. "Please don't bother him. It's almost five. I'll just wait."

But the door to Alan's office opened. He stuck his head out and smiled. "Darling! I thought I heard your voice. What a lovely surprise!"

He was already walking toward her, arms outstretched, a sight to behold, really, tall and trim in his three-piece suit. He was twelve years older than Cora, but his dark brown hair was still full. She glanced at the typists just long enough to see she had their full attention, as if she were the heroine in a silent film. Alan leaned down to kiss her cheek, smelling faintly of a cigar. She thought she heard someone sigh.

"You're damp," he said, using two fingers to touch the brim of her hat. His tone was lightly scolding.

"It's just sprinkling now, but it might start up again." She spoke in a low voice. "I stopped by to see if you wanted a ride home. I didn't mean to interrupt."

It was no bother, he assured her. He introduced her to the typists, praising their skills even as he gently steered her back to his office, his hand on the back of her waist. There were some fellows he wanted her to meet, he said, some new clients from the oil and gas company. Three men stood when she entered, and she greeted them all politely, trying to memorize faces and names. They were pleased to meet her, one said: her husband had spoken so highly of her. Cora feigned surprise, her smile so practiced it seemed real.

And then it was five o'clock, time to go. Alan shook hands with the men, put on his hat, took his umbrella from the stand, and jokingly apologized for having to catch his ride home in a hurry. The men smiled at him, at her. Someone suggested a future get-together. His wife could call Cora to see what would be a good evening. "That would be lovely," she said.

When they got outside, the rain had indeed grown more serious. He offered to bring the car around to the front, but she insisted she would be fine if he shared his umbrella. They ran to the car together, huddled close, heads lowered. He held open her door and gave her his arm as she climbed up into the passenger seat, his umbrella over her head until she was safe inside.

In the car, they were still friendly, though the air between them was always different when they were alone. She told him about the library and the children's room, and he congratulated her on her good deed. She said she hadn't been home for most of the day. She would have to warm up some soup for supper, but she had been to the market, and she could make a good salad, and there was bread. A light supper would be fine with him, he said. It wasn't the same, sitting down for a big meal now that the boys were gone, and yet they better get used to it. If they had a quick meal, he added, the two of them could go to a movie later, and see whatever was playing. Cora agreed, pleased with the idea. Hers was the only husband she knew of who would go see anything with her, who had actually sat through *The Sheik* without rolling his eyes at Valentino. She was lucky in that way. She was lucky in many ways.

Still, she cleared her throat.

"Alan. Do you know Leonard Brooks?"

She waited for his nod, though she already knew the answer. Alan knew all the other lawyers in town.

"Well," she said, "his eldest daughter got into a dance school in New York. He and his wife would like a married woman to chaperone her. For the month of July, and some of August." She rubbed her lips together. "I think I'll go."

She glanced at him only briefly, seeing his surprise, before she turned back to her window. They were already close to home, moving down the tree-lined streets, past their neighbors' pretty houses and neat lawns. There was much that she would miss while she was away: club meetings and ladies' teas, the summer picnic in the Flint Hills. She would likely miss the birth of a friend's fourth child, which was unfortunate, as she was to be the child's godmother. She would miss her friends, and of course, she would miss Alan. And these familiar streets. But her world would still be here when she returned, and this was her chance to go.

Alan was silent until he pulled in front of the house. When he did speak, his voice was quiet, careful. "When did you decide this?"

"Today." She took off her glove and touched a fingertip to the glass, tracing a raindrop's path. "Don't worry. I'll come back. It's just a little adventure. It's like the twins, going to the farm. I'll be back before they leave for school."

She looked up at the house, lovely even in the rain, though far too big for them. It was a house built — and bought — for a large family, but given the way things turned out, they'd never used the third floor for anything but a playroom, and then for storage. Still, even now that the twins had moved out, neither she nor Alan wanted to sell. They both still loved the quiet neighborhood, and they loved the house, how majestic it looked from the street with its wraparound porch and pointed turret. They reasoned that it would be nice for the twins to be able to come home to a familiar place. They'd kept their rooms as the boys had left them, their beds made, their old books on the shelves, the better to lure them home for summers and holiday breaks.

"New York City?" Alan asked.

She nodded.

"Any reason in particular you want to go there?"

She turned, taking in his warm eyes, his cleft, clean-shaven chin. She had been just a girl when she first saw his face. Nineteen years they had lived together. He knew the particular reason.

"I might do some digging," she said.

"You're sure that's for the best?"

"I can speak with Della in the morning about coming in earlier, or staying later. Or both." She smiled. "If anything, you'll gain weight. She's a far better cook than I am."

"Cora." He shook his head. "You know that's not what I'm asking."

She turned away, her hand on the door. That was the end of the discussion. She'd made up her mind to go, and as they both understood very well, for them, that was all there was to it.

Two

The Brookses lived on North Topeka Street, close enough to Cora's house that the walk might have taken another woman less than a quarter of an hour. But it took Cora much longer because, as had long been her habit, every time she heard the motor of a passing car, she lifted her parasol to see if it might be anyone she knew. If a friend or a friend of Alan's was kind enough to stop to ask if she needed a ride or to comment on the lovely June morning, she was happy to stay and chat for a few minutes. She appreciated neighborliness, especially in this little city that still seemed so big to her after all these years. On this morning, however, she turned down all offers for rides, and would only say that she was on her way to meet a friend.

Still, she reached her destination on time, having left the house early to allow for diversions, and it was eleven o'clock exactly when the Brooks home came into view.

Even painted a dull gray, it was a difficult edifice to miss. On a block of large houses, it was easily the largest, all three stories stretching more than halfway to the back alley; really, it seemed overgrown, too big for its average-sized plot. All the front windows were open to the breeze, except for one with a jagged crack across the frame, perhaps too fragile to lift. The surrounding lawn was freshly mown, and several lilac bushes, still in bloom, framed the shaded limestone porch. When Cora made her way up the steps, a bumblebee circled her twice before losing interest and buzzing away.

Myra opened the door with a smile, and Cora was at once reminded of and surprised by her hostess's relative smallness. Cora was just shy of average height herself, and she wasn't used to looking down at another grown woman, but she had at least four inches on Myra. She didn't think of Myra as being short — she hardly appeared short when at a podium, and she had the low speaking voice of a taller woman. Despite her tiny frame, Cora had never heard anyone describe Myra Brooks as "cute" or "adorable" or even "pretty." She was called "beautiful" or "captivating" or "appealing." Today, even Myra's pale neck appeared long, rising up from a white silk blouse with a flat collar, and her skirt, with its nipped waist and demure hemline just above her ankles, made her body seem longer, too. One dark strand of hair, escaped from a twist in back, hung down almost to her shoulder.

"Cora. So good to see you." Her voice was soothing, melodious, and almost convincing. On the telephone, she'd pretended to know who Cora was. Now she clasped Cora's free hand and took her parasol with the other. "You walked? In this heat? That's impressive. I wilt in this sun, I swear."

"It's only a few blocks," Cora said, though her back felt damp with sweat. She fished her handkerchief out of her purse and dabbed at her forehead. Myra waited, looking, on closer inspection, a little frazzled herself. The pearl buttons of her blouse had been buttoned incorrectly, leaving an extra hole at her throat and an extra pearl at the bottom.

"Please come sit. I can get you some lemonade. Or some tea? And I apologize for the condition of the house." She shook her head, turning away. "Our girl usually comes at nine, but for some reason, no sign of her today. Of course she doesn't have a telephone." She threw her hands in the air and sighed. "Nothing to do but wait."

Cora nodded, empathetic, though she always tried to clean as best she could before Della even arrived, not wanting to leave a bad impression, to have Della go home and tell her people what a slob her white employer was. As she followed Myra into the parlor, it became clear that her hostess was not burdened by this kind of worry. The room itself was lovely, spacious and full of light, with a breeze drifting in from two large windows. But there was clutter everywhere. On the floor, in no discernible design, lay a spoon, a fountain pen, a badminton racquet, a shoe horn, and also a naked doll with one blue eye missing. Farther on, not quite under a lovely brocaded settee, a pair of soiled socks lay next to an open-faced copy of *Candide.* Cora pretended not to notice the socks, and she tried to breathe through her mouth. Despite the open windows, the distinct smell of burnt bread permeated the air.

Myra sighed. "I've been upstairs working all morning. I'm giving a talk on Wagner next week." She stooped to pick up the spoon, the doll, and the racquet. "The children are driving me crazy. They're not even supposed to be in the parlor. I'm really so embarrassed. I'll be right back. Tea? You'd like tea, you said? Or lemonade?"

Cora took a moment to answer. She had expected perfection, rooms as lovely as Myra herself. "Lemonade is fine."

Myra moved through a pocket door, pulling it closed behind her. Cora stood where she was, wondering if she should kick the dirty socks under the settee. After a moment of hesitation, she did, and then, pleased with the result, surveyed the room again. Books, she noticed, were everywhere. *Latin Made Simple* rested on the window seat, a frayed green ribbon of a bookmark fluttering in the breeze. A small stack of books sat on the center table. She took a step closer, peering at the titles. *The Poems of Goethe. An Artist in Corfu. The Adventures of Sherlock Holmes. The Origin of Species.* Under an upholstered chair, like a waiting footrest, crouched *The Collected Works of Shakespeare.*

Quick feet descended a creaking staircase, and a moment later, a curly-haired child of maybe seven wandered in from the hallway, using a spoon to eat what appeared to be chocolate icing out of a teacup. The chocolate was smeared against her pale cheeks, the front of her shirt, and the tip of her nose. She startled when she noticed Cora.

"Hello," Cora said in her gentlest voice. "I'm Mrs. Carlisle. I'm a friend of your mother. I'm just here waiting for her."

The girl swallowed another spoonful of chocolate. "Where is she?"

Cora nodded at the closed pocket door. "In there, I think."

The door slid open. Myra glided back into the parlor, a glass of lemonade in each hand. Her smile faded when she saw the girl.

"Darling, what are you eating?" Her voice remained low and soft, though she handed Cora both of the lemonades so she could take the teacup and spoon from the girl. She looked into the cup and scowled. "June. This is not an acceptable lunch. I don't think I need to tell you that. Go to the bathroom and wash your face, and then go find Theo."

"He's playing badminton with himself," said the girl. "He said he didn't want a partner."

"Nonsense. I just found the other racquet where he was not supposed to leave it, and now it's by the back door. After you wash up, go get it, and then go outside and find Theo. Mother has company. That will be all."

With that, Myra turned to Cora, her smile restored, and took back one of the lemonades. Her blouse, Cora noticed, was now buttoned correctly. "Please," she said, gesturing to the upholstered chair.

"I'm so impressed with all these books," Cora said. As she sat, she was careful not to kick the Shakespeare beneath her chair.

"Oh." Myra rolled her eyes. "The children leave those lying about. They can't keep them in the library because of Leonard's law books. That side of the house is actually sinking because he keeps so many, and they're heavy." She saw Cora's smile and shook her head. "No. Really. The foundation has slipped fourteen inches. That's why the windows are cracking. And he won't get rid of one book."

Cora tried to think of some mild complaint she could make about Alan, just to show understanding. But she couldn't think of anything comparable. Alan, too, had many law books, but if the foundation started slipping under their weight, she was sure he would part with a few.

They looked at each other. It seemed to Cora that Myra should start.

"Beautiful girl," Cora said, nodding to the pocket door through which June had disappeared.

"Thank you. Wait till you see Louise."

Cora stared.

Myra took in her expression and shrugged.

"You haven't yet, I take it. I'm sorry. I'm just being frank. I feel I must be, given the nature of the . . . mission for which you've volunteered." She looked at Cora skeptically. "You should know that you'll be chaperoning a girl who is not only exceptionally pretty, but also very willful."

Cora was again taken aback. Apparently, no conversation was necessary: Myra had already decided that Cora was a suitable chaperone. Cora had expected eventual approval and even gratitude, but she had also expected that Myra would ask a few questions first, some pretense of an interview.

"I've heard she's quite pretty," Cora said.

"What else have you heard?"

Cora straightened.

"Oh! I don't mean anything horrendous!" Myra leaned forward and gave Cora's arm a reassuring pat. She had big hands for such a small woman, her fingers narrow and long. "I didn't mean to alarm you. I only . . . I imagine you have many friends in town." She leaned back, crossing her ankles. "I wondered if you'd spoken with, for example, Alice Campbell?"

Cora shook her head. The lemonade was too tart to sip. She had to work not to pucker her mouth.

"Oh. Well. Alice Campbell teaches dance

and elocution at the Wichita College of Music." Myra said this last phrase as if it were laughable, a joke in and of itself. "Louise studied with her for a few years. They butted heads, so to speak. Mrs. Campbell found her" — she glanced out one of the big windows, as if searching for the exact words — "spoiled, bad-tempered, and insulting. There were other adjectives, I recall. At any rate, she dismissed Louise from all classes."

Cora frowned. She was going to New York. She'd already decided. If she backed out now, she might never go. Yet this information did complicate her idea of what kind of trip lay in store.

"I won't say any of those things aren't true of Louise," Myra continued, setting her glass on the table. "Or at least, they're true on occasion." She smiled. "I dare say I know how difficult she can be better than anyone. But what I also know is that as hard as Louise can be on others, she's always hardest on herself." She made a dismissive gesture with one hand. "She has an artistic temperament. And honestly, she's already far more talented than Mrs. Campbell ever will be, and she has been for some time. She realized it while still a pupil. That was really the problem."

Something heavy thumped the floor over their heads. A male voice called out, "Idiot!" Cora's gaze moved upward. Myra appeared to hear nothing.

"Are you saying she'll be . . . unruly?" Cora asked.

"No. On the contrary. I want to allay your fears. You see, whatever Louise's temperament, you'll have far more leverage than anyone has ever had with her, myself included. You're her ticket to New York, and she knows it. Once you get there, you'll continue to have enormous leverage, because if you decide to come home, she has to come home, too. Her father has already made that clear."

Somewhere above them, glass shattered. That was quickly followed by a feminine, but guttural, shout. Again, Cora looked at the ceiling, and then at her hostess's untroubled face.

"So with you," Myra continued, "our little lion should be as docile as a lamb. She knows how hard I worked to get her father to agree to let her go, and she won't jeopardize the result. Studying under Ted Shawn and Ruth St. Denis will be an enormous opportunity for her. You're familiar with Denishawn?"

This last question seemed an afterthought,

a question that didn't really need an answer. Cora almost nodded before realizing she should be honest and shake her head.

Myra appeared confused. "You don't know the Denishawn Dance Company?"

Cora shook her head again.

"Well. They're the most innovative dance company in the nation. Didn't you see them when they came through last November? At the Crawford?"

Cora, irritated now, shook her head again. She recalled, vaguely, advertisements for a dancing group, but neither she nor Alan had been interested. Myra gazed back at her under slightly furrowed brows. Clearly, an opinion had been formed.

"You missed something, then. Ted Shawn and Martha Graham were the leads, and they were sensational. There was none of the tripe we usually get out here in the hinterlands." She gazed out the front window, frowning. "Denishawn does modern dance that is truly modern, artistic. Their choreography owes something to Isadora Duncan, but not entirely. They themselves are innovative. And they're the best." She paused, looking down at her own hands. "I'm really so happy for Louise."

Cora heard a distinct slap, and another scream that could have been attributed to

41

an injured party of either gender. She cleared her throat, pointing at the ceiling. "Shouldn't we . . . investigate?"

Myra gazed at the ceiling. "No need," she muttered, smoothing her skirt. "You can be sure — she'll come to us."

Footsteps moved down a staircase, even quicker and lighter than June's. "MOTHER!"

Myra gave no answer.

"MOTHER!"

"We're in here, darling," Myra called out. "In the parlor. Being civilized."

A girl appeared in the doorway, her right hand pressed against her left shoulder, her dark eyes glassy with tears. Cora had no doubt she was looking at Louise: even crying, the skin around her eyes puffed with rage, she was strikingly beautiful. She was short and small like her mother, with the same pale skin and heart-shaped face, the same dark eyes and dark hair. But her jaw was firmer, and her cheeks were still as cherubic as young June's. Framing all this was the remarkable black hair, shiny and straight and cropped just below her ears, the ends tapering forward on both sides as if forming arrows to her full lips. A smooth curtain of thick bangs stopped abruptly above her brows. Viola was right. For all her resemblance to her mother, really, this girl looked like no one else.

"Martin hit me," she said.

"Hit?" Myra asked. "Or slapped? After years of living with you both, I suppose I can hear the difference, even a floor away."

"It left a mark!" Louise moved her hand and lifted the sleeve of her cream-colored frock to reveal a patch of skin that was not only red, but beginning to bruise along the top. Cora gasped. Louise looked at her, but only for a moment.

"He's bigger than I am. He's older. And he was in my room, reading my diary! How can you tolerate that level of insolence from him?" She pointed to her arm. "And violence?"

Myra smirked, clearly amused by the drama of the girl's words. But to Cora, both questions seemed legitimate. The mark on the girl's arm was ugly. If this Martin person was older than Louise, he must be close to the age of the twins, and she couldn't imagine either Howard or Earle striking a younger girl, or any girl for that matter. They simply wouldn't do it. And if one of them lost his head and did, he would have to answer to both Cora and Alan, who would take such an incident far more seriously than the still-smirking woman seated across from her now.

"Your brother's insolence and violence won't be your problem much longer," Myra said, stifling a yawn. "And you can keep your precious diary safe in New York, thanks to this woman here. Louise, I'd like you to meet Cora Carlisle."

The girl looked at Cora. She said nothing, but the expression on her face was a clear mix of revulsion and forbearance. Cora couldn't imagine what about her might invite such feelings. She'd taken care to look nice for this visit. She was wearing a modest but fashionable dress, and even a long strand of beads. She was certainly dressed as nicely as Myra. But there was no mistaking the contempt in the girl's eyes. It was the way a child looked at the broccoli that must be eaten before dessert, the room that must be cleaned before playtime. It was a gaze of dread, made all the more punishing by the girl's youth and beauty, her pale skin and pouting lips. Cora felt herself blushing. She had not been the subject of this sort of condescension in years.

She stood quickly, extending her hand. "Hello," she said, smiling, her eyes locked onto the girl's. The height difference, she decided, would be a help. "It's nice to meet you. I hope we're in for a wonderful trip."

"Nice to meet you," the girl stammered. She wasn't half as smooth a liar as her mother. She gave Cora's hand a limp shake and then cradled her sore arm again.

"I'm sorry about your arm. It looks as if it hurts."

It was only the truth, but she'd said it kindly, and it was as if she had turned an invisible key. The lovely eyes filled with tears again, and seemed to take Cora in anew.

"Thank you," she said. "It does hurt."

"She's never heard of Denishawn," Myra said. She remained seated, smiling up at her daughter, expectant. Cora felt the first risings of strong dislike.

"You've never heard of Denishawn?" Louise, too, seemed confused.

"No," Cora said. She hoped that if she were clear on this, they would perhaps stop asking.

The girl and her mother exchanged looks. They stared up at Cora with matching dark eyes, looking more alike than before.

"Why are you going then?" Myra asked in a pleasant voice, though her smile seemed unpleasant. "What draws you to New York?"

Cora swallowed. She should have anticipated the question, and prepared an answer. Vague associations with New York City floated through her mind: The Statue of

45

Liberty. Immigrants. Bootleggers. Tenement squalor. Broadway.

"I love good theater," she said.

Louise gasped. Her smile was nothing like her mother's — her pleasure was as sincere as her earlier scorn. "Well then! You're not so bad after all!"

Cora wasn't sure what to make of this.

"I think live theater is the snake's hips. I want to go to all the Broadway shows."

Cora nodded amiably. She didn't mind theater.

Myra tilted her head at Cora. "Funny. I don't think I've ever noticed you at plays here in town."

Cora worked to recall any play she had seen in the last five years. Nothing. She preferred the movies, seeing the faces up close. She didn't mind reading along.

"She didn't say she liked *local* theater, Mother." Louise turned back to Cora. "You mean quality theater, don't you? I don't blame you at all. It's a dreadful scene around her, just like with dance. I can't wait to see a real show."

"Nor I," Cora said. She and Louise smiled at each other. She supposed she would like Broadway well enough.

"Louise dear," Myra said, though she kept her gaze on Cora, "I'm so glad you two will be chummy. But Mrs. Carlisle and I have a few more things we need to discuss."

Louise looked at her mother, and then at Cora, as if hoping to discern what, exactly, would be the subject of the discussion. When no sign was given, she shrugged and turned to go. As she passed the center table, she picked up the book from the top of the stack without looking at its title. She looked back over her shoulder. "See you in July," she called out. She waved with the hand that held the book, and gave Cora the quickest of winks.

Myra filled her in on the particulars: she and Louise would be staying in an apartment building near Riverside Drive that Denishawn had recommended. Leonard had already purchased their train tickets and paid in full for the apartment, although, Myra cautioned, it would probably be better to let Louise think he was paying rent by the week. Cora would be in charge of the spending money; he would give her at least a week's worth when he saw them off at the station, and he would wire the rest at her request. The funds were hardly endless, but she needn't be especially frugal: they wanted Louise to experience New York, or at least some of it. Museums. Theater.

Restaurants. Really, any wholesome entertainment would be fine.

Watching Myra tell her all this, Cora softened a bit. Perhaps all the Denishawn snobbery obscured jealousy, or simple maternal worry. Perhaps Myra wished that she could be the one to accompany Louise. It couldn't be easy, sending your daughter off with a mere acquaintance. And Myra had taken the trouble to arrange a chaperone, to require one. Obviously, she cared. Perhaps she was just worried, as any mother might be.

So when it was time to go, and she and Myra were standing in the cavernous entryway, Cora summoned her courage. "I want you to know," she told Myra, slouching a bit so she wouldn't feel so tall, "that I appreciate you telling me about that dance instructor, the one Louise didn't get along with. But really, it seems to me that your daughter is a lovely young woman. I heard she even goes to my church."

"She used to," Myra said flatly.

"Oh. Well. In any case, I want you to know, you needn't feel anxious about the trip. I know I talked about going to plays, but I assure you, I'll take my primary responsibility seriously. I'm sure Louise is a decent girl, but I'll be sure to keep her safe."

Myra lifted her brows, smiling as if Cora had said something funny. "Leonard insisted on a chaperone," she said, opening the door to the sunlight and heat. She shielded her eyes with the flat of her palm, though her smile remained unchanged. "Finding you was his idea. I just want her to go."

THREE

Union Station was, perhaps, the most elegant building in Wichita. It was still relatively new, built just a few years before the war, its front entrance adorned with granite columns and arched windows more than twenty feet high. Inside, it was all one grand space, and on this bright July morning, long slants of sunlight fell across the marble floor. People holding tickets and suitcases walked purposefully between shadow and light, their footfalls and chatter echoing. Cora and Alan, along with Leonard Brooks, sat on one of the wooden benches on the perimeter. The high-backed bench looked and felt like a church pew, and Cora sat very straight, occasionally looking up at the large clock positioned high on a wall. Louise had left to use the ladies' room over twenty minutes ago.

"You'll take the Santa Fe as far as Chicago," Alan said, looking down at Cora's ticket. "You'll have two hours to change trains, which is plenty of time. But you should probably find your connection right away." He gave her a meaningful look, using a handkerchief to wipe his brow. "Chicago's station can be overwhelming."

Cora managed a nod, her gloved hands clasped tightly in her lap. She was seventeen when she first arrived in Wichita, literally right off the farm, her train pulling into the old depot, which was so much smaller and less impressive than this new one. Yet at the time, she had been both thrilled and anxious at the sight of so many people and so much movement, and all the fashionable women with corseted figures wearing belted skirts and high-collared shirtwaists. To Cora, even now, Wichita was the big city. Alan had grown up here, taking the crowds and the bustle for granted, and he'd been to law conferences all over the country. Now he was telling her that even he could be over-whelmed by Chicago's Union Station, which she would be navigating early tomor-row, so she could get on another train to an even larger city, all with her young charge in tow.

"That's if your train arrives on time." Leonard Brooks leaned back and pulled a pocket watch from his vest, ignoring the clocks on the column. "This strike could go on all summer. Harding needs to step in."

He was a small but intense-looking man, his eyes more black than brown, his hair as dark as Louise's and Myra's. He wasn't much taller than either one, but he, too, gave the impression of being at least average height. He had a long, pointed nose and a habit of staring off into nothing in a way that implied deep thought. Leonard Brooks had an excellent mind, according to Alan, with a solid chance of an appointment to the bench. He did seem obsessed with his work, Cora noticed. Moments after he'd cut a path across the station with a suitcase in each hand, Louise keeping stride beside him, he'd tried to strike up a conversation with Alan about a recent ruling on property taxes. Only after Alan cleared his throat and gave Cora a long look had Mr. Brooks seemed to recall that his business at hand was with her. Once focused, he was gracious, saying how pleased he and Myra were that Cora was taking on Louise. But now he was going on about the railroad strike, even though his daughter, who had yet to return from her exceedingly long trip to the ladies' room, was about to embark on her first real journey from home.

"It's an interesting debate," he said, looking up at Alan. "The workers have the right to strike, but reliable transport seems a right of the people."

"I'm going to check on Louise," Cora said, her voice as smooth as she could make it. She didn't want to give the impression that she was uncertain of the girl's whereabouts before they even boarded the train. But she was getting worried, and she could hardly come up with another reason for going after her. Cora herself had just returned from the ladies' room when Louise decided she needed to go. Now, as Cora made her way across the station, her low heels clicking on the marble, it occurred to her that the girl may have purposefully staggered their excursions.

That suspicion seemed more likely after she turned a corner around a shoeshine and found Louise leaning against a wall and drinking a Coca-Cola right out of the bottle. A tall boy in a dapper coat and flat-brimmed hat stood beside her, one arm against the wall, the better to turn toward Louise and get a better view, which he was clearly enjoying.

"Louise. There you are."

They both straightened. Louise moved the bottle away from her mouth. The boy, Cora saw now, was actually a young man, in his late twenties at least, blond stubble on his chin. His light eyes took in Cora with an expression of utter disappointment.

Cora looked at Louise. "I worried you'd gotten lost," she said, and then regretted it, the obvious lie.

Louise nodded. Without another look in the man's direction, she walked quickly toward Cora. She was wearing an ivory calf-length dress with a Peter Pan collar, no hat, and very high heels, so high, in fact, that her head was almost level with Cora's. She smiled, but her dark eyes were trained on Cora's face, clearly trying to read it. *"Are you going to make trouble?"* she seemed to ask. *"Right from the start? When we could get along so well?"*

"He's just an old friend from school."

Cora gave no response. It seemed far more likely that in less than half an hour, Louise had met a perfect stranger, perhaps from out of town, and let him buy her a pop. But there was no way to know for certain, and it seemed unwise to start an argument she could not prove.

"We should get back," she said amiably. "We'll be boarding soon."

"Would you like a sip?" Louise tipped the bottle toward her.

Cora shook her head. When they got to

New York, there would be no more questions of previous acquaintance, and she would be in a better position to explain to Louise the hazards — to her person and to her reputation — of allowing a strange man to buy her anything. She was a child, Cora remembered. Innocent. *Motherless,* Viola had said. She probably longed for guidance. The girl had gone to Sunday school, and by her own volition, for goodness' sakes. She simply needed attention and instruction. As soon as they got on the train, Cora planned to provide her with both.

She said goodbye to Alan on the platform. The sky was too bright for her to look up at him, so she gazed at her hands, held in his. They'd spent time apart before. When the boys were small, she'd taken them to visit his sister and her children in Lawrence while he stayed in Wichita to work. But she'd never been gone for over a month. And she'd never gone so far.

"Your trunk was checked," he said. "It should be delivered the night you arrive. But you'll let me know if you need anything." He spoke in a low voice, perhaps not wanting to imply to Leonard Brooks that there might be some need he had overlooked. "Don't hesitate," he added.

"Anything at all."

She nodded, and, sensing his face moving down and toward her, held up her cheek for him to kiss. Over his shoulder, she saw Louise brazenly watching, her hand flat under the straight bangs. Their eyes met. The girl's eyes narrowed. Cora looked away.

"Now I want you to mind Mrs. Carlisle," Leonard Brooks was saying, primarily to Louise, but loud enough for Cora and Alan to hear. He bobbed forward on his toes, his thumbs hooked on his suspenders. In heels, his daughter was taller than he was. "I trust I'll only get reports of your hard work and good behavior."

Louise lowered her head and gazed down at him, holding her small travel bag behind her back. "You will, Daddy. I promise." She could look so youthful, Cora thought, so girlish. But only sometimes. And the trick seemed to be in her command.

Her father wiped his brow, squinting past her to the waiting train. "With what that school is charging, I expect that when you come back, you'll be the best dancer in Wichita."

Cora and Alan smiled. But Louise only looked at him and blinked. She appeared momentarily at a loss for words, wounded even, her beautiful pout pronounced. She aged before Cora's eyes, her gaze wizened as she lowered her chin.

"Don't be stupid. I already am."

She softened the words, as much as they could be softened, with an afterthought of a smile. To Cora's surprise, Leonard Brooks seemed only amused at his daughter's condescension. Either that, or he couldn't be bothered to give what seemed the necessary reprimand. Cora herself would have put a check on such rudeness. But it wasn't her place. Not yet.

Of course in just a few years, Cora would better understand Louise's annoyance with her father's ignorance: being the best dancer in Wichita was hardly the end of her ambition. In just a few years, they would be reading about her in magazines, about her films, about her wild social life. She would receive over two thousand pieces of fan mail a week, and women all over the country would be trying to copy her hair. Before the decade was out, she would be famous on two continents. By then, if Leonard Brooks wanted to see his eldest daughter dance and dazzle, he would have to pay at a theater like everyone else, and gaze up at a thirty-foot screen.

On the train, they had their own open section, Cora's double seat facing Louise's. The windows had drawn curtains made of the same maroon velvet as the seats, and overhead, they each had a small reading lamp. They wouldn't need berths until they got to Chicago, so no partitions separated the sections. Normally, Cora liked the openness of day cars, but on this particular trip, she felt wary. Before they even left the station, a man from across the aisle, who appeared about Cora's age, asked if he could help lower their top window. The man had not, Cora noticed, offered to lower the window of the two elderly women in the section directly behind them — and he addressed Louise directly. Cora quickly answered for her: telling him she would let him know if and when their window needed lowering. Her tone was polite but firm, and her real message was clear: she was the guard at the gate.

If Louise was distressed by her sequestering, she didn't show it. The brightness of her face seemed both irrepressible and general, directed at no one in particular. No matter where she looked — at the ceiling of the car, at the other passengers, at her view from the trestle over Douglas Avenue — her glee was obvious, and, it seemed, as private as if she were alone. She did not speak to

Cora, but as the gears of the train whinnied and clicked, she smiled, her fingers drumming on her lap. She tapped her toes. When the whistle finally blew and the train lurched forward, she tilted her chin up, closed her eyes, and exhaled with a sigh.

"It is exciting," Cora ventured. The boys had loved train trips when they were small, and even when they were older. They'd both insisted on sitting by the window, watching for puffs of steam, and for years, it seemed, on every journey, she'd had to ask the conductor if they could visit the engine.

"Is it ever!" Louise rewarded her with a dazzling smile before turning back to the glass. Cora breathed in cigarette smoke and the scent of talcum powder. Diagonally across the aisle, a baby cried in its mother's arms. The mother was trying to comfort the child with coos and kisses, and when her efforts failed, she turned and gave her neighbors an apologetic look. Cora caught her eye and smiled.

"Goodbye, Wichita!" Louise waved down at Douglas Avenue, the busy stream of dark cars disappearing under the trestle. "Wish I could say I'll miss you! But I don't think I will!"

Cora started to reach for her arm. Certainly some of their fellow passengers were from Wichita, and hadn't yet forsaken their home. There was no need to offend. But the warning was unnecessary. Louise was finished saying goodbye. Even as they rolled by and away from the streets of her childhood, the square brick buildings and one-story homes, the treed parks and church steeples, she showed no interest in the view. Instead, she opened her bag and pulled out her reading material, of which Cora took sly and quick inventory: the July issue of *Harper's Bazaar*, the June issue of *Vanity Fair*, and a book entitled *The Philosophy of Arthur Schopenhauer*. Before they were out of the city, the paved streets giving way to dirt roads and fields, Louise appeared immersed in the book. Occasionally, she set it open in her lap, using a blue-ink pen to underline something or mark the pages. But usually, the book was a wall in front of her face. Its cover was a dreary brown.

Fine, Cora thought. She didn't need the girl to be social. She'd come prepared with her own reading, which she now took out of her bag. Perhaps she didn't keep all sorts of books lying around her parlor, but she enjoyed a good story as much as anyone. For this trip, she'd brought a *Ladies' Home Journal* and the new novel by Edith Wharton. Normally, she might have stuck with her preferred indulgence, something by Temple Bailey, who could be counted on to deliver satisfying tales of plucky heroines outwitting painted vamps and bringing wayward husbands back into the fold. But for this trip, understanding that whatever title she chose would fall under the girl's critical gaze, and would no doubt be reported back to Myra, Cora had gone to the bookstore and purchased *The Age of Innocence,* which, although it was written by a woman, had just won the Pulitzer Prize, and therefore seemed beyond reproach from even the worst kind of snob. It was also set in New York City, and though it was set in the previous century, Cora thought it would be interesting to read about the very place that they were headed, to picture long-dead characters walking the very streets that would soon be under her feet. She liked the story so far. And the historical details were lovely, all those carriages and sweeping gowns. Even as the train rumbled through open fields, and the air in the car grew warm with the rising sun, Cora turned the pages easily, feeling virtuous and smart.

"What are you reading?"

She looked up. Louise was staring at her, her own book in her lap. The black hair, even in the heat, was as smooth as glass.

"Just this." Cora held her place with her finger and showed the girl the cover. The sky was brighter now. She adjusted the brim of her hat.

"Oh." Louise wrinkled her nose. "I read that. So did Mother."

"You didn't like it?" Cora asked, though the answer was already clear from the girl's expression. The only question was whether Louise and Myra had agreed on the matter. Cora suspected they had.

"*The House of Mirth* was better. But in general, historical fiction bores me." There was a hint of apology in the girl's voice, just enough to vex. "Everything is so stuffy. All those ridiculous rules and manners about who gets invited to a party, and who can be seen with whom." She reached into her bag and took out a pack of chewing gum. "It's just tedious and fake. I couldn't care about it."

"It won the Pulitzer."

"And that hero, if that's what you want to call him. He turns out to be so pathetic, such a coward." She slipped a piece of gum in her mouth and offered another to Cora, who refused. "He's in love with the Countess Olenska, the only authentic woman in the book. But she's out of bounds just because she's been divorced? What bunk.

And then he marries that boring, dumb May Welland and feels so noble for it. He's an idiot. He deserves his misery. But I don't know that he deserves a book."

Cora looked down at the book. In love with the Countess Olenska? A divorced woman? Cora hadn't expected that. In lust with, yes. Perhaps the girl misunderstood. Perhaps she didn't yet know the difference.

"Oh." Louise, childlike again, put her fingers to her lips. "Did I ruin it for you? Sorry."

"Not at all," Cora said. "I read for the language, not the story." She'd heard someone say that once, and now seemed a good time to repeat it. She gazed out the window, the girl's black hair in her peripheral vision. Outside, the prairie looked hot and windless. A herd of Angus stood knee-deep in a muddied pond, most of them clustered under the shade of a lone willow. The train would probably go by the old farm, not right by it, but close. She remembered lying in bed at night, in perfect darkness, listening for the whistles.

"Your husband is handsome."

Cora looked at her, surprised. "Oh. Yes. Thank you."

"How old is he?"

"Pardon?"

"How old is he?"

"He's forty-eight."

"A lot older than you."

"Not so much," Cora said. She wasn't sure if she was being flattered.

"My father is almost twenty years older than my mother. He's as old as her father."

"Oh." Cora smiled. "Well. That's not unusual. Often when the man is older, it makes for a good match."

The girl stared at Cora as if she had said something wise and not generally known.

"Dear? Are you all right?"

She nodded, a strand of black catching on her cheek. "Yeah." She gazed at her own hands in her lap. And then, as if forcibly breaking a spell, she blinked, looking up. "My mother regrets it. Marrying him, I mean."

Cora drew in a quick breath. "You shouldn't tell me that. It isn't my business." She looked away, to show she meant it.

"She wouldn't care. It's not personal. Nothing against him. Or us. She just doesn't like her life. She didn't want to get married, but her father made her because my father had money. She didn't want children, either."

Cora looked back at her. "Who told you that?"

"She did. And she told him, back when they got married. She said if he really wanted to get married, fine, and if he wanted children, she would have them, but he would have to find someone else to take care of us." Louise shrugged. "He didn't."

Cora waited, wanting to choose her words carefully. Perhaps Myra had said this in a joking tone, the way some women did. Cora had never cared for that kind of humor. It wasn't a funny thing to tell a child she wasn't wanted. She thought of little June, wandering around the house.

"I'm sure she didn't mean it."

"She meant it."

Louise looked and sounded amused, which Cora didn't understand. Such a statement by a mother must hurt. She shook her head. What a horrible woman Myra was. And how unfair the world.

"Perhaps she felt that way for a time," Cora said, giving Louise the kindest of looks. "But I'm certain she cherishes all you children now. She must understand her good fortune."

Louise frowned. "She didn't say it in a mean way, if that's what you think. I told you it's not personal." She looked at Cora coolly, leaning back in her seat. "It's nothing against us. She had six little brothers and sisters, the ones who lived, I mean. Her mother was always sick, and she always had to take care of them. So even before she met my father, she was already tired of babies. I can't blame her for that."

Cora was silent, chastened. She had not suspected Myra Brooks of a difficult upbringing.

Louise held her gaze. "The only reason she knows how to read is because she's so smart, because she loves books and music so much. She taught herself." She lifted her chin. "She taught herself everything. And she knows far more than most people know."

Cora nodded, eager to concede this point. She'd not meant to make the girl defensive about her mother. She touched her hand to her left temple. The air in the car had gotten warmer.

"Anyway." Louise paused to pop her gum. "I'm never having a bunch of brats. Or even one. That's for sure."

Cora smiled. "Well. You have plenty of time to change your mind."

"I won't."

They rolled on in silence, Louise looking out the window, Cora staring into the aisle. It would be wise, she knew, to let this argument go, to let the girl think what she wanted. Time would tell. But she was irritated. There was something *entitled* in the girl's voice, something proud and unthinking.

"You'll feel differently when you fall in love," Cora said. "You may not think so now, but you might want to marry someday."

"Hmm." Louise smiled and lifted her book. "Schopenhauer writes about marriage. He says getting married is like grasping blind into a sack of snakes and hoping to find an eel."

"Does he." Cora gave the book a disparaging look.

"Actually," Louise said, lowering the book again, "I think I'd like to get married someday. I just don't want children."

Cora almost laughed at the girl's innocence. She didn't yet understand about babies, and how they came through marriage, decided on or not. But then, looking into Louise's eyes, she realized what the girl meant, what she was getting at, wasn't innocent at all. Cora looked out the window, up at the sky, feigning interest in a blue-bottomed cloud. There wasn't much else she could do. Just a few months earlier, Margaret Sanger had been arrested for publicly asking if birth control was moral.

Obscene, she was called. And that was in New York, if Cora recalled correctly. In any case, Cora wasn't about to attempt a similar discussion on a train in Kansas, not with anyone, thank you very much.

Certainly not with an adolescent girl.

When the conductor called out for Kansas City, Louise looked up from her book and bounced a little in her seat. "That means we crossed the state line." She looked at Cora, and then at the rounded ceiling of the car, her hands pressed together in theatrical prayer. "I'm out of Kansas! Thank you, God! I actually made it out!"

Cora looked out the window. Kansas City's Union Station was like Wichita's station grown stout, just as beautiful, but twice, or even three times, the size. That was how it was going to be, she realized. As they moved east, slow and steady, everything would get bigger.

"You've been out of state before?" Louise gave her a friendly, inquisitive look.

"No." Cora leaned back against her seat. "I've traveled around Kansas, but that's all." She smoothed her hair, and adjusted a pin in back, purposefully avoiding Louise's reaction. She didn't need to see it. She could imagine the look of disappointment, even disgust. It would be a worse crime than not knowing about Denishawn, Cora's openly admitting the smallness of her life.

The truth would have worked in her favor, impressing the girl, perhaps. But the old lie had moved easily through her lips — she'd told it so many times it felt true, even now, with the steady rumbling of the wheels on the track pulling up memories. She had been only a child on her other long trip, traveling with other children but also alone, headed west instead of east. She'd been hungry. Her seat, she remembered, had been hard wood, and the nights long and absolutely dark. But the sounds were the same, the whistles and the gears. So was the rocking feeling, which was what she remembered best. Then, as now, she'd been almost sick with both dread and longing, moving fast toward another world, and all she didn't yet know.

FOUR

She didn't recall what the building looked like. Perhaps she never saw it from the outside. But she remembered the roof, which was flat, and covered with gravel, and long enough that if a girl called out from one end on a windy day, a girl on the other end wouldn't hear her. On every side was a beige-brick wall that was too high for Cora, or even the older girls, to see over, even when standing on a chair. Metal hooks stuck out of the walls, but they were not allowed to use them for climbing. If you tried and you were caught, woe to you, as the nuns liked to say. The hooks were for knotting the clotheslines, stretched taut across the roof. Pigeons, and sometimes seagulls, would land on the wall, give Cora their one-eyed stare, then turn and fly away.

The older girls carried wet clothes up the stairs in baskets, each attached to a tag with the owner's name. Cora and the other younger girls would pin them up, sometimes standing on chairs. She couldn't read the names on the tags, but the nuns had shown them how to keep each basket at the head of each line, so the clothes wouldn't get confused. All items had to be pinned with care as they belonged to paying customers. If the wind blew a pair of trousers or a skirt down into the gravel, it had to be washed again, and the older girls would get sore. They already worked hard enough. Most of them had scars on their hands and forearms, burns from flatirons or scalding water. Imogene, who was almost fourteen and nice, had let Cora touch the burn on the back of her hand. It didn't hurt anymore, she said. The skin had healed over, a lopsided heart of brownish red, rough under Cora's fingers.

On Sundays, they got to go out to the backyard, as long as they were careful of the garden. There was a tree, Cora remembered. They were not allowed to climb it. The older girls would sit under it and talk, or braid one another's hair. They all jumped rope, using a clothesline with a knot in the middle to weight it down. Some girls played blindman's bluff. When it snowed they played fox and geese.

Inside, there was a sleeping room, Cora's bed one in a row of many. In the winter, you got a sweater, and you slept in it, not just because it was cold but because if you lost your sweater, woe to you. They ate downstairs in a big room with long tables and cross-barred windows. They were not to speak unless spoken to. Some of the nuns were kind, and patient, but some were not, and they all wore habits, making it difficult to distinguish one from another until one was close and looking right at you. Sister Josephine might turn and become Sister Mary, or Sister Delores, who was young and pretty, but who also carried a wooden paddle. It was best to always follow the rules, and show respect at all times.

It was the New York Home for Friendless Girls. Mary Jane, who knew how to read, said the words were painted on a sign out front. This name made no sense to Cora. She wasn't Friendless. Mary Jane was her friend, and so was Little Rose, and Patricia, and Betsy, all of the younger girls and even Imogene if Cora didn't bother her too much. It means no parents, Mary Jane said. Orphans. But that didn't make sense, either. Rose's father came by almost every Sunday. Rose said he would be coming for her and her older sister soon. He would take them home. And Patricia's mother was in the hospital, sick with tuberculosis, but alive.

Cora herself did not have parents, none that she knew. She had only a flash of a memory, or a memory of a memory, or maybe just a dream: a woman with dark hair, curly like her own, and wearing a red knit shawl. It was her voice Cora remembered, or imagined, most clearly, saying unknown words in a strange language, and also, clearly, Cora's name.

"Am I an orphan?" Cora asked.

"You are," said Mary Jane. The older girls called Mary Jane Irish, because of the way she talked. "We all are. That's why we're here."

The nuns said grace before every meal. *Because you rescued the poor who cried for help, and the fatherless who had none to assist them.* The girls only had to wait and then cross themselves and say, *In the name of the Father, the Son, and the Holy Spirit* and *amen.* They ate oatmeal for every breakfast and every dinner. The nuns ate oatmeal, too. They put raisins in when they had them, and when they did, Cora ate with an elbow on each side of her plate, because some of the older girls had long fingers. For supper, there was bean soup with vegetables, and if anyone was stupid enough to complain, what they got was a lecture about gratitude, and about how many thousands of children on the very streets of New York would give anything to get three meals a day, not to mention a roof over their heads. If the complainer wasn't happy, a nun would suggest, she might leave, and make room for a truly hungry child who would be glad to take her bed and her place at the table. She could be sure there were plenty waiting in line.

That seemed to be true. Whenever a new girl came in, she was almost always bonier and far dirtier than Cora and the other girls. The nuns had to shave new girls' hair off because so many of them came right from the slums or even the streets and lice were always a concern. New girls ate their oatmeal fast, spoons scraping the bowls, and the nuns would give them seconds and even thirds until they caught up and lost the dead look in their eyes, their hair finally starting to grow back. Only Patricia had come in plump, her pretty blond hair never shaved, and she was the one who sulked about the food, who made faces when the nuns weren't looking. Patricia told Cora that even when she was awake, she dreamed of pie and cheese and smoked meat. Cora knew about smoked meat, because sometimes the air on the roof smelled so good she wanted to bite at it, and another girl said this was the smell of meat cooking on a stove. But she'd never tasted the other things Patricia said she dreamed of, at least not that she could remember, and so she, unlike Patricia, wasn't tormented by their loss.

Cora didn't remember being anywhere but the home. Big Bess, who was almost thirteen, said she remembered when Cora arrived, and that she hadn't been a baby but a toddler, chubby, and already walking and looking up when she heard her name. But that was all she knew. Cora once asked Sister Josephine who had brought her, and where she had been before, and even Sister Josephine, who was the nicest nun by far, her missing teeth plain to see when she smiled, the only one who never even threatened to use the paddle, even she had told Cora firmly that such questions were impertinent, and that she should consider herself a child of God, and a fortunate one at that.

One day, not long after she had lost her first tooth, Cora became even more fortunate. At least that was what she was told at the time. Sister Delores would be taking her on a little trip, along with six of the other younger girls. They would need to be on their best behavior, leaving quietly while the other girls were in the laundry. They would need to leave right away. They would need to button their sweaters, as there was a chill in the air.

Cora, holding Mary Jane's hand, assumed she would be back in time for supper. She felt only excitement, a thrilling break from the routine, as she and Mary Jane followed Patricia and Little Rose and the other lucky girls, who followed Sister Delores, down the steps and through the big front door, and finally, out the front gate onto the street, which Cora had only seen from the upstairs window. Even Mary Jane, who'd already lost all her baby teeth and grown new ones back, who could do a perfect backbend, seemed afraid. They followed Sister Delores around a corner, and all at once, there were people everywhere, some walking, some in carriages, the horses going *clip clop clip clop,* everyone moving quickly. They had to take big steps to avoid piles of filth that came from the horses. Cora pulled the collar of her sweater against her nose, breathing through the wool. Sister Delores had to lift her habit from time to time, and Cora saw her black stockings. They were torn above each heel, the white of her skin showing through.

At the next corner, Sister Delores stopped walking, and told them they would wait there for an omnibus. None of them knew what an omnibus was, but they were all too afraid of Sister Delores to ask. On the omnibus, she said, they were to sit quietly, as close to her as possible. They were not to talk with any strangers or try to make any friends. She wanted them to know that there would be a rope stretching the length of the omnibus, and that it was attached to the ankle of the driver. She knew they would be curious about the rope, and so she would tell them now it was to let the driver know when to stop. If someone wanted to get off at a certain location, he or she pulled the rope, and the driver would stop the horses. Sister Delores hoped all the girls understood that she would be the only one in their group who would touch the rope, as she was the only one who knew where they were going. If one of the girls thought it would be clever to pull the rope and make the driver stop with no reason, that was fine. But the clever girl should understand that when the omnibus stopped, the clever girl would, in fact, be getting off, and getting off alone.

On the omnibus, which turned out to be a covered cart with benches, pulled by a sad brown horse, the girls were very quiet, their hands clasped in their laps. No one touched, or even looked at, the rope.

Their destination was a redbrick building with high windows and a cod-liver smell. As they walked in, Sister Delores said hello to a woman in spectacles who was not a nun and told her she and her girls would need a private moment. The woman with spectacles smiled and showed them into a room with a cross and a painting of Jesus and a flag of the United States. There were wooden chairs, most of them sized for children. When the woman who was not a nun left, Sister Delores asked the girls to sit, and then she sat in a bigger chair, and smiled at them with her pretty face, and told them they were not on a little trip at all. In fact, she said, still smiling, they were about to be sent on a great adventure, courtesy of the Children's Aid Society, which had raised great sums of money to help girls just like them.

"You're being placed out," she told them, looking kinder and happier than she ever had, her blue eyes large and, for the first and only time Cora could remember, twinkling. "In just a few hours, you're going for a train ride. You're going to go very, very far away, because there are good people in the Middle West, in places like Ohio and Missouri and Nebraska, who want to bring a child into their home." Still smiling, she pressed her palms together. "You're each going to find a family."

Cora, sitting in her little wooden chair, felt her blood go still. She looked at Mary Jane, who appeared too stunned to move, but with a strange smile on her face. Cora shook her head. She was afraid of Sister Delores, but she was more afraid of the train. She didn't want to go to Ohio. And Betsy. Betsy wasn't with them.

"I have a family," Patricia said. She already had the panicked voice of someone about to cry. "My mother's in the hospital. She won't know where I am."

Rose said that she couldn't leave New York, either. Her father was coming to get her any day. Her and her older sister.

"This has all been decided," Sister Delores said quietly. Her hard look, the one they knew better, had already returned. "If you were placed with us, it's because you've got no one else. Some of your parents may have made you promises that they can't keep. You can't rely on them."

"My father's coming for me," said Rose.

"Your father's a drunk." Sister Delores looked at her without blinking. "If he would stay sober through the week, he could keep

79

a job, and he could come get you as he says he will. But he hasn't done that, has he? Has he? No. And he won't. I'm sorry. I don't mean to be unkind, but you are too gullible. It's been a year now, Rose. We can't throw away a chance like this so you can wait around on an empty promise."

Rose started to cry, her whimpers louder and higher-pitched than Patricia's. She took the tips of her brown braids and held them against her eyes. Cora felt heat behind her own eyes, her bottom lip starting to tremble. This train, this horrible train, was leaving in a few hours. They wouldn't be able to go back to the home. She wouldn't see Sister Josephine again. Or Imogene. Or Betsy. They would give her bed away to a skinny girl with a shaved head. Perhaps they already had.

"Stop that. Stop that crying. You don't understand what good fortune this is." Sister Delores looked at them and shook her head. "I wasn't going to tell you this. But before you even get on the train, you'll each get a new dress."

Mary Jane turned to Cora, her eyes bright with excitement. She reached over and squeezed Cora's hand. She thought Cora was like her. Neither of them had a mother in the hospital, or a father with good intentions, or an older sister to leave behind. Not as far as they knew. But Cora shook her head again. She didn't care if Sister saw her. She didn't know if her mother was in the hospital or if she had a father coming to get her. But she might. The train would take her away from all she knew, from who she was.

"I won't go," Patricia said. Now she was crying full on. "I won't go. I don't want a new family. I have a mother."

Sister Delores stood quickly. There was no telling if she had the paddle. Patricia shrank from her reach.

Cora looked up at a high window, at the sliver of gray sky beyond. Even if she could reach the window, and somehow fly through it, where would she go? They'd had breakfast before they left, and already she was hungry again.

"How very selfish," Sister Delores said, still looking at Patricia. She shook her head, her veil brushing her shoulders. "That you would deny another child a place to sleep and enough to eat because you refuse to take advantage of an opportunity."

"Let someone else go in my place," Patricia said. "They can go to the Middle West."

"Stupid girl." Sister Delores frowned.

"These are good homes. They can't place someone right off the street."

From the other side of the door, an infant cried. They heard a young voice, different from theirs. A boy's.

"Why just us?" Mary Jane asked. "Why not the other girls?"

Sister Delores nodded, as if to thank someone, finally, for asking a logical question. "They only had seven spots for us," she said. "Out of a hundred and fifty. And they told us the younger ones do better. We've been sending our babies out for a while."

"Betsy's younger than I am," Cora said. She was not defending her young friend. She was hoping Sister would realize her mistake, take her back to the home, and make Betsy get on the train.

Sister Delores shook her head. "Betsy's slow in the head. You can see it, looking in her eyes. They said no one would want her." She gazed up at the picture of Jesus. The girls understood that they should not speak. Even in profile, the veil obscuring half her face, Sister Delores's weariness was clear.

"We love all of God's children." She continued to look at the picture. "But only some can get on the train."

She took a deep breath and pulled her

shoulders back. She didn't raise her voice. She didn't need to. Her quiet voice, her hard blue stare, was enough.

"I'm going to tell you once more, and once more only. If you're sitting here now, you are a very lucky girl. And for your own good, I guarantee you are each getting on that train."

They didn't know they were part of an exodus, a mass migration that spanned over seventy years. They didn't know that the Children's Aid Society had already filled, and would continue to fill, train after train with the Great City's destitute children, sending, before the end of the program, almost two hundred thousand of them off to what was usually an easier life among the farm families of the Middle West, with its abundant fields and fresher air, its clean Main Streets and church picnics, its earnest young couples who wanted a child.

Or a field hand. A young slave. An indentured servant who could be made to work long hours in the cold and the heat, who wouldn't need much food. A prisoner whom no one would miss, who could be beaten, starved, tormented, undressed and violated, all within the privacy of one's home.

The routine was almost always the same.

Flyers would be mailed a few weeks before a train went out: Homes for Children Wanted. Various Ages. Both Sexes. Well-Disciplined. Caucasian went without saying. The address, time, and place of distribution would be announced at a later date.

The trains didn't go to the same towns every year. The Society kept them in rotation, thinking the chances would be better if a community wasn't already thick with orphans, if the orphans they had were anomalies, not a real threat to the demographic. And there were so many little towns to choose from, their little downtowns snug against the tracks. The agents, the women with the rosters who rode the trains as well, told the children not to worry if they weren't selected at the first few stops. People always went for the babies first. Once they were all spoken for, the agents promised, the older ones would have a chance.

Still, they were coached. They were taught to smile when smiled at, and to sing "Jesus Loves Me" on command. The girls were told that if potential parents asked them to lift their skirts, they should, to show that their legs were straight. People had the right to know what they were taking on. Two red-haired boys had the seat in front of Cora. They held hands even when asleep. The older boy told the agent they were brothers, and that they couldn't be separated. She told them she would do her best.

When the train arrived at a new town, the children were cleaned up, their faces and hands washed, their hair combed, their clothes changed. Before they even left New York, they had each been given a bath, and not just one nice set of clothes, but two: one set for travel, and a nicer set for the selections. They had warm coats and new shoes that actually fit, caps for the boys, hair ribbons for the girls. The agents were experts at braiding hair and tying shoelaces and erasing evidence of tears or interrupted naps. When the children were clean and presentable, they were led onto some kind of stage, usually at a church or a theater or an opera house. There was always a crowd. People would come out just to watch.

Even at the time, Cora understood the danger she was in, standing on stage after stage, staying quiet as adults milled about, looking her and the other children over, telling some to open their mouths and show their teeth. She was glad not to be a boy. Men and women squeezed boys' skinny arms to feel for muscle, and pressed hands against their knees and slim hips. Some were clear about their needs. *Have you ever milked a cow? Have you ever shucked corn? Are you sickly? Were your parents sickly? Do you know what it means to work?* But it wasn't so good to be a girl, either. At one stop, Cora listened as a man with a long beard told an older girl with thick black braids how pretty she was, and how he had lost his wife a few years back, and how it was just him in the house, alone, but that it was a big house, and did she like babies? Instead of answering, the girl had started to cough, hard and purposeful, not even putting her hand to her mouth, her face red as if she were choking, until the man stepped away. When he walked past Cora, his face grim, she started coughing, too.

Rose was the first of her group to go. Cora didn't see who chose her. She'd been so nervous, standing on the stage, that she didn't even notice Rose was gone until they were back on the train, and she had the seat to herself. Mary Jane was picked at the next stop, practically jumping into the arms of a young man with a black coat and a cane who asked her if she would like her own pony. His wife was pretty, with a long green skirt and a matching, smart-looking jacket, her blond hair in coils under her hat. Walking out between them, Mary Jane had turned back and waved at Cora, a flash of loss in her eyes before she looked up at the man, smiled again, and disappeared through the door.

Cora didn't see Patricia go, either.

By the first stop in Kansas, over half of the children were gone, but Cora still hadn't been picked. She knew this was partly her fault. Some of the children sang the Jesus song on every stage, and it was true that they got more attention. But Cora was too shy. And in her young way, too suspicious. She remembered stories Sister Josephine had told, *Hansel and Gretel* and *Little Snow White.* Surely the people who showed up at the stages were as capable of disguise, of appearing good and kind as the agents looked on, only to transform into witches and child-eating goblins once they were out of sight. She wondered what would happen if she were never picked, if, stop after stop, and stage after stage, she had to keep getting back on the train, until finally — what? The train couldn't go on forever. The agents would have to go back to New York. If she were still with them, she could go back as well.

This was what was in her head when she first saw the Kaufmanns. They were both tall people, pale-faced and lanky. Cora stared up at them more with curiosity than personal interest. The man was older than the woman, his forehead deeply lined, his lips thin and bloodless. The woman was younger, his daughter, perhaps, but she was not pretty like the woman in the green dress who had taken Mary Jane. This woman had small, pale eyes, and a pointy nose. A gingham bonnet covered her hair.

"Hello," she said to Cora.

Both the man and the woman crouched low, their faces level with hers. Cora could not cough or pretend to be slow: one of the agents was right there, watching. The man asked her name, and she told him. He asked her age, and she said she didn't know, but that she'd just lost her first tooth. Both the man and the woman laughed as if Cora had said something terribly funny, as if she were one of the children singing the Jesus song, trying hard to be cute. She gave them a hard look, but they continued to smile. The man looked at the woman. The woman nodded.

"We'd like you to come live with us," the man said. "We'd like you to be our little girl."

"We have a room all set up. Your room." The woman smiled, showing overgrown front teeth. "With a window, and a bed. And a little dresser."

Cora looked at them, revealing nothing. They couldn't be her parents. They didn't look anything like her. And they'd said nothing about a pony. Also, this was a strange place, the main street of the town dry and dusty. And windy. On the walk from the station, the wind had nearly knocked her down.

Then the agent's hands were on her shoulders. "She's shy. And tired, no doubt. They've been on the train for days."

"Hungry, I imagine," the woman said. She seemed distressed about this.

The agent, still behind Cora, gave her a push forward. "Go on now," she said, with no question in her voice. "And be grateful, why don't you. It seems to me you're a lucky little girl."

FIVE

At a blow of the whistle, she blinked awake, her hat crooked on her head. Louise was not in her seat. She turned, looking around the car. The fat baby across the aisle, silent but awake in its mother's lap, looked back at her with a stern expression. Many seats were empty. She fixed her hat and rubbed her neck. No need for alarm. Louise might just be using the bathroom. She'd been considerate, slipping into the aisle without waking Cora. She would likely be back any minute.

The train rolled past a field of corn, the stalks summer high, the golden tips peeking out of the green, straining toward the sun. Cora searched her seat for her book and frowned when she saw it on the floor. She wouldn't be able to reach for it, not in her corset. She tried to lift the book between her shoes, but her soles were too stiff, and she only managed to scoot it under Louise's seat. She looked over at Louise's empty seat. The Schopenhauer book lay open-faced on top of the magazines. Cora turned, glancing up and down the aisle. Seeing no sign of Louise, she leaned forward as far as she could and grabbed the Schopenhauer. She checked the aisle again, then skimmed the pages until she found something underlined in the girl's blue-inked pen.

It would be better if there were nothing. Since there is more pain than pleasure on earth, every satisfaction is only transitory, creating new desires and new distresses, and the agony of the devoured animal is always far greater than the pleasure of the devourer.

There were blue-ink doodles along the margins. Three-dimensional arrows. Staring eyes. Spiraling vines with leaves. Another passage had stars around it.

We will gradually become indifferent to what goes on in the minds of other people when we acquire a knowledge of the superficial nature of their thoughts, the narrowness of their views and of the number of their errors. Whoever attaches a lot of value to the opinions of others pays them too much honor.

Frowning, Cora closed the book and put it back as she'd found it, on top of the magazines.

As it was just after noon, the dining cars were busy, with waiters holding trays high over their heads and sliding fast past each other in the aisles. Nearly every booth was full. But Louise, wearing no hat, was easy to spot. She was facing Cora, her crossed legs turned toward the aisle, a heeled shoe dangling off of one foot. The man who had offered to lower their window sat beside her, smoking a cigar. An electric fan sat on a corner of the table, blowing smoke over his shoulder out the window. The man's free arm rested on the back of their seat, close to Louise's shoulder.

A black man in a spotless white coat ducked to speak to Cora quietly. "Ma'am? Table for one?"

"No, thank you. I —"

"Cora!" Louise waved a white linen napkin. "Cora! I'm over here!"

She did not fool Cora for a moment, pretending she thought everything was fine. Myra could have raised her in a barn, and still, a girl her age knew better than to sit at a table with a man she did not know.

"Come join us!" Louise waved the napkin again. "Please help! I'll never finish this lunch alone."

The train leaned around a curve, and Cora grabbed on to a pole. She didn't know what to do. She couldn't stomp out of the dining car and leave Louise. She couldn't grab her by the arm and drag her out as well — she would only draw attention to the indiscretion. Also, she needed to eat. If she left now, she'd just have to come back, and either bring Louise with her or leave her unattended in their section. Louise's new friend smiled, apparently untroubled by her invitation. He'd left his bowler on a peg by the table, revealing salt-and-pepper hair that was just starting to thin at the temples. He was at least middle-aged, Cora saw now, closer to Alan's age, and he was powerfully built, wide at the shoulders. Next to him, hatless Louise looked even smaller and younger than she was.

"Ma'am? Will you be joining them?" The waiter gestured toward the table. If he knew of Cora's predicament, or the awfulness of the situation, he showed no interest whatsoever.

She nodded and followed him to the booth, glancing at the other diners, watch-

93

ing for expressions of disapproval, or worse, recognition. She intended to slink into the seat facing Louise and the man, but when she tried, still glancing around the car, she found herself, to her horror, in the lap of another man.

"Oh my goodness!" She jumped up, almost bumping into the waiter, who, instead of helping to steady her, took a quick step away, his hands behind his back.

Louise's laugh was more of a whoop. She actually leaned back in her seat and clapped. "Oh, Cora. I thought you would see him!"

"Terribly sorry," said the other man, who was sliding out of the booth now, trying to stand. "Terribly sorry," he repeated, though it was clear from his voice that he was as amused as Louise. He was younger than the other man, a little younger than Cora, with high cheekbones and thick blond hair. "I didn't realize . . ."

"My mistake. Please sit. Please," Cora whispered. She needed him to sit so she could sit. Heat crept up her neck. The man obliged, and she sat beside him. He smiled politely at her, but his gaze moved back to Louise.

"Sorry I crept off without you." Louise reached across the table to touch Cora's arm. "I was just famished, and you looked so peaceful. Did you have a nice nap?"

"Yes. Thank you." Cora tilted her head so the brim of her hat would hide her face from the men, and gave Louise a steely look. Louise smiled and resumed cutting into a very large piece of chicken.

"Anyway, when I got here, all the tables were full, and these gentlemen were kind enough to offer me a seat. Cora, this is Mr. Ross, and this is his nephew, also Mr. Ross. Isn't that nice?" She stabbed her fork into the chicken. "Twice as easy to remember."

"Call me Joe," the older man said, with a pleasant nod of his head.

"I'm Norman," said the younger man.

"Mrs. Carlisle." Cora smiled curtly. Despite the steady whirl of the electric fan, cigar smoke stung her eyes. A waiter set a glass of water by her plate, along with a menu. Cora, coughing a bit, asked for lemonade.

"Are you hungry?" Louise used her fork to point to her plate, on which remained over half of a chicken breast, and another, still untouched. "The chicken is good. But the portions are humongous. Do you just want some of mine? I can't eat all this."

The chicken did look good, roasted the way Cora liked it. And even with the cigar smoke wafting through the air, even with the heat, she was hungry. If she simply ate what the girl couldn't, they would be able to leave the table that much more quickly. Both men seemed to have finished eating, their plates gone, linen napkins rumpled in front of them.

Cora looked at Louise. "Thank you. It's too bad they couldn't offer you something smaller, something from the children's menu. Did you tell them that you're only fifteen?"

Louise narrowed her eyes. Now Cora smiled, using her knife and fork to transfer the piece of chicken onto her own plate. There were rolls, too, she saw now, and she took one from the basket. She would have to pace herself. The corset only allowed her to eat a little at a time.

The older man moved his hand away from Louise's shoulder. He crossed his arms in front of him, looking across the table at Cora. His expression seemed to beg her pardon.

"Mrs. Carlisle." His voice was friendly. "Are you from Wichita as well?"

She nodded. The waiter walked up with her lemonade, saw the secondhand chicken on her plate, and, with the slightest of sneers, took her menu away.

Louise leaned across the table. "These two

are Wichita firemen. Isn't that something? Everybody loves firemen. And we get to sit at their table."

Cora frowned. She'd had the men pegged as salesmen, or somehow involved in something coarse. It would be harder to be short with men who regularly risked their lives to save people from burning buildings. Then again, firemen or not, they didn't seem entirely noble. On the older man's left hand, which had just moved away from Louise's shoulder, Cora spied the glint of a wedding ring.

"We're on our way to Chicago. Fire school." He tapped the butt of his cigar into a silver ashtray.

"Fire school." Cora sipped her lemonade, which was perfect, not too sweet and surprisingly cold. "I didn't know there was such a thing."

"Certainly. There's a lot for us to know. We don't just aim the hoses and spray. We have to learn about building materials. Chemistry. We'll see all the newest tools and techniques." He smiled at Cora. "How long have you lived in Wichita?"

"Since my marriage."

"And before that?"

"McPherson."

"You don't say!" The man gestured toward

97

his nephew. "His father and I are both from McPherson! I'm a bit older than you, I believe. But what was your maiden name?"

"Kaufmann."

He shook his head, looking closely at her face.

"We lived far out. We had a farm."

"Ah, a country girl." He smiled at her in a way that seemed too familiar. Louise looked at Cora and flexed her brows.

Cora held up her finger as she was chewing, and even after she swallowed, she made a point of not returning the smile. "Not so much anymore," she said. "My husband and I have been in Wichita for a while now." She felt more at ease, mentioning Alan.

"Are your people still in McPherson?"

"No. It was just me and my parents. They both died some time ago."

"I see." His gaze moved over her face. "Well. Your young friend tells us you're on your way to New York." The uncle puffed out a ring of smoke. "I've been there a few times. That's a whole different level of city. Two women alone in New York? That sounds worrisome to me. Have you ever been there?"

Cora shook her head. She didn't like his tone. *Two women alone.* She was glad he and his nephew would be getting off in

Chicago. She chewed quickly and swallowed.

"It can be a rough place," he continued, "especially these days. Kansas is used to liquor laws, but New York is still getting used to them." He looked at his water glass and frowned. "I think the temperance movement may have overreached. New York won't put up with Prohibition for long."

"Good," Louise said, her elbow on the table, her chin in her hand. "I think Prohibition is stupid."

"I couldn't agree more," the nephew said, trying to lean into her line of vision. He appeared incapable of even glancing at anyone or anything but her.

"That's because you don't know anything different." Cora used her napkin to dab at her lips. She, too, looked at Louise. "I know it's fashionable for young people to think nothing could be more fun than legalized alcohol, but you've grown up in a dry state, dear. You've never seen the effects of rampant abuse. You've never seen men drink up their wages and forget about their families, their children." Now she turned her gaze to the older man. "I suspect there are more than a few married women in New York who will be grateful to live as Kansas wives have for years."

99

Louise scoffed. "Unless they like a good drink." The younger man shook his head and laughed, but again failed to catch her gaze.

The uncle looked at Cora thoughtfully, taking another puff of his cigar. "Forgive me," he said politely, "but you said you grew up in Kansas, which has been dry for forty years. You don't look old enough to know anything but Prohibition, either." He shrugged. "Perhaps the troubles you're recalling simply prove liquor laws don't mean people won't drink."

Louise smiled and nudged his arm, as if their team had just scored a point.

"No," Cora said, unruffled. "That's not it at all. I've simply known older women who do remember the bad days. When I was a girl, I heard Carry Nation speak. If *you* grew up in Kansas, I'm sure you did as well. And as I recall, she had plenty to say about her first husband drinking himself to death. From what I understand, she was hardly alone in that experience."

The older man raised his water glass. "Now we'll all be punished together."

"That's one way to look at it." Cora fixed her knife and fork on the side of her plate, nodding at the waiter. She'd eaten all the corset would permit, enough to hold her over until dinner. "We'll have to agree to disagree."

"I'll drink to that!" the man said. He winced and smiled, tapping his head. "Damn. I'm not allowed."

Louise clicked her glass against his. "Unless you can be sneaky about it."

Cora put her napkin on the table. "Louise. I think we're both done eating. Nice meeting you, gentlemen. We should get back to our seats." She rose and undid the clasp of her purse.

"Please." The older man waved his hand. "Please! Don't think of paying. We asked the young lady to sit with us. And your company was a pleasure as well."

"Thank you, but I insist." She put a dollar on the table, fixing him with a look that ensured no further argument. She wished he would quit smiling at her like that. They were old enemies — the drinking man and the voting woman. She didn't need his esteem.

"Thanks for trying," Louise told them. As she stood, she glanced at the younger man and smiled at his uncle. Cora waited until Louise was in front of her, her tall heels moving fast and assured down the aisle, before she turned back, ever so briefly, to wish the men good day.

■ ■ ■ ■

She wanted to take Louise to task as soon as they got back to their seats. But first she had to ask her to retrieve *The Age of Innocence,* which she hoped was still on the floor.

"I have a bad back," she explained. They were both still standing in the aisle.

Louise looked up at her skeptically. "Bet your corset doesn't help much, either." Thankfully, she'd lowered her voice to a whisper. "Don't deny it. I've been picking things up for Mother my whole life."

Cora watched as Louise crouched down and searched under the seat. She moved so easily, so lightly. Cora knew many girls didn't wear corsets these days. They wore just brassieres that actually flattened their breasts — it was the new fashion, apparently, to try to look like a child, a young girl or even a boy. Cora couldn't tell if Louise's breasts were bound or if she was naturally small-chested. But everything about her seemed girlish — her haircut, her big eyes, her small stature. Yet with wise eyes and full lips.

Louise jumped up with a triumphant smile, and handed her the book.

"Thank you." Cora lowered her voice as well. "And now I'd like a word with you. I think you know about what."

Louise sank into her seat with a sigh. Instead of returning to the facing seat, Cora sat directly beside her. She needed to keep the imminent conversation as private, and as quiet, as possible. Louise, clearly unappreciative of Cora's discretion, crossed her legs and leaned toward the window. They were going over a brown, slow-moving river. Two boys wearing overalls stood on a rowboat, waving at the train with their caps.

"I'm not your enemy," Cora said. She was talking to the shiny back of the black hair, and the inch of pale neck just beneath it. "I'm not here to harass you, or to make you miserable, or to stop you from having fun. I'm here to protect you, actually."

Louise turned, annoyed. "From what? From those men? What did you think they were going to do? Have their way with me right in the dining car? Drag me under the table?"

That took Cora back. She had to swallow to regain her composure.

"Louise, a girl your age does not have lunch with men she doesn't know. Not without a chaperone."

"Why not?"

"Because it's not done."

"Why not?"

"Because it isn't."

"Why not?"

"Because of the appearance of impropriety."

They stared at each other until Louise looked away. "Circular reasoning," she muttered. "Round and round and round."

"We could turn round in Chicago," Cora offered. "We can go back to Kansas right now."

It was a mistake. Louise seemed afraid for only a moment. Then she looked into Cora's eyes, and right then, it seemed, saw the bluff. She couldn't have known why Cora wouldn't turn back, why her older companion needed the momentum of this train they'd already gotten on, moving east at a steady pace. But the girl — so watchful, so sensitive to vulnerability — seemed to sense some advantage.

"I suppose we could," she agreed. Still meeting Cora's gaze, she smiled.

"I'd rather not take such measures." Cora scratched her neck and turned away. She could smell her own dried sweat on her blouse. "But if you force me to, I will. Your parents have entrusted me with a great responsibility." She turned back to Louise.

"To be clear: I've come along not just to watch out for you but to watch out for your reputation. Do you understand? I'm here to protect you, even from speculation. My very presence on this trip ensures that no one could even suspect a compromising situation."

"Oh." Louise waved her hand. "Then you can relax. I don't care about that."

Cora had to smile. For someone so bookish, Louise certainly came across as naive. Had her mother really never explained any of this to her? This simple concept of damage? It was no wonder she seemed annoyed to have Cora along for the trip — she truly didn't understand why she needed a chaperone at all.

"Louise, those men were from Wichita — they live where we live. And so do many people on this train. You may not know them, but they might know who you are. They could go back and tell stories about your behavior. They could even embellish, not that they would have to, with you lunching on your own with firemen. And then when you come back to Wichita at the end of the summer, your reputation would be compromised."

"So?"

Cora took a breath, summoning patience.

"So you've told me you might like to marry someday. You'd like to be a bride."

Louise looked back at her beneath lowered brows, seemingly still confused. Cora sighed, fanning herself with her book. She didn't know how to be clearer. She'd talked to the boys about this sort of thing, but it was a different conversation. She'd simply warned them to stay away from a certain kind of girl, the kind who had a dismal future, the kind who might compromise theirs as well. Whether her sons had listened to this advice, she didn't know. They'd each had steady girlfriends, as well as girls who seemed less steady, who'd shown up for a while and then disappeared. She knew there were a few she'd never met. But there hadn't been any trouble, not that she knew of, and both Howard and Earle would go to college unfettered.

But Cora felt a girl needed a stronger warning — if only because the world was unfair. There were some inequities that wouldn't change. Maybe they couldn't. In any case, it was simply the way things were.

She glanced over her shoulder before leaning in. "Louise, I'll put it to you plainly. Men don't want candy that's been unwrapped. Maybe for a lark, but not when it comes to marriage. It may still be perfectly

106

clean, but if it's unwrapped, they don't know where it's been."

Louise stared, her lovely face absolutely still. Finally, Cora thought, she had gotten through. She'd had to use a crude analogy, and one she hadn't thought of or heard in years.

Louise put her hand to her mouth, clearly trying not to laugh. "That's the dumbest thing I've ever heard. Unwrapped candy? Oh, that's dreadful. Really, Cora. You sound like some old Italian mama. Who in the world taught you that?"

Cora stiffened. "I can assure you I've said nothing funny."

Louise leaned against her window. Her cheeks were flushed, her eyes bright. No matter how she shifted in the window's light, it seemed to love her face, its angles and its softness, her pale skin framed by the black hair. Cora stared at her grimly. Louise could afford to laugh. She was the beautiful daughter of indulging parents. She believed she was above everyone. Rules didn't apply to her.

"Go ahead and make fun if you want." Cora picked her book up off the seat. "But it's not just tedious morals from history, or whatever you want to call it. That's the way it is, the way it always has been, and the way it will be for a very long time." She was surprised by the anger in her voice. "You don't know what a slippery slope you're on, young lady, but I can assure you it has an edge." She stopped, embarrassed. She lowered her voice. "I only tell you this because I care."

With that, she stood, steadied herself, and eased into her own seat. She didn't look at Louise, but she was aware that the girl was still watching her. Cora opened her book to her marked place and did her best to look untroubled. She wasn't going to take back her words or hear any more backtalk. That wasn't what was needed now. Louise was well on her way to becoming the kind of girl she'd warned her own boys to stay away from. She was doing the girl a favor, coming down so hard.

She tried to calm her breath, focusing on the words on the page. But she heard crinkling, and she sensed movement on the other side of the table. She didn't look up. She heard the unfolding and opening of a paper bag. More rustling. The loud and pointed smack of lips.

Cora looked up warily.

Louise smiled. "Lollipop?"

On the girl's side of the table, spread out on a long sheet of wrinkled wax paper, were several uneven squares of hard, translucent candy, with a toothpick stuck in each.

"They're homemade." She gave Cora the same patronizing smile she'd given her father on the platform. "So they're a little uneven. But I've got such a sweet tooth. I made a big batch before I left."

Cora looked at the candy. She wouldn't have thought Louise would be interested in baking. But of course, she would have needed to learn to make her own treats, having distracted, unhappy Myra for a mother.

Louise put her elbow on the table, leaning in. "And since I made them myself, I can assure you I know where they've been." Her voice was stage-whisper loud. "I'm absolutely certain they're clean."

Cora stared back at her. She was being mocked. She was being mocked, and there was nothing she could do.

"Suit yourself." Louise slipped a candy into her mouth, so just the toothpick showed through her spit-shined lips, and closed her eyes with what seemed honest pleasure.

Six

Cora had first been told that a girl was like candy, either wrapped or unwrapped, when she was in Sunday school, and still too young to understand. The church outside McPherson only had one classroom, and because the boys had been sent out to the sanctuary for their own lesson that Sunday, there was no means to further separate the younger girls from the older. Or perhaps it was simply decided that even the younger girls were better off learning about un- wrapped candy too soon rather than too late. In any case, Cora, around seven at the time, was confused enough by the candy lesson to ask what it meant that very night, when Mother Kaufmann was tucking her in.

"Oh, goodness," Mother Kaufmann said, her small blue eyes widening before she looked away. "They're already teaching you that?" Cora's room was almost dark, the candle in its holder far from the bed, and still, in just that faint, flickering glow, reflected in the mirror over her bureau, she could see Mother Kaufmann was embarrassed, pink blooming on her pale cheeks. She smoothed the hem of the cotton quilt under Cora's chin, finally meeting her gaze. "They mean you girls need to save yourselves for marriage. That's all they mean by that."

Cora didn't want to further embarrass Mother Kaufmann, or herself, by asking any more questions, but she stayed awake for a long time that night, even more confused than before. How did you save yourself for marriage? How could you get used up? If you got used up, did it mean that you died? If not, what was left over? Could other people tell you'd been used up? How would they tell? Most importantly, how could Cora stop this using up from happening to her? Because she understood that not letting it happen, saving herself, was important. The lesson about the candy had been more somber, and more sternly presented, than the regular Sunday lessons when the boys were mixed in with the girls. And the other girls, all of them, appeared to have listened more attentively than they did during the regular Sunday lessons about loving their neighbors and doing unto others and such. But then, Cora considered, that wasn't saying much — neither the girls nor the boys seemed to have taken those lessons seriously at all. For these were the same girls and boys that Cora went to school with, and though Cora was their neighbor, they did not pretend to love her. They did not do unto Cora as they would have Cora do unto them.

During the week, she was one of fourteen, aged six through fifteen, nine girls and five boys, all of them sharing one room, one teacher, one stove, and not enough readers or slates. In so many ways, Cora was just like them. They all missed school during planting, and then again during harvest. They all did chores in the morning and tried not to fall asleep at their desks. Their mothers sewed them each a new outfit every school year, no nicer or worse than the new dress Mother Kaufmann sewed every year for Cora. They walked the same main road into school. And yet not one of them would walk with Cora. It was an older girl who finally told Cora the reason, and she seemed sad to be the one to have to bear the unfortunate news. It was as simple as this, the girl said: their parents knew Cora had come in on the train, and that she'd come from New York City. Cora likely had unmarried parents — her mother could have been a prostitute, or an imbecile, or mad, or a drunk. And maybe someone just off the boat — Cora had, after all, dark eyes and dark hair. In any case, if her parents had to give her up, she probably came from bad stock.

The teacher, who wasn't much older than a girl herself, who said "it don't matter none" when someone asked a question she couldn't answer, seemed to like Cora just fine. She told Cora she was a good girl who never caused any trouble, and that she had excellent penmanship. And so the learning part of school was fine. But in the play yard, Cora sat by herself while the boys roughhoused and the other girls played a game where they each held two wooden wands, using them to toss and catch a wooden circle the size of a hatband, with a ribbon wrapped all around it. Graces, they called the game, because it made you graceful. The girls only had two rings between them, and so they had to share, but they played every day, keeping track of who could catch the ring ten times first, the winner going on to play a challenger. They would not let Cora play, and sometimes when she was sitting in the play yard, her loneliness as sharp as thirst, she wished she were back in New York, still jumping rope and playing blindman's bluff with girls who were no better than she was, even though since she'd come to Kansas, almost every day, she ate beef or chicken or pork and buttered corn and Mother Kaufmann's fruit pies with real whipping cream; even though she was tucked in bed under a soft quilt every night with a kiss; and even though on Sundays, she rode to church in the wagon between the Kaufmanns, and when they walked inside the church, the Kaufmanns, both of them so tall and fair and not looking anything like her, each held one of her hands, with no care of what anyone thought.

One morning in October, Cora told Mother Kaufmann she no longer wanted to go to school. They were sitting back-to-back, each of them milking a Jersey, the air in the barn cold enough that Cora could see her breath by the light of the lantern. She said she would be happier at home, helping with the work. At first, Mother Kaufmann was irritated. She told Cora that her education was important, and a privilege, and that she didn't want to hear that kind of foolish talk again. But then Cora told her why she hated going to school: how the others knew she'd come on the train, and how she had to sit by herself and watch the girls play graces. For a while, there was only the sound of the milk hitting the sides of the buckets, and Lida shuffling in her stall, and then Mother Kaufmann said, "Graces. I remember that game. Well, it's good for our hearts to be strengthened by grace. Theirs, too, I suppose." She turned then, her wet fingers and thumb gently tugging Cora's ear. "Hear me, love? We'll show those girls more grace than they've ever known."

At first, Cora worried Mother Kaufmann meant to go down to the school and scare the other children into being nice. She likely could have. Mother Kaufmann was thin all over; still, she could look very serious with her pointy nose, and she was tall enough to wear her husband's trousers under her calico skirts on the days she helped him in the fields. But she never came down to the schoolyard. Instead, just a few days later, Mr. Kaufmann presented Cora with her own graces ring. He had carved it to Mother Kaufmann's specifications, using the sharp knife he called his Arkansas toothpick and a piece of wood from the big branch of oak that had fallen the previous summer. Mother Kaufmann had wound a red ribbon around the ring, leaving the knotted extra hanging, just like the rings of the girls at school.

"And here are the wands," Mr. Kaufmann said, his pale eyes bright, clearly pleased with the bewilderment on Cora's face. She still didn't know him so well. Except on Sundays, he only came in for meals and sleep, even when there was snow. At the table, he frequently talked about rain — when it would rain, how long it would rain, how hard. When it was cold, he worried aloud about frost and frozen ground. Cora understood, on some level, that his preoccupation with weather and work was as necessary to her well-being as anything Mother Kaufmann did or said. But she also understood, with the same intuition, that he didn't need her the way Mother Kaufmann did, and that Cora had been, in a sense, his present for his young wife. Mr. Kaufmann had children from his first marriage. His wife, the first Mrs. Kaufmann, died of pneumonia, but three of their children, two sons and a daughter, were still alive. The sons were doing well out west, and the daughter was married, a mother herself, and living in Kansas City. Every year, just after harvest, Mr. Kaufmann took the train to Kansas City to visit this daughter while Cora and Mother Kaufmann stayed behind to look after the animals. The daughter had never come to visit them. They shouldn't judge, Mother Kaufmann said. It would be hard to come back to your childhood home, and find your father's new wife and child.

"Thank you," Cora said, holding the ring and wands out in front of her. She was anxious about how much time Mr. Kaufmann had spent carving the ring, and what, exactly, they expected her to achieve with it. It wouldn't be enough for her to just take the ring and the wands to school. Was that what they were thinking? That it would be so easy? The problem was where she had come from — and the ring and wands wouldn't help with that.

"We should start right away," Mother Kaufmann said. She was already in the mudroom, putting on her heavy brown boots. "It's a little wet out. We can go to the barn. Bring the lantern for when it gets dark."

Cora was almost as stunned as she was thrilled — Mother Kaufmann had never played any kind of game with her. She was always busy, always getting something done. She got the fire going under the big tub to wash the clothes and sheets; she killed chickens with the clothesline before hanging them by their feet on the hook for plucking; she shoveled manure; she strained milk; she gathered eggs; she washed the strainers and the milk pails; she cooked the meals and canned pears and asparagus; she hauled in water to wash the dishes; she sewed tears in clothing. Cora helped with all this when she wasn't at school, but she was given time to loaf, to pet the animals, and to lie on her back in the grass to look up at clouds. Still, she'd always done her loafing alone.

Once Mr. Kaufmann made the ring, however, Cora and Mother Kaufmann went out to the barn every evening, both of them staying up late to make the time. Mother Kaufmann was patient, especially at the beginning, when Cora was still learning how to uncross the wands at the right speed and angle to shoot the ring into the air. When she failed, after many tries, Mother Kaufmann told her she wasn't moving the wands quickly enough. She showed her how to do it and told her to try again. And again. Again. Even in the cold, Cora would sweat in her dress, breathing hard. But she was so happy to be playing graces, to be playing anything with another person. They only had Cora's two wands, so Mother Kaufmann didn't use any — she caught the ring with just her hands before tossing it back to Cora. When Cora pointed out that this wasn't exactly fair, Mother Kaufmann looked impatient and said fairness wasn't the point.

She started tossing the ring from farther away. When it got late, she would blink at the lantern, and her tosses would get less controlled and even harder to catch.

But after a while, Cora was good enough to send the ring up high enough that she had time to run under it and catch it with one wand or two. She was allowed to stay up late and play on her own. She thought about the game even when she wasn't playing it — the satisfying click the ring made when it landed just right on the wands. By Christmas, she could throw the ring up, spin around twice, and catch it with both wands. She could catch the ring behind her back. She could catch it with her arms crossed at the elbow. She tossed it up high enough to make one of the hired hands take off his hat and say, "Whoo-wee!" She could even catch the ring with her eyes closed, but after succeeding at this twice, she'd almost broken her nose, and she was too scared to try again.

The Kaufmanns agreed it was time for her to take the ring to school.

"You don't need to ask them anything," Mother Kaufmann said. "You just stand there and show them what you can do. Smile if you want. But they can come to you."

On the cold, sunny morning when Cora first walked into the school yard with her wands and her ring, they ignored her. The girls playing graces kept tossing and throwing, and the others waited for their turn. The boys were over by the tree. Cora heard pebbles shift under her shoes as she rocked back and forth, getting ready. She pushed her braids behind her shoulders. It was just like at home, she told herself, the same ring, the same wands. But her hands trembled as she crossed the sticks beneath her ring.

She caught several high tosses in a row. She caught the ring behind her back, and then she did it again. She knew they were watching when the clicking sounds of the other girls' rings and wands stopped. She flew the ring up again, still higher than before, and this time when she caught it with the wands behind her back, someone, a boy — she would never know which one — yelled, "Darn, Cora. Bully for you!" And really, that was the moment, the exact moment, when everything started to change. Two of the older girls came up to her, just as Mother Kaufmann had said they would.

They wanted to know how she could throw the ring up so high and always catch it. Could she show them? Where had she learned to play so well?

"New York," Cora said, still throwing the ring high, high, high, in the air. She wasn't ready to look at them just yet. "Everyone there is good at this."

It was surprising, and a little perplexing, how easy things were from then on. The girls fought over who would play with her. Some started being friendly all the time, even when they weren't playing. Cora was never invited to anyone's house, but they were all a little nicer, and some risked the wrath of their parents by walking home with her from school. "You're perfectly nice," one girl told her. "My father said some people can overcome their backgrounds."

All because of a game, a ring and wands, a set of rules. Really, it was as if she had tricked them. After all, she was the same person she had always been. She was still from New York City, with unknown heritage and dark hair. The game hadn't really made her more graceful, or more anything, except more able to toss and catch a ring with wands. It wasn't even that interesting of a game — there were only so many variations of the same toss and catch, and after a

while, there was little room for further chal-
lenge or improvement. But she kept playing, long after she grew bored, for the same
reason she started in the first place.

"I think you likely came from good people,"
Mother Kaufmann told Cora once. It was
her fourteenth birthday, or what they called
her birthday, the anniversary of the day
she'd come on the train. She and Mother
Kaufmann were in the kitchen, washing and
slicing potatoes, Mother Kaufmann watching Cora to make sure she sliced away from
her hand. The cake was in the copper-
trimmed oven, and though it was a cold day,
the air in the kitchen was warm enough that
a glaze of mist had settled on the four-paned
window.

"I never told you this." She paused in her
slicing to look down at Cora. "But you're
older now and I think you can hear it." She
started slicing again, still watching Cora's
hands. "When I told Mrs. Lindquist next
door that we were thinking of getting a child
from the train, she told me not to, not unless I only wanted a worker. She didn't
mean breeding and all that." She glanced
down at Cora shyly. "She said you wouldn't
love me. She said children can't respond to
affection if they're without from the start."

Cora considered this, still slicing and listening to the rain fall from the eave over the window. Mrs. Lindquist was wrong. It was ridiculous. How could she not love Mother Kaufmann, who sang "Black Is the Color of My True Love's Hair" as she and Cora pulled weeds in the garden, who could get very mad sometimes, but who had never laid a hand on her with anything but softness? How could she not love being in the kitchen with her, the scent of the cake in the oven, the sound of their slicing knives?

"She said it was scientifically proven." Mother Kaufmann plunged two more potatoes in the bucket of water, rubbing off the mud with the pads of her thumbs. "But then we got you, and you wanted to be cuddled from the start. Not at the very first, but fairly quickly." She looked down at Cora and smiled. When Cora was younger, she'd thought of Mother Kaufmann's front teeth as little people, leaning into and against one another. "We'd hug you, and you'd hug back. We'd kiss your cheeks, and you'd kiss right back. You'd come up and sit in my lap. In Mr. Kaufmann's, too. Mrs. Lindquist said someone must have held you when you were a baby. But you said the nuns didn't hug and kiss."

Cora had to laugh at the thought of it.

123

Mother Kaufmann reached over to steady the knife. Even with all her work in the sun, her skin was much paler than Cora's.

"Maybe the other girls then?"

Maybe. Cora remembered holding hands with Mary Jane. And there was the earliest memory, the one of the dark-haired woman with the knit shawl. Was she a real memory, then? And not just a lonely dream? Was that who had held her, and taught her to be held? She'd known her own name when she first came to the orphanage. That's what the older girls said.

She glanced up at Mother Kaufmann. She'd never told her about the woman with the shawl. She'd worried the telling would hurt her, this woman who fed her vegetables but also cake and made her clothes and tied ribbons in her braids and stayed by her bed when she had a fever. She was betraying her now, perhaps, even thinking about the woman with the shawl. Cora leaned her forehead against Mother Kaufmann's shoulder as a silent apology, and breathed in the lavender smell of her dress. When she looked up again, Mother Kaufmann's blue eyes were bright and blinking fast.

"It doesn't matter," she said, smoothing Cora's hair. "We're here for you now."

■ ■ ■ ■

But one day, all at once and forever, they weren't.

It happened in early November, when the days were still warm, but the cool evenings were lovely, the mosquitoes gone. Two cuttings of hay were stacked neatly in the barn, and Cora was back at school. On that day, she'd made a map of the solar system, writing each planet's name neatly beside it. She was sixteen, the oldest student by far, and she spent a good part of her time at school helping the teacher with lessons for the younger children. She was good at drawing and explaining things. Mother Kaufmann had said maybe she could be a teacher herself — not in this town, but maybe one close by.

One of the hired workers found her as she was walking home. He was a young man, a Norwegian with good English who could lift a squealing hog, full grown, as if it were nothing, but when he stopped in front of Cora he was sweating, panting. He'd run toward the school to find her, and now that he had, he didn't talk.

"What?" she asked. A perfect breeze, cool and light, moved across her face, kicking up dust farther down the road. She could see the windmill, the top of the barn. It had never occurred to her this new world could be lost, just as quickly and permanently as the old one.

He was so sorry to tell her. There'd been an accident.

She backed away, and he followed, making sure she understood. Just an hour before, he had climbed up the silo, looked in, and seen their bodies already blue, but peaceful-looking, lying on top of the grain, her right next to him. As if they had fallen asleep in the cold. He didn't think they had fallen. Or maybe one fell, and the other went in after. It was more likely that they'd both jumped in, as they often had, to tramp the clotted grain down. It was the gas, he said. From the grain. They must have thought enough time had passed. A quick death. And not painful. Another worker had already left to get the minister.

Cora ran around the Norwegian and toward them, cutting through the field to the silo, her hands in tight fists with her nails digging into her palms, her boots hard and fast on the dirt and yellowed stalks, grasshoppers springing all around. The dogs ran alongside her, barking, thinking she meant to play. She smelled manure and turned earth, everything familiar holding fear. She kicked a dog out of her way. Her hair fell out of its bun, and by the time she lunged for the ladder, she was crazed, her blood hot in her throat. The workers held her back, and told her she couldn't go in, and that she shouldn't climb up. They would need time to safely get the bodies out. You couldn't see or smell the gas, and if she went in, she would for certain die with them. She tried for the ladder again. It took two of them to get her back in the house.

The Lindquists came for her that night, their white-haired heads hovering over her bed, saying her name until she heard them. She shouldn't be alone, they said. Their own children were grown; they had spare rooms. The Kaufmanns had been good neighbors, and it was the least they could do. They insisted. Just for a while, Mr. Lindquist said, until decisions were made about the farm. Even if Cora could function and keep the house running, it wouldn't be right, a girl by herself. The Norwegian and another man were staying on to care for the livestock and fields.

Later, Mrs. Lindquist would apologize for taking Cora from her home. "We didn't know we were making it easier for them to turn you out with nothing," she said, using a fork to slide the remainder of Cora's lunch into the slop jar. She glared out her own window to the Kaufmann farm. "The sheriff would have had to put you out, but at least it would have been harder."

Mrs. Lindquist would also tell Cora, over and over, that the Kaufmanns had had no way of knowing they would be taken up so suddenly, or so relatively young. If they had, Mrs. Lindquist was certain, they would have made a will, or made Cora one of their legal heirs. Of course they would have. They had loved her as a daughter. Mrs. Lindquist had heard just that many times, straight from her neighbor's mouth, and she would testify to it in any court. It was a shame, she said, the way the Kaufmann girl and her brothers were denying Cora any inheritance. The laws needed to be changed.

The Kaufmann girl. Cora, too, looked through the window, over the autumn-cropped fields to her old home. When Mrs. Lindquist said the Kaufmann girl, she did not mean Cora but Mr. Kaufmann's daughter in Kansas City, who had a lawyer, and who was adamant that Cora should not be considered an heir, as she was not related by blood or marriage. As the lawyer pointed out, her selection had been arbitrary. The

Kaufmanns could have picked any child from the train. It was unfortunate if Cora had truly misinterpreted their kindness as the familial love she was so sadly lacking. But if they'd wanted her in the will, they would have put her in.

Cora had no energy to be outraged. Her grief was a weight on her chest that she felt as soon as she woke. The Lindquists had gone back to get all her things, including her nightclothes, but at night, Cora couldn't summon the energy to undress. She slept in her dress, and also lay awake in it, thinking about the Kaufmanns, how the Norwegian said they'd looked peaceful, but also that they had turned blue. At some point, she stopped combing her hair. Mrs. Lindquist, who'd had four daughters and lost only one to diphtheria, used bacon grease to get out the tangles. She'd warned Cora that next time, scissors would be required, and wouldn't that be a shame, because the curly hair was so pretty in her opinion. Cora made herself use a comb. She felt bad for looking so terrible when she was taking up space in their home. The Lindquists had only thought she would be with them for a few days, maybe a week. But now she had nowhere to go.

Mr. Lindquist talked to the minister, who

agreed that Cora was being cheated out of her share. He remembered the Kaufmanns had once mentioned that they hoped to formally adopt Cora, and he could testify that they had never thought of her as a servant. They simply hadn't gotten around to adopting her. And there was good news. The minister had described Cora and her situation to his son, who lived in Wichita, and who happened to know a skilled attorney, who was doing well enough that he was looking for some pro bono work. He wanted to meet with Cora and see if he could help.

Mr. Carlisle, as Cora called him then, was the first man she had ever seen wearing a waistcoat, a jacket that matched his trousers, and shoes that were perfectly clean. When he first appeared on the Lindquists' dusty front porch, tipping his hat and saying her name, both of the Lindquists came out to stare at him as well. It was hard for any of them to believe that this man, important enough to have a driver waiting outside with the horse and carriage, would come so far out into the country to help Cora with her case.

"And he's something to look at, isn't he?" Mrs. Lindquist whispered as she and Cora set the chipped cups on the flowered saucers and waited for the water to boil. "No wedding ring, and he looks about thirty. The women of Wichita must be stupid or blind."

Cora looked at the shiny teapot, the distorted reflection of her face. She didn't care if her lawyer was handsome. She didn't even care about the case. The real Kaufmann daughter had sent legal papers, and on them, Cora's name was Cora X. When Cora first saw this X by her name, she'd felt as if the rhythm of her breathing was permanently altered, and she would never again get enough air into her lungs. That feeling had not gone away. If she did get money from the sale of the farm, she would no longer be a burden to the Lindquists. The Kaufmanns would still be gone, though. And she would still be Cora X.

Out in the parlor, Mr. Carlisle, before he even took a sip of tea, read over the legal papers and said the X by her name was ridiculous, and that he would help her with that issue as well. He sat on the edge of the Lindquists' wooden rocker, not rocking, a pad of paper balanced on his knee. He had a nick on his cheek from shaving. He pointed out that the minister, at least when he spoke with him, had referred to Cora as Cora Kaufmann. Was that what she had

131

been called in school? Cora, sitting next to Mrs. Lindquist on the sofa, nodded, watching him closely. She registered that he was indeed handsome, his hair the color of strong tea, his profile strong. And he clearly meant to help her, to do the best he could.

"I'll need to ask you questions about your history. Details about your life with the Kaufmanns, how they treated you. And before that." He looked at his pocket watch and took out a steel-nibbed pen. "It shouldn't take longer than an hour. Are you up to it?"

She nodded again. Mrs. Lindquist, leaning over the table to pour the tea, gave her an encouraging smile. The Lindquists had been so patient with her, and so helpful, going to the minister to plead her case. And now old Mrs. Lindquist, who usually napped at this hour, had to sit here with them because it wouldn't be proper for her to leave Cora and the lawyer alone in the parlor. Cora was taking up her time, and the lawyer's time as well. The least she could do was be compliant.

She spoke with a clear voice, answering every question as best she could. She was never a servant, she said. She did chores like any child, but the Kaufmanns treated her as their own. Mr. Kaufmann had carved

132

toys and dolls for her, and Mother Kaufmann had made them clothes. Yes, she said, Mother Kaufmann. That's how I addressed her. Whose idea? She couldn't recall. She told him how the three of them had sat together in church, and how they made her go to school even when she didn't want to, and how she was grateful for that now. She told him about her little room in the house, with the bed and the dresser, and how the Kaufmanns had first told her she would have her own room before they'd even brought her home from the station.

"The station?" He looked up from his notepad, apologetic.

At that precise moment, Mrs. Lindquist, who Cora thought had just been sitting quietly beside her, started to snore, her mouth open, her head resting on the top of the sofa's cushioned back. Cora smiled. Her first smile since the accident. The stretch of her lips felt strange.

"And here I thought I was so interesting," she said.

Mr. Carlisle smiled as well. "Should we wake her?"

Cora shook her head. She was already thinking about the train, and how she had felt as a child, riding through those dark nights without knowing what was in store

— very much how she felt now. But she went on speaking clearly, telling him of the day she met the Kaufmanns and how they had asked her to be their little girl. She told him about the train, and all the stops it made before she was chosen, and how she and the other children had been taught to sing "Jesus Loves Me" on stages and the front steps of city halls and churches. When you didn't get picked, you got back on the train. There was a jar of water at the front of the car, she remembered, and a ladle, and if you got thirsty you could make your way to the front and take a drink.

At some point, he stopped writing and rested his chin in his hand, his elbow propped on the rocking chair's arm.

"Oh my," Cora said. "I hope I won't put you to sleep as well."

"Not at all." He held her gaze before looking back at his notepad. "Did you have a family in New York?"

She blinked at the flowered edge of her teacup. Her only memory might not even be real. But she could still see the woman clearly, too clearly to have dreamed her. She could see the frayed edges of the red shawl.

"I'm sorry. I can see this is difficult for you." He put down his pen, took a white handkerchief out of his pocket and started

134

to offer it to her, and then, seeing she would not cry, put the handkerchief back in his pocket.

"I'm fine," she said. "I just haven't thought about that in a long time. That sounds strange, perhaps." She looked back up at him, waiting. She really didn't know.

He shrugged. "I couldn't tell you. I grew up with my parents and my sister in Wichita. No one put me on a train when I was six."

Mrs. Lindquist snored on.

Cora smiled again, her gaze resting on his hands. His fingernails were clean and neatly trimmed. "I don't know that I can explain. Coming out here, it was like becoming a new person. I think we all understood that, even though we were young. We knew, or at least I knew, we would have to be good, which meant we would have to become whatever they wanted us to be. In my case, it was their daughter, which was lucky. But even then, I couldn't hold on to who I was. Or maybe I just started to think that, by and by." She looked away and shook her head. "I don't know if that makes any sense."

"It does."

She was surprised by the conviction in his voice. He was looking at her so intently. She brushed her hand across her face, wondering if something was there. But no. And really, that wasn't the kind of look he was giving her. She didn't know what to make of it.

"I appreciate you helping me like this," she said. "I wish I could pay you. I'm sorry I didn't say that from the start. I'm not myself right now."

"Of course not." Finally, he looked away. "And I'm honored to represent you. It seems to me you're a very decent young woman who has had a difficult time. And borne it well, I should add. You don't seem bitter in any way."

She didn't know what to say to that. Even with Mrs. Lindquist's snoring, she could hear the ticking of his pocket watch. Hadn't he said he would only stay for an hour? She didn't know the time, but surely they'd been talking for longer than that.

"Would you like more tea?"

He shook his head, and still, he made no move to leave. She didn't know why not, what should happen now. She'd already told him she couldn't pay.

"It must be very exciting to live in a city." It was all that she could think of.

"It is." He smiled warmly. "So much to do. We have a soda shop now, with mirrored walls, and electric fans in the ceiling." He gestured up to the Lindquists' bare ceiling, twirling his hand. "You can get penny candy, all different kinds, and malted milk shakes."

It made no sense to Cora, how he was looking at her, how long he was staying, the focus of his kind gaze. Mother Kaufmann had told her she had a strong face, an interesting face, and that it was beautiful in a unique way. Cora believed this when she was young, but as she got older, she suspected Mother Kaufmann of flattery. She had observed the behavior of the boys at school, the way they acted around certain girls, and she knew real beauty would have trumped everything, even her sketchy origins. Yet even after she was the champion of graces, the boys at school were polite to her at best. And yet — yes, it was true — this very handsome lawyer had been sitting in the Lindquists' parlor for longer than he had to, staring back at her as if she really were something to behold.

"That sounds wonderful," she said, her voice perhaps too full of breath, too loud. Mrs. Lindquist woke with a cough. Cora and the lawyer fell silent, both of them looking away to give her time to compose herself. When they looked back, Mrs. Lindquist was sitting up straight. She smiled at Cora, sipping her tea as if it was still hot to her lips, and no time had passed at all.

"I should be on my way." Mr. Carlisle lifted his briefcase, opened it, and put the notepad inside. "Thank you, Mrs. Lindquist. Thank you, Miss Kaufmann." He looked at Cora meaningfully and stood. She stood, too, the top of her head barely reaching his shoulders. She realized, only now, that for at least an hour, she'd had a short recess from her squeezing grief.

Mrs. Lindquist stood beside her. "Dear? Are you all right?"

She nodded. At that moment, unbelievably, she was.

He helped, and he helped quickly. There wasn't even a trial. By the start of the new year, the Kaufmann daughter and her brothers had agreed to a settlement. Cora wouldn't get a full fourth of the profit from the farm, but she would get enough to pay the Lindquists something, and, when she did move out, to afford her board and security until she married or found a vocation. The money did make her feel better, more hopeful for the future. But it was her new legal name that truly raised her spirits. She was officially Cora Kaufmann now, as recognized by the State of Kansas.

She sent a letter to Mr. Carlisle's office in Wichita, letting him know what she planned to do with the money the following autumn: she would go to Wichita herself, to Fairmount College, and train to be a teacher. She thanked him for his kindness. She wrote how much his compassion and charity had meant to her, and she signed the letter "with gratitude and deep respect," which wasn't nearly what she felt. In truth, she had replayed those hours with him in the Lindquists' parlor many times, letting herself imagine that she would somehow see him again, after she moved to Wichita. It wasn't that large of a city — surely they would bump into each other. And perhaps he really wasn't married yet. But in her more somber moments, which were frequent, she understood these imaginings as fantasy, not likely to actually happen. If Cora ever did see him in Wichita, she would be lucky if he remembered her at all. In so many ways, they weren't on the same level. He had just helped her because he was kind.

But a week after she sent the letter, he was back at the Lindquists' door, this time holding a bouquet of red carnations and seeming more nervous than before.

His courtship made perfect sense to Mrs.

Lindquist — and yes, she said, it was clearly a courtship; she knew a man with intentions when she saw one. And she had to say, she wasn't surprised at all — Cora was a lovely young woman, pure of heart and pure of virtue, and what man wouldn't want just that in a wife? Mrs. Lindquist imagined many men, even wealthy, sophisticated men, would prefer an unsullied country girl to a hardened woman of the city. The legal situation had simply given Mr. Carlisle a chance to get to know her. True, he was older and more educated, but wasn't that often the case for a husband and wife? He didn't seem to lord anything over her. He was as smitten as she was. It was clear to anyone with eyes.

It was clear even to Cora. Alan — *Alan,* she called him now — brightened at the sight of her. He wanted to be with her all the time, this handsome, considerate man. It was unsettling for her, this giddiness, this excitement, this thrilling at the touch of his hand on her arm, so soon after the misery of the previous fall and winter. Mrs. Lindquist said she shouldn't feel guilty. The Kaufmanns would want this happiness for her. They would agree that she deserved it.

"And I did some checking for you," she added, her voice lowered, though Mr.

140

Lindquist was out with the pigs and they were alone in the house. "His family is very respectable. I have cousins in Wichita, and they talked to the mother once. They said you could tell she had good schooling, she spoke so nicely."

The next day, Cora walked to the schoolhouse and begged her old teacher for any book she could study that might help her with her grammar. The teacher told her she already spoke just fine, better than most of her other students; but Cora persisted, and the teacher eventually lent her *Lessons in Language* by Horace Sumner Tarbell. The preface assured her that self-confidence was the key to success with any art, and that regular study would provide her self-confidence, though the book's subsequent warnings made her anxious. (*Caution: Be careful not to say don't for doesn't. Caution: Never say ain't, hain't, 'tain't, or mayn't.*) At night, after the Lindquists had gone to bed, she stayed up with the book and a candle, going over subject-verb agreement and proper use of adverbs and the error of the split infinitive. Some of the rules she knew from school, but not all of them. She did the exercises. She learned when to say "lie" and when to say "lay," when to say "me" and when to say "I," and to never say "irregardless," and though she was most urgently concerned about her speech, she read and studied the sections on punctuation and capitalization and proper salutations, just in case the time came when she would have to write Alan's well-spoken mother a note.

When Alan first took her to Wichita for dinner at his parents' house, which was so beautiful and modern, with an indoor bathroom that had a little pull chain above the toilet that made it flush, she was nervous, certain they would be disappointed in her youth and plainness, even though she wore the flower-trimmed hat and the smart dress with the narrow skirt that Alan had purchased and sent to her at the Lindquists'. The very fact that he'd bought clothes for her to wear to the dinner suggested that his parents would be observing her closely, and she found another book on table etiquette and memorized its every instruction, worried that if she didn't, she would be soon found out as the bumpkin that she was.

But to her surprise, she was greeted warmly. Alan's parents and his pretty sister appeared charmed by every practiced sentence that came out of her mouth. His mother, a very tall woman with Alan's eyes, declared Cora just as good-natured and naturally intelligent as her son had described. Alan's father smiled as he made a toast to Cora's "wholesome loveliness." After dinner, Alan's mother took her hand and said she understood Cora had suffered a horrible loss with the death of her parents, and that she hoped their family could bring her some solace. Cora was struck to see real kindness in the woman's face — there was no hint of the judgment or ridicule she'd been afraid of.

Later, Alan told her he'd been honest with his parents, telling them everything about Cora's legal case, and even her coming from New York on the train. She had their sympathy, he said. But there was a reason they had said nothing about her life before the Kaufmanns. His parents strongly believed it would be best, for Cora, and for everyone — as Alan and Cora were spending so much time together — if her origins weren't publicly discussed. As far as they were concerned, Cora was a nice young woman who had grown up on a farm outside McPherson, and that was as much of the story as people needed to hear.

Cora was quick to agree. She was much in favor of a fresh start. There was no need for anyone in Wichita to know she'd come in on the train, that she'd ever been Cora

X. And if Mrs. Lindquist was correct, and if her own greatest wish came true, she would soon be Mrs. Cora Kaufmann Carlisle, and that would be the name that mattered. She would be Alan's wife, part of his family, and she would fully embrace her good fortune, his surprising and irrational love, just as she had when she first met the Kaufmanns, all those years ago.

■ ■ ■ ■

Part Two

■ ■ ■ ■

Ah, no, he did not want May to have that
kind of innocence, the innocence that
seals the mind against imagination and
the heart against experience . . .
— EDITH WHARTON,
The Age of Innocence

SEVEN

They were still out on the sidewalk of West Eighty-sixth Street, the taxi pulling away, when Louise put down her travel bag, raised both arms, and declared herself in love with New York City.

"It's *exactly* as I imagined it!" She let her arms fall and looked out at the street, at the honking, halting parade of cars, headlights bright in the dusking air. She turned to Cora with glistening eyes. "I've always known it, my whole life. This is where I'm meant to be."

Cora, though exhausted, managed a smile. Louise had been like this since the moment they stepped into the main concourse of Grand Central Station. Even with people just behind them and just in front of them, so many speaking strange languages and wearing the dark clothes of foreigners, some smoking, some coughing, all exhaling too closely, Louise said she felt as if she were walking into her dreams. Cora had only nodded in response, her gaze moving around the concourse, taking in the arched blue ceiling and the wide exits on every side. It was a magnificent space, brighter than the station in Wichita and big enough to swallow it whole. But if she'd been there before, if the train she'd boarded with the other children had left from that very station, she didn't remember. Nothing felt familiar. Maybe it would have, if she'd had more time there. But once Louise saw the exit for Forty-second Street, she walked toward it quickly, saying she couldn't wait to get out on the famous street and breathe in the city's air.

The attraction, from what Cora saw, was mutual. As she and Louise made their way through the big doors and into the muggy air, even with the rush of so many people moving in and out, all kinds of men — laborers in shirtsleeves, sailors, even well-dressed men who seemed to be in a hurry — let their gazes linger on Louise's face before moving down the length of her figure. Beautiful women in silk dresses turned to look at her haircut, the blunt bangs so unusual even among so many bob-haired heads. At least Cora hoped the hair was why they stared. That morning on the train, Louise had returned from the ladies' lounge in a light green skirt and a white short-sleeved blouse with such a low V-necked collar that she had to swear to Cora that her mother not only approved of the blouse — she'd bought it for her. Cora surrendered the argument. Either Louise was lying, or Myra had very poor judgment, and Cora hadn't felt up to making a case for either. And so Louise had sauntered into the streets of New York with so many eyes on her lovely face and striking hair and rosebud décolletage. She pretended not to notice the attention she garnered, but Cora, glancing at her from the side, suspected that she did.

Cora herself, on the other hand, knew she did not look her best. She was in need of a bath; the train windows had been open for most of the trip from Chicago, and she felt as if she'd been basted in grease, thoroughly heated, and finally dipped in dust. And she was tired. Despite her more sensible, lower-heeled shoes, she trailed Louise across a wide street with its vaguely observed cross-walk to the taxi stand, struggling to keep up. "People move more quickly here," Louise said, looking back over her shoulder. "Have you noticed? They walk faster, talk faster, everything! It's swell!"

It really was something, all the bustle and commotion, so many people everywhere. Cora didn't let herself look up at the buildings, gawking like the newcomer she was. She'd taken the warnings of people back home seriously, and she was on guard for pickpockets and hustlers, though during the short wait for the taxi, neither a pickpocket nor a hustler appeared. Once she and Louise were in a cab, with its relative safe and quiet, she tried to take it all in, looking out at more buildings and cars and trains and trolleys than she had ever even pictured in one place. She'd seen photographs of New York, street scenes and pictures of parades in the newspaper. For years she'd studied them, searching for anything — a street corner, a building's façade, a passerby's expression — that might remind her of her early life. But she couldn't have imagined the noise of the actual city, all the engines and horns and jackhammers and drills and the jarring clatter of elevated trains. The only way she could think of New York, the only way she would be able to describe it when she got home, was as a hundred Douglas Avenues on the busiest day of the year, all of them pushed up against each other and on top of one another. She was at once amazed and overwhelmed.

But Louise's enthusiasm was unrelenting, even after they arrived at the squat apartment building, even after they climbed three flights of stairs, even after they found the key under the loose board by the door just as the landlord had told Leonard Brooks they would, and gained entrance to the disappointing apartment.

"It's not so bad," Louise announced, trying and failing to turn on a lamp, which Cora hoped only needed a new bulb. The front room was small, with pale yellow walls, most of the floor space taken up by a writing desk and a circular table with three chairs. There was no window, just a framed oil painting of a Siamese cat hung above the desk. Cora followed Louise into and through a narrow kitchen that doubled as a hallway to the bedroom, which was shaped exactly like the front room, though the walls were painted pea green. The bedroom did have a window, and a ceiling fan. But no rug. A door by the bed led to a bathroom. The bedroom itself had no door.

Louise plopped on the bed, declared it very comfortable, and said New Yorkers didn't really care about their apartments because they were never home. "That's just fine with me," she said, her voice growing louder to compensate for Cora turning on the faucet in the bathroom. "I'd live in a closet and be happy, as long as it's by everything that matters."

"We have warm water," Cora called out. The bathroom had its own small window looking into an airshaft, and walls that had been painted, for some reason, blood red. But there could have been orange stripes on the walls for all Cora cared. A bath was all she needed. Easing out of her shoes, she stuck her head into the bedroom.

"I'm going to take a bath, dear. Do you need to use the bathroom before I get in?"

"I'm fine. Go ahead." Louise crouched by an electric socket, plugging in the fan. "Just don't take too long. I can't wait to go out."

Cora leaned against the bathroom doorway, fanning herself with her hand. "Are you hungry?" She had to talk over the running water. "We had that big supper on the train."

"No, I'm not hungry. We should go to Times Square. We could take the subway."

"Oh, Louise." Cora shook her head. She was so tired. The sleeping berths on the train had been as comfortable as they could be, with drawn curtains and porter-fluffed pillows; still, she'd been too aware of strangers across the aisle, not to mention the steady rocking. She hadn't slept very well.

"I figured you might be tired." Louise tugged on the low neck of her blouse. "That's all right. Is there anything you want me to get?"

Cora stared at her. In the street below, a car backfired. Louise blinked back at her, smiling, as if what she'd just said made perfect sense.

"It's almost dark." Cora nodded toward the bedroom window, which, aside from the whirling fan, held only a view of a brick wall maybe six feet away. "And you have your first class in the morning."

"Not until ten. I'll be fine." She slid past Cora into the bathroom, looked in the mirror, and gave her reflection a brief but appreciative glance. She looked beautiful. She did not smell at all. It was as if for her, even in these warm rooms, even after the long journey on the train, sweat and dust and fatigue did not exist. She was still in heels. Cora had already eased out of hers, and so in the mirror, they appeared the same height.

"Louise," she sighed, bracing herself. There would be no avoiding an argument. She glanced back at the tub, checking the height of the water. "I'm sorry. I can't let you go out by yourself."

Louise looked back, her smile gone. She

took in a deep breath, lowered her head, and moved past Cora into the bedroom. "I won't go far. I'll just walk around here for a while. Don't worry. I'll stay close."

"I can't let you go out by yourself at all." Cora leaned against the doorway. "Honestly, I think you know that."

Louise turned, the dark head slightly lowered. Like a bull, Cora thought.

"I don't know anything." She crossed her arms, standing between the pea-green wall and the bed. Because of the low-cut blouse, Cora could see the flush across her pale chest. "I didn't know I was a prisoner. What's my crime anyway? What exactly have I been charged with?"

Cora rubbed her eyes. She was in no mood for this nonsense. And if she didn't take her corset off soon, she would burst out of it like an overstuffed sausage.

"I am hungry." Louise raised her chin. "I just realized it. I'll go around the block and find something to eat while you're in the bath. I won't be long."

"If you're truly hungry, I'll put my shoes back on and go downstairs with you. I saw a luncheonette on our way here, and it was still open. On this block, I think. We can go to the market tomorrow to get some things for the kitchen."

Louise clicked her tongue and gazed up at the ceiling. "It's so stupid. I just want to walk around. Why do I need an escort?"

Cora looked up at the bedroom's ceiling as well. A large water stain in the middle was shaped like a rabbit's head. "For your protection."

"From what?"

Exasperating. They had been over this. Cora shook her head. She wouldn't tolerate more of Louise playing dumb, asking ridiculous questions to get answers that she would either laugh at or question again.

"Protection from what, Cora? From what someone in Wichita might think of me? My future husband's gossiping friends?" She smiled, shaking her head. "That doesn't matter here. No one knows who I am." She looked up again, batting her eyes, her fingers laced against her cheek. "Just think. I can actually walk down a street by myself and still hope to get married someday!"

"Do you want to be raped?"

The girl was silent, clearly startled. It was satisfying for Cora, finally, to be the one to shock. Still leaning against the door frame, she flexed her feet and toes, feeling the cool of the tile floor through her stockings.

"You seem to like being frank, Louise. So I thought I might be frank with you. My

155

apologies if you're taken aback. But yes, that is one of the very good reasons I can't let you go out in a strange city by yourself at night, especially dressed like that."

Louise looked down at her blouse, her fingers grazing the collar.

"And then there's your tendency to make friends with men you don't know. Letting them buy you things so they can get you off into a corner. You're not exactly discriminating." Cora lifted her travel bag onto the bed, unsnapped it, and took out her long cotton gown. "Honestly, if something happened to you, something horrible, I'd have a hard time making the case that you weren't partly to blame."

Carousing voices, both male and female, sang from the street below. *Oh the Bowery! The Bowery! I'll never go there any more!"* A man yelled out something unintelligible, and a woman's laughter faded into the steady rumble of traffic.

"Fine," Louise said quietly. She was looking hard at Cora's face, memorizing it, it seemed. "I'll stay in."

Cora nodded. She didn't wish to be stern. But apparently, she needed to be stern to get the girl to listen. "Again, if you'd like to go down and get something to eat, I can go with —"

"I'm not hungry." She turned away. "You can take your bath. Don't worry. I'll be right here."

It felt wonderful to undress, to free her belly and hips from the corset, and her legs from the stockings and garters, and her hair from the pins, and climb into the steaming tub. But she had to admit, it was getting away from Louise, even with just a closed door between them, that gave her real relief. Cora appreciated the girl's wounded sulking even less than all the backtalk and teasing. If she was truly wounded, it was her own fault. Neither of Cora's boys had ever talked to her so disrespectfully: if they disagreed with her and Alan's rules, they bore it in silence, like the honorable young men they were. They certainly didn't try to wear her down with constant argument and dramatic changes in mood. She thought of Myra, and the dance teacher in Wichita. They had both wanted Louise gone. It was becoming apparent why.

She sank farther down into the water, her soaked hair heavy on her shoulders. Let the girl sulk. Cora needed this quiet time to think, and to consider where she was. Today in the taxi, she had perhaps ridden past streets that her mother, and maybe her father, had walked on, maybe carrying her once. She had seen buildings that they would have recognized. Had they had other children? Her sisters and brothers? Did they speak the language of the woman with the shawl? Did they look like her? Would they know her if they saw her on the street? Her own people? Would she know them? She cautioned herself not to get too hopeful. But even if she never found them, even if they were dead, unable to ever meet her or Howard and Earle, she would at least spend the next few weeks walking the same streets they might have walked.

On the other side of the door, the bed-springs creaked. Cora stretched her sore toes against the faucet, listening over hissing pipes for any other sign of movement. What would she do if Louise just ran out to Times Square while she was in the tub, too naked to get out and stop her? Who was to say she wouldn't? Louise was a different creature than Cora herself had been at her age. She had needed the Kaufmanns so badly — she wouldn't have risked such behavior. Uneasy with the quiet, Cora unplugged the drain and carefully stood. The mirror was steamed over, and she used one of the thin but clean towels she'd found in the tiny closet to wipe it clear, revealing her reddened cheeks and her hair, still wet at the shoulders but already curling. She looked down at her body, her breasts and hips, where the pressure marks from her corset were just now starting to fade. She pressed her finger to a mark, red skin turning white, painful to the touch. Perhaps if she had a different sort of figure, she could, on occasion, go without.

She'd just put on her nightgown when she heard men's voices, then knocking. She cracked opened the bathroom door. Louise, who was stretched out on the bed, still dressed and reading the Schopenhauer, did not look up.

"Louise!"

More knocking. Louise appeared to hear nothing.

"Ello? Ello? Ve have, ah, luggage for Brooks, ah, luggage for Carliss-lay?"

"Louise!" Cora hissed. "Our trunks! I completely forgot. Would you please get the door?" She gestured at her own body. "I'm in my nightgown!"

Without looking at Cora, Louise closed the book and stood. She seemed surprisingly short, no longer wearing the heels.

"Wait. I have to get the receipts." Cora moved to her purse. "And we need to tip." She tried to figure. Two trunks. Three flights of stairs. Did one tip more in a large city? She gave Louise two dollars and told her to have them leave the trunks in the front room.

Louise took the money without a word, without looking her in the eye. She walked through the kitchen to the front room. Cora stayed in the bedroom, hiding behind the wall.

"Sorry. Hello." She heard Louise open the door. "Thank you. Yes, I have the receipts. Carlisle and Brooks. Right here is fine. Thank you."

Cora heard grunting, heavy footsteps. A man spoke gruffly to the other in a language she didn't recognize. Turning off the bedroom light, she peeked through the kitchen to the living room and saw her own Indestructo trunk in the arms of a stout, dark-haired man wearing only a sweat-soaked undershirt and suspended trousers. He moved out of her vision as another man, bearded and equally sweaty, walked by holding another trunk by its handles. She could smell the men from across the apartment — nothing but sweat-soaked clothes, but the stench was strong enough to burn her eyes.

There was more talking that she couldn't understand. Louise moved into her view, taking a small clipboard and pen from one of the men. Louise looked distressed as she signed, and Cora wondered how she could bear it, standing so close. She was still wearing the low-cut blouse, but the man waiting for the clipboard seemed indifferent to it. As Louise signed the paper on the clipboard, he wiped his arm over his forehead.

Louise gave him the money and said thank you again, looking up at him for longer than seemed necessary. Dear God, Cora thought. Did the girl not have any discernment at all? Was every man's attention and desire necessary?

Louise handed the clipboard back to the man.

"Do you want some water?" she asked.

Silence. From the dark bedroom, Cora watched the girl put her hand to her mouth and pretend to drink from a cup. There was a response from the men, and then Louise was in the kitchen, opening the cupboards to search for cups. Cora shrank back in the darkness as Louise ran the faucet. A moment later, she asked if they wanted more, and again the answer must have been positive, because the whole process was repeated before the men said brief words Cora didn't understand and moved back toward the front door.

Even after they were gone, the door closed and locked behind them, the stench of their sweat lingered. Cora walked through the kitchen, her hand over her nose and mouth, and almost bumped into Louise, who was putting the two empty cups in the sink. Cora took her hand away, looking into the girl's dark eyes. Was she still angry? Would she be hostile? Would she start up another fight?

"Your hair," Louise said. "It's curly." Her voice and expression were neutral. If she was still upset, it didn't show. "I didn't know. It's pretty."

Cora smiled briefly, tucking the sides behind her ears. Alan always said that, too. "Thank you. And that was nice of you to offer them water."

It had been. Indeed, Cora felt sheepish, even ashamed, that she hadn't thought of it herself. That the men would be thirsty just hadn't occurred to her. But Louise didn't need to know that.

A baby, maybe in the room right above them, started to sputter and cry. Louise seemed calm, but newly distant, not looking her in the eye.

"I'm going to change and go to bed." She nodded toward her trunk. "I'll unpack this in the morning." She gave Cora a perfunctory smile. "Good night."

"Good night, dear."

In the front room, Cora sat at the table. She wanted to give Louise some privacy, a little time to herself. And she had the familiar sensation of having forgotten something crucial, but not knowing what it was. She looked down at the trunks. Louise had an Indestructo, too. Top of the line. *Arrived Safe* was the slogan. And really, it was amazing that the trunks had arrived safe, both of them, having been in the care of strangers for their long journey to and through this massive city, with so much risk of damage or loss. Anything could have happened to either one of them. Yet here they sat, unharmed.

The next morning, they had eggs and coffee at the luncheonette across the street, where the young man behind the counter assured them that Seventy-second and Broadway was only a mile away. He said they would be better off just walking: the subway was stifling this time of year, and the trolleys were always crowded. He drew them a map on a napkin, using the pen from behind his ear.

"Where are you two from anyway? I thought I'd heard every accent in the world." He looked at Louise as he refilled someone's coffee.

"Kansas," Louise said, spooning sugar into her mug.

"Kee-ansas?" He stepped back, his hand flexed under his bow tie, as if she'd said something funny. "You come straight from the feeerm?" A few other diners at the counter chuckled. Cora smiled politely.

Louise's gaze went cold. "I don't sound like that," she said.

He picked up a spoon, tossed it high in the air, caught it, and gave her a friendly smile. "Sorry, beautiful, but you do."

On their way out, Cora tried to console her. "He was flirting," she said, adjusting her hat to block the sun. She wasn't worried — from what she'd seen of Louise's reaction, the counter boy didn't stand a chance. "You don't have an accent."

Louise rolled her eyes. "You don't hear it because you have the same one. We can't hear ourselves. We sound like hicks and we don't even know it." She shook her head, frowning. "I should thank him." She was speaking slowly, pronouncing every word with care. "He did me a favor."

He'd also drawn them a good map. Even in the dizzying heat of the morning, they had no trouble finding the church where

Louise's classes would be held. Cora was relieved when they were directed to the basement — just going down the carpeted steps, the air felt cooler against her sweat-damp skin, though the basement hallway held the faint odor of musty, uncirculated air. A muffled piano played a waltz, the music turning loud when they opened a door to a large, low-ceilinged room with no windows and a mirrored wall. Maybe twenty young women and four young men, all barefoot, and all wearing sleeveless bathing costumes, were stretching bare arms and legs against waist-high wooden bars that ran the lengths of the walls adjacent to the mirror. The piano was played by a spectacled woman glaring at the sheet music.

"I am going to change," Louise said, enunciating each word. She gestured toward a red door that more young women were coming out of. Cora nodded and smiled. She wanted to say something encouraging, something kind, perhaps telling Louise not to be nervous. But then, Louise didn't look nervous. She looked completely calm, not in need of encouragement, or of anything, for that matter. Cora, along with a few of the dancers, watched her walk away.

Within twenty minutes of the instructed

warm-up, which consisted of a lithe woman with bobbed red hair calling out French commands the students all seemed to know, Cora, sitting in a metal chair in the corner, understood why Louise hadn't seemed anxious. She was a good dancer. Her legs were shorter and a little plumper than most of the other dancers', and still she landed from jumps more gracefully, and she could hold a pose longer without trembling. She was strong. In general, she seemed to move more easily than anyone, even the instructor. Cora understood little about dance, but a tall man and a turbaned woman, standing by the mirror and occasionally conferring with each other, gave a strong impression of authority, and they seemed to notice Louise as well. When she performed a jump in front of the rest of the class, the turbaned woman looked up at the man and nodded.

When the turbaned woman raised her hand, the piano stopped. The dancers went still. Despite the relative cool of the basement, they were all sweating, even Louise, the chests and backs of their black wool suits soaked through. But aside from the panting breath of a few students, they were perfectly quiet, every one of them looking at the couple with reverence. When the turbaned woman told them to sit, they sat, right there on the hardwood floor.

"Welcome, all of you, to Denishawn. I am Ruth St. Denis."

Cora could only guess what the counter boy at the luncheonette would have made of Ruth St. Denis's accent. She didn't sound foreign, but she spoke with a dramatic rhythm, emphasizing each word.

She held out both hands and smiled. "Please, call me Miss Ruth."

She wore a sleeveless calf-length dress, deep red, with a brown silk scarf knotted on one side of her narrow hips. Like the dancers, she was barefoot. The few strands of hair that were free of the turban were milk white, but her face didn't look much older than Cora's. She'd tweezed her brows into thin half-moons.

"And this" — she bowed slightly, extending a sinewy arm to her right — "is my husband and partner, Ted Shawn."

The man smiled at the students. He wore a white collarless shirt and white flannels, and he also had bare feet. He seemed relaxed, calm, yet his posture was perfect.

"You may call me Papa Shawn," he said, with no accent or strange intonation. "Once we get to know each other better, you probably will."

The students laughed, some of them,

including Louise, looking a little dazzled. Ted Shawn was over six feet tall, and well muscled, with a broad chest. His hair was thin, his hairline receding, but he looked younger than his wife. Something in his manner made Cora think of Alan. He smiled at St. Denis as she spoke.

"Unfortunately," she said, "I will not be able to stay in New York and watch you grow as dancers. As you likely know, we have a studio in Los Angeles, and I need to spend at least part of the summer there. But I will see you some of the time, and I wanted to meet you today, and perhaps give some guidance and inspiration."

As she spoke, she stared at a point on the wall just above Cora's head, her eyes narrowed as if she saw something there, though after a while, Cora looked up and saw only blank white wall above her. St. Denis told the students that as of this moment, they were all personal representatives of Denishawn, and that she expected them to behave that way on and off the premises. Other persons interested in modern dance had unfortunately linked the art with sordid behavior, at least in the public's mind, but she and her husband intended to correct that misperception. Young women who were Denishawn students wore hats, stockings, and gloves when out in public. They did not roll their stockings. Male students wore hats in public. Obviously, no smoking or drinking would be permitted for either gender, on or off the premises.

"Dance is a *spiritual* experience," she said, her taut jaw raised, her gaze now moving over the faces of students. "It will not *tolerate* indecency or self-corruption."

Only now did Louise appear less than enamored. Cora could see her face in the mirror, twisting her mouth to one side, the sole student not gazing up. If St. Denis noticed this subtle defection, she gave no sign. She told the class they were at the forefront in a revolution in American dance. She wasn't interested in having them memorize steps or show off pointless athleticism or dexterity. She certainly wasn't interested in high kicks or cartwheels. Technical skill, she said, was only a tool that allowed the body to reveal its natural understanding of the rhythm of the universe, allowing all people, all races, to comprehend God, Buddha, and Allah and all forms of divinity. Dance was a visualization of divinity, a way for dancers to realize that they were not in their bodies — their bodies were inside of them.

Cora had no idea what she was talking

169

about. But everyone else in the room appeared to understand, and so Cora was very still and quiet. She'd brought *The Age of Innocence,* but she didn't open it. She didn't want to embarrass herself, looking as if comprehension of something artistic were beyond her. And truly, she wanted to hear what this woman was saying, even what she couldn't understand.

"I want you to learn to feel the music," St. Denis said, pressing her palms together. "Not to count nonsense numbers in your head. Certain composers facilitate feeling. Who here is familiar with Debussy?"

No one moved or spoke. St. Denis gave them a reassuring smile and started to speak. Louise raised her hand.

"I am. Of course. My mother plays him all the time."

A few other students turned to see who was talking. Some of them glanced at each other.

After St. Denis and Shawn stepped off to the side, the red-haired instructor resumed class by asking the students to stand and move their heads from side to side while their shoulders remained perfectly still. The cobra, she called it. Louise excelled at this move as well, her cropped hair and pale neck seemingly disconnected from her shoulders. Cora, feeling inconspicuous in her corner, tried an abbreviated version herself, her head moving just slightly, her back straight and unmoving in her chair.

"Hello?"

She looked up. Ruth St. Denis was walking toward her, her bare feet silent on the floor.

"Oh, hello." Cora stood, feeling bovine and graceless. Even in shoes, she was no taller than St. Denis, but she was certainly wider. Frumpier. Her hand went to her hair. "I hope it's all right that I stayed. I'm with Louise Brooks. I'm her chaperone."

"Ah yes. From Kansas." St. Denis seemed amused. "So nice to meet you." She glanced back over her shoulder. "I heard Louise would be traveling with a companion. I thought that was wise on her mother's part."

"Oh. Have you met Myra?"

She shook her head. "I wasn't on that tour. But Ted met both Louise and her mother when they came backstage after the show in . . ." She closed her eyes and tapped her turban.

"Wichita," Cora said.

"Wichita." She smiled. "The two of them made quite an impression." She gave Cora a knowing look. "So. She seems arrogant. Is she?"

Cora looked back out at Louise, who stood with her arms crossed, her eyes focused as she watched the instructor. Cora wasn't sure how to answer. Of course the honest reply was yes, but she felt suddenly, oddly, protective. "Well," she tried, "she has good qualities."

"Mmm." St. Denis smiled, her thinned eyebrows raised. "Almost everyone does."

The instructor had handed each dancer a square of diaphanous orange material. She fluttered and twirled her orange square over her head, and the dancers followed suit.

"But she is talented, isn't she?" Cora watched Louise. "I don't know anything about dance. But I've been sitting here watching, and she seems talented to me."

St. Denis nodded slowly. "It does seem that way. For a beginner." She smiled at Cora. "But then, we knew that would likely be the case." She looked back out at Louise. "Ted told me what the mother was like backstage. We've seen that type before. Show me a mother with that much thwarted ambition, and I'll show you a daughter born for success."

Cora watched Louise turn in a slow, controlled circle, both arms raised and perfectly straight. Her face, glistening with perspiration, was tilted up to one of the basement's overhead lights. It was something to think that St. Denis was right, that as beautiful and talented as Louise was, she was only here because of her mother's drive. Surely some of her grace and talent belonged to her alone. But what would she have been without Myra? If young Louise had been sent off on a train to another life, never knowing the mother whom she resembled so much, would she have fared better? Worse? What would have been different about her?

The instructor called out to the dancers, "Turn. Again. Again."

St. Denis touched Cora's arm. "It was nice meeting you. And I meant to say, you're welcome to come to the classes and watch, but they'll be at it five hours a day. You should feel safe leaving her here. We keep them perfectly in line." She smiled. "Even during the break."

Cora had no doubt that even after St. Denis left for Los Angeles, her expectations would remain the law. She was clearly the sovereign, or at least one of two, ruling over this little world. She could leave Louise here without worry. Her afternoons would be free.

"You should go out and see the city." St.

173

Denis looked up at the ceiling of the basement, as if all of New York City were contained in the church above. "Have you been here before?"

Cora shook her head. Again, the easy lie. The instructor stood in the middle of the dancers, holding her orange scarf above her head. With an elegant turn, she wrapped it around her shoulders like a shawl, her face tilted down, her expression hidden.

Cora had to look away. She'd come so far, and now she was here. The address was in her purse.

She thanked St. Denis for the suggestion and agreed: Yes. There was so much she wanted to learn about the city. She would of course take advantage of the time.

The New York Home for Friendless Girls
355 W. 15th Street
New York, New York

Mrs. Alan Carlisle
194 North St. Francis Street
Wichita, Kansas

November 23, 1908

Dear Mrs. Carlisle,
Thank you for your generous donation,

which we received last week. As much as we appreciate and rely on such charity to feed, clothe, and educate the girls in our care, we cannot respond to your third request, or any future requests, for information about your birth parents. We are delighted to know that you are now a married woman, blessed with two little boys of your own, and that you are doing well enough to help us in this way. Please consider that this success has come to you because of the opportunity you were given to start a new life away from the city, and to break ties with a burdened past. It is our policy to protect the privacy of birth parents, who may not wish to be known, and also the well-being of our former charges, who we believe are better off focusing on their current lives, and not their troubled origins.

I read what you wrote of your longing and confusion. Please know you will be in my prayers.

God bless,
Sister Eugenia Malley

EIGHT

Cora walked back up Broadway alone, grateful for the continuous shade of buildings that blocked the mid-morning sun. By the time she reached the luncheonette it was crowded. She waved away cigar and cigarette smoke as she made her way to the counter. The bow-tied young man who had flirted with Louise was still behind it. He smiled, tilting his head at two bar stools.

"Hello again." He cleared dirty plates as he looked around. "Where's your Kee-ansas friend?"

Cora slid onto a bar stool. "At class. I'll take an iced tea, please."

He nodded, clearly disappointed, though he adjusted an electric fan so it blew toward Cora. She glanced at him as he poured coffee for another customer. He wasn't crazy to ask about Louise, to think he might have a chance. He was a good-looking boy, a little older than Howard and Earle, with sun-streaked brown hair and green eyes that the average teenage girl would likely swoon over. Louise hadn't seemed to notice.

"What kind of class?" He set a glass and a sugar bowl in front of her.

"Dance." She gave him a disapproving look. She wouldn't give him any more information.

"She seemed like she might be a dancer or something." He poured the tea without looking up. "She looks like she could be in pictures. I just asked what kind of class she went to because I thought she might be in summer school, and I wondered where. I go to Columbia. I just work here summers to help pay for it." Now he looked up. "Maybe you could mention that to her for me?" He smiled and bobbed his eyebrows. "There's a free iced tea in it for you."

Before she could answer, a bell rang, and he turned to pick up an order of pancakes from the little window to the kitchen. Poor boy, Cora thought. Already smitten. But there were no points to be scored. Louise, she imagined, wouldn't be impressed by his imminent degree. She could marry this college boy, be the envy of all, and still end up like her mother.

When he returned to offer her a refill, he leaned on the counter and lowered his voice. "I'm Floyd, by the way. Floyd Smithers. So are you two sisters or something?"

She rolled her eyes. He was trying a new tactic, flattering the guard. She took the paper with the address out of her purse. "I can pay for the tea," she said casually, "but I'm hoping you can tell me how to best get to this address."

He looked at the paper. "You should take the subway." He took the pen from behind his ear and again sketched a map with directions on a napkin, this one on a bigger scale, less intricate than the map he'd drawn for them the previous morning. Cora looked over her shoulder. A woman with bobbed blond hair and a skirt clearly showing bare knees sat at a table by herself, smoking a cigarette. She turned, caught Cora watching, and Cora, embarrassed, looked away.

He slid the napkin across the counter. "That'll get you there. Say, what do you need down on Fifteenth Street?"

"Oh." Cora adjusted her hat. "Just looking up an old friend."

"Yeah?" He tilted his head.

"Why? Is it a bad area?"

"It's okay." He shrugged. "It's by the docks."

Cora looked at the steel counter, her

blurred reflection. Yes. *Yes.* She remembered the low horns of ships. She touched her tea glass to steady her hand.

"It's not terrible." He lowered his voice. "Mostly Irish. Italians. All kinds, really. You'll be fine if you hold your purse tight. Some of those kids are quick." He nodded at her hand. "You might leave that ring at home. Somebody could pawn that and feed a family of ten for a year."

She looked at her wedding ring, the European-cut diamond. She and Alan had picked it out together. She looked back up.

"Aw jeez. I didn't mean to scare you. It's not all bad down there. Not at all. You know what? You'll be just a few blocks from the Hotel Chelsea. It's famous. Mark Twain stayed there. And Lillian Gish. Beautiful homes around there. Here. I'll put it on my map." He leaned over again, making new marks. "Just walk up Eighth Avenue if you want to see it." When he slid the napkin to her, he seemed worried. "Hey, I didn't mean there was anything wrong with the docks, with the people around there. I didn't mean that. Just a lot of foreigners, hungry kids. But it's not bad."

"Thank you." She opened her purse again and took out three dimes, payment with a generous tip. Yesterday, he'd told Louise the hard truth about her accent. Now he'd done Cora a favor, preparing her with a hard truth as well.

"Hey, hey," he said, stepping away. "It was on me, remember? You were going to put in a good word for me?" He gestured at her, and then at himself. "I thought we were in cahoots."

She had to laugh. Floyd Smithers. He was a nice boy. He made her think of her own Howard, four minutes older than his brother, and from then on, it seemed, so fearless, so eager to go out and bargain with the world. She missed them both. And she worried. She would write to them tonight, and remind them to be careful. So many ways to get hurt on a farm.

"Thank you for the directions." She pulled on her gloves and picked up the napkin map. "I'm afraid I can't help you with my young friend. She is young, by the way. Fifteen. She's here to study dance. And I've come along to keep her safe."

"But I just want to —"

Cora held up her palm. "You should direct your hopes elsewhere."

He looked at her as if she should feel guilty, as if she were in the wrong, as if she'd stolen something from him. Still, she felt no remorse as she walked away. He was a good boy, with a fine future. She'd done him a favor, too.

The subway was indeed stifling. She had hoped it would be cooler, down out of the sun, but there were so many people, and the air in the car felt stale and humid, smelling of urine and unwashed bodies. Still, she could tell the train was moving fast, and that was exciting, racing underground, unimpeded. The seats were all taken, so she stood and held a strap, listening to two old men having what sounded like an argument in French and someone repeatedly coughing. She tried not to look at anyone in particular. When a streetcar back home was this crowded, she always stared out the windows, not so much for the scenery as for the wish to be polite. People did that here, too, though there was nothing outside but the tunnel wall.

The stops were short and frequent. She moved aside to let people pass, tilting her head to protect the brim of her hat, aware that each brief stop brought her closer to her own. Despite the fetid air, she wished the ride could continue indefinitely, until she was ready to actually be where she was headed. She still had trouble conceiving of the New York Home for Friendless Girls as an actual physical location, a brown-brick building that existed on a street, and not just a haunting in her mind. What would it do to her to actually see it? To touch the same bricks with her hands?

When she did climb the stairs from the subway back into the bright sunlight, she moved aside to let people pass and took a moment to study the map. She was close. According to Floyd Smithers's map, the address was right around the corner. She dabbed at sweat on her forehead, dampening the tips of her gloves. Soon, too soon, she would be standing outside the orphanage's door. She put the map away. The streets and avenues were numbered logically. If she went for a walk to calm her nerves, there was little chance of getting lost. She opened her parasol, and, with her free hand, held her purse close to her chest.

Floyd Smithers had been right about the neighborhood — the Irish, or at least their names — were everywhere. McCormick's Shoe Repair. Kelly's Auto and Tire. Paddy's was just Paddy's; the word "Saloon" had been painted over thinly. She passed a Catholic church. Many of the people around her looked and sounded native born, though an old woman did lean out a high window to yell, "Daniel Mulligan O'Brien! You get your arse back up here now!" (No one but Cora — apparently not even the boy being summoned — turned to look.) She heard other languages here and there. Spanish. French. Along a side street thick with rumbling cars and trucks, a group of girls in braids bounced a rubber ball off a front stoop, calling to one another in a language Cora didn't recognize. Over their heads, stretched across the street from window to window, were dozens of long clotheslines, from which hung undergarments and clothes, mostly sized for children — little vests and little shirts, short pants with patched seats and little dresses with ragged hemlines.

The more she walked, the more children she saw. And then they were everywhere. On one street, each stoop sported at least five or six throwing balls against the steps or balancing on the railings. Some children walked with their mothers, or with men in stevedore caps. More moved down the sidewalk in packs, all girls or all boys. Many looked as if they'd just been swimming in their clothes, their hair still slicked back and dripping, though none looked particularly clean. They gave one another light pushes and laughed, the barefoot ones hopping fast on the hot sidewalk. Cora saw a blond-haired girl of about eight reach into a garbage can, pull out a half-eaten apple, and take a delighted bite. When her friends gathered round, she handed over the apple, and they each took a bite as well.

She passed a pregnant woman with a bruised cheek and a rumpled hat, a child on her hip and another trailing behind her. When she noticed Cora staring, she glared.

And babies. So many babies. They cried from open windows and in the arms of other children. They rolled by in wobbling carriages and slept in slings tied around their mothers' necks. A woman in a long black dress nursed an infant on a bench in front of a pool hall, her swollen breast bared for all the world to see. When she noticed Cora's shocked stare, she misunderstood, smiled, and said something cheerful in Italian.

Cora felt dizzy. It was the heat, or perhaps the smells, which varied widely from storefront to storefront. Fresh baked bread. Cat urine. Melting cheese. Laundry soap. Roasting meat. She started to walk into a café, only to realize, too late, that all the patrons were male. As she hurried out, they called to her in another language, saying things she guessed to be, at best, disrespectful.

She got out the map again. She still didn't feel ready, not in the least. But she was hot, and tired.

Three shrieking girls in dingy dresses rushed past her from behind. The smallest knocked her bony shoulder against Cora's skirt. The girl kept running, her dark braid swinging behind her, but she called out, "Sorry, ma'am," and briefly turned back, flashing a radiant, chipped-tooth smile.

She almost walked past the building. She wouldn't have known it if not for the address — she'd remembered it as larger than it was. It was just four stories, each floor five windows across, with the windowless wall on top. An adjacent lot, which she didn't recall, had been paved and fenced, with a wide gate closed to the street and a two-story wooden outbuilding. But the brown brick of the main building was just as she remembered, and there was the little gold plaque by the door, engraved with a cross and black letters: *The New York Home for Friendless Girls.* Cora stared at it grimly. After all these years, really. They could have found a better name.

The air on the street smelled sweet and buttery, like cookies right out of the oven. If she had smelled such treats as a hungry child, she certainly would have remembered. Did they give orphan girls cookies now? Or did the girls bake them for sale? Other changes were clear. Inside the fence, there was a rudimentary swing set, the seats made out of the lids of packing crates. There was a climbing rope, too, knotted at the bottom. But some things were the same. Just next to the swing set, a pile of stuffed canvas bags waited by the door. Incoming laundry. Cora gazed up at the roof.

"Can I help you?"

She turned. A young nun with a faint dark mustache was hurrying up the steps, followed by a man in overalls carrying a wooden crate.

"Oh. Yes," Cora said, climbing the steps as well. "I . . . I'd like to speak with someone."

"Regarding?" The nun looked at her pleasantly, taking one side of the crate while the man, still bearing most of its weight, took a ring of keys from the pocket of his overalls.

Cora hesitated. But the nun was clearly in a hurry.

"I used to live here," she blurted out. "As a child."

The man, who wore wire-rim spectacles, glanced at Cora as he turned a key in the lock. He nodded at the nun, took the crate, and carried it inside.

186

"I see," the nun said, wiping one hand against the other. Rushed as she was, her expression seemed pointedly neutral; it was impossible to tell if Cora had shocked her, or if grown orphans came by every day. "I'm afraid we have Mass now. We'll all be upstairs until one. You could come back tomorrow, either before twelve-thirty or after one."

Cora worked to hide her disappointment. After all these years, she was still that conditioned to show only calm acceptance to a nun, to not talk back, to not be disagreeable or show ingratitude, even with the look on her face. But that was ridiculous. She wasn't a child now. She was an adult, a married woman. She had nothing to fear.

"Could I just wait inside?" Cora smiled pleasantly, masking her own surprise. "I don't know that I'll be able to come back," she added. "And I've come a very long way."

The nun nodded, and Cora followed her up the stairs and through the door. The entry was small and painted white, with a stairway to the right and, straight ahead, a long hallway leading to a window-bright kitchen. Cora could see part of a stove from where she stood. The cookie smell from outside was gone; now she only smelled bleach.

"Thank you, Joseph," the nun called out, though the man had disappeared. She shut the front door, turning the lock. "I'm sorry. I shouldn't be late." She was already moving up the stairs, using both hands to lift the hem of her habit. "Just go down the hallway and through the kitchen to the dining hall. You're welcome to sit and wait there."

Cora stood in the entry, listening to a muffled piano coming from somewhere above. The wooden crate had been set by the door. It was full of girls' shoes, she saw now, scuffed and used, each pair held together by a rubber band. She looked at the front door, the brass knob in the middle of an oval-shaped plate with beaded edges. Nothing about it was familiar. But then, it wouldn't be. It wasn't as if she'd spent much time by the front door, coming and going as she pleased.

She moved down the hallway to the kitchen, the smell of bleach growing stronger. She passed two doors, both closed, and spaced evenly apart. She still heard the piano overhead, and now, the voices of girls singing. *Sing, my tongue, the Virgin's trophies / Who for us her Maker bore.* Cora went still, looking up at the low ceiling. She knew this song, remembered it. Without thinking, she moved her lips to the words. *For the curse of old inflicted / Peace and blessing to restore.*

The kitchen was unfamiliar. Both the sink and the green enamel stove looked modern, newer. Three cylindrical containers of bulk oats sat on a shelf next to the icebox. She almost laughed. After all these years, they were still serving oatmeal. Maybe the nuns put sugar or syrup in it now. Or maybe they didn't still serve it twice a day, every day. In any case, when she was here, she hadn't minded the oatmeal. She'd been happy for anything that eased her hunger, even if for only a few hours. And she hadn't known anything better — that had helped. But after just a few days at the Kaufmanns', eating scrambled eggs and potatoes and roasted chicken and peaches, she'd decided she would never eat oatmeal again. It didn't matter if Mother Kaufmann put brown sugar in it, or butter, or syrup. It was the texture Cora remembered. She hadn't had a bowl since.

Through the open doorway to her right, she saw the ends of two straight-edged tables. And benches, and light coming in through square, cross-barred windows. She walked into the dining room, sweat cooling on her forehead. The room was smaller than she remembered, and the four tables, arranged two by two, weren't as long as the ones where she had eaten all those silent meals with the other girls and the nuns. But they were the same tables, of course. Everything seemed large when she was small. They'd had to eat in shifts, she remembered, the younger girls before the older.

She sank onto a bench, her gloved hands resting cautiously on the table.

"Hello."

She turned. The man in overalls had entered from a door on the other side of the room. He carried a folded ladder to the center, just beneath a small circle of exposed wires. Before he opened the ladder, he stopped, the spectacles glinting in the sunlight.

"You are fine?"

He had some kind of accent. She wasn't sure what. He had an angular face, his hair thinning and blond.

"I'm fine, thank you." She coughed, her throat dry. "I'm just waiting."

"I can get you something to drink?"

"Oh. Yes. Some water would be wonderful. Thank you."

She heard him opening the ladder, and then his footsteps to the kitchen, the keys jangling in his pocket. She removed her gloves. When she heard him running the water, she placed her hands on the table, her fingertips tracing the groove of the wood. After every meal, they'd wiped the tables down with boiled rags. She looked out the back window. The grass in the yard was summer dead, and there was just a stump where the big tree had been.

The handyman returned, and a glass of water was set in front of her.

"Thank you," she said, glancing up.

He smiled, not moving away. She looked down at her hands. She'd taken Floyd Smithers's advice and left her wedding ring back at the apartment.

"I'm fine now, really," she said. She waited until he had walked back to the ladder to lift the glass to her lips with both hands. As soon as the cold water touched her lips, her body seemed to take over, and she drank it all, gulp after gulp, her eyes closed, her head tilted back.

The handyman, up on the ladder now, started to whistle.

She turned away, setting the empty glass on the table. She didn't wish to be rude, but she didn't want to talk. She opened her purse and took out *The Age of Innocence,* more as a buffer to any conversation than an actual desire to read. She couldn't read right now. She could only stare at the pages, trying to calm herself.

The handyman stopped whistling. Without thinking, she looked up. He nodded at her book and started to say something, but before he could, she turned her whole body away from him, staring down at the pages, the swimming, unread words. She glanced at her watch. It was already a quarter till one. Her fingers tingled, and she felt a rushing in her arms, as if her very blood knew where she was.

Sister Delores. Cora recognized her at once — the high cheekbones, the blue eyes — and had to work not to gasp. Of course. The nuns who had been old when she was a child would all be dead by now. But Sister Delores was only middle-aged, with deep lines between her faint brows, and especially around her mouth. If anything, even in the austere black habit, she looked less frightening than in memory. She seemed smaller, like the tables, and the dining room itself. Cora wondered if she still carried the paddle.

"You'll have to forgive me," she said, leaning a little across the desk. Her voice was the same, low and commanding. "I used to think I would remember the face of each girl who lived within these walls." She shook her head, peering at Cora.

They were in an office, behind one of the two doors that opened to the hallway. Just above the nun's head was a framed painting of Jesus in Gethsemane, and, beside that, a framed photograph of the new Pope. The wooden desk was free of clutter, with just a typewriter, a pen, and a stack of paper weighted down with a silver cross. The only window was somewhat obscured by a long lace curtain, which fluttered a little with the warm breeze, its patterned shadow flickering on the hardwood floor.

"I don't expect you to remember me," Cora said. In truth, she was glad Sister Delores had no memory of her as a child. She had introduced herself as Cora Kaufmann from McPherson, Kansas, not Mrs. Alan Carlisle from Wichita, who had already pestered them with three letters, who had already been told no.

"You're in Kansas now, you say." The blue eyes focused on Cora's. "You went out on the train, then?"

Cora nodded. Overhead, she heard water moving through pipes, and the shuffling of many feet. The girls were getting started on the laundry, taking the soiled clothes and sheets from the bags. All these years, while she had lived with the Kaufmanns and gone to school, and then married Alan, and brought up the boys in Wichita, back here, the laundry bags had still been arriving every day, at the same time, with different small hands doing the scrubbing and the hanging.

"Was your placement good?" The nun winced, as if preparing for a blow.

"It was, Sister. Wonderful people chose me. I couldn't have been more fortunate."

Sister Delores closed her eyes and smiled. "Praise God. That's nice to hear." She opened her eyes. "That's been true, more often than not, of the girls we've sent out, the ones we've heard from. Not always. But more often than not."

"You've heard from other girls who went out on the train?"

"A few."

"Mary Jane? I don't remember her last name. But she was here when I was, and she was on the train with me. Or Little Rose?"

"No. Just a few girls, I said. Are you still with the Church?"

Cora considered lying. But even now, the blue eyes scared her. Through the lace curtain, she saw the shadow of a seagull on the sill.

"No, Sister. They weren't Catholics, the people who took me."

Sister Delores frowned. Her left hand had a tremble. She stopped it by laying her right hand over it on the desk. "They were supposed to put you all in Catholic homes." She brought her hands beneath her chin and gave Cora an accusing look. "They hardly ever did, though. Isn't that nice? Our own children, who we fed and clothed, could now be donning white hoods against us."

Cora shook her head. "I've had nothing to do with white hoods."

"What church do you attend now?"

"Presbyterian. My adoptive parents were Methodists, but now I'm Presbyterian."

It was as if she'd answered First Church of Satan. Sister Delores stared.

"Well." The nun again rested her hands on her desk. "We got wise to what they were pulling. Now we send out our own trains. The Church does, I mean."

"Still? Children still go out on trains?"

"Certainly. When we get financing. It's been a very good program for most." She turned her hands over, showing her palms. "You're sitting there in very fine clothes. You just said you had a positive experience."

"I did," Cora said. "I'm grateful."

It was true. She would be the first to say how lucky she was. If not for the train, she could have grown up here, her hands ruined from laundry, her mind dull from lack of school. She knew the train had given her an easier life, and more importantly, the Kaufmanns. But that had just been luck.

"I want to learn about my birth parents, Sister, who and where I came from."

"I can't help you with that."

"Why not?"

"The records are confidential."

"You have records?"

"It doesn't matter. I couldn't share them with you."

"Why not?"

"Those are the rules."

"Why?"

"Because no good can come of that knowledge." There was the hard look Cora remembered, the blue eyes unblinking and still. "Miss Kaufmann, it's likely that your parents are dead, and that they were dead before you even came here. What good would knowing more do you?"

"I want to know," Cora said. "Even if they're dead." She smiled. "Actually, I'd like to learn more about my Catholic roots."

The nun's eyes narrowed. "You can do that on your own."

"I want to know who I am." Cora looked at her lap. She didn't want to beg, but she would. "Who I would have been, without charity."

"It doesn't matter. You're a child of God. You're you. Do you need to find out the sad tale? Would it bring you real peace? No." She made her hand flat, slicing it through the air. "It would do you no practical good. And if they're not dead, then that's a bigger problem. We don't betray the birth mothers' privacy. If they're alive, they don't want to be found."

"How do you know?"

"I know."

"How?"

She leaned back in her chair, sighing. "You want me to be frank, Miss Kaufmann? I'll be frank. If your mother was alive when she gave you up, you were likely conceived in some sort of sordidness. Drinking. Drugs. Adultery. Prostitution. Rape. Do you want me to go on?" She sat up straight, her eyes still on Cora's. "That wouldn't be your fault. No one is saying that it would be. That was the whole point of caring for you, and certainly the point of sending you out on the train. Consider the trouble that people went to, the expense, to get you girls into decent homes so you could have decent lives. What? Are you a homing pigeon for misery? You want to undo all the time and money that was spent on your behalf, coming back here to find the very squalor we lifted you out of?"

Cora swallowed. She shouldn't be scared, not of the annoyance in the nun's gaze, the sureness of her questions. She was an adult now. A married woman. She could talk back.

"But some of the girls just had sick parents," she said, her voice steady. "One girl's mother was in the hospital. I remember. That's not squalor. That's sickness. What if she got better?"

"She probably didn't. And do you know why she was in the hospital? You don't. Not really. What the girl was told and what was true may have been two different things. We would likely have spared a child knowing what would have been too much for her."

"But I'm not a child now," Cora said. "I don't want to be lied to." She held the nun's gaze, not looking away. She wanted her to understand. Nothing would be too much for her. Even if her parents were sordid, or mad, or drunks, or dead, she wanted to know who they were. And they couldn't be all bad. She saw them — she was sure she saw them — in her own boys. Earle was quiet and thoughtful like his father, but

198

where had Howard gotten his pluck, his daring? No one in Alan's family had a grin like that. And where had Earle gotten his talent for drawing? She didn't care about sordidness or squalor. She knew the story would likely be ugly. But she wanted to know it. She did.

"When I was first brought here," she said calmly, "I wasn't an infant. I was already walking, and I knew my name. The older girls told me. I was chubby, they said. I'd been cared for. I have a memory of a woman holding me, speaking to me kindly. And in some other language, not English."

"Then hold on to that." The nun shrugged. "Know that you were loved. Don't soil it with details that will only ruin what you remember. And consider your adoptive parents, who you just told me were the best you could have hoped for. Why betray the people who cared for you as if you were their own?"

Cora looked at the lace curtain through blurred eyes. It was a smart tactic, shaming her with the Kaufmanns. But it wasn't fair. Hadn't Mr. Kaufmann himself taken her to the cemetery in McPherson to show her the graves of the Kaufmann parents and grandparents who had settled the land and taught him to farm? And hadn't Mother Kaufmann told her about her grandfather the abolitionist, so committed to his cause that he'd moved his Massachusetts family out to Kansas? Sister Delores was telling her bloodlines meant nothing, when most people's entire lives were shaped by who their parents and grandparents were. Look at Louise. Myra wasn't a dream mother by any stretch, but Louise had grown up so confident, so sure of what she was meant for.

Sister Delores stood slowly, steadying herself by leaning on the desk. Cora understood. The interview was over. The answer was, and would be, no. Cora nodded, standing as well. There wasn't anything else to do. It wouldn't matter if she cried or laughed or screamed or got on her knees and begged.

Cora managed a polite thank you. At least she had gotten this far. She was looking into the face of someone who had known her as a child, in the first home she remembered. Still, that was not what she had come for, and even as she followed the nun back into the hallway and to the front door, as obedient as the child she had been, she felt the same anger as when she'd received Sister Eugenia's letter, back in Wichita. Who were these old women, with their cloistered lives, to tell her what she could and couldn't know? What she needed and what she didn't?

"I see that you're disappointed," Sister Delores said. Her voice was softer now, but the pale eyes didn't blink. "I understand that. But please know, my goal is to protect you. From yourself. You think you want to know more than you really do."

The front door opened, and the handyman walked in. He looked at Cora, right at her face, as if her distress was any of his concern. She lowered her gaze and moved by. And then, these were the facts: the sweet-smelling air as she stepped outside, and the sound of the door closing, and locking, behind her.

NINE

At intermission, Louise said that the problem with the Ziegfeld Follies was that she'd come with high expectations.

"The comedy is good," she told Cora, fingering the strand of beads around her neck. "But the chorus girls? Pretty faces and elaborate costumes. Boring. Maybe one or two girls are *authentically* beautiful. That's it. I've never seen so many fake smiles."

"Lower your voice," Cora whispered. The theater's big foyer was crowded with men and women talking in little groups. A sign gave directions to the Men's Smoking Lounge, but many of the women were smoking as well, and, from what Cora could see, neither gender seemed interested in separation.

"Mark my words," Louise said, with only a slight decrease in volume. "When I'm on stage, I won't smile just because someone tells me to. I'll only smile when it's real."

Cora sighed, looking up at the foyer's glass-dome ceiling. Every inch of the New Amsterdam's interior was ornate, with swirling vines and flowers and birds carved into the walls, and matching patterns on the green and mauve carpets. In her opinion, just being in such a beautiful space, not to mention feeling the ice-cooled air blown in by electric fans, was worth the price of admission. All of it had cheered her spirits, taking her mind, at least temporarily, off of her quick defeat by Sister Delores. She'd had to pull herself together before collecting Louise, who apparently wasn't as good at detecting a forced gaiety as she thought. Either that, or Cora was a better actress than the chorus girls.

And now, truthfully, she was enjoying the show, and grateful for all its distractions. She couldn't wait to tell the boys and Alan that she'd gone to the Ziegfeld Follies and seen Will Rogers in person, not to mention funny Fanny Brice doing an impersonation of a ballerina. Cora thought the chorus girls were beautiful, though she didn't see why, even in the number where each girl was supposed to be a different flower in a wedding wreath, they had to wear such immodest costumes, with nothing at all covering their legs and the midriffs showing on some. She would have preferred it if the chorus girls had taken off their elaborate, feathered headwear and used it to cover their thighs.

She turned to Louise. "How could you possibly tell if their smiles were fake? We're in the back row of the mezzanine."

"I could tell. They were that fake."

Staring out into the crowd, Louise pulled her necklace up to her mouth, moving a bead in between her lips. Cora touched the girl's hand and shook her head. It was hard to know when she was just trying to provoke or get attention, and when she just wasn't thinking. Tonight, she was wearing a sleeveless dress as black as her hair, and when she wasn't gumming her jewelry, she looked more sophisticated than any older woman in the room.

"I thought you loved theater," Cora said. "Don't stage people have to fake emotions all the time? Isn't that their job?"

Louise winced before looking up at Cora as if she were the most tiresome idiot on the planet. Even with the blunt bangs, she could resemble Myra so much.

"Acting is not fakery, Cora. At least not good acting." She shook her head, clearly disgusted. "A real actress, a real artist, feels whatever emotion she's showing. You just saw Fanny Brice's performance. You're telling me that you can't tell the difference between her expressions and those idiotic chorus girls'?"

"Fanny Brice is just being funny."

"She's a genius."

Ah, Cora thought, smiling a little. Someone actually had the girl's approval. Louise also admired her mother, of course, as well as the older girl named Martha at Denishawn who Louise said was the best dancer she'd ever seen. So it was a club of only three. Everyone else, as far as Cora could tell, only earned the girl's scorn.

A silver-haired man in a dark suit walked by them, openly staring at Louise. Louise stared back, dark eyes gleaming, before turning to Cora.

"It's an elegant crowd, isn't it?"

Cora nodded. She had just been thinking how strange it was that this theater full of women in beaded dresses and silk gowns, so many with long strands of pearls or steel-cut beads, a few holding cigarettes in holders out for men in suits to light, was just some thirty blocks from the neighborhood by the orphanage. It was hard to fathom that they belonged to the same city, the same side of Manhattan, even. There might as well have been an ocean in between.

"You do think the crowd is elegant?" Louise looked at her, waiting.

"Certainly." Cora glanced back at her, suspicious. It wasn't like Louise to solicit her opinion on anything.

"Hmm." Louise smiled, fingering the beads again. "You'll notice many of the women are wearing paint."

Cora rolled her lips in. So there was the trap. Before they left the apartment that evening, they'd had an argument over whether or not Louise could wear rouge and lipstick out to the theater. Cora had held firm, and made Louise wash her face clean. She had not believed the girl's protests that Myra regularly allowed her to paint her face like a harlot. As far as Cora knew, obviously painted cheeks and lips marked women of a certain profession.

Looking around her now, however, she saw that many, if not most, of the women in attendance had unabashedly shadowed their eyelids and lined their eyes, and reddened and glossed their lips. More than a few wore skirts that just grazed their knees. Of course, compared to the very painted and nearly naked Ziegfeld girls that they had all just applauded and paid to see, the women in the foyer looked like nuns. None of it would have been conceivable when Cora was Louise's age. Maybe Louise was right.

Maybe the old rules were changing. Cora caught sight of herself in a gold-framed mirror: her long, high-collared dress, her pinned hair, her unpainted face. When she'd left the apartment, she'd thought she looked nice, wearing her good rose gown with the sash that made her waist look small, or smaller. But none of the younger women in the foyer wore a skirt as long as hers, and none had a collar as high.

Maybe she was falling behind the times, as provincial and outmoded in her thinking as in her dress. Maybe she was like the old women who had told her generation that they were behaving unnaturally, bothering legislators and asking strangers in the street to sign petitions, trying to get the vote.

Yet Cora couldn't believe all standards were truly so ephemeral. And how far would these new fashions go? Where would it end? Would women be expected, in a few more years, to walk around with their thighs and midriffs showing or risk being called a prude? Or maybe women wouldn't be clothed at all? They would just wear makeup and underwear. All for the sake of being modern? How would you tell if a particular woman was of a certain profession if all women started dressing the part?

She turned to Louise, lowering her voice

to a whisper. "Even if wearing paint is more common now, I still think it looks tawdry. And many people agree."

"You just said they looked ele—"

"By elegant I meant wealthy. But wealthy or not, obvious paint makes a woman look desperate. Everyone knows that. A woman wearing rouge might as well put a sign around her saying, 'Hello. I'm really trying to be attractive.'"

"What's wrong with trying to look pretty?"

"It's not about trying to look pretty, Louise. You look perfectly pretty right now, a soap-and-water girl, fresh-faced. You're prettier than any of them."

"I know *that*."

"I mean the paint. Women wearing that much paint just look . . ." She glanced over each of her shoulders. "Available."

"And what's wrong with that?"

Cora looked away. She would not be roped into another ridiculous argument over something so obvious. Louise just liked to fight, to bounce back every answer like a ball off a stoop. Cora wished she could take the girl down to Fifteenth Street and let her go head-to-head with Sister Delores to see who would get the last word. She didn't think Louise would make any more headway than she had, but just imagining the two forces in full combat was entertaining.

"I wish we had better seats," Louise said.

Cora turned back to her, grateful. It wasn't much of an olive branch, but she had at least tried a subject they could agree on.

"I do, too. My neck hurts from trying to see around that balcony support. We'll get tickets earlier from now on." She'd had no idea the show would be nearly sold out on a weeknight, especially in such a big theater. "I saw a few empty seats that were closer. We could try to move up."

Louise wrinkled her nose. "How will we know if the seat belongs to someone just getting back late? People could come back for their seats after the show is started, and we'll have to move. How embarrassing." She scowled out at the crowd. "I have a better idea. I'll be right back."

She was already walking away. Cora had to pull her back by her elbow.

"Where are you going?"

She looked down, clearly offended, at Cora's hand on her elbow. Cora didn't let go.

"I'm going to talk to an usher." She lowered her voice to a hostile whisper. "Cora, it's true he'll likely be male. But neither of your prior objections to me talking with a man holds up in this case. One,

209

we aren't in Wichita, nor are we surrounded by Wichitans. We are surrounded by strangers who cannot affect my reputation back home. Two, we are in a crowded foyer of a theater, and you, my watchful chaperone, will only be about twenty feet away, making it difficult, even for me, to be assaulted."

With that, she twisted her arm so her elbow moved out of Cora's hand. "Give me three minutes."

"I'll come with you."

"No." She glanced back over her shoulder. "If you do, it won't work as well."

From where Cora stood, she could see two ushers, each man standing by an exit. They wore the same light gray coats and white shirts and black ties. Both men, oddly, were tall and very thin, though one didn't look much older than Louise, and the other was at least Cora's age. Louise stood between them for a moment, looking at one, and then the other, before she made her way through the crowd to the older man. When she reached him, she kept her hands laced behind her back, twisting her body back and forth a little. Cora watched as the man leaned down to better hear her voice. His face was kind, but he shook his head no. Louise gestured toward the auditorium, the same hand then grazing her hair, then touching her bare shoulder. The man touched his ear and shook his head. Louise stood on tiptoe, her heels just leaving the floor, her hand balanced on his arm.

Cora moved as quickly as she could, excusing herself as she cut through the crowd, her gaze angry and hard on the back of the girl's head. But she was only halfway across the foyer when Louise turned around and pointed her out to the usher. The usher glanced at her, and nodded before smiling back down at Louise. Louise stepped away from him, turning back to Cora with a smile.

She looked like a child. It was something in her face, an easy, naive pleasure in her smile, with no sign of the strong will or cynicism that Cora had come to know in her. It was so strange, the way she seemed to be able to change from younger than she was to older than she was, then back again, with so much ease. Had the usher, with his small authority, brought the little girl out in her? Or had she brought out the look of a girl like a trusted tool before he even spoke a word?

"Louise," Cora said sharply.

"Cora!" She was still smiling, but the sharpness returned to her eyes. "So glad you found me." She looked back over her shoulder and said something to the usher as Cora took her by the arm. "For a minute there I felt like an unleashed dog."

"Do we need to go home?" Cora hissed, steering her back across the foyer.

"Home?" Louise looked at her with wide eyes. "You mean the apartment? Or are you threatening Kansas again?"

"Stop it."

"I don't see why we should consider either." She leaned in. "Especially because my new friend said when the lights start to flicker, we can follow him to our box seats."

Cora stopped walking and stared.

"I know." Louise shrugged. "Certainly not my first choice. Mother says box seats are for people who want to be seen at the theater, not for people who want to see theater. But they'll be a lot better than the back row of the mezzanine."

"Louise, did you make some kind of *arrangement* with that man?"

"Don't be revolting. I just asked him nicely. That's all most men really want."

Cora gave her a wary look. But she wasn't sure what to do. Really, maybe Louise hadn't done anything wrong. She'd gotten what she wanted, with no real risk or harm. No sense in faulting her for her confidence and the generosity of ushers. Maybe she,

212

Cora, was the one with the crass mind, an old Mrs. Grundy harping on the young, seeing sin and scandal at every turn.

"You can thank me later," Louise said, the black eyes gazing up as the lights began to flicker. "Next time, if you want orchestra seating, you might let me wear a little rouge."

She wasn't anxious so much as silently frenzied, as if she'd had too much tea, or sugar, her mind alert and focused, even in the midday heat. For almost twenty minutes, she'd been waiting under the shade of a striped awning outside a drugstore. Her watch was back at the apartment, along with her pearl earrings and wedding ring, but if she turned and looked through the window of the drugstore, she could see the clock over the counter, next to a picture of the Holy Virgin and an advertisement for Juicy Fruit gum. She was a block away from the orphanage. In three minutes, she would start walking.

It had rained that morning. She'd used an umbrella when she walked Louise to class, and by the time she returned to the apartment alone, her hair was still more or less dry under her hat, but her curls, enlivened by the humidity, had begun a wild mutiny,

213

with several strands springing free of her hairpins and making her reflection in the bathroom mirror appear, as she saw it, a little deranged. She'd redone her hair, pulling it up into a new and tighter twist, though a few frizzy strands had again broken rank during the miserable subway ride.

She looked back at the drugstore's clock again. At exactly half past noon, she started walking. She'd thought it all through the night before, lying awake in bed, Louise asleep beside her. If she had miscalculated, if Sister Delores or another nun answered the door, she could say she was missing her parasol, and just wondering if, the other day, she had left it behind. She told herself this, rehearsed saying it, even as she walked down Fifteenth Street, even as she climbed the steps to knock.

The handyman opened the door, wearing the same pair of overalls. Or a different pair. They looked clean.

"I'm sorry," he said, no sign of friendliness. "The sisters have Mass. Every day at this time."

She stepped away, and had to turn quickly to check the stairs behind her. He was German. She hadn't realized before — he'd said so little. But now she was almost certain.

214

During the war, there were vaudeville skits about the Kaiser, usually some jokester with a fake curling mustache, marching around and yelling with an accent until he got a pie in the face.

"Oh," she said. "May I wait again?"

He nodded.

"Thank you," she said, her smile as friendly as any Ziegfeld girl's.

He stepped aside, gesturing into the entry. He was only a little taller than she was, though his shoulders were broad, his forearms thick. She moved past him, waiting as he closed and locked the door. Upstairs, the girls were singing, the piano playing along.

He led her down the hallway, keys jangling from a side loop on the overalls. Her gaze focused on the balding back of his head, the blond hair cut short at the sides.

"It was a nice rain we had this morning, wasn't it?" she asked. "So refreshing."

He barely looked over his shoulder, but he nodded. She followed him through the kitchen into the dining room. Three of the long tables were as clean and bare as they'd been the other day, but the table in the far corner was covered by a white oilcloth, and on top of that sat a mahogany box about a foot high, surrounded by tools and screws.

"You would like some water?"

"Oh! Oh yes! Thank you." She continued to smile. "You were so thoughtful the other day, and today, too, of course. Offering water again, I mean."

He gave her an odd look before moving back into the kitchen. She touched her hair beneath the brim of her hat. She was talking too quickly, perhaps. Maybe his English wasn't so good. She turned, looking out the cross-barred windows as she unbuttoned her gloves. There was no point in thinking of Alan.

He didn't always think of her.

"Sorry for the mess," the German said, handing her the water. "I am working on something."

"Thank you so much." She took the glass and walked over to the far table, moving lightly, like Louise, she hoped. She didn't have to be herself. She could be anyone. She would never see this man again. "Your mess looks interesting. What is it?"

"Well," he said, following, "it was a radio."

She looked at the box, which she now saw was missing its front panel, an interior of black wires and clear tubes exposed. The front panel, with one of the glass dials shattered, lay flat on the table. But she recognized it as the same model that Alan had showed her in a hardware store just before she left. He was going to decide between it and another model while she was gone. She would love having a radio, he said. Wichita's new station was still mostly broadcasting crop prices and weather reports, but they were going to add in more music and lectures, things she would be interested in.

She touched a finger to the shattered dial. "What happened to it?"

"It was going on or coming off a ship. I don't know which. Someone dropped it, and it broke, and they throw it away." He stood beside her, looking down at the radio, his arms crossed in front of his chest. "My friend told me, and I went to get it."

"Oh. Are you good at fixing things?"

"Sometimes." He looked at her again, his eyes small and green behind the spectacles. She smiled, and with her free hand, touched her shoulder. She had worn her only short-sleeved dress.

"What are you hoping to listen to?"

He gave her another odd look. His thinning hair, she saw, made him look older than he was, at least from far away. He was around her age, with only a few lines around his eyes. "For the girls," he said, pointing at the ceiling. "For them to listen."

"That's so nice of you!"

He didn't have to keep looking at her like

217

that. She was just making conversation. She took a sip of water. She was fine. There were nuns and children upstairs. If he misunderstood, if he was a bad man, she could scream for help.

"You are not from here?"

She shook her head. "I'm from Kansas." She paused. "It's in the middle of the country. West of the Missouri River."

He smiled. "Yes. I know." He pointed to his own mouth. "I could tell you are not from here from how you talk."

She nodded, looking back at the radio. She wouldn't think he would want to bring up accents and places of origin. "How will so many girls share the headset?" she asked. "They'll have to take turns."

"No. They can use a horn, as with a phonograph." He pointed to the horn on the oilcloth. "They will all be able to hear together."

"Wonderful!" She continued to smile. It was hard to touch her hair, since she was wearing a hat, but she did her best. "You've really figured this out!"

He shrugged, blinking at her from behind his spectacles. "You are being much nicer than you were the other day."

She had to think to continue to smile. Perhaps in New York, or in Germany, this kind of frankness was not considered rude. She set down her water glass.

"Yes," she said carefully. "I was short with you the other day. I thought about it, and I'm sorry. I wanted to tell you I was sorry. I was just upset. I was very upset."

He nodded, meeting her gaze. "It's fine."

"You see, I came a long way, all the way from Kansas, to find my records. And I think that they're in this building. But the sisters don't think I should see them." She lowered her head, raising her eyes to look up at him. "I think I should decide that for myself. I'm an adult, after all. Isn't that right?" She swallowed, still trying to smile.

She couldn't tell what he was thinking. He stared back at her, his face neutral. Perhaps he was not intelligent. The spectacles gave him the look of a scholar, but he was just a handyman. In any case, she didn't have much more time. Thinking too much, she decided, was the enemy of confidence.

"I was thinking you seemed so nice . . ." She laced her hands behind her back. "And that you maybe knew where the records were kept, and . . . I thought maybe you would be more sympathetic?"

He moved his fingertips along the stubble of his chin, his eyes cool inside the wire rims. He pointed to her, and then to himself.

"You are . . . you are trying to be seductive?"

He smiled, skin crinkling around his eyes.

Heat moved up her throat. She picked up her gloves, backing away.

"I look so desperate?" He held out his hands and looked down at himself, his clean overalls, his scuffed shoes. "You know, if I want to pay a woman to be nice to me, I can find a . . . professional woman, and I don't risk losing my job."

"I'm shocked by what you're insinuating." She didn't look at him, pulling on a glove. She felt as if she were falling inside her own body, the drop nauseating and fast.

He chuckled again. "You think I should be so grateful."

She was going to faint. The perimeter of her vision was going dark. She turned and started toward the kitchen anyway. Better to collapse outside, out on the street, than in front of this horrible man, this handyman Kaiser. She was almost to the kitchen when she felt herself going down. She grabbed the edge of a table.

"You should sit." He put his hand under her elbow.

She reached back to wave him away and accidentally swatted him in the face. She felt the spectacles beneath her glove, and heard them clatter on the floor.

"Just sit." He pressed down on her shoulder. "You must sit."

"Don't touch me."

"Fine." He laughed again, and she understood the meaning, the cruelty, in that. He did not want to touch her. That was the joke. The immigrant handyman did not want to touch her.

"I'm all right," she said, though she was crying now, completely against her will. She turned away, holding the edge of the bench. She was only wearing one glove. She'd dropped the other one somewhere.

"I'm going to get your water. If you get up now, you will go to the floor. Don't. Just wait." He started to walk away, then stopped. "Can you . . . you should try to bend forward, and your head low, between your knees."

She shook her head. She really couldn't. Not in the corset. She felt a loose curl, stuck to her neck with sweat. "You've misunderstood," she said, the words garbled. But she needed him to know. "I was asking nicely. That's all. I was asking nicely for something I need."

He came back with the water. She took it, and he sat on the far end of the bench.

He was wearing the spectacles again.

"Drink," he said.

She looked down, trying to get the one glove off.

"What are you doing?" He scooted closer. "Leave the glove. Drink."

She turned away from him, holding the glass, and drank as best she could. Her nose was running. But it was fine. It would all be fine. No one from home, from the real world, would ever know about this. She could walk out the door, and eventually, put on a smile, and it would be like it never happened. She knew that better than anyone.

"Okay," he said. "I will help you."

She turned back to him. "What?"

"I will help you. I know where the records are." He shook his head. "But today is too late. They will be down soon. You have to come back another day, and I'll let you in."

Cora stared. "Why? Why will you help me?"

He shrugged.

"You feel sorry for me."

He shrugged again. "Ya."

She turned away, her hands in fists at the sides of her face, looking down at her sensible shoes. She should be pleased. He was going to help her. That was all she'd wanted from him. She should have just tried for pity from the start — that had always been her strong suit. What had she been thinking? That she was some great beauty? Or even charming? She was not Louise. She had never been Louise, even when she was young. If Alan could see her now, knowing everything, he, too, would likely feel only pity. That was the main feeling she inspired in men. And oddly, admiration. Alan said so all the time. That he admired her. He admired her so very much.

"You are fine?" the handyman asked. He rested the backs of his elbows on the table, his legs crossed so that his ankle was propped up on his other knee. He was looking at her, waiting, but there was no cruelty or judgment in his gaze — she saw that, now that she was calmer. He had a thoughtful face.

"Just embarrassed," she said, straightening her posture. "But yes. I'm fine. Thank you. I can't come over the weekend. But I'll be here on Monday if that's all right."

Still looking at her, he smiled, the spectacles lifting a little.

Ten

She woke too early, just before dawn, and already warm and sweating in her gown. It was Saturday, the first morning with no dance class, and so, not wanting to wake Louise, she closed the bathroom door while she ran a bath. She stayed in the tub for some time, reading and occasionally running more lukewarm water over her toes. She assumed that if Louise woke and needed something, she would knock.

But when she got out of the bath and put on her robe, she opened the door to an empty room. She walked out into the front room, her wet hair still cool against her neck, and found the note. It was written on a page ripped from one of Louise's magazines, an advertisement for Palmolive soap with a picture of a young bride in white urging readers to *Keep that wedding day complexion.* Louise had crossed out the words and written her own in a speech bubble connected to the bride's mouth:

Good Morning, Cora. I hope you're having a nice bath. I really need to use the bathroom, so I'm going across the street to use theirs. I might get something to eat.

P. S. Don't cast a kitten.

L

Cora found her at the luncheonette's counter, talking with Floyd Smithers, who was leaning on the counter, clearly more interested in whatever she was saying than in the needs of his other customers. When he saw Cora, he straightened and turned his attention to a smoking woman and her little boy. Cora slid onto the bar stool next to Louise, who was fiddling with the straw of her drink. It was hard to tell if she'd dressed in a hurry or by design. She did not appear to be wearing any kind of undergarment — even a brassiere — under her thin dress. But the black hair was brushed and smooth.

She looked up. "Oh. Hi." She did not seem particularly pleased or displeased. She lowered her head, peering up under Cora's hat. "Your hair is still wet. I hope you didn't rush over here."

"It's just cooler this way." Cora fanned herself with a paper menu. She'd already decided she would avoid another battle. No harm would come from the girl walking across the street for breakfast on her own. "Thank you for leaving a note."

"Oh, did you like it? The blushing bride? I thought you might." She nodded over to Floyd, who had returned to get Cora's order. "I've just been over here getting free elocution lessons from my learned friend. Did you know our counter boy goes to Columbia?"

Cora smiled warily at Floyd. "I think I heard something about that."

Floyd wouldn't meet her gaze, focusing instead on his notepad, his pen at the ready. Of course he was still trying for Louise, she thought. That was his nature, as a young man. He couldn't be expected to be too concerned with Louise's age. It was Cora's job to keep him in check.

He thanked her for her order, but said nothing more. Apparently, the elocution lessons were over. Cora waited until he walked away before she spoke to Louise.

"If you're truly worried about your speech, I'm sure your parents would pay for real lessons."

Louise shook her head. "People who take

226

lessons always sound like frauds, like they're faking an English accent." She nodded at Floyd again, who was now engaged with the little boy in a pleasant discussion about pancakes. "This is far better. His speech is perfect, unaccented American. And he said he doesn't mind helping me."

"Imagine that." Cora looked at Louise's glass. "Is that a chocolate milk shake?"

Louise frowned at the mixture in her glass, though she took another long sip. "I know," she finally said, dabbing at her mouth with a napkin. "You're right. I need to watch it. I'm getting fat."

"That's not what I meant."

She pushed the glass away. "No. You're right. I need to be on all sixes. They'll only pick a few girls to join the company at the end of the course, or maybe not any at all. Mother thinks I have a good chance, but I'll never make it if I'm fat."

Cora had to work not to roll her eyes. Then again, Louise, small as she was, was actually thicker in the hips than most of the girls Cora saw in magazines these days. Models and actresses had gotten so thin, not just in the waist like a Gibson Girl, but in the hips, too, and most with nothing at all for breasts. All these girls had thrown away their corsets, claiming liberation, but apparently, they weren't supposed to eat.

"That's just silly," Cora said, taking off her gloves. "You have a lovely figure. Milk shakes aren't a good breakfast for anyone. You can have some of my eggs and toast when they come." She patted Louise's arm. She hadn't known that the girl had real hopes of joining Denishawn, and that the goal, for Myra as well, was for Louise not to return to Wichita at all. "And you get a break from dancing today," she added. "Our first weekend. What would you like to do?"

Louise frowned. "Do?"

"Yes. What would you like to do today? I imagine you'd like to see something of the city besides Broadway and that church basement. I've been looking at my guidebook. We're not at all far away from Grant's Tomb, which I hear is very impressive. But we could easily get to the Natural History Museum. I'd like to see the Statue of Liberty sometime."

Louise groaned. "Sorry. I have no interest in playing the Midwestern tourist. Can't you do all that while I'm at class?" She turned to Cora, perplexed. "What *do* you do while I'm at class?"

Cora wasn't sure what to say. Telling Louise about the orphanage would be a mistake. It was all too tender, too painful. Any

228

mockery would be more than she could bear.

"I just rest at the apartment," Cora said. "I get in the bath and read."

Louise put her hands on the small of her back and flexed her shoulders. "That sounds wonderful. That's all I want to do today. I don't know that my body has ever been so sore. I'll probably just go back up to the apartment and nap. I have to write Mother a letter, too." She turned to Cora. "And we're going to that show tonight. Did you get the tickets?"

"Orchestra seats." Cora frowned. "The theater is all the way out on Sixty-third Street. Why is it so far away from all the others?"

Louise shrugged. She pulled the milk shake close again and took another sip from the straw. Floyd set the eggs and toast in front of Cora, asking, very professionally, if she needed anything else.

"Another plate, please. And more silverware."

He retrieved both without another word, giving Louise a wistful look before again moving away. Cora used her knife and fork to push half of the eggs and toast onto the second plate, which she slid in front of Louise.

"Eat," she said. "And I do understand you just wanting to rest today. But as for tomorrow, I found a beautiful Presbyterian church not far from here at all."

If Louise was pleased with the idea, it hardly showed. She put her hand over her mouth as she chewed. "Church? I didn't know you were religious."

Cora smiled. She was hardly devout. She and Alan missed services all the time, especially now that the boys were gone. She thought they would go tomorrow for Louise's sake. And she herself wouldn't mind — with the week she'd had, she was longing for something of home, some ritual she knew and understood.

"I actually thought you were religious," she told Louise. "You liked to go to Sunday school back in Wichita. Isn't that right?"

Louise put her fork down. She was suddenly, unmistakably, angry. The black eyes focused on Cora's. "How do you know about that?"

Cora didn't know what to say.

"Did my mother tell you that?"

"No . . . I just heard it."

"You heard it." Louise lifted her chin. "From whom? From whom did you hear this tidbit, Cora?"

"Louise, I —"

"From whom?"

"I'm friends with Effie Vincent," she stammered. "Her husband teaches Sunday school." It was a half lie, leaving out Viola. Cora didn't want to say that she'd heard Louise went to Sunday school because her friend was friends with the Sunday school teacher's wife. It just sounded so convoluted, as if they'd had some big meeting about it. And she did know Effie Vincent, a nice woman, who never said a bad word about anyone. "We're friends," she said again.

"Are you." Louise looked at her coolly. They were quiet, surrounded by the clatter of plates and the ring of the kitchen's bell. "What else did Effie Vincent have to say?"

"Nothing. Just that you liked to go to Sunday school. That's hardly gossip, Louise. It's a nice thing for people to say about you. I don't understand why you're upset."

Cora wanted to reach out and touch her on the arm, gently, to show she meant no harm. But something told her not to. Was Louise just being dramatic? Was this the famed moodiness of the adolescent girl? Her boys had never been like this, imagining a slight where there was none. Earle could get distant and quiet when he was down, but neither of her sons ever got so angry or cross-examined her over the most innocent remark.

Louise nudged her plate away. "I'm not upset." She looked up and gave Cora a pitying smile, exactly like the one she'd given to her father on the platform back in Wichita. "I'm just astounded that you good ladies are able to keep such a close tab on everyone. It's really something, how much you all know."

The 63rd Street Music Hall was not only outside the theater district, it held none of the grand opulence of the New Amsterdam. It was just an old lecture hall, really, with a crammed-in orchestra pit and seats with torn upholstery. Cora and Louise were among the first of the audience to arrive, and the theater was still quiet enough that they could hear a persistent telephone ringing, without pause or response, from whatever space was to the left of the auditorium. But Louise had sworn that *Shuffle Along* was one of the biggest hits of the year, and that the review she'd read promised there was no coarse humor or language. Sure enough, the seats began to fill with respectable-looking people, and Cora relaxed, taking her book out of her purse. She had no option of conversation. Louise, sitting to her left, had pulled out the Schopenhauer the moment they took their seats.

They were both still reading when someone tapped Cora's shoulder. She looked up to see a tall colored man in a three-piece suit.

"Pardon us," he said.

Behind him stood a woman, also colored, and wearing an organdy silk dress and pearls.

Cora stared up at them, uncertain. She didn't want any trouble.

"Cora." Louise laughed, nudging her arm. She was already standing. "They need to get to their seats."

Cora's gaze moved over the other seats. She saw now that at least four colored people were sitting in the orchestra pit, closer to the stage than she was.

"Oh yes, of course," she said, standing quickly. Her seat sprang up behind her. "Sorry," she said, glancing at the couple. She leaned back to give them space. After they passed, she sat slowly, her eyes moving side to side. She wasn't sure what was happening, if this was some sort of protest or instigation. A few years ago in Wichita, a group of colored men had tried to sit on the ground floor of a theater, but they'd been arrested before the show began.

But no one here, black or white, seemed at all distressed.

She looked at her program. The drawing on the cover was innocuous, just the legs of a few men and women in a row, their upper bodies obscured by the title. She opened the program and looked at the cast list, the names of the characters. *Syncopating Sunflower. Happy Honeysuckle. Jazz Jasmine.*

She swallowed and touched Louise's arm.

"Louise," she whispered. "What kind of show is this?"

Louise looked up, her expression both blank and annoyed, as if she didn't know what Cora was asking, as if nothing were out of the ordinary, which was just maddening, because of course colored people taking seats on the main floor of a theater *was* out of the ordinary, even for New York. At the New Amsterdam, colored people had sat up in the balcony, just as they did in every theater Cora had ever been to. She'd never heard of anyplace, anywhere in the country, where things were different.

"It's supposed to be a very good show," Louise said, looking back down at her book. She waved her hand at the seats in front of them. "It's obviously very popular."

Cora's gaze moved over the seats, then back down to her program. The fact that there was a character named "Jazz" seemed especially worrisome. Was it a jazz show? A radical one with mixed seating? She wasn't much of a chaperone, sitting there passively with Louise, waiting for the music to start. Just the year before, there'd been an article in *Ladies' Home Journal* that warned that the new jazz craze was a real threat to young people, as it regularly led to a base form of dancing that stirred up the lower nature. Even just hearing jazz was bad, the article said: its primitive rhythms and moaning saxophones were purposefully sensuous, and capable of hypnotizing young people. Cora knew that Viola had told her daughters in no uncertain terms that they were not to listen to jazz music, ever.

"Louise. I think we should go."

"I'm not going anywhere." She didn't even look up.

Cora might have insisted, or tried to insist, but just then, a colored woman took the seat to her right. Cora glanced up, and the woman, who had bobbed hair with a Marcel wave, smiled briefly before she looked up at the curtained stage. A skinny colored boy of about twelve sat on her other side, his program rolled like a telescope against one of his eyes. Cora, her heart pounding, folded her program in half, and then in quarters.

They couldn't get up and leave now — not without giving the impression that they were fleeing from the proximity of this woman and the boy, that they were somehow personally offended by them, which wasn't the case at all. Cora had no problem with colored people. She liked Della, for example, very much. She made a point of telling her how much she valued her as a talented housekeeper and cook. She was the one who had told Alan they should give Della a raise last year, and she'd always tried to be understanding and gracious when Della had to stay home with one of her own children.

She'd just never expected to sit next to a colored person at a theater. She'd always heard that colored people, unless they were troublemakers or communists, preferred to have their own space up in the balcony, and that most of them weren't interested in theater anyway.

She had just managed to calm herself when the orchestra walked out into the pit. She stared. The musicians were colored, not white musicians in blackface, but actual colored musicians. All of them. Back home, she'd seen colored pianists at minstrel shows, goofing and grinning, their faces further darkened with grease paint or burnt cork. But this was clearly something else. She had never seen a show with colored violinists and colored oboists and colored saxophonists, and she had certainly never seen a colored conductor looking relaxed in a three-piece suit and shined shoes. Her eyes slid to her left. Louise. Louise must have known that this was not a regular Broadway show. Did she think this was some kind of joke, having Cora buy them tickets for this? Was getting the housewife from Kansas to a radical theater some kind of hilarious trick?

What Cora didn't know was that she wasn't alone: although the theatergoers around her were playing it cool, much of New York had been similarly taken aback by *Shuffle Along.* Before the show opened in 1921, no one believed a white audience would pay to see a musical that was written, produced, directed, and performed solely by black people. The producers took the hall on Sixty-third Street because it was the only venue they could get, but after opening, the show proceeded to fill the seats with an enamored, cheering audience — both black and white — for over five hundred nights.

The show made all kinds of history. Some fifty years later, when Cora's godson, the dentist, who was born in Wichita the very summer Cora was in New York with Louise, and who at the age of twenty had fought under General Eisenhower in North Africa during World War II, discovered that his old godmother had seen the 1922 Broadway production of *Shuffle Along,* he asked her if she had any memory of a beautiful black girl, who certainly would have stolen the show, the same girl who would go on to become Josephine Baker, or the most gorgeous woman in the world, so insanely popular in her adopted France that even the occupying Nazis were afraid to touch her, the same girl who would become the Bronze Venus, or the Black Pearl, or just La Baker, as she was called when she performed for the Allied troops and whipped Cora's young godson into such an obsessive frenzy that when he came home from the war he read everything in print about La Baker, as if that would improve his chances with her if she ever decided to leave France and return to America, and maybe someday happen into Wichita, where she might develop a toothache, sashay into his practice, so he could forsake his wife and proclaim his enduring love.

No, Cora had to say, sorry to disappoint him. She didn't remember a particular girl.

The godson looked disappointed only for a moment before he tapped his own head and said, of course, of course, Josephine Baker had auditioned for *Shuffle Along* on Broadway, but they'd rejected her at first, saying she was too skinny and too dark for the stage. They let her work backstage as dresser, helping the stars with costume changes, secretly memorizing the lines and routines. Months later, when a chorus girl had to leave, Josephine Baker would step into her role like the natural she was, like the legend she would become, and show them all. But the night Cora and Louise went to see *Shuffle Along,* Josephine Baker, born the same year as Louise, was still backstage, just a costume girl, unseen and simmering.

Was that what was in the air that July? All that talent and ambition and yearning so close that Cora couldn't help but breathe it in? Because even so many years later, she would remember how on that warm evening on Sixty-third Street, despite all her discomfort and fear, she had at some point stopped worrying, stopped silently raging at Louise, and started to enjoy the show, her shoe-cramped toes tapping to the syncopated rhythms, and her eyes tearing up at the end of the slow ballad "Love Will Find a Way."

That had surprised her. She'd never seen a real love story between colored people, and the very idea of it had seemed so odd and silly to her, but by the end of the song, it didn't.

Cora would be in her early seventies when a group of young black people in Wichita decided to sit at the counter of Dockum Drugs every day, from open till close, until they were served. They endured cursing, threats, and boredom, but after a month, Dockum's owner, tired of losing frightened or displaced customers, finally relented and served the protesters at the counter. Plenty of white people in Wichita believed they had cause for concern, because now that Dockum was serving colored people, they might think they were welcome anywhere. Cora, if she were honest, would have to admit she might have been one of them had it not been for that night back in 1922 when she sat between Louise and the black woman with the Marcel wave, and she watched a black man conduct a black orchestra while black men and women talked and danced and sang "I'm Just Wild About Harry," and black and white people applauded them together, and nothing terrible happened. In fact, even though she'd gone into the theater with her own troubles and sadness that night, she'd had a wonderful evening, as she would later assure the frightened ladies in her circle, many of whom, in 1958, were far younger than she was. An integrated lunch counter, Cora would tell them, was not the end of civilization, and integrated schools and theaters wouldn't be the end, either. It would be fine, she assured friends, thinking back to that night in New York. Really. It would be more than fine.

She would owe this understanding to her time in New York, and even more to Louise. That's what spending time with the young can do — it's the big payoff for all the pain. The young can exasperate, of course, and frighten, and condescend, and insult, and cut you with their still unrounded edges. But they can also drag you, as you protest and scold and try to pull away, right up to the window of the future, and even push you through.

She read the postcard the next afternoon, while Louise was in the bath. She didn't mean to read it. She'd never scavenged through her sons' rooms, even when she'd been tempted, and she'd learned not to look through Alan's things. But Louise's postcard had fallen from the writing table to the floor of the front room, and Cora, while sweeping, had crouched down to pick it up, and her eye went to her own name in Louise's compact but readable script.

. . . Cora Carlisle is such a flat tire, and quite the rube. And she has a rich, handsome husband, which makes absolutely no sense. I keep wishing she'd fall into the Hudson or get hit by a trolley or something, but every day, she . . .

Cora put the postcard down, writing side down, so she could only see the back, a picture of Charlie Chaplin. She looked at the yellow walls, and the painting of the Siamese cat. It didn't matter. She was fine. She wasn't concerned with what a fifteen-year-old snob thought of her. And anyway, she shouldn't have read it, even the bit that she had. She crossed her arms, looking down at the postcard. Had she written that to her mother? It was too awful to consider, Louise writing such cruelties to Myra. Cora circled the table once, and then again, before reaching to retrieve the postcard.

Dear Theo Darling,

Cora put the card down. Theo was the brother. Not the older brother Louise had fought with, but the younger one, who'd wanted to play badminton by himself. It didn't matter. If Louise had written the same to Myra, so what? So what. She wasn't going to look at the other postcards. She didn't care. She moved away from the table.

She went into the kitchen and poured herself a glass of milk. She sipped it slowly, listening to the steady drip of melting ice in the ice-box. On the other side of the wall, the tub was draining, and she heard Louise humming a languid version of "Ain't We Got Fun?" She put down the glass and tapped her fingertips on the stovetop. That Louise had called her a bore and a rube wasn't such a surprise. The girl said as much with her eyes and tone of voice almost every time they spoke; Cora could hardly call her dishonest. What hurt her, what felt like a physical blow to Cora's chest, was the girl's cruel but astute observation about Alan, about how mismatched they seemed. It was too bad that Cora had not known Louise the summer Cora was married, when she perhaps could have used an acquaintance with such brutal honesty.

Louise walked into the kitchen wearing a pink wrap, her hair slicked back and wet. Her forehead was wide and prominent, Cora noticed, almost protruding. She wasn't as striking without the bangs. She still looked young and pretty, but not uncommonly so.

"Oh my God, that bath was wonderful." She tilted her head from side to side. "But I've been out for exactly three minutes, and I'm already sweating. The theater tonight had better be ice-cooled."

Cora nodded and sipped her milk.

"What's the matter?"

"Nothing." Cora looked at her and smiled. "You're right. It does seem warmer today."

Louise stretched her arms up with an exaggerated yawn, and started talking about *Blossom Time,* and how she hoped it would be as good as the reviewers said. Cora leaned against the stove and listened with an interested, pleasant expression. There was no point in bringing up the postcard or what Louise had written about Alan, and there never would be. So even while the hurt was still there, a heaviness in her mind and heart, she acted as if nothing were amiss, and of course, Louise believed her. The girl may have sworn off fake smiles, but Cora knew how necessary they could be, and hers was well-practiced and convincing.

Eleven

Mr. Alan Carlisle of Wichita and Miss Cora Kaufmann of McPherson were united in marriage yesterday under a canopy of white roses and carnations outside the boathouse of Riverside Park, with Pastor John Harsen of the First Presbyterian Church of Wichita presiding. The ceremony was immediately followed by a grand and festive reception at the Eaton Hotel, where over a hundred guests dined on generous portions of roast beef, sweet potato croquettes, assorted cheeses, fruits and vegetables, and a multi-tiered wedding cake. A small orchestra accompanied the happy couple as they danced a graceful waltz, and family and friends soon joined them on the floor.

The bride was perfectly lovely in a white lawn dress with a high lace collar and a V-insert of patterned lace and pintucks. She wore her hair in a high pompadour adorned with real orange blossoms, a gift from Miss Harriet Carlisle, her new sister-in-law and Maid of Honor. The tall and elegant groom wore the conventional black, his striped tie worn ascot fashion and held with a silver pin.

Mr. Carlisle, a prosperous lawyer, is well and favorably known in Wichita, and when and whom he would marry has long been the subject of speculation among our city's single ladies. By all accounts, he is smitten with his young bride, who was recently orphaned in a tragic farm accident, and who seems a very worthy young lady with a sweet disposition. The new Mrs. Carlisle has already made many friends here in her adopted community.

— *"Society News,"* The Wichita Eagle,
June 7, 1903

Cora would long appreciate that the reporter left out the low point of her wedding's festivities, which was when Raymond Walker, a farm boy turned defense attorney who sometimes played cards with Alan but who hadn't even come to their engagement party, attempted to make the first toast at the reception, apparently forgetting, or not caring, that he was drunk. Raymond Walker was shorter than Cora, but wide in the shoulders, with flame-colored hair, and a deep, theatrical voice that made it easy to command attention. When he stood and started talking about friendship and love, even the busy waiters turned to look.

"Alan!" he boomed, raising his glass of lemonade. "What a good, decent man you are!"

This statement was met with a burst of applause, with other guests raising their lemonades and adding, "Hear! Hear!" and Cora laughing and nodding in agreement. But then Raymond Walker, still standing, set his lemonade on the table and nonchalantly removed a silver flask from the interior pocket of his jacket and proceeded to take a long, audible gulp. Cora glanced at Alan, who sat beside her, staring at Raymond Walker with a forlorn expression and shaking his head in tiny, almost imperceptible movements.

"Some people marry for love," Raymond continued, giving the entire head table a misty-eyed look. "But, Alan, you've shown us all that real propriety, and real charity, begins at home."

Alan stood. But his two uncles and a cousin were already moving toward Raymond, their faces grim. Someone wondered aloud if they should take the flask away, but

247

someone else said, "No, just get him out." Raymond Walker shook the men off and said he was leaving on his own. He staggered out, big shoulders back, under a collective glare of disapproval, although Cora could only stare, stunned, at her dinner plate. An orange blossom fell from her hair, landing in her roast beef.

He was just a drunk, she told herself. And he was wrong. It wasn't charity — Alan loved her, loved her as much as she loved him. He'd told her so, many times, and he'd said it with such sincerity, and with such hope and kindness in his eyes. He was the one with good fortune, he'd said. He'd been looking for her his whole life.

The door was barely closed behind Raymond Walker when Alan's father stood, raised his lemonade, and in his most venerable voice told Alan, who was still standing, how very happy he and his mother were to invite a young woman as fine as Cora into the family, and that he had made them very proud, and that they wished them many children and happy years. He walked across the room, shook Alan's hand, and then embraced him to loud applause, and then it was as if the horrible moment with Raymond Walker simply hadn't happened. When Alan took his seat again, reaching for her hand, she was surprised to see he had tears in his eyes. Her humiliation already receding, she was moved to see that his father's words meant so very much.

The only advice Cora ever got about sex came from Mrs. Lindquist, who told her, just a few weeks before the wedding, that she didn't want to scare her, but she felt she ought to know that a man was different from a woman in that he was often a slave to his physical self, with far more desire than necessary for a happy home with a reasonable amount of children. It was a wife's duty, she told Cora, to both submit to this desire and to temper it, for it was a powerful force, and a husband, even a gentleman, could not always be expected to think with his mind.

"It's the same as feeding horses and dogs," she added, cracking an egg on the side of a bowl. "You don't want to starve them. But they always want more than they need."

Cora wasn't scared. In fact, she was intrigued by the idea that at least in this one arena of her marriage to Alan, she would be the one in charge. She wouldn't abuse this power. She had no intention, to borrow Mrs. Lindquist's terms, of starving her handsome fiancé, or even letting him go hungry for long. Still, he was older than she was, and more educated, and more used to society and having money and living in a city. As much as her speech had improved through diligent study of grammar and the way Alan and his family lived, Cora hardly felt his equal, especially when they were out in public. But if Mrs. Lindquist was correct, when it came to the intimacies of marriage, even with all she didn't know, he would be at her feet.

And truly, during their first nights together as husband and wife, her refined and mannered Alan did seem like a man possessed, his gentle caresses ceasing as he began to labor over her, his hands gripping the pillow above her shoulders, as if he needed to hold tight to something else to avoid doing her harm. If it weren't for the peppermint smell of his aftershave, she wouldn't have recognized him as the same man who, during the daytime, laughingly complained about lazy court clerks and taught her to play chess and held out his arm for her on their strolls down Douglas Avenue. In her room, she couldn't see him. He only came to her after dark, and he never brought a lantern. She was grateful. With any light, she would have had to worry how her expression should be — forbearing? Determined? She didn't know. She had seen animals mating on the farm, so she understood the mechanics of sex, but she knew nothing of how she should behave as a human, as a woman. She doubted Alan, given his advanced age, was a virgin as well, and she worried that in her ignorance, she would do something unheard of and embarrass herself. Even in darkness, she didn't know if she was supposed to just lie still, or if it would be all right to let her arms and legs wrap around him, as they kept wanting to do. She didn't want to appear sex-crazed. But she didn't want him to think she was bored, because if anything, her body and her mind wanted him to go on longer, and she felt oddly bereft every time he slumped over her with a quiet cry, and it was done. She wasn't sure what he would think, if she let on about that.

Afterward, reaching across the bed to hold her hand, he would ask if she was all right, as if he had damaged her somehow, which she didn't understand, because she was his wife. And she had told him, even before they were married, how much she wanted a child, how she didn't want to wait, how much it would mean to her to know someone, even a little baby, who shared her blood. And she wasn't hurt. In fact, even when he was holding her hand and what she needed from him for a child was already released inside her, even then, she wanted to crawl across the bed and move her hand against his side and press her face into the warm skin of his chest.

But that might be strange, or too forward.

"Cora? Darling? Are you all right?"

"I'm fine," she would say, squeezing his hand, because she couldn't say more than that.

Having the twins nearly killed her. She wasn't due for another three weeks when she woke with what felt like a pickax in her belly, her mouth and throat so parched that at first, she couldn't cry out. When she finally did, the pickax moved, slicing into her on each side, but Alan appeared in the doorway of her room, still wearing his pajamas, his mouth going slack at the sight of her.

Later, he told her she was so pale, even her lips drained of color, that it was like she was already a corpse, but writhing in agony on the bed.

They were lucky to have a phone. Most people still didn't, and it saved time, which the doctor said later had been crucial —

she could have bled to death. As soon as Alan made the call, he returned to her with water and a wet cloth that she grabbed from him and bit down on. Her vision began to blur and darken, but she could hear him crying, begging her not to go. That scared her. He kissed her forehead, the morning stubble of his chin rough against her cheek, and whispered that he was so sorry. He kept saying how sorry he was. She was irritated, even as the pickax burrowed in. He hadn't done anything wrong. He'd only been a husband. It wasn't his fault that something in her body was going horribly wrong. It was her own defective machinery, likely bad since her own birth. Regular childbirth was Eve's curse, a bearable pain for all women, but this, hers, was something else.

When the doctor arrived, he asked Cora if her own mother had suffered from toxemia. Or a sister? Or an aunt, perhaps? Had any of them had any trouble with childbirth at all? Any blood clots?

She gripped Alan's hand, dug her nails into his skin.

"She doesn't know," he told the doctor. And then more firmly: "Don't agitate her with these questions."

She would never understand how she survived it, bearing down while she could barely breathe, the doctor and nurse urging her on, even when she told them about the pickax, even as she was shrieking and begging them to stop the pain. It was the placenta, the doctor told her. It was tearing off too early, and they had to get the baby out. He couldn't use chloroform. He would need her help to push and save the baby, and to save herself as well.

Alan was banished from the room. She didn't know he'd gone, or how long he was away. He told Cora later that he heard Howard's first hearty cry from the parlor, and that he'd been on his knees, his forehead pressed against the sofa's armrest. Cora heard Howard's first cry, too, though she never heard Earle's — by the time he was delivered, she was losing blood, fading in and out. Even when she could hear, she couldn't move, or feel, her arms or her legs. But she no longer felt the pickax, either, and she was peaceful, ready to sleep, even with her unquenched thirst, even having just heard the first cry of her child. She was that tired, and that afraid of the pickax's return. "We're losing her," the doctor said, quietly, but she heard it, and still all she wanted was to rest, to stop having to fight, to just go with what nature intended and lay her head down on the grain. But hands pressed against her, shook her awake. "Don't breathe in the poison," Mother Kaufmann said. "Cora? Love? You can't see it or smell it, but it'll kill you." They were both with her, their hands on her, shaking her awake though she couldn't see them, even as they pushed and pulled her to the silo's ladder. "Go on," Mr. Kaufmann said, with a not-so-gentle shove. "Go on, now." She couldn't turn around. She had to keep looking up at the silo's blue-sky opening, grasping for it, but she could hear them both behind her, urging her to keep climbing through the thickness on the slippery rungs, to go on and let herself be the happy woman and the very good mother they'd always known she would be.

They already had an older Swedish woman coming in on washday, but after the twins were born, Alan asked Helgi to come in every day to do the housework and the cooking, too. So Cora spent the first months of her sons' lives recovering in bed as the doctor suggested, a bassinet on each side, both within easy reach for breastfeeding. Despite Cora's lingering weakness, Alan's mother had insisted that a wet nurse was out of the question, as most wet nurses were unmarried mothers and immigrants, she said, and there was no telling what unseen weaknesses or vices babies ingested along with the milk. When the senior Mrs. Carlisle said things like this, Cora didn't know if she had simply forgotten about Cora's own murky background. Her mother-in-law was always kind, and she never brought up the fact that Cora could easily be illegitimate herself. But Cora knew she knew.

So even before she was strong enough to go down the stairs by herself, Cora worked to prove herself not just adequate, but excellent at nursing her ravenous boys, who both seemed a little angry for being expelled too early from the womb, and so thin and desperate for nourishment. She sang "Black Is the Color of My True Love's Hair" to them, marveling at Howard's fair hair and strong grip, and how Earle, with his serious eyes, already looked so much like Alan. Twins. The surprise of it made her laugh, albeit with exhaustion. Alan's family had no history of twins. Perhaps her side did.

Alan handled the shopping. Almost every day, on his way home from work, he went to the grocery and the bakery and vegetable stands and purchased what Helgi needed to cook whatever Cora was craving. He regularly brought home calf's liver, which the doctor had suggested to restore her blood and iron, though Cora did not crave this at all. He brought her novels and constructed a little bookstand so she could read while she nursed. The phonograph was moved upstairs by her bed, and Alan purchased records he thought she and the babies might like to hear. He would bring up her dinner and sit with her at the table in the corner of her room, holding both of the boys so she could eat. Fatherhood agreed with him. He seemed so happy, beaming down at their little faces, or, if one or both started to cry, walking them around the room and assuring them, in his low, patient voice, that they would be fine, that their mother had been through a lot, and they should give her some time to rest.

Once she was able to get up and down the stairs without feeling light-headed, she and Alan started eating in the dining room again, leaving the twins upstairs asleep, the heavy door to her room pulled shut for just that half hour, so, Alan said, she wouldn't hear if one of them woke and started to cry. Cora appreciated that he insisted they spend this uninterrupted time together, and that he always worked to amuse her with stories of warring secretaries and belligerent judges. But it was an effort to keep up her end of the conversation — her days consisted of repeated, short cycles of sleeping, eating, nursing, and changing diapers, and there was no way to get too many anecdotes or charming observations out of that. She could ask him about things she'd read in the paper — had he heard about the fire at the ice plant? Did he really think it would cost twenty-five thousand dollars to build a new one? Had he heard Henry Ford had invented an automobile that could go over ninety miles an hour? She would plan these topics in advance, not wanting to appear such a dullard, but then, when Alan actually tried to discuss them with her, her tired mind would lose focus. Even with the door upstairs shut she might hear one or both of the boys crying, and the front of her dress would be wet with milk and she wouldn't hear Alan at all.

She felt sorry for him. Before the end of her pregnancy, they'd gone out to parties and dances together. Now she felt like a walking eyesore, her body still too swollen to squeeze into a corset, her breasts too large with milk. And really, she didn't want to be away from the twins for long. But having people over for dinner also seemed too challenging — and embarrassing, as she was still an exhausted and potentially leaky vessel. She was only comfortable with visits from Alan's family, for whom it seemed she could do no wrong.

Alan said it was ridiculous of her to apologize, that she didn't have anything to be sorry for. Of course she needed time to recover.

"You almost died," he reminded her, taking a bite of a pancake coated with sugar, a favorite dessert of Helgi. "And I'm hardly dissatisfied. We've been married a year, and we have two healthy sons. You've been a devoted mother to them." He smiled across the table. "I have no complaints whatsoever."

She cut into her pancake and glanced up at him. He was still dressed for court, still wearing his coat, even, though he'd removed his tie and unbuttoned the top button of his shirt. The skin beneath was a faint shadow in the glow of the table's candles. Her gaze moved to his hands.

"Thank you," she said. "But I want you to know . . ." She swallowed and looked down at her plate. "I want you to know that I look forward to my full recovery, when I can be a wife to you again as well."

There. She had said it, as plainly as she could. She didn't know what else to do. He hadn't been in her bed since she told him she was pregnant. She'd assumed that this was a common practice, and that having relations when she was pregnant would harm the child in some way, and that her doctor was too embarrassed to tell her. And Alan, so considerate, might still think her too tired or fragile for relations. But now, looking at him in the candlelight, even with Helgi still cleaning up in the kitchen, she wanted to go to him and sit in his lap and put her arms around his broad shoulders, and press her nose against his Adam's apple, breathing in the peppermint and the scent of warm skin underneath. She didn't want him to be considerate forever.

She heard him set down his spoon. When she looked up, his smile was gone. He turned toward her, his knee grazing hers under the table.

"Cora," he said, reaching over the table's corner to take her hand. "I'm afraid I have to tell you something."

She held her breath, waiting. His hand was warm against hers.

"We can't have any more children. Or we shouldn't. I didn't want to tell you while you were still weak, but the doctor was clear." He stared at her. "What happened with the twins' birth could likely happen again, and he can't guarantee you would be as fortunate."

She looked into the candle's flame. He wasn't telling her anything she hadn't already suspected. But she'd put the thought out of her mind — she'd long dreamed of a big family with Alan, finally, to make up for the years of being alone. She'd wanted to be one of those women with a house full of children who would know only love and togetherness, all of them calling her Mother and wanting for nothing. She'd wanted this so badly that it had felt like a need, a mission. But now, hearing the hard facts, her fear trumped all that. Alan was right. She loved the twins more than these imagined children. She wouldn't risk leaving them motherless. And really, it was more than that. She remembered with clarity the feeling of life truly pulling away from her. She didn't want to die, or ever feel that pickax again. She wanted to live a long life and be in this world with her beautiful husband and her baby boys and her pretty house with the turret and the afternoon sunlight slanting across the wooden floors. Even for herself, even without the twins, she didn't want to bleed to death. She was grateful Alan hadn't left the choice up to her, or implied they might try for another child anyway. Because she wanted to live even more than she wanted more children, but saying that aloud would sound unwomanly, and cowardly, and selfish.

She leaned down to kiss Alan's hand. "You don't mind?" she asked, looking up.

He smoothed back her hair and shook his head. "I couldn't bear it if something went wrong," he said. "We need you to live."

He never came to her bed again. He kissed her cheek, and kissed her hand, and sometimes moved his hand over her hair, but even when the twins were sleeping through the night in their own room at the end of the hall, and even when she could fit in her corset again, and wear pretty dresses and dance with him at parties, he stayed in his own room at night. She understood he was being chivalrous, protecting her from his desire.

But she also wondered, from time to time, if so much chivalry was necessary. Surely not all relations led to babies. Many women she knew had ten or more children, but some had only three or four, and it was hard to believe that all of the married women who weren't having babies each year lay alone in bed every night as she did. And what about bad women? They certainly couldn't risk a baby every time they had relations. There must be some trick, something other women knew and she didn't. Would it be safe if they just didn't complete the act? If they stopped before he spilled out? That would certainly be better than nothing. But who could she ask? Not the doctor. Not Viola or Harriet. Either one would likely be offended, or horrified, and think her some sort of bad woman. She could say she was just asking for Alan's sake, for the sake of a happy marriage, but she might just embarrass herself.

She wondered if he went to bad women. If he did, then he was right to stay out of her room. There had been a notice in the paper that had bluntly warned men not to visit bad women unless they wanted to bring syphilis and all sorts of other diseases home to their wives and likely make them infertile. Cora knew a nice woman who had been married five years, with no children at all, and Viola Hammond said she was sterile because her husband had visited a bad woman and brought home a disease. It happened all the time, Viola said, and then she'd looked at Cora so steadily that Cora wondered if she was implying that Alan was similarly responsible for the twins' difficult birth, which for all she knew, he could have been. Would the doctor have told her? She didn't know. There was so much she didn't know, and no way to find any of it out.

But she couldn't come out and accuse him. Not on such shaky ground. And not when he was so good to her and the boys. Once Howard and Earle were toddling around, Alan would get down on the floor to play with them, even after a long day at work, letting them climb up on his back and crawl underneath him, laughing and blowing raspberries into their bellies until they were laughing, too. And he often surprised Cora with a present — a new hat from the Innes store, or something nice for the house. If she would remind him that it wasn't her birthday or Christmas, he would tell her he was aware of that, but that he was also aware of what a wonderful wife and mother she was, and that it wasn't his fault that she had the kind of head that looked good in any hat.

When the twins were four, Cora thought it would be fun to take them to Wonderland, which was just over the Douglas Avenue Bridge, a trolley park with a carousel, a roller rink, and even a roller coaster called The Great Thriller. Out of her own excitement, she made the mistake of telling the boys her plan in advance, and she was so pleased with their thrilled response that she promised to take them the very next Saturday if the weather was good. Alan had been working long hours, but he said he was curious about Wonderland himself, and he thought he could manage to free himself for a Saturday. Harriet and her new husband, Milt, said they wanted to come along as well, as they would soon be moving to Lawrence, and they knew how much they would miss their little nephews, not to mention Cora and Alan, once they were three hours away.

But when Saturday came, a cloudless morning suggesting a beautiful day, Alan said he didn't feel well. It was just a headache, he said, tightening the belt of his robe. And maybe something with his stomach. He didn't need a doctor, just some rest at home. They should go on without him.

"You're sure?" Cora asked, reaching up to press her hand against his forehead. They were in his room with the green velvet curtains, the same fabric covering the bed. Five years they had been married, and she'd hardly been in this room. She'd never so much as sat on the bed. "We could just go another day."

He took her hand from his forehead and kissed it. Even now, she found him so arresting to look at. He'd grown a mustache like Teddy Roosevelt's, and she was surprised at how much she liked it on him.

"I'd hate to disappoint the boys," he said. "It's all they've been thinking about. Really. I just need some rest. I'll be fine."

Before they left the house, her own head started to ache a bit. She tried to ignore it, because the boys were already sad that their father wasn't coming and she was determined to make the best of things. But by the time they met up with Harriet and Milt on the trolley, the ache was making her snappish with the boys, too sensitive to their collective volume. She realized she was shivering a little, too, though the sun was shining and everyone else said the breeze felt good. If Alan hadn't fallen ill that morning, she might have kept pushing herself, but since her symptoms trailed his by just a few hours, it seemed likely that she really was getting sick. And though she'd been looking forward to seeing the boys have fun, a day at the amusement park with two excited children hardly seemed what she needed now.

After a few minutes of hushed consultation, Harriet agreed that Cora should probably go home.

"Darlings," she said, turning around in her seat to address the boys. "Your mommy is sick, maybe with what your daddy has, and she needs to go home and rest. You can go home with her and try to be very quiet all day and maybe not have anyone make you something to eat, or you can come to Wonderland with me and your uncle Milt, and you can go on roller coasters and carousels and have us fill you up with sweets, and take you home only when you're good and tired."

Cora was surprised, and touched, to see that the twins actually had some trouble with the decision. They wanted her to come to Wonderland, they said. Earle started to cry, and it was only when Cora promised that she would take them again the very next Saturday when she was feeling better, and let them show her around, that they agreed to go along with their aunt and uncle. When they got off the trolley and she stayed on, she was a little heartbroken, though she waved and smiled and called for them to be brave boys. If she and Alan were both laid up, it would be best to have them out of the house.

She was quiet when she came in, slipping off her shoes in the entry. She thought he might be sleeping and she didn't want to disturb him. But on the turn of the stairs, she heard a sigh, or maybe a yawn, and she decided she would let him know that she was home, and see if he needed anything. But when she got to his door, her gloved hand already balled in a fist, ready to knock, she found not a closed door but a sunlit view of her husband lying naked and almost on top of Raymond Walker, who was also naked, the sheet pulled up to their waists, one of Alan's hands embedded in the flame-colored hair, the fingers of his other hand moving slowly over Raymond's freckled shoulder. Raymond's eyes were closed, and Alan was staring down at him so intently he didn't notice her standing there.

She was still. She'd once been kicked in the chin by a calf while helping Mr. Kaufmann in the barn. She remembered her head snapping back, that first flash with no pain, just the certainty that pain would come.

"Oh God," she said, and put her hand to her mouth. Her other hand went to her belly.

Alan sat up, looked at her. She stared. She'd never seen his naked chest, the tufts of dark hair around his nipples.

"Shut the door!"

His voice was so commanding, and so loud that she complied, or tried to, reaching out for the knob. But her corset was tight against her ribs, and she couldn't breathe. She grabbed the edge of the door frame, believing she would faint, hoping she would faint, if only to escape what was happening, what she had just seen, and fall into nothingness as she had during the twins' birth. But something obstinate in her wouldn't fade out, and wouldn't go down to the ground. She was still conscious, still standing, still horribly aware. She turned away, wheezing, and started for the stairs, wanting only to get away, to get out of the house, but her vision darkened and she couldn't get a good breath. She turned back, her eyes closed tight as she stumbled past Alan's doorway to her own room, humiliated by the guttural gasps she couldn't stop. She fell onto the bed, yanking off her gloves so she could undo the buttons on her collar. A button came off in her hand. She threw it, and it ricocheted off the wall. She unhooked the belt of her skirt and reached up to tug at the front ribbon of her corset. And still her terrified mind would not go out, would not let her forget what she'd seen.

Her life was over. That was clear. Her husband, the father of her children, was wicked, debased. Nothing was as she'd thought.

As her breathing quieted, she heard their murmuring voices, and the clink of a belt buckle, the snap of suspenders, and then feet moving fast down the stairs, the front door opening and slamming shut. Were they leaving together? All she could see, with her eyes open or closed tight, was Alan's fingers moving over the freckled shoulder. So loving. She thought she would retch.

She heard water running and then slow, heavy footsteps coming up the stairs. She tried to get up and close her door, but she couldn't get up fast enough, and then Alan was already there in the doorway, wearing his green robe and black pajama bottoms, holding out a glass of water. His eyes were mournful, stricken.

"Take this," he said.

She shook her head, turning away from him. The window was open. A bird chirped, and she felt a cool breeze against her face. Alan walked past her to a chair at the little table in the corner of her room. He put the water on the table and sat with his knees apart, an elbow resting on each, his fingers together and his head bowed. She shifted, and he looked up.

"Where are the boys?" he asked.

For a frightening moment, she didn't know. And then she remembered.

"With Harriet and Milt," she said. "I wasn't feeling well, so I came home."

They stared at each other. Everything was gone. He was a monster. This man, her husband, was a monster. Depraved.

"I'm sorry, Cora. I'm so sorry."

"You're disgusting. That was a vile, horrible thing."

He sat up straight, looking away.

"It's a sin. It says so in the Bible."

"Yes. I'm aware of that."

"And in our home? You brought that horrible man to our home?"

"I shouldn't have done that." He lowered his voice. "He isn't horrible."

"What?"

"He isn't horrible."

Her hand reached for the little crystal bowl by her bed. She threw it at his head, but her aim was off. It shattered on the floor. He stared at the pieces, pulling on the end of his mustache.

"That was the same drunk who behaved so abominably at our wedding?" Her voice was rising, hysterical. She couldn't help it. "Who insulted me?"

"He doesn't usually drink." He looked up at her. "He feels terrible about that. That was a hard day for him."

She put up her palm, to stop him from

saying more. She was still cold and achy, as she'd been on the trolley, but that was nothing, nothing, compared to the falling fear she felt now. And yet it was all getting worse. For he wasn't even sorry, not really. Not shamed, not on his knees.

"What are you saying?"

He stared back at her.

"Why was it hard for him?" She almost laughed. "Was he jealous? Did he want to be your wife?" Her mocking smile faded as she looked at him, the anguish on his face. She turned away, holding the edge of the bed. She thought of his hands moving through the flame-colored hair, the way they'd reached for the freckled shoulders.

She was a fool. That happy day, she'd been a fool in white, with orange blossoms in her hair.

"Even then? When we married?"

He nodded. He reached down to pick up a piece of crystal and set it on the table, looking at its jagged edge.

"You were doing that with him, even then?"

"No. We'd agreed to stop."

"Stop?" It was as if the house were falling down around her, a flimsy set on a vaudeville stage. "When did it start?"

"We met in law school."

She shook her head. She couldn't speak. This. This was why he didn't touch her.

"I didn't mean to hurt you, Cora. I wanted to help you."

She narrowed her eyes. "You used me."

"No. No, I didn't. I thought we could stop. I thought I could. I tried. You don't know how I tried."

She looked at the broken crystal piece on the table. She could get up and grab it, and slice her throat, or his. But the boys. They were at Wonderland, maybe riding the carousel. They would be home for dinner, both of them tired and wanting a cuddle. But what if they'd come home early with her? What if she and Harriet hadn't convinced them to go on without her, and one of them had run upstairs and seen what she'd seen? This perversion in their home?

"You're vile."

"Cora. Don't say that. It's not true, and you know it." His eyes were shining, locked on hers. "You know me."

"I know nothing. You told me you loved me. You said it so sincerely."

"I did. I do." He swallowed. One tear and then another moved down his cheeks, soaking into his mustache. She felt no pity. Nothing.

"I do love you, Cora."

"And yet you do vile things. With that man. And you don't touch your own wife."

"We agreed to no more children."

She shook her head. She would not abide that fatherly tone, his patient appeal to logic. It wasn't logical what he was saying. She would not be confused. "You can't exactly have a baby with another man, now can you, Alan? And that doesn't stop you."

"It's different for men."

She grimaced. This was madness. This made no sense, what he was saying. "It's different for you, Alan. Other men don't do this. Other husbands don't do this. For you, Alan. Just you. Don't act as if you're like other men. You want to have relations with another man."

He hesitated, then nodded.

"But you needed a wife so no one would know. So no one would even guess."

He nodded again.

"And you could have picked any woman in Wichita, a more beautiful woman, or a richer woman or a woman from a good family, but you picked me because I was young and stupid and poor with no family, and I wouldn't know any better."

He leaned back in the chair. "I picked you because I liked you." His eyes still glistened, pink around the edges, but he smiled. He actually smiled, wiping his cheeks with the back of his hand. "I admired you, Cora. Right from the start. And I thought I could help you." He covered his eyes. "I knew I wouldn't love any wife, in that way, the way men are supposed to love their wives, but I knew I could help you, and give you a better life. I thought that would make up for it."

She laughed, and it turned into a gasp for breath. "For what? For doing vile things behind my back? Well, it doesn't, thank you. I'd rather be a maid somewhere, all alone."

"No. No. We'd stopped. For loving him, I mean. I couldn't help that."

For some time, there was only the sound of the chirping bird, and a horse walking slowly in the street. She was a fool. She would never stop cringing, thinking of how in this very bed she'd lain under him, so certain of his desire. But everyone had been fooled. *By all accounts, he is smitten with his new bride.* How she'd loved reading that in the paper. What an idiot she was.

"I want you out of the house," she said. "I want you out today, before they come back." She turned away. If he was truly sorry, and truly ashamed, he could only crawl away from her sight. But he didn't move. She turned back to him, enraged. "Go!"

"Are you sure?" he asked, still looking down. "Take a moment to think, Cora. Think about your life, what you have. The boys. The house. No wanting for anything. A good life with friends. And me, Cora. I love you. I do."

"It's a lie."

"No it isn't." He looked up, wounded. "Haven't I always taken care of you?"

"I don't need you to take care of me anymore. You're a . . . sodomite." She was spitting her words. Her rage made her certain, strong. "I could tell any judge what I just saw, and I'd be granted a divorce and everything you have."

He stood up, rubbing his jaw. "If you do that," he said quietly, "I'm ruined. And maybe dead. Understand that. I won't be able to practice, or make any money for you and the boys to live on." He looked at her. "And know that there are people who would have me killed if they knew what you saw. Think about the boys, at least, and what that would do to them, their hearts, and their chances. Please, Cora. Think about that."

"Perhaps you should have thought about that."

He said nothing. He didn't have to. Howard and Earle were now in her mind's eye, their untroubled faces before her. She held up her hand.

"Fine," she said. "I just want a divorce. And you'll have to support me and the boys." She closed her eyes at the thought of it. She'd be a divorced woman, a scandal. And how would she explain it? If she told no one the truth, she would be the one in disgrace. She would have to endure it, the shame of a divorce, the whispered assumptions and isolation. The future stretched out before her, long and dark. She would never be happy again.

"Think on it," he said. He put his hands in his hair and tugged back so hard his pinked eyes bulged like a fish's. "If you want a divorce, I'll give you one. Obviously. You have me over a barrel. But ask yourself if it's worth so much turmoil for the boys, for any of us?"

It occurred to her, at that very moment, that he'd rehearsed all of this, this little speech, just as he would rehearse a closing argument for any jury. He'd thought over his strong points, logical and emotional, well in advance. And she was still stunned, crazy. She didn't stand a chance.

"Cora, I'll give you everything you desire for the rest of our days. Ask yourself what you're really lacking. You can't have any more children. You have the boys. You have my love and devotion, as you always have."

"What am I lacking?" She asked the question with indignation, and yet, really, she couldn't answer. She knew only that she hated him. She really did. She reached behind her and threw a pillow at his head. And then another. She looked around for something harder, but there was just the good lamp, which she liked.

"Did you give me some disease?" she asked. "Did this disgusting thing you do give me a disease? Answer me honestly, for God's sake. Is that why I almost died?"

He lowered his brows, finally startled as well. "What? No, Cora. It was nothing like that. What happened was just something in you. The doctor said. It had nothing to do with me. I swear it."

She put her face in her hands.

"Cora."

"You wished I would have died," she said. "Then you could have played the sad widower. All that sympathy for losing a wife you didn't love in the first place."

"If I wanted you dead, I would have insisted on more children."

The cruelty in this astounded her, but when she looked up at him, he only seemed tired. He walked toward her and started to sit, but she cringed away, and told him to get out of her room and to please not say anything else. He had already made his case: she'd gotten so much, in exchange for so little. She had everything a woman could want, except more children, which wasn't his fault. She might not be angry, but grateful.

Bowing to her desire, and not wishing to upset her further, he left her alone with the decision.

TWELVE

Cora had only knocked twice, and softly, when the German opened the door. She averted her eyes as she said hello. She was still so embarrassed.

"You are on time," he said, stepping aside. Some kind of dark oil was smeared on the bib of his overalls.

She nodded and moved past him into the entry, peering down the long hallway into the bright kitchen. Not a nun in sight. Upstairs, she heard the girls singing, the off-key piano almost drowning them out.

He shut the door and gestured for her to follow him down the hallway, past the closed door to Sister Delores's office. At the second closed door, he stopped. She waited, looking at the back of his balding head, exactly at eye level, while he searched through his ring of keys. All weekend, she'd cautioned herself not to be too hopeful, not to anticipate. But now she was here, and the German really was going to let her in, just as he'd said. In less than half an hour, she might walk out of this room knowing her last name at birth, or her mother's first name, or her father's.

Though maybe not. She took a handkerchief out of her purse and dabbed at her hairline. The part of her who knew and remembered disappointment sent out a stern warning. It was possible she wouldn't even have a file, or if she did, that it would tell her nothing. It was possible that, despite all this effort, she would have to go back to Wichita knowing no more than she did now. And then what? She would go on, of course. She would slip back into her life, resigned.

"This is the one," the German said, holding up a silver key. He turned and frowned at her wrist. "You have no watch?"

"Sorry. I have it here." She took her watch out of her purse. She'd again followed Floyd Smithers's advice about wearing jewelry in this neighborhood.

"Good." He raised his thick forearm to look at his own watch, with its worn leather band. "You will have to be gone in twenty minutes. I will eat my lunch on the stairs. If someone comes down early, you will hear my voice. That means don't come out, and

281

wait until you hear me tell you it is fine."
He gave her a solemn look. "If this happens,
you will be waiting in there until they go to
bed, so it is better if you are gone in twenty
minutes."

She nodded. Satisfied, he turned the key
in the lock and opened the door to a small
room with a barred window, a desk, a chair,
and, flush against a wall, a wooden filing
cabinet that was as tall as she was and a
little wider across than she could stretch
her arms. There were four columns of drawers. Each drawer had a little brass handle.

"Twenty minutes, yes?" He moved into
the hallway. "You understand?"

"I promise." She turned back to face him.
"And thank you," she said, meaning it. He
hadn't even asked for money.

He shrugged and glanced at the ceiling.
"It is nothing," he said. "Every day I eat
lunch on the stairs." He closed the door,
leaving her alone. The piano had grown
softer, and she could hear the girls singing
in Latin, their voices high and wistful.

She wasted almost five minutes figuring out
that the records were sometimes organized
by year of birth, and sometimes by year of
admittance. Within each folder, papers were
held together with straight pins. Because of

the heat, she removed her gloves, and she pricked herself right away, drawing blood. Sucking on her wounded finger, she sifted through the files with her free hand, her eyes moving over cardstock tabs with names. *DONOVAN, Mary Jane. STONE, Patricia. GORDON, Ginny.* She flipped past them. Overhead, the girls had stopped singing.

She found it, her own file, in the drawer for 1889, her name written in capital letters on a tab — *CORA,* and nothing else. No last name. She pulled the file out. If she'd had more time, she might have taken a moment, bracing herself.

The top page wasn't yellowed or wrinkled, and the typed script was easy to read.

Cora, 3, from FNM.
Hair: Brown.
Eyes: Brown.
Seems in good health, of good intelligence, sweet natured; current distress likely due to transition. Had been at FNM (29 Bleecker St.) for some time.
Parentage: unknown

On the bottom of the page, someone had handwritten:

Sent out on train with Children's Aid

283

Society, November, 1892. Placed.

She unpinned the file. The second page was a handwritten letter on lined paper with a flowered border. The envelope was gone, but there were two creases where the letter had been folded in thirds.

November 10, 1899

To the kind people at the New York Home for Frendless Girls,

I write this letter with much admiration for the good work that you do. My husband and I are the happy adoptif parents of Cora, now thirteen years of age, who resided at your home in her erly years, and who was brought to us in Kansas on an orfan train seven years ago. We believe she is as pleesed with her coming to Kansas as we are. However, we also think she would like to know more about her history and natchural parentege, as we think she will wonder about this even more as she gets older. Pleese know that my husband and I would not feel in any way upset if you sent any news about Cora's peeple or history. We would, in fact, be greatful, as we think any truth would bring our girl some comfert.

God bless,
Naomi Kaufmann
PO Box 1782
McPherson, Kansas

Cora stared at the signature. She had likely written it, Cora knew, sitting at the kitchen table with her good pen and her little brass inkwell shaped like a mouse, perhaps after Cora had gone to bed. She'd never told Cora she'd written the nuns. She likely hadn't wanted to get her hopes up, and for good reason, as it turned out. If the sisters had written back, and Cora doubted that they had, it was only to say that there was nothing to say. Parentage unknown. But even with this blow, how good to know that Mother Kaufmann had tried, her concern for Cora bigger than any jealousy or fear. Cora picked the letter up and brought the thin paper just under her mouth and nose, wanting to somehow breathe her in. When she opened her eyes, she looked down, and saw the other letter.

It was on good stationery, heavy cream paper, with no lines or decoration. The script was neat, the letters made with the alternating thick and thin lines that came from deft use of a fountain pen.

May 1, 1902

Dear Sisters,

It has come to my attention that a brown-eyed girl with the Christian name of Cora, born in the spring of 1886 at the Florence Night Mission, may have been placed in your care in her early years. I am close with this child's birth mother, who longs to know something of how the child fared, but who must insist on discretion, which is why I write to you instead. Please know that my friend has no intention of troubling Cora or intruding on her life in any way. But she tells me that she often wonders about the little baby she had to part with, and that any information, good or bad, would bring her no small measure of peace.

I've enclosed a self-addressed envelope in the happy event that you are able and willing to pass along any news about Cora. You'll notice that the return address is already written as the Hibernia Relief Fund. I apologize for the deceit, and hope that you won't be troubled by it — my only intent is to spare myself any questions that a letter from your good organization would elicit, and thus cause me to choose between lying in person to my questioners, and betraying the confidence of my friend.

With gratitude,
Mrs. Mary O'Dell
10 Maple Street
Haverhill, Massachusetts

Cora read the letter again, and then again, crinkling the stationery from holding each side too tightly. It wasn't just the content that thrilled her, that frightened her. Cora had never in her life seen forward-slanting but narrow-lettered handwriting so similar to her own. This Mary O'Dell, this "friend," looped her *y*'s the way Cora did. She crossed her *t*'s at the same height and angle. It was as if Cora had written the letter in her own hand.

The girls were no longer singing above; she could hear the priest's droning voice, though she couldn't make out his words. She looked at her watch. Five minutes. She had time to copy the name and address onto the pad of paper in her purse. But she stood still for a moment, and then, with a satisfying thrill, took both letters out of the folder and tucked them into her purse. She put the file back, straight pin refastened, her name showing on the tab just as it had been, and closed the file drawers.

She stood back to make sure the room looked exactly as she'd found it — she owed the German that much. But she didn't feel bad about the theft. She doubted the sisters would ever open her file, and what she had taken belonged to her.

When the German saw her, he stood, and met her at the low curve of the stairs.

"You found what you needed?" he asked quietly, leaning down. He smelled like salted peanuts.

"Yes!" she whispered. She had the crazed urge to embrace him, to risk getting oil on the front of her dress. She was that ecstatic. She put her gloved hand to her throat. "I have an address! An actual name and address! Thank you so very much!"

He frowned and looked at his watch. "We will go outside," he said.

She understood he was ushering her off the property, getting her out the door as quickly as possible. That was fine with her. Outside, she nearly ran down the steps, her feet as light and nimble as a girl's. She almost knocked into a passing stout woman who wore no hat. Even after Cora apologized, the woman gave her a warning look.

"You are all right?" The German was still

coming down the steps, putting on his cap.

"Yes!" She breathed in the cookie-sweet air and smiled. "But thank you! Thank you so much!"

"You seem very . . ." He frowned again and flapped his hands. "Excited. Maybe you should sit?"

"I'm fine," she assured him. A truck sputtered by, and she raised her voice. "I'm delighted, actually! I can't tell you." She couldn't. She couldn't explain to him what this meant to her, what he had made possible. She'd get a letter in the post by tomorrow. It would likely reach Haverhill, Massachusetts, in just a few days. The German seemed happy for her, his eyes bright behind his spectacles.

"You've been so kind, and you don't even know me. I wish I could thank you somehow."

"I could use a cold drink," he said.

Her smile was still. Was he joking? She didn't understand. Was he taunting her about her foolishness the previous week? But he looked serious. And he was waiting.

"Right now?" she asked. It would have to be now. She certainly wasn't going to arrange an appointment, or some kind of date, for later. She wasn't coming back here again. "Aren't you working?"

"I am always working. I live on-site, upstairs there." He pointed through the gate to the second floor of the outbuilding across the lot. Metal stairs led to a door. "I can leave as soon as Mass gets out. As long as everything is running, I take breaks as I like."

"Oh," she said. She glanced about her, at the people walking past them on the sidewalk, the cars going by on the street. She was being asked to get a drink with a foreign handyman, and she wasn't wearing her ring. But if anyone around her cared, they didn't let on at all.

"There's a drugstore around the corner," he said.

She nodded, not meaning that she'd agreed to the plan, only that she had heard him. She wasn't sure what to do. In truth, she did feel like celebrating, and he was the only person she could celebrate with, and certainly, he deserved a thank you. In any case, he didn't have designs on her — he'd made that clear the other week. She would mention that she was married, work it into the conversation. There was nothing wrong with a public drink in the middle of the day. And anyway, it didn't matter, as no one she knew would see her.

■ ■ ■ ■

The drugstore had both an American flag and an Italian flag in the window, as well as signs advertising trusses, Mentholatum, and cold drinks. The air inside smelled of garlic and witch hazel, and Cora and the German were the only customers. The light was dim, at least compared to the sun-bright sidewalk, but there were familiar goods on the shelves behind the counters: talcum powder and Hypo-Cod, Ayer's Hair Vigor, cigars, Mag-Lac toothpaste, and tatting yarn. It could have been a drugstore in Wichita, except for a sign, hung from the cash register, that read *Benvenuti!* in bold red letters, which Cora guessed to be some kind of warning.

An apple-shaped woman with dark hair nodded at the German from behind the counter. "Oh, hello to you. What today?" She was taking rubber hot-water bottles out of a cardboard box and hanging them from wall pegs. She wore a black dress with a high neck, and sleeves down to her wrists.

Cora turned to the German. "Whatever you like is fine," she said. She was still effervescent, floating. Mrs. Mary O'Dell. She would put a letter in the post by tomorrow.

"I will have an Orange Quench. Thank you." He removed his spectacles, rubbing each lens on the folded sleeve of his white shirt.

"I'll take the same," Cora told the woman. She wasn't sure how slowly she should speak, if the woman truly knew English. She held up two fingers. "Two, please. Two."

The woman put the chilled bottles on the counter. Cora put a quarter on the counter, and when she looked up, she saw the German was watching her. He looked away.

The woman slid her change across the counter with small, wrinkled hands stained purplish red. *"Scusi,"* she said kindly, wiggling her fingers. *"È solo l'uva."*

Cora smiled as if she understood, thanked her, and followed the German, who carried both bottles, to one of the three empty tables at the back of the store. Flies buzzed all around, but he pushed a lever on a pivoting fan and angled the steady whirl at one of the tables. He pulled out a wire-backed chair for her before he sat in his own.

"Thank you," she murmured.

"And thank you." He lifted his bottle as if making a toast.

"Do you know what she said?" Cora whispered.

"What?" He leaned in to hear over the fan.

Cora gave a quick glance to the woman at the counter. "What did she say about her hands? The stain?" Cora worried it was some kind of rash. Her drink was still on the table. She wouldn't touch it until she knew.

"I do not know Italian." He took a sip of his orange drink. "But I think she has been making wine."

Cora looked at him. He had a gold streak in one of his eyes, from the white to the pupil, like a slant of sunlight. "You're serious?"

He nodded.

She glanced up at the woman, who was still hanging up hot-water bottles. She was at least in her sixties. A gold cross hung from her neck.

"That's terrible," Cora said. "She could be arrested."

"That is terrible. Yes."

"I mean it's terrible that she's doing it," Cora clarified. "Are you saying she's selling it? Like a bootlegger?"

He smiled. "It is probably for her family. Italians drink the wine like milk."

She looked back at the woman. "And what if a Prohibition agent were to come in here and see her hands?"

He sipped his drink. "She would be caught

red-handed, ya?"

She worked not to smile. "That's not funny. I'm truly concerned."

"Then write to your senator." He lifted his soda. "Tell him to repeal the Volstead."

She rolled her eyes. "Oh. You're in that camp."

"And you are not?"

"Correct." She sat up straight, taking off her gloves. She was thirsty, and her glass bottle looked perfectly cold, sitting and sweating on the table. A trace of grapes wouldn't hurt her.

He watched her with narrowed eyes. "You would put her in jail? That woman?"

The orange drink was sweet and bubbly. She held a sip in her mouth before she swallowed. "If she's really selling poison that ruins families and lives, yes. Yes I would."

"Hmm."

He seemed as if he didn't quite believe her. Well. She knew her mind. And she'd educated simpler men than him. She took another sip and set her bottle down.

"Tell me that this isn't a better country since we got rid of the booze." She raised her voice a little. It would be good for the Italian woman to hear her. "You know right here in New York they've had to close down entire floors of hospitals, floors that were once reserved for people who had poisoned their blood? I believe that's considered progress."

"But now more people are being shot in the street."

She shrugged. "Criminals, maybe."

"No. Not always. And it seems to me more people are dying drinking bathtub gin." He tilted his bottle to his chest, to the oiled bib of his overalls. "I used to serve the best beer in the state. It looked like gold in a glass. It was healthy and pure and good. No one ever got sick from that."

She scowled. "You worked in a saloon?"

He set his bottle on the table. "I owned a beer garden. In Queens. It was a good place, with no one getting shot, no gangsters." He crossed his arms. "People would bring their children, their babies. How is this bad? No one was drunk. My wife would bring the baby and get her dinner there."

"Oh," Cora said. She hadn't guessed there was a wife, and a baby, and now she felt even more embarrassed about the way she'd behaved the week before and her silly fretting over buying him a drink. She tried to imagine a whole family living in the small space above the orphanage's shed. No wonder he was bitter, then, if he'd owned his own business before. But every change, even a good one, had its casualties. And whatever he wanted to think, a beer garden didn't sound like any place for a child.

He waved his hand. "It does not matter. This is not what I want to tell you." He was sitting so close to the fan that the breeze pushed a bead of sweat sideways across his broad forehead. "I want to talk about your records. I know it is not my business. But I let you in, and now I feel responsible."

"Responsible?" She brought her bottle to her lips.

"Ya."

"For me?"

"Ya."

She almost laughed. "Well, that's very sweet." She started to lean back in her chair, mirroring his posture, but her corset wouldn't let her. "I can assure you I'll be fine. I'm a grown woman."

"I can see."

She glanced up. His face was neutral. She couldn't tell if he was being suggestive. He'd just told her about his wife and child. But she'd heard about European men.

He leaned forward, his elbows on the table. "I just do not want . . . The nuns have reasons for keeping the records private. I have been working there for a few years now, and I have seen the people who bring their children, and the people who come to visit."

"Please." She raised her palm. "The sister already gave me this lecture. I know my mother could have been a drunk or . . . a woman of . . . ill repute. I know all this, thank you." Her purse, with its wonderful new contents, was nestled against her side. "But I don't care. I have an address. I came looking for answers, and now I might find them. That's all that matters to me."

"That is good." His brows lowered behind the silver frames. He seemed not to require more from her, but now she wanted to talk, to say these words to another person, this stranger, her sudden confidant.

"So I don't care if she's a drunk or . . . or . . . anything. But you know, she could very well be a decent person. I remember the parents who came to visit. Some of them were just poor. Some were just sick. It's not as if they're all bad people."

"I hope not." He nodded, looking at the table. "My own daughter stays there now."

Cora tilted her head. "Your daughter? She's . . ." She couldn't think of how to ask. If she was his daughter, she wasn't an orphan.

"My wife died. The influenza."

"I'm so sorry," Cora said. She'd heard the

flu had been especially bad in New York. In Kansas, in just 1918, more than ten thousand had been killed, including Alan's sister and her husband in Lawrence. Everyone at the funeral, except for the minister, had worn a paper mask, and Alan, even in his grief, had yelled at Howard for yanking his off after the service. When they returned home, they'd been too scared to even get on a streetcar, and Cora, terrified, had kept the boys home from school for months.

"I'm glad you survived," she said. "For the sake of your daughter." She didn't know what to say. "Did you . . . did you fall ill at all?"

"I wasn't with her." He rubbed the blond stubble of his chin. "I was gone for most of the war and a little after. Down in Georgia. Fort Oglethorpe. I was interned."

"Interned?" She frowned. "You mean imprisoned?"

"Ya, it was the same. Only with prison, you get a trial."

She leaned a little away from him. "What did you do?"

"It was what I did not do." He held her gaze. "I didn't get down on my knees at the request of a mob. I wouldn't kiss the flag, not for them. So I was a spy. They had about four thousand of us spies down there.

Only we did not know we were spies until they tell us."

She was silent. He could be lying. Perhaps he'd really been a spy. Or maybe he'd been secretly sending money to Germany, the way she'd heard some immigrants were doing. Perhaps he'd deserved to be sent to Georgia. But then, maybe not. In Wichita, at the start of the war, a foreigner who sold popcorn from a cart on Douglas Avenue was nearly killed by a mob. Alan had been there, just walking down the street, and he said it was the most frightening moment of his life, seeing so many people screaming at this man who was on his knees pleading, trying to explain that he'd misplaced his war bond, and that he hadn't hung the flag from his cart because it was torn and he hadn't been able to mend it. The police finally arrived and got the man to safety. Later, she and Alan heard the man wasn't even German, but a Polish Jew.

"Your wife died while you were there?"

"Ya. And I did not know. They only sometimes gave us our mail. I never got the letter." He shrugged. "There was nothing I could have done. It was all barb-wired." He pointed up at the low ceiling of the drugstore, his finger moving in a slow half circle. "There were men in towers with machine guns. When they let me out, I make my way back, and that is when I found out about Andrea. The neighbors said a charity took the baby. I spend three months to track her down, and find out she was placed down here." He lifted the bottle, then set it down. "But then I could not take her out. My business was gone. I had no money. I could not work and care for her. I told the sisters I know how to fix things, and they take mercy on me and hire me. So now, at least, I get to see her every day. And I know she is safe." He rubbed his chin. "She is almost six."

Cora lowered her gaze. "You must be angry," she said quietly. "About being sent away."

He sighed, puffing out his cheeks. "No. Like you tell me, I am lucky to be living. I can go crazy, thinking about what would be if I had not been sent to Georgia." He shrugged. "Maybe it was good luck. The flu was in Oglethorpe, too. There were bodies going out every night. But I think it was worse in Queens, on our street, in our building. If I was not interned, I would have been with her, but maybe I get sick and die, too. And then what for our daughter? She would be a full orphan, not a half one." He met Cora's gaze. "She might have already gone out on a train."

Cora was silent. It was so hard to believe that the trains were still going out, that other children were still, maybe at this very moment, headed west into anything, into so much good luck or bad. "It's true," she finally said. "It's hard to know what could have been."

"You should think about that." He leaned forward on his elbows, and the table creaked. "So what will you do now? You will write to this person?"

"Yes," Cora said. "It's someone who knows, or knew, my . . . mother. She wrote from Haverhill, Massachusetts. She might still be at that address." She felt insensitive now, talking about her own good fortune. But he was looking at her intently. Quite intently.

"Have you ever heard of the Florence Night Mission?"

He shook his head.

"On Bleecker Street?"

"That is in the Village. Not far."

"The records said that was where I came from. I might go down there, just to see." Might nothing, Cora thought. She would go to Bleecker Street tomorrow, as soon as she got Louise to class.

"You might as well. You have come all the

way from Kansas."

She smiled. He had a good memory. Her gaze rested on his hands. They needed cream, she thought. The pads of his thumbs were callused.

"I think the sisters were wrong not to let you see the records," he said. "That is why I show you. But you should know they aren't just mean and crazy, the nuns. They have reasons." He held up his hands. "Have open eyes. That is what I mean."

She nodded, looking at him shyly. It was nice to be shown such caring. She'd been feeling a little beaten down, perhaps, spending so much time with just Louise. And she'd thought everyone in New York would be so cold and hard. But here she'd already made a friend. A German handyman ex-prisoner, whom she'd never see again, but a friend nonetheless.

"Thank you," she said, meaning it. "Thank you for taking the time."

He nodded, his gaze moving over her face in a way she would long remember.

"It was a pleasure."

She stood quickly, saying she had to hurry and catch the subway; her young charge would be getting out of class soon. She really had to run. On her way out of the store, she walked fast and kept her head low, concerned that she was blushing. But the woman behind the counter only called for her to please come again, with a little wave of her grape-stained hand.

THIRTEEN

"I hate movies." Louise sat under the painting of the Siamese cat, fanning herself with a section of the newspaper. "Really. I don't care what's playing. I absolutely won't go."

Cora looked up from the listings, irritated. Heat and humidity this early in the morning did nothing for her patience. "How can you hate the movies, Louise? You love theater. You have to read with the movies, but that's the only difference."

"Blasphemer." She closed her eyes, still fanning. "Please don't say that in my presence again."

Cora frowned. After only a week of diction lessons from Floyd Smithers, free with the purchase of a daily milk shake, Louise's way of speaking had already changed. The difference was subtle — she didn't, in fact, sound as if she were faking a British accent. But she no longer sounded like herself, either, or like anyone from back home. Her vowels were more rounded, her consonants more distinct. She'd accomplished her goal in a matter of days: she had no accent at all.

"They're hardly the same," she continued, her eyes open now, fixing Cora with a pitying stare. "Movies are manufactured and packaged for the masses, served cold. Wichita sees what Los Angeles sees, and Manhattan sees what Toledo sees. It's all the same because it's all dead." She put down the newspaper and fluttered a hand over the table between them. "Live theater is like dance. It's alive and ephemeral. You have just one night between the dancer and the audience, everyone breathing the same air." She sighed, as if realizing the futility of trying to explain any of this to Cora. "Besides," she said, "you can see all the movies you like back in Wichita, but you won't be able to go to Broadway once you get back."

Cora had for some time noticed that Louise always said "once *you* get back to Wichita," not "once *we* get back to Wichita," and Cora suspected that Louise was not simply hoping to be offered one of the permanent spots at Denishawn, but planning on it. Cora worried how Louise would react if it didn't happen, how she (and therefore they) would survive the long trip home. It wasn't that Louise never suffered

305

insecurity. She was always criticizing herself on the way home from class, saying that her jumps had been too sloppy or that her legs were still too fat for a dancer's. At the same time, she seemed so bent on success that Cora doubted she had any kind of contingency plan, or even any capacity to accept a different kind of life if things just didn't work out. Part of her thought she should caution Louise, to warn her that life didn't always go according to one's wishes, if only to prepare her for the possibility of disappointment. But most of her understood that this conversation would not go well, and she managed to hold her tongue.

Nevertheless, Cora cautioned herself against hope, even as she waited for a letter from Haverhill, watching for the postman from her window like a hawk watching from a tree. A letter was her only hope. She'd already gone down to Greenwich Village and wandered its curving streets until she found 29 Bleecker Street, which was just a three-story building that appeared broken up into several apartments. Cora asked the greengrocer on the corner if he knew where she might find the Florence Night Mission, and although the grocer had never heard of it, he translated her question to Italian for an elderly man sitting by a barrel of apples, who apparently told the grocer to tell Cora that the Florence Night Mission had been across the street some thirty years ago, but wasn't anymore.

And the old man, wrinkled and toothless as he was, looked her up and down.

So the Florence Night Mission was gone, a dead end. She tried not to be too anxious about the letter. Even if Mary O'Dell were still alive and living at the same address in Haverhill, even if she still wanted contact, it might be several days before Cora received her response. But probably not much longer than that. Cora had been clear in her letter that she would only be in New York for a few more weeks. She would either hear from Haverhill soon, or not at all. She knew that of the two possibilities, the latter was more likely. If that was the case, she would bear it. She was not like Louise, unfamiliar with disappointments, needing everything to go her way. If she got no reply, if Mary O'Dell was dead or otherwise unreachable, Cora would find a way to be grateful that she'd at least discovered that her mother, whoever she was, had wanted to know her. That might have to be enough.

She tried to distract herself, playing the tourist the rest of the week. While Louise was at class, she visited Grant's Tomb. She spent a whole day at the Museum of Natural History and several art museums. She went for a ride in an open-air bus, and she took a guided walking tour of Central Park, where she saw a veritable flock of grazing sheep, oblivious to the cityscape behind them.

And through it all, she was so lonely. The intensity caught her off guard. She'd spent plenty of time alone back home — days when Alan was at work and the boys were at school. She'd always liked having time to herself, to read, to think, to pretty up the house. But she'd had her friends and her volunteer work, or a pleasant exchange with Della or a neighbor to break up the time. This was a different kind of solitude, unrelenting and thorough. She moved through the crowded sidewalks as a stranger to everyone, without even a chance of bumping into anyone who might recognize her and call out. This was how it felt to be a foreigner, she thought, with no one knowing who you were or where you came from. It was as if she had become a person not just unknown but unknowable, and it bothered her to think that her grasp on herself was so weak that she needed steady reminding from people at home who knew her to feel like herself at all.

The German was foreign, of course, and he had seemed at ease.

On Friday, she paid a dime to take an express elevator, so fast it felt like a thrill ride, to the top of the Woolworth Building, so she could look out at the city from its highest point some sixty floors up. It was something, really, to be up that high, higher than she'd ever imagined she would be, surrounded by windows and looking down at the tiered and tapered tops of regal buildings that were all at least twice as tall as the tallest building in Wichita. She could see the great bridges, and the Statue of Liberty, so far away they looked small, and the embracing arms of the blue, surrounding water, and in the distance, it seemed, the very curve of the earth. But even then, even in her wonder, she couldn't help but think that from up in the high and quiet, behind the glass of the observation booth, the city finally looked and sounded as apart from her as it felt. And after spending so much time alone with herself, she wondered if she were in Wichita, somehow looking down from such a great height over the quieter streets and surrounding prairie she knew so well, full of people she would recognize and love, she might still find the distance fitting.

■ ■ ■ ■

She purchased postcards with sepia-toned pictures of famous landmarks. She wrote Alan and the boys and Viola that the city was even bigger than she had imagined, and that there was so much to see in such a short time. That was true. Then again, the idea of spending even one more week in so much solitude, going hours without speaking to anyone except to say "thank you" and "excuse me" and "one ticket, please," filled her with a heavy dread.

There was still no reply from Massachusetts, though enough days had passed that a reply was possible. Every afternoon when they returned from dance class, Cora checked the little locked mailbox on the first floor of their building. Louise got a letter from Theo, but nothing, Cora noticed, from either of her parents. Cora herself got a nice letter from Alan, saying that she was missed, but that Wichita in July was Wichita in July, and that she wasn't missing much. He wrote that he'd driven over to Winfield to visit the boys, and he could report that they were still in good health, though they both seemed a little disenchanted with farm life, and they were both looking forward to starting their more sedentary studies in the fall. They sent their love to her through him, he wrote, and hoped she would understand that they didn't write only because they worked right up until sunset, and fell asleep the moment they could. *They both seemed to know your young charge,* he added. *They said Louise B. was a real "looker," and that everyone knew who she was. But they doubted she would know of them, since she seemed bored with every boy in school. Can you imagine that? A cheeky freshman ignoring even our wonderful boys? I'm sure you have your work cut out for you, as they say. I can only send you my best wishes.*

And money, of course. He'd wired a good amount to a Western Union, and told her she should go claim it at once. He hoped she would buy herself something pretty, he wrote, something she could show off when she came home.

She supposed she should have been excited. She'd gone walking past the big department stores on Broadway, and she'd seen so many beautiful things in the window displays: afternoon dresses of crepe de chine, and hats trimmed in taffeta bows or smart feathers. There were many times at home when just the feel of new silk or a pretty shoe had brought her real comfort, and there was the satisfaction in usually being able, with the assistance of a good corset, to fasten a button on a narrow waist. But now the idea of shopping for clothes, even expensive New York clothes, only depressed her. She was irritated by the way he had written his suggestion. She wasn't sure if it was the *show off* or the *home* that made her feel tired, even of taffeta and silk. She never knew when a gift was just a gift, truly given in caring, or just part of the charade.

In any case, she had a better idea.

"You're back," the German said. He looked happy to see her, and surprised. But he blocked the doorway as he glanced at his watch. "Mass is almost over," he whispered. "The sisters will come down very soon."

She nodded. She'd timed it exactly right. "I know," she said. "I have a different mission today."

He waited, looking at her pleasantly. For a moment, she forgot what she'd planned to say.

"The radio," she said. "I wondered if you were able to fix the radio." She kept her face businesslike.

"No. It was . . . kaput. Why?"

"Well, I was thinking you were right, that

it would be nice for the girls to have one. And I just happened upon a little extra money. I was thinking I would buy one for them."

He tilted his head. "They are expensive."

She nodded. "I passed a place that sold them a few blocks away. They had one with a single-tube receiver that seemed good." She pointed vaguely behind her. "But they didn't seem keen on delivery."

He raised his brows and laughed. "I am not surprised."

She was relieved. In truth, she hadn't asked about delivery. "Well, if you do think the girls would still like a radio, I'd be happy to go buy one now. But it'll be heavy, of course. I was hoping you could come with me and help me carry it back."

His gaze was as steady on her face as it had been the other day. She focused on the truth, which was that she really did want to get a radio for the girls. That was part of it.

"I am Joseph Schmidt," he said, holding out his hand.

"Oh." She smiled, and in her nervousness, shook hands as if she were a man, her hand vertical, her grip tight. "I'm Cora." There was no need to give him a last name.

Even after she loosened her grip, he held on longer than he might have, his callused thumb rough against her palm. "Cora," he said, with careful pronunciation, as if learning a new word for something familiar. "I will get my cap."

He brought an old baby buggy to carry the radio. A Chelsea Model-T, he called it, because almost everyone in the neighborhood used one to get things from here to there. His buggy had a torn green sunshade and a wobbly tire, but the radio fit inside it just fine. They got a bit of a laugh, with him pushing it down the street, both of them smiling at passersby like proud new parents. "He's got your eyes," she said, feeling bold, and when this made him laugh, she went light in the head, but in a good way, as if she were breathing differently, and taking in more oxygen than usual. He steered the buggy over sidewalk cracks and past chattering Italians, or maybe Greeks, and around gangs of children, going slowly enough that she could keep up in her heels, and the whole time she was giddy with the idea that during this little holiday, she was not Cora Kaufmann or Cora Carlisle or even Cora X. She was only Cora in the neighborhood where she used to live and where, now, no one knew her. She could act as she liked without any consequence or anyone from home even finding out, providing she did no real harm or get herself arrested.

"What's the sweet smell?" she asked, holding her hat down against the breeze. She liked walking with a man her height, not always having to look up. "It always smells like baking treats around here."

"That is National Biscuit." He looked at her, then away, then back. "Nabisco? You eat the Fig Newtons? They are made here."

She had to laugh. How many packages of Fig Newtons had she bought over the years? She bought them for the boys and Alan, and to serve at tea parties, and she'd eaten quite a few herself, with no idea they'd been baked within sniffing distance of the New York Home for Friendless Girls. Her street in Kansas, with its wide lawns and shade trees, seemed a separate world from this crowded Babel of a neighborhood, with no possibility for overlap, and yet for years, without her knowledge, mere cookies had passed between them.

"What's that ya got in there?" A damp and shoeless boy pushed past Cora to look into the buggy. "That's a radio. Does it work?" Cora turned to see more boys, all wet-haired and dirty-looking, some with shoes, some without, crowding them from behind, trying to see into the buggy. It was confusing to be afraid of them. The oldest was twelve at the most, but there were six of them, and then seven, and they were fanning out, coming around to the buggy from the sides, hands quick and reaching in. All around on the sidewalk, other adults kept walking by as if nothing were out of the ordinary.

"Get away!" Joseph crouched and put his arm across the buggy. "I know what you do!" The boys backed away, but only a few steps, as if only waiting for another chance to pounce. Cora didn't know what to do. The boys were so dirty, and they smelled foul, but they had sweet, little-boy faces and the scrawniest legs, and one reminded Cora of Howard as a boy, with apple cheeks and eyes that seemed to give off their own light. She was thinking how sad it was that a boy who looked like Howard could be so bone thin and dirty when she felt a hard tug on her purse. She turned fast to find an even younger boy, no older than five, smiling up at her even as he was still tugging. She held tight, and told him to get away.

"Okay, okay, there you go." Joseph brought a fist out of his pocket. "Pennies, okay? And one nickel for who gets it." He turned away from the buggy and rolled a handful of change down the sidewalk. The boys whooped and ran after the coins.

"Walk fast." He took Cora by the arm, his other hand on the buggy's push bar. They hurried around a corner, one wheel of the buggy squeaking. When they were halfway down the street, he let go of her arm, but she could still feel where his hand had been, the pressure of his fingers through her sleeve.

"They got a few coins out of you," she said. "How often do you have to do that?"

He shrugged. "Maybe they will get something to eat. They will probably buy candy, though."

Cora looked down at her purse. She didn't have much in it, now that they'd bought the radio. But she wished she would have thought to reach in and throw down some coins herself. "Why were they all in wet clothes?"

He eyed her strangely, as if she'd asked a trick question. "They swim," he said. "The river is just down there. They jump off the docks and go up and down, from one street to the next."

"Well, that's nice, that they can cool off, at least."

He made a face. "The water is filthy. They have to breaststroke to push away the garbage." He pantomimed this for Cora, one hand pushing away, the other covering his mouth and nose. "They all go in, though, to cool off. Except for our girls. The nuns do not let them swim in the river. They walk them to the public baths once a week, and that is it."

Cora was quiet. A bath once a week, in this heat. And they were the lucky ones. She'd known she was lucky, even as a child. The nuns provided steady shelter and enough to eat — nothing tasty, but enough for health — and that was no small thing.

"What's your daughter's name?"

"She is Greta."

"Does she go to school? It's the law now, isn't it?"

"The nuns give lessons in the home. They don't want the girls at a public school. They have to work around the laundry schedule, too." He paused to ease the buggy over a curb. "I have been saving, though, for an apartment. Maybe next year, and I can go to work while she goes to the public school. Right now, she just hangs clothes on the roof. But they will have her in the laundry soon if we do not go. I know the sisters have to do the laundry, to keep the home with money. But I don't want Greta working so hard, not when she is so young."

Cora remembered seeing the older girls' hands, the burns from the boiling water. Her own hands, under her gloves, were unscarred and soft. "What will you do for a job?"

"Anything. I already work extra around the neighborhood, fixing things. People know me." He took a hand off the push bar and pointed at his mouth. "But my accent makes it hard." He smiled with resignation. "I am the Hun."

"Why don't you go back?" She kept her voice soft, so quiet that even she could barely hear herself over the squeaking tire and the cars in the street. She was really just asking, wanting to know, not making a rude suggestion.

"To Germany? No. Things are bad with inflation, and the reparations. We would have more trouble there." He shook his head. "And it is more than that. I have been in America from when I was nineteen. And before that, all I wanted was to come here." He looked out at the street, the rumbling cars. "I like this country, the idea of it. I was thinking to enlist when they sent me to Oglethorpe."

Cora almost pointed out that if he'd just made these statements at the beginning of the war, to whomever demanded an answer, and gone ahead and knelt to kiss the flag, he might not have been sent to Oglethorpe in the first place. But of course there was a difference between loving a country, truly loving what it stood for, and letting someone tell you to get on your knees and prove it.

"Ah, look at this," he said, slowing the buggy. "It is our old place."

Cora looked up. They were in front of the drugstore where they'd had the orange drinks. Cora could see the older Italian woman behind the counter inside.

"Since you bought the girls the expensive present, I will at least buy you an orange drink." He watched her eyes. "Do you have time?"

She hesitated. It was just another soda. But he was poor, saving everything he could, and she hated to think of him spending even a nickel on her. Still, it was likely a point of pride for him. And he was looking at her with such affection, as if they were already great friends. She didn't want to leave him just yet.

She was quiet as they waited by the counter, even though the Italian woman, her hands no longer stained, recognized her and smiled, and pointed at the buggy and made a joke about their radio *bambino*. Joseph explained to her that it was Cora who had purchased the radio for the girls in the orphanage, and the woman nodded, though it was unclear if she really understood him. Cora watched him talk. He'd taken off his cap when they came in, and she considered that his face had strong bones — he didn't really need a full head of hair. He paid the Italian woman and gave Cora a smile, sincere and open. She followed him, wondering about his dead wife, how young she'd been, how pretty.

"Tell me about your life in Kansas," he said. He sat in the adjacent chair, one elbow on the table, the other on the back of his chair. "You know all things about me, and I know not much about you."

She looked down, pretending to be overwhelmed by the task of unbuttoning her gloves. She didn't want to answer. She would have been glad to just keep hearing about him, or the orphanage, or the neighborhood, all the while feeling a little intoxicated by his focused attention, the gold streak in his eye, the pleasing lowness of his voice. But the vacation was over. He'd asked. And she didn't have it in her to actively lie, to kill off her family, even in word.

"I'm married," she said. "We have two

sons, twins. They'll leave for college in the fall."

His brows went low behind the silver frames. He didn't seem angry, but she could guess what he was thinking, what opinions he was forming of her now. He was in no position to accuse her of withholding information. She'd only been friendly, she could say, and this was the first time he'd asked about her life. But she'd known very well how he was looking at her. And now he thought her dishonest and careless, a married woman with no ring. It was so unfair. He wouldn't know what this afternoon had meant to her, these few hours of not being herself, stepping out of her life. Perhaps she could just be honest. She'd never told anyone about Alan. She couldn't risk it, with even the closest friend. But Joseph Schmidt had a thoughtful face, and she would never see him again. He didn't know her last name, or even what city she was from. He could do Alan no harm. And what a relief it would be to say the words aloud, to have someone else in the world truly know her.

And so right there, while sitting at the little table with the whirling fan muffling her voice, she explained her life to him, the truth of it, as plainly as she could. The Italian woman was over by the counter, reading a magazine, and Joseph was still and quiet as Cora talked. She told him about Howard and Earle and how much she loved them, and how even they didn't know. She told him that even she and Alan talked and acted as if nothing were amiss between them, as if she really didn't know that he was still meeting with Raymond at his office after hours, as if she didn't know they bought each other presents — a watch engraved with *R. W.* and a Latin phrase she didn't understand, books of poetry with lines underlined. *I am he that aches with love.*

Joseph said nothing. She didn't know what he was thinking, but she kept talking. She didn't stop to take a sip of her drink. It was as if she needed to talk to breathe. She told him how young she'd been when she married, and how alone, and she was careful to explain that it really wasn't as terrible as it sounded, that Alan was not a bad person, that he was good to her in many ways, and certainly an excellent father.

"But not a husband to you."

She shook her head. He twisted his lips to one side. For a moment, she thought he might spit.

"I had a cousin like that, back in Germany," he said. "He was a good man. He

323

was a good person."

Cora frowned, waited.

"Beaten. We did not know who, but we knew why." He rubbed his cheek. "Your husband is maybe right to be secret."

She put her face in her hands. Alan. She couldn't bear it if he were harmed. She was as stuck as she'd ever been. It hadn't changed anything, her telling Joseph Schmidt.

"What you do now?" he asked.

She looked up. "What do you mean?"

"Your boys are grown. That was why you stayed, you said. They're grown now. This is right?"

"Oh. I don't want a divorce."

He raised his eyebrows.

"I don't." She tried to explain. "I don't want to be divorced." She shook her head. She didn't want to be divorced. Of course she didn't.

"Why not?"

She almost laughed. "How would I explain it? What would I tell people? What would I tell my sons?"

"That you want to be happy."

"That's not enough."

"No?" He leaned closer, just a little. She drew back, looking away. The Italian woman had gone out in front of the store to sweep.

"What a waste," he said.

She looked up. They stared at each other unblinking, with just the sound of the fan and the distant scuffing of the Italian woman's broom. She couldn't move, or she didn't. Alan had once looked at her with so much hope and kindness, but not like this, never like this. Unchecked joy rose up in her, only for an instant, but somehow he saw it, or just knew, for without another word, he reached up under the brim of her hat and pushed a loose curl behind her ear. She didn't move, not even as his rough fingertips trailed behind her ear along her damp hairline.

She could hear her own breathing, her pulse just under his fingers. His watch ticked by her neck.

"What time is it?" she asked.

He lowered his hand and looked at his watch. "Twenty to three."

"I have to go." Her chair screeched against the floor as she pushed it out. She picked up her purse and her gloves. She would put the gloves on outside.

He caught her hand. "Don't go," he said. "Not yet."

"I really have to," she said, more firmly. "I have to go now. I forgot. I just forgot. I'll already be late." It was true. She couldn't be late, and give Louise that kind of leverage.

"Cora."

She shook her head. She needed to get away. But she was still flushed and smiling, even as she pulled her hand away. She felt lightheaded. To be looked at like that, to be held on to like that, it was intoxicating — she was not herself. "I'll come back," she said, a promise as much to herself as to him.

But by the time she was back out in the street, walking fast to the subway in the bright sunlight, she had a clearer head.

She was hurrying up Broadway when she saw Louise walking toward her. Even on the crowded sidewalk, as small as Louise was, she was easy to spot, her face glistening, the black hair tucked behind her ears. A man whistled at her, but she moved past him as if she heard nothing, staring straight ahead. She walked past Cora, too. When Cora said her name, she turned, looking both annoyed and surprised.

"Oh. Hi." She didn't smile. "You were late, so I started walking."

"I'm sorry." Cora swallowed and tried to steady her breath. "But you really should just wait for me. What if I hadn't seen you?" Cora had actually run the last block, worried Louise would use her tardiness as an excuse to go off on some solo adventure. But of course the hours of dance class had left her both sweaty and exhausted. Louise wouldn't want to go anywhere until she had a bath and a nap.

"What's wrong?" She frowned at Cora. "You look strange. Your cheeks are red."

"Oh." Cora touched her wrist against her warm forehead. "Well, I knew I was late. I've been hurrying in the heat. Are we headed home then?" It was a little heady, being the one to evade and distract.

Louise resumed walking, though she glanced at Cora. "I hope you're not coming down with something."

For a moment, Cora was touched by her concern. But Louise went on to say that they would need to be careful to use different glassware, just to be certain. She couldn't afford to get sick while she was here, not before they made the selection for the troupe. Cora reassured her that she was not ill, and that she was just tired, but after that, as they walked along, she was silent. Louise talked about Ted Shawn doing his Japanese Spear Dance, and how beautiful it was, how perfectly it showed off his skill and excellent form. Cora nodded, half listening, dazed by the heat. No, she thought. She wouldn't go back to see Joseph Schmidt, not tomorrow, and not ever again. She thought of the hero of *The Age of Innocence,* who'd had a brief moment of forgetting himself, unbuttoning the Countess's glove, but understood he could have no more. It was the way things had to be.

And just deciding this, it seemed, she got her reward. When she and Louise got back to their building, waiting in the mailbox was a pale yellow envelope for Cora, postmarked Haverhill, Mass.

FOURTEEN

On her way to Grand Central Terminal, Cora stopped to buy a bouquet of yellow roses, which she hadn't planned to do until the very moment she saw them, bright and lovely, at a corner stand. Still, she arrived at the terminal twenty minutes early, and she had an easy time finding the big clock above the information booth. So there was nothing to do but just stand there, shifting the roses from arm to arm and gazing up at the ceiling. The first time she passed through Grand Central, when she and Louise had just arrived in the city, she'd been so overwhelmed and rushed she hadn't even noticed, for example, that the blue of the ceiling was the background for a map of the heavens, the constellations outlined in gold. But today she had time to marvel, taking in the ceiling as well as the glittering chandeliers and the terraces overlooking the main concourse, and the polished marble floor that went on and on, and how cool the building felt on such a warm day, even with so many bodies rushing about inside.

But mostly, she looked at the clock. Very soon now. Very soon.

As it got closer to noon, she paid more attention to the travelers approaching the booth from all directions. Mary O'Dell had written that she would be wearing a gray matron's hat with white beading on the front. There had been no time for Cora to write back with any more questions, or to say what she would be wearing. So she scanned the crowds for a gray hat, turning every time she heard fast-approaching heels, only to watch each woman move past her or run to embrace someone else.

But there was no reason to worry. Not yet. It was still a few minutes before noon. That morning, she woke before dawn, jittery before even a sip of tea, and she'd had to work not to show impatience with Louise's slow morning routine, the way she lounged in bed until the last possible moment. Cora had literally counted the minutes until she could deliver the girl to Denishawn. Now she was free and here, at the appointed time, exactly where she was supposed to be. She'd done her best to look nice. She was wearing her good silk dress, her pearls, and a pretty hat with a lavender ribbon.

She smoothed down her dress, though it didn't need smoothing, and tried not to keep looking at the clock. There was, after all, plenty to distract. Clearly, Mary O'Dell was not the first person to suggest the clock as a meeting place. On every side of the information booth, it seemed, a happy reunion was taking place. An old man with a cane bent low to embrace a running child in pigtails. Two grown women held hands and jumped up and down like schoolgirls. A man in a white suit strode past Cora to a young woman in a sleeveless dress. When he reached the woman, they didn't speak. The man leaned down to kiss the woman, dropping his cloth bag on the floor so he could put both hands on the small of her back, pulling her against him. The woman's bare hands moved up to his shoulders. Her fingernails were painted red.

It was only when they both glanced at Cora that she realized she was staring.

She touched her hand to her neck and turned toward the booth, where a man in a turban was asking about a train to Chicago, his English halting and careful. He held the hand of a boy in short pants, who was gazing up at the ceiling with an open mouth, probably seeing it for the first time as well.

He tugged on his father's jacket and said something in another language, and when the father didn't look down, the boy, perhaps sensing Cora watching him, looked at her and moved closer to his father. He continued to stare up at her, and Cora tried to imagine what he saw in her face, how strange she might seem to him if he was new to America and not just Grand Central. She gave him what she hoped was an encouraging smile, then turned away so as not to scare him.

She loved the city today, loved the beehive feel of where she was standing, loved the signs listing arrival times of trains from Albany, Cleveland, and Detroit, as well as smaller towns she'd never heard of. She loved the little boy standing by his turbaned father, and she loved the man with a pungent cigar and a briefcase sprinting across the concourse as if there would never be another train, and she loved the two old men with sideburns and black hats looking just like some of the Jews back in Wichita and having a good laugh about something. She even loved the man and the young woman who had been kissing, who were now walking out to Lexington Avenue, the woman's body pressed close to the man's, his hand moving down from her waist to the curve of her hip for everyone to see.

Cora lowered her nose to the roses, breathing in. She wouldn't begrudge anyone a reunion today.

She would love her. She already knew it. She would love Mary O'Dell no matter what kind of person she turned out to be. Even if she was not her mother, even if she really turned out to be just a concerned friend, and the similar handwriting was a strange coincidence, Cora would still love her for being such a caring friend or such a good person in general that she would take a train all the way down from Massachusetts just to give a stranger some solace. She would love her for even having known her mother, who might be dead now, found too late. Whoever got off the train would tell her more than she'd ever known. She would be grateful for that.

She searched the floor for a woman with dark hair, curly like her own. That was when she noticed an older woman wearing a gray matron's hat walk up to the booth. Cora would always remember it, the shock of seeing her mouth, her exact mouth, on the face of another person. This woman was stouter, and older, but she had the same full lips, the same slight overbite, and her square jaw was still firm. She stood on the toes of sensible gray heels to survey the crowd. Cora moved toward her without feeling her feet.

"Mary?" The name came out high-pitched, strange. "Mary O'Dell?"

The woman looked at Cora, but didn't speak. Her hair was reddish-blond, and though the bulk of it was pinned up under the matron's hat, Cora could see its texture was nothing like her own, and nothing like the hair of the woman in her memory, the woman with the shawl. In fact, nothing about this woman before her was like anything she'd remembered or imagined. This woman was dressed beautifully, in a gray linen dress that was wrinkled at the hips, the front panel embroidered with flowers. A short strand of pearls, small and dainty, circled her well-creased neck.

"Cora?" They were the same height. Her eyes were gray and larger than Cora's.

Cora nodded. People were all around them, standing, waiting, walking, looking up at the clock. But really, it was as if they were alone in that enormous space, taking each other in.

"You're my mother," Cora said, with no accusation, but with no question in her voice. All she had to do was look at the other woman's mouth and chin, even her

334

nose. "You. You're not a friend. You're my mother."

She stepped back from Cora, looking nervous.

Cora shook her head. No. She wasn't angry. And then it was as if the child in her were bursting forth, too excited, too thrilled to be contained, and too impatient for misunderstanding. Cora opened her arms and moved forward, and then she was breathing in the woman's unfamiliar smell and the roses still clutched in her own hand. The body against hers felt stiff and still. But she was not pushed away. She was embraced back, held tight, just as in her wildest hopes. But this was real. Without letting go, she looked up at the blue ceiling with its glinting zodiac, her vision blurred, her nose running.

They stepped back from each other. Cora realized she'd lost her hat. She stooped to pick it up. They both laughed, and then stopped, staring at each other.

"Well." Mary O'Dell reached up to touch her glove to Cora's cheek. "There's no point in denying it, now is there? Not when you're the spitting image." She had an Irish brogue. It was pretty, Cora thought, gentle. The voice she should have known.

"These are for you." Cora held out the

335

roses, and still her words were high-pitched and strained, though she'd managed to blink her eyes dry. She pressed her hat back over her hair, feeling foolish. "I don't know where to begin," she said.

Mary O'Dell took the roses and nodded solemnly, as if agreeing that yes, this was the problem, not knowing where to begin.

She could only stay for an hour, she said. She was sorry, but she would have to catch the one-fifteen to Boston in order to get home in time. She didn't say in time for what, and Cora decided it best not to press for details. Not yet, at least. Cora also told herself not to be disappointed. This woman, her mother, had spent all morning on a train, and she would spend all afternoon getting home. One hour was fine for a beginning.

The Dining Concourse was one floor down, as busy and crowded as the great room upstairs, but with none of its light and beauty. They stood in line to order iced teas, which they carried to the only free table they could find. It still had a dusting of crumbs from its previous tenant, so they sat across a corner from each other and held their tea glasses upright in their laps, the roses in an empty chair on the other side of the table. They sat the same way, backs straight, feet tucked under chairs, legs crossed at ankles.

She nodded at Cora's ring. "You're married," she said with approval.

"Yes!" Cora felt shaky, too awake. She put her tea on the table. "Almost twenty years now. He's wonderful. A lawyer. We have two grown boys." She opened her purse and took out a photograph of Howard and Earle, taken in a studio the afternoon they graduated, both of them in cap and gown and looking so serious, even Howard. She slid the photograph across the table and watched her mother's mouth, so much like her own, break into a smile. How many times had she fantasized about this very moment, the first time she could show evidence of her beautiful sons to her own mother, who Cora now could see had the same slanting right eyebrow as Howard. The boys. She would tell them the truth as soon as she got home, now that there was good reason. Her mind surged ahead — there might be a visit? At Christmas, perhaps, when Howard and Earle would be home from school? Or Thanksgiving, rather. They'd already lost so much time.

At the next table, a man reading a newspaper reached into the pocket of his suit, brought out a silver flask, and flipped open the lid without once looking up from his paper.

"Oh my." Mary O'Dell looked up from the photograph. "Oh goodness. What fine young men. You don't know what a comfort this is, to see that you've done so well." Her voice seemed anxious, fragile. She used the back of her bare hand to whisk crumbs off part of the table before setting the photo down. "I can't tell you how I've worried and wondered about you. I didn't know if you'd even . . . survived, if your name was the same. I didn't know if you were suffering somewhere. I knew nothing."

"I was fine," Cora said, smiling. "I was well cared for. Good people adopted me." Not really the truth. Not legally. But it was the truth that the Kaufmanns had been good to her, and that was what she wished to convey.

"Thank you. Thank you for telling me that." She nodded as if still trying to re-assure herself, the matron's hat bobbing up and down. "I think that really, I always knew you were all right. I would get scared, but I was sure I would have known if you were suffering." She laughed a little, touching her pinkie to the corner of her eye. "I never dreamed you were off in Kansas, though, out on a farm with horses and cows. I always thought you were here, in New York."

"I always thought you were here. I never guessed Massachusetts."

She couldn't quit staring at the familiar mouth, the lips. She had the strange sensation that she wasn't simply looking at her mother, but also, aside from the different-colored hair, a prophetic vision of how she herself would look in less than twenty years.

Cora nodded at her hand. "You're married, too."

She nodded, held up her ring. The diamond was as big as Cora's.

"Not to my father?" Cora asked. She was being indelicate. But they didn't have much time.

Mary O'Dell glanced at the man with the flask, and then to the table on their other side, where two girls with leather-encased tennis racquets frowned at an unfolded map.

"No." She spoke so quietly that Cora had to strain to hear her over the surrounding chatter. "I met my husband when I was twenty-one. I had you when I was seventeen."

Cora nodded, her face pointedly neutral. She'd known that answer was likely. "And my father?"

"A boy at a dance." She adjusted the gray

hat. "That sounds bad, worse than it was. I mean that's where we met. He and I were together for a while. I was working in Boston, living in. They used to have these big dances on Thursdays. It was the day off for domestics, you know, our one night to ourselves. We knew each other for a month, maybe." She lowered her gaze, then looked at Cora shyly. "You probably think I'm low class, hearing that."

Cora shook her head. It wasn't so bad, the story. Not compared to what Sister Delores had prepared her for. Prostitution. Rape. But in her fantasies, her parents had loved each other, and for much longer than a month.

"Well, it was just ignorance." Mary O'Dell's voice had grown so quiet that Cora had to lean in a little to hear. "I'd been to school back in Ireland, and I wasn't dumb in books. But I didn't know anything about boys and babies. My mother told me nothing except go to church and keep my skirt down." Her mouth curled into a half smile, just the way Howard's often did. "I mean nothing. I got my first curse on the boat coming over. I was by myself, and I didn't tell anyone because I thought I was dying. You see? That's how little I knew. I didn't know it was normal. I was sure I was being punished for impure thoughts. I had no idea about anything."

"I understand," Cora said.

"As for your father, I don't know that he knew much more." She winced. "He was only fifteen."

"He was Irish? He was Irish, too?"

She looked offended. "Of course."

"Where is he now?"

"Don't know. I heard he went west. He left after I told him I was pregnant. I only know what his friends told me, and they didn't tell me much."

Fifteen, Cora thought. Just Louise's age. Three years younger than her own boys. He would be a different person now. She looked down at her hands, pale and folded in her lap. She'd always disliked how large her knuckles were. Mary O'Dell's knuckles were ladylike and small.

"What was his name?"

"Why?"

"Because I want to know my father's name. It might have been mine."

She scoffed, looking away. "That was never going to be your name. I can tell you that from the way he took the news."

"I still want to know."

"Fine. Jack Murphy." She gave Cora a dull look. "God as my witness, I'm not lying.

341

But if you want to search the great West for a Jack Murphy from Ireland by way of Boston, you should rest up. You'll have a lot of interviewing to do."

Cora blinked. So that was that. She would never know her father. Even if she could find him, this man with a common story and a commoner name, he likely didn't want to be found. He'd run away as soon as he'd known there would be a baby, wanting nothing to do with her. Sister Delores had been half right.

"You got his hair," her mother said, as if making a concession. "I don't mean you should hate him. I did then, but I don't now. He was just young and scared. I remember he came from a big family, poor. He didn't want more of the same, I imagine." She shrugged, her face matter-of-fact. But when she lifted her tea to her lips, Cora saw her hand was trembling.

"I'm sorry," Cora said. "That must have been terrible for you."

"Well, I was sorry for you. That's who I was sorry for." She looked at Cora, then away. "But I couldn't have cared for you on my own, unmarried. I didn't have a choice."

"I know," Cora said. She did. Her understanding was ready and waiting, easy to summon. She reached across the table to touch the back of Mary O'Dell's small hand, which was rougher than she would have guessed, even on the back. "I don't blame you. I don't blame you at all." Mary O'Dell's hand did not move, did not respond to the gesture. Uncertain, Cora put her own hand back in her lap.

"Well, I blamed myself. God knows." She again glanced at the surrounding tables. "I hated leaving you there."

"Leaving me where?"

"At the mission. The Florence Night Mission. The people who ran it were good, and I knew they'd find a place for you. But it was a terrible time for me, staying there. The other women were low class, actual street-walkers." She reached up, moving her hand over her pearls. "And some still practicing, mind you. They'd come in just to get out of the cold. I was the only one having a baby, and maybe the only one from a decent background who'd just made one mistake. But I didn't know where else to go. I couldn't have stayed in Boston. My cousins were there, my aunts, my uncle. I would have been a humiliation to all of them. They would have sent me back to Ireland, and I'd have been a Magdalene for sure. So I said I got a good domestic job in New York, and I came down and hid in the mission until I

343

had you. And then I went back to Boston without you, and I said I'd been robbed of my earnings at the point of a knife." Again, she half smiled. "Everyone felt sorry for me."

Cora waited. "And then what?"

"Then nothing. I went on with my life. I never told anyone about it. It was as if it didn't happen." She lifted her chin. "It didn't follow me, didn't hurt me in any way. I married a good man, and we've done well. Two of our sons are in politics." She straightened her shoulders. "Our daughter just married into a very good family."

"So I have . . ." Cora could hardly get the words out. "I have brothers? And a sister? In Haverhill?"

She hesitated. "Half. They're half."

"But still, I —"

"They don't know about you. I told you. No one does."

Cora lowered her gaze, understanding. Of course she understood. She could imagine the ridicule if one of the grand old dames of Wichita, one of the women from the club, suddenly owned up to a baby born out of wedlock. It wouldn't matter if that baby was now thirty-six years old, if the woman herself was now a grandmother. A transgression was a transgression. Cora would be the agent of the entire family's humiliation, and likely resented as such.

"You're not going to tell them about me."

"No." There was no shade in this response, no room for argument, the pronunciation brief and firm. "And since I don't know you, or what your plans are, I'll make myself very clear." The brogue had grown more distinct, and it no longer sounded soft. "I guarantee my children won't be any more interested in you bringing shame upon me than I am. We do stick together. If you make any trouble, you'll find that out yourself."

Cora looked away. The warning was both shrewd and unyielding, which made sense. Mary O'Dell, her mother, was a shrewd and unyielding woman; she certainly was when she was seventeen and pregnant, when Cora had first been a danger to her survival. Cora shouldn't expect any sentiment to undo her now. Cora did not know her, and likely would not be allowed to know her, but she had at least learned this about her mother: this was a woman who, when still a girl, had pulled herself from a fire, who knew what it took to survive. How many, at seventeen, would have been able to keep a secret like that? But she'd done it. She'd had her baby and she'd gone back to Massachusetts and acted as if all she'd lost was her pay, acted

345

as if a life had not moved through her, looking everyone in the eye. And now she thought Cora wanted to come to Massachusetts and be the ruin of her legitimate family, her marriage, her dignity, everything she'd suffered for and lied for and left her baby for, all those years ago. She didn't know that such a threatening display was unnecessary, that Cora already understood, all too well, everything she feared.

"I won't trouble you." Cora's voice was surprisingly calm. She picked up the photo of the boys and slipped it back in her purse.

Mary O'Dell looked at the spot where the picture had been. "I'm sorry," she whispered. "I wish things could be different."

"I understand. I won't go to Haverhill unless I'm invited." She tried to laugh, miserable. "And it seems I'm not invited."

"It's Hay-ver-ill. Just so you know. You don't say the second *h.*"

Cora could have slapped her. Thrown the tea in her face. That's how fast the anger came on, the indignation. She'd been trying, hard, to show grace and kindness, even in her disappointment. She understood the predicament, why she had to be kept away. She understood. But no, she hadn't known that it was Hay-verill, and not Haver-hill. How could she have known, this special pronunciation of the town where her extended family lived, this town where her siblings had grown up together, this town that Cora had never heard of until two weeks ago? No. She hadn't known about the silent *h.*

But she said nothing. It would do no good to show her rage, to try to hurt this woman who really had no other choice. It would do no good. The man with the flask stared down at his table, bleary-eyed.

"Why did you write the orphanage?" Cora asked. "Why did you even come here today?"

She turned so Cora couldn't see her face, just the beaded helmet of the gray hat. "I told you. I needed to see who you were, who you turned out to be. It's tormented me for so long." Her voice was still quiet, wavering. "I was going to tell you I was just a friend of your mother's, someone who'd known her. Stupid. I don't know what I was thinking." She looked back and smiled at Cora with her familiar mouth. "But I'm glad I came. I'm so relieved, so happy, to see you, and to know that you're just fine, that you didn't grow up on the streets, that you turned out so well and proper."

Cora nodded. Well and proper. As if that were the same as fine.

"You've given me such a gift today." She reached across the table, cupping Cora's cheek. "It's true that if you ever came to Haverhill, you would be a thorn in my side. But know this. If we part now, and never meet again, you'll always be a rose in my heart."

Cora could barely mask her disgust. It was as if she were breathing in a bad odor, yet trying not to change her expression. A rose in her heart? Pathetic. A ridiculous thing to say. This woman — this shrewd, pragmatic woman — had come up with bad poetry, that tripe, as a consolation. Had she really thought in those terms, flowers and thorns, when she lay in her bed at night, plotting out this visit, strategizing how she might get what she wanted without losing what she held more dear? Cora could see the misery, the real anguish in her eyes. But a rose in her heart? Was that really all she had to offer them both?

Still, when it was time to go, Cora walked her to her train. She didn't have time to be angry: these last few minutes were all she had. Mary O'Dell had not asked for her address in Kansas. She did not even pretend there would be another meeting. It was as final as death, the goodbye that was coming. Unhappy as she was, Cora would hang on until the very end.

Later, she would be glad for these last few minutes, and for her inability to throw them away. Because it was only when they were on the dim, underground platform, with other passengers already boarding, that Cora had time to consider what she'd already known, and how it compared to what she'd just learned.

"Mary." It seemed the only name for Cora to call her. This woman beside her wasn't Mother. But "Mrs. O'Dell" just sounded cruel. "How old was I when you left?"

She didn't turn toward Cora, her glazed gaze on the waiting train. In profile, or perhaps at that moment, Cora thought she looked suddenly older, more worn down, her pale skin sagging beneath her eyes. "You were six months old. Exactly six. They said I should stay to nurse you at least that long."

Six months old. Exactly. So she had left the first day she'd been allowed. No use in stretching things out. But Cora thought of the twins at six months, their milky smell, their grasping hands. As ill as she'd been after their births, she would have cut off both her arms rather than walk away from them, and she, too, had been seventeen. But then, it wasn't fair to compare. Mary O'Dell had had no husband, no solicitous Alan, just the mettle to save herself. And there was no point in being angry, not now, when there was little time and more to ask.

"But I didn't go to the orphanage until I was three," Cora said. "The records said I'd come right from the Florence Night Mission, so I must have been there for years. Without you."

She looked at Cora, wincing. "I'm sorry," she said. "I told them to take you to a home, a Catholic home, right away. I didn't want to leave you there, around those . . . the kind of women they took in." She drew in her shoulders. "I was scared one of them would try to take you. They didn't like me much, that was clear, but they all wanted to hold you and pass you around. It made me so anxious. These were streetwalkers, you understand. Or at least very immoral girls. Some of them had diseases, or they were ruined with drink. They likely couldn't have their own children."

Cora turned away. Such little sympathy. But she had to ask. It was now or never. "Do you remember a woman with long dark hair? And a shawl? She didn't speak English?"

"Ach. That sounds like most of them. They walked around with their hair loose, their ankles showing. And I was the only one with a proper coat." She said this as if it were an accomplishment. "But I don't remember a particular shawl, or a particular woman." She looked at Cora, frowning. "Why?"

"No reason," Cora said. She never considered that the woman with the shawl could be a true memory — yet still hold no significance. Perhaps the woman she remembered had held her just once. Or perhaps she was just one of many women at the mission who'd held her, at seven months old, at eight months, at two years. In any case, there was no one left to look for. And Mary O'Dell needed to go back to Massachusetts without the thorn in her side, just the rose in her heart. Good thing, Cora thought, for she'd left her bouquet of real, yellow roses on the chair in the Dining Concourse. Cora had noticed them when they started to walk away from the table, and she almost said something, but then realized they might have been purposefully left behind. After all, it was likely no one in Haverhill even knew this respectable matriarch had come to New York today. In any case, coming home to Mr. O'Dell with an armful of roses would force a more elaborate lie.

That was fine, Cora decided, as the train

started to click and sputter, preparing for forward motion. The bouquet had been expensive, but perhaps some lucky stranger would find it and be pleased.

"I have to go," Mary O'Dell said, turning to Cora. Her voice was certain. But there was something so despairing in her gray eyes that Cora was again moved to step forward and put her arms around her. She did it more slowly, carefully this time, nothing childlike or impulsive about it. Mary O'Dell's shoulders, narrow like her own, again felt stiff under her arms, but she held Cora back and didn't let go until the train's conductor called out the window for her to board, then she stepped back, staring at Cora, the gray hat a little askew.

"It was nice meeting you," Cora said, not really thinking. Her bland politeness was so ingrained.

But it didn't matter what she said, or whether it was true. The train sighed again, serious this time, and Mary O'Dell turned to go. She didn't look back, not once. But Cora, unwilling to forfeit even a final glimpse, watched her lift the skirt of her dress and make a ladylike climb onto the train.

FIFTEEN

Despite the heat, and the fact that other dance students were already coming out the door, Cora waited outside until exactly three o'clock before going in to get Louise. She wanted just a few more minutes to collect herself before what promised to be a long evening of protecting her new wounds, still open and bleeding, from the salt of Louise's provocations. The only way to do that, she decided, was to pretend, even to herself, to not be wounded at all. She would be disciplined in her thoughts, and not let herself think about Haverhill, Massachusetts, or thorns in sides, or the fact that her heart felt physically swollen with grief. At least it wasn't the weekend, with two full days of chaperoning before her. In the morning, she could escort Louise back to dance class, return to the empty apartment, where, for almost five blessed hours, she could give way to her sorrow in private.

She didn't necessarily want to be alone. If anything, she wished she could go talk with Joseph Schmidt, sitting at the drugstore and having orange sodas. Maybe because she'd already told him so much. Maybe. It didn't matter.

Fortunately, the Louise she expected that afternoon, the sullen, post-dance-class Louise, would not be too difficult to endure. Louise was usually too tired to consciously provoke on their hot walks home in the afternoons. If she did speak, it was not to converse with Cora, but only to inform her on a variety of subjects — the grace of Ted Shawn, the stupidity of the other dancers, or how she couldn't wait to get home to take her bath — nothing that required or even sought an answer or opinion from her chaperone. That would be fine today. Cora would welcome either silence or the distraction of whatever Louise wanted to talk about. She just didn't want to be antagonized, not when she could still recall the smell of the roses at Grand Central, and the wrinkled back of Mary O'Dell's dress as she boarded the train, not when she was so pathetic, still flexing her eyebrows high and swallowing so she wouldn't cry on the corner of Seventy-second and Broadway.

She could only hope today's dance class

had been particularly demanding and hot.

But when she finally went in and started down the stairs to the basement, Louise called out to her from the foot of the stairs, and then ran halfway up to meet her. Her eyes were bright, her smile wide, and though she was still in her dance wear, she looked more exhilarated than fatigued.

"They chose me!" She seized Cora's elbow with a warm, damp hand. "For the troupe, Cora! They chose me! Miss Ruth is back, and they made the decision. She's waiting to talk with you in the studio. They only chose one student to join them." She pointed to the chest of her soaked wool suit. "Me."

"Oh, Louise!" Cora clasped her hands. "I'm so pleased for you!" It was true. For a moment, all her own disappointment was forgotten. Cora knew how much she'd wanted a spot, how hard she had worked for it. It was a pleasure to witness a dream coming true, even someone else's.

"Isn't it the bee's knees? Isn't it? I have to telegram Mother right away. We can do it on the way home."

A tall, thin girl, her narrow face shiny with sweat, emerged from the door to the studio. Passing them on the stairs, she gave Louise a hostile look. Louise responded with a wave and a smile.

"Who would've thunk it?" she called up to the back of the girl's head. "Little old me! The only one they chose!" When the girl disappeared at the top of the stairs, Louise turned back to Cora, beaming. "They want me to start right away. I'm going to Philadelphia and performing with the troupe tomorrow night."

"Philadelphia?" Cora leaned against the stairway's railing. "Tomorrow? I don't understand."

"I knew you wouldn't believe me. I told them you wouldn't. Miss Ruth will tell you." She tugged, not too gently, at Cora's elbow. "Come down and ask her. Ask her yourself. She's waiting for you."

Downstairs in the studio, Ruth St. Denis stood with perfect posture by the piano, her white hair pulled back in a low bun, her bare feet just visible beneath the low hem of a full, black skirt. She confirmed to Cora that yes, everything Louise had told her was true. Louise should come to class tomorrow morning with an overnight bag. The troupe, now including Louise, would leave for Philadelphia immediately after class. She expected the performance to end late, and they would stay the night in a Philadelphia hotel, but they would start out early in the morning and be back in time for the next day's lesson.

"There is no need to worry," she told Cora. A jade bracelet slid to her elbow as she raised her hand in a dismissive wave. "I will be on the trip, and I will be personally responsible for Louise." She turned to Louise. "She and I will be rooming together."

Louise, who apparently still had a rule against forced smiles, managed a neutral expression.

"And if Philadelphia goes well," St. Denis continued, giving Louise a steady look, "meaning the entire trip, meaning Louise proves she can adhere to the moral code as well as the aesthetic demands of Denishawn, she may join the troupe." She turned back to Cora. "As a member, she could move into the boarding house we use as early as the end of next week. We have separate floors for men and women, and our own chaperone, of course."

Louise looked at Cora pleasantly. "So you can go home," she said. "You could probably leave tomorrow if you wanted. I'm sure that would be fine."

Without waiting for Cora's response, she turned and walked back to the dressing room. Cora watched her go, stoic. Clearly, even with the formidable St. Denis as a replacement, Louise considered Cora's early departure good news, perhaps on par with the trip to Philadelphia and the invitation to join the troupe. Well, she was right, Cora thought. It was good news. She certainly had no reason or wish to stay any longer. She'd accomplished her goal in coming to New York, as surely as Louise had. She'd come with questions, and now she had answers, dismal as they were. Perhaps when she was back in Wichita, the sorrow she felt now would ease, and she would be glad, in the end, that she'd come to New York, grateful that she'd at least gotten to speak with her mother, even just once, and learned her father's name. And she could go home with the memories of Broadway shows and subway rides and a building sixty stories high. And she could go home with the memory of Joseph Schmidt, of moving down the street with the radio in the baby carriage, of feeling so light and free, and then the touch of his fingers on the back of her neck, his gaze on hers. She would remember desire, felt and inspired. Would she be worse off for these memories? She didn't know. She would find out when she got back.

For dinner, Louise insisted they sit at the

counter across the street so she could tell Floyd Smithers the good news and work on her diction one last time. Cora agreed, in part because Louise deserved a celebration, in part because she wasn't up for a fight, but mostly because she wasn't up for a conversation, especially with Louise, and she guessed Floyd would be a good distraction. She was right about that. For a good half hour, Cora picked at a grilled-cheese sandwich while Louise ate a fudge sundae and occasionally smiled at Floyd's last, desperate effort to impress her. He did his very best. His other customers got only rudimentary attention, but Louise's sundae was given a fresh topping of whipped cream each time she requested it. He gave her an extra maraschino cherry, too, which she sucked on like a lollipop, the little stem sticking out between her lips, until her lips were bright red, as if she were wearing paint. Even then, Cora didn't intervene. Louise would soon be Ruth St. Denis's problem, and perhaps she could address the girl's issues with proper decorum. Cora was on her way out, and more than happy to pass on the torch.

It was only when Floyd started whispering to Louise over the counter, too quietly for Cora to hear, that Cora cleared her throat and declared they would be on their way.

"Why? Why do we have to go?" Louise bit the cherry off the stem, chewing it like gum. "If you're ready to go, fine. I'll be up in a minute."

"You'll come with me now," Cora said, the ache in her chest moving into her voice, making it sharp and brittle. "Because enough is enough, Louise. Really. Enough is enough." She stood, waiting, and the look on her face must have been something, as without any further protest, Louise dabbed her mouth with a napkin, and told Floyd to have a good night.

Later, when she was in bed, trying to read the last few pages of *The Age of Innocence,* Louise asked what she was so sore about.

"You've had your face all scrunched up all evening." She stood next to the bed in her nightgown, which was a pale pink silk, sleeveless and barely falling to her knees. It looked like something from a bridal trousseau, and Cora couldn't imagine why or how she'd gotten it. She continued to read, or to try to read, but she could feel the girl standing there, watching her. For someone who liked to hold a book up to her own face so often, Louise certainly didn't seem to mind interrupting someone else's reading.

"What's the story? Should I be afraid? You look like you want to slug somebody."

"I'm fine." Cora looked up and managed a smile. But her jaw ached, and she knew she'd been clenching her teeth. She wasn't angry, though. She wasn't. She was just sad, just full of disappointment, fatigued from the miserable day.

"Mother says making faces like that is what makes you wrinkled. Not you in particular, I mean. But don't say I didn't warn you." She stepped into her heels, clicked back across the floor into the bathroom, and shut the door. Cora looked back down at her book. If Louise wanted to see what her nightgown looked like with heels, Cora supposed she could, provided she stay in the bathroom. She had no wish to start any argument. She only wished to be left alone, to read her book in peace. But even the book was bothering her. Louise had been right about the hero, who wasn't a hero at all — even now that he was old, and the wife he hadn't loved was long dead, even then he couldn't muster the strength to look his real love, now old as well, in the eye. Cora read with narrowed eyes. A horrible end for a book. Yet she took in every word, even as her jaw ached, even as her vision blurred. When she finished the last line, she closed the book and crossed her arms, staring at the pea-green wall. A terrible ending for a book. A foolish man, a waste. She could feel herself scowling, the lines of her face settling in. Louise and her mother were probably right — she was making herself look old. And now Cora knew just how she would age, what she would look like in twenty years, maybe less. She would look like Mary O'Dell.

Louise opened the bathroom door. She stood in the doorway, silent, clearly waiting for Cora to look up. Cora did, irritated, but then Louise looked away, a strand of black hair catching on her mouth. She was still wearing the heels, moving the hem of her gown around her knees as she shifted from side to side.

"Did you hear about the shooting last night?"

Cora shook her head, though Louise was still looking away. Louise looked back at her, waiting.

"No," Cora said, "I didn't."

"Oh. Well. It should be in the paper tomorrow. A girl was talking about it in class. It was just one block up from where she lives." She held on to the doorway as she stepped out of her shoes. "She said a

Prohibition agent got a tip about a still, and when the police went in to check it out, somebody started shooting. This boy was killed on the stoop. The girl in my class said there was blood and maybe his brains all over the stoop."

Cora squinted, her mind going right to Howard and Earle, as it always did when she heard of some boy, any boy, harmed or killed. "That's terrible," she said.

"Yeah." Louise walked to the bed, a shoe in each hand. "She said her neighborhood has been a lot scarier since Prohibition started. She said things like that never used to happen. It used to be safe."

Cora nodded, wary again. Of course Louise had an agenda. She wanted an argument. "I'm not sure about that," Cora murmured. She shimmied down under the sheet, her head flat to the pillow. "It's too bad the boy chose to get mixed up with bootlegging and stills."

"He didn't." Louise dropped her shoes next to her side of the bed. "He didn't have anything to do with the still. He just lived in the building with his family, and he happened to be on the stoop. The girl in my class said she'd known him forever, and that he was just a nice boy."

Cora was silent, listening to the whirling

fan. She would not be provoked into an argument. She didn't have one in her tonight.

Louise sighed as she lay down on the bed, smelling of dental cream and talcum powder. The nights had been so warm that they slept with just the top sheet over them, the thin cotton bedspread folded at the foot of the bed. "It's so stupid," Louise said, pulling the sheet up. "People are still drinking. And they always will. People want to drink. That's all there is to it." She squinted at the collar of Cora's gown. "Is that thing comfortable to sleep in? I mean, that lace at the neck. It can't be comfortable. And what does your husband think?"

Cora didn't answer. She reached for the lamp. She would not engage, not about her gown, not about Prohibition, not about anything. She just wanted to go to sleep, to feel nothing, to make this long day finally come to an end.

And she did sleep, almost right away. But she fell into dreams, and she would remember one dream the next morning, and even long after that: She was still in her nightgown — she could feel the lace at the collar, the soft cotton against her legs — but she was back at her dining room table in Wichita. Alan and Raymond Walker were sitting there with her, both of them wearing suits and drinking out of teacups. They were being nice to her, making pleasant conversation, but one of Alan's hands was under the table, and one of Raymond Walker's hands was under the table, too, and she knew by the looks on their faces that something illicit was going on out of view. She didn't look under the table because she didn't have to. She could tell by the smiles on their faces, their mischievous grins. And she was mad, mad about it. But then she lifted her own teacup to her mouth, and it was beer, which in her dream tasted sweet, like tea sweetened with honey. "Like liquid gold," Alan said, raising his cup as if making a toast, a toast, it seemed, to her. She could hear sirens outside, coming closer, maybe real New York sirens in the dark streets outside that became part of her dream, but she was thirsty, so thirsty, and so she stopped being mad and stopped worrying about the sirens and took a long drink from her own teacup, and the sweetness of the beer was so perfect, so cool and wonderful, that she tilted back her head to empty her cup. Alan smiled and said she would be fine. They would have to stay hidden, but they weren't bad people. They were just people who wanted a drink.

She never knew what woke her. She would realize later that the room had been quiet for hours, with no movement aside from the whirling fan. But for some reason, maybe the heat, maybe a car backfiring, she became conscious in the darkness, even as her eyes were still closed. She lay still for a while, recalling the strange dream and the imagined sweetness of the beer. Just a dream, not a memory. A car rolled by on the street, followed by another with a louder engine, and she opened her eyes. The thin curtain was aglow, illuminated by an orange streetlight, and she turned away from it, careful to move gently so as not to disturb Louise. In just the past few weeks, she'd grown used to sharing a bed with another body, staying confined to one side, not letting her arms and legs flail about as she did in her big bed at home. And so now she peered through the semidarkness to locate Louise's head, to measure just how much space she had.

She could only see the white of the pillow.

She sat up, making certain, her hands moving over the sheet.

"Louise?"

The fan whirled. She reached over to turn on the lamp, shielding her eyes from its brightness. The bathroom was dark. She pushed back the sheet and got out of bed.

"Louise? Are you here? Answer me."

She checked the bathroom, just to be sure, and moved quickly through the kitchen. In the front room, she pulled the chain on the low lamp. The painted Siamese cat stared.

She ran back to the bedroom, snatching her watch from the nightstand. Twenty past three. She hiked up her long gown, rested one knee on the bed, and peered over the edge of the other side, where Louise had dropped her shoes just hours before. They were gone. Of course they were. Louise had left them out on purpose, boldly, right in front of her. When had that been? Ten o'clock? Almost five hours ago, and there was no way to know what time she'd left. Cora went to the window and pulled aside the curtain, looking down at the street. Even at this early-morning hour, people were still out, men and women bobbing down the sidewalk, getting into taxis, huddled at the corners in little groups. She could see a few lit windows in the building across the street. But the luncheonette was closed, its electric sign dark, its windows dimmed. From the sidewalk, a man with no jacket waved up at her, while his two friends laughed, as if with all the bare-kneed girls in the street, Cora was the one who'd been putting on a show for them, in her prim gown with the ribbon at the collar, her hair loose to her shoulders. She stepped out of sight, her heart pounding, her arms crossed over her chest.

She didn't know what to do. Wake the neighbors? The few people she'd seen in the hallway and on the stairway never even said hello. Should she go down to the street and start screaming? Ask a stranger how she might find the police? So they could what? File a report? Her fingers grazed her lace collar, the skin of her neck. No. There was no need for real alarm. Louise was fine. She'd gone out for a lark, but she would come back soon, and when she did, Cora would give her a good scolding, a terrific scolding, letting her know how much she'd frightened her, and how absolutely stupid she'd been to go out by herself in New York City in the middle of the night. Didn't she know that Cora would only have to say one word about this to Ruth St. Denis, just one word, and Louise could forget about Philadelphia and joining the troupe?

Cora turned off the lamp so she could again look out the window, unseen. Stupid girl, she thought, even as her gaze moved worriedly up and down the street. Perhaps she should tell St. Denis. It would serve Louise right to have to go back to Kansas now, to lose everything because of her childish behavior. But even as she thought this, she knew that if Louise would just come back, Cora would say nothing to Ruth St. Denis. Louise needed punishment, yes, but Cora didn't want her to lose everything, not when she was so close, the only student they picked.

She didn't know how much time passed before she spotted them, two people moving oddly down the sidewalk, the taller one almost upright and half supporting, half dragging the other. The smaller, leaning figure wore a sleeveless dress, light-colored. Cora pressed her forehead against the window, cupped her hands over her eyes, and saw the cropped black hair. She picked up the key and ran down the stairs in her bare feet, one hand alternately gripping and sliding down the narrow banister. She could hear her own breathing as she turned the first landing, her nostrils flared like an enraged bull's. She reached the bottom of the stairway, ran across the gritty floor of the entry, and tried to fling open the door to the street, realizing only now that it was kept locked at night. She undid the lock and

369

pushed the door so hard it swung open and hit the exterior wall.

"Oh. Hello."

Before her, on the covered stoop, Floyd Smithers, his bow tie dangling from his collar, stood very still, doing his best to hold up Louise, who slouched against him like a soft doll. She was still in the nightgown, wearing the heels. She raised her head, looked at Cora through hooded eyes.

"Oh fuck. Not her. Please? Take me anywhere else. Not her. Not now." She frowned at Cora. "That's a goddam ugly nightgown, by the way. You look like Little Bo Peep."

Floyd met Cora's gaze. He looked alarmed, and perfectly sober.

"I just wanted to get her home," he said.

For a moment, Cora couldn't even speak. She wanted to scratch his handsome, college-boy face, the door key sharp in her palm. He was at fault for this, more than Louise, even. Now Cora knew what they'd been whispering about over the counter at dinner. He'd plotted it all out, getting a fifteen-year-old girl out alone and so drunk she couldn't stand up, so he could . . . what? The night was still warm, muggy, but she felt a chill of real fear.

"You're disgusting," she hissed. "I should call the police."

He shook his head. "I didn't mean to . . ."
Louise started to swoon away from him, and
he widened his stance for better support.

"I can guess your intentions." She moved
to Louise's other side, looping one bare,
limp arm over her neck. "I'll take it from
here, thank you. But don't worry. You'll be
hearing from me soon. And from the au-
thorities. She's a child, fifteen. You knew
that."

He disentangled himself and stepped
away. Louise's full weight slumped against
Cora, and they staggered backward, almost
falling against the wall. For such a small
person, Louise was surprisingly heavy,
dense like a soaked sponge, and the silk
nightgown hard to hold on to. Cora righted
herself, hooking her free arm around Louise's waist, and took a careful step toward
the stairway. Louise rolled her head in and
whispered something indecipherable. Her
breath smelled of sour milk and pine.

"Floyd." Cora turned her own head away,
breathing hard. She wasn't sure if he was
still there. "Floyd?"

"Yes."

She closed her eyes. "It's three flights up.
I need your help."

In a moment, he was beside them. He put
one arm under Louise's knees, one arm

371

under her shoulders. Without comment, he made his way to the stairs. As soon as he began to climb, Louise started to kick and slap his back, muttering protests. One of her heels fell off on the second landing, but Cora, following, didn't pick it up. She wouldn't. Maybe the shoe would be there in the morning. Maybe it wouldn't. It seemed to Cora she deserved to lose it.

At their door, Floyd waited, breathing heavily, as Cora pushed the key into the lock. Louise, somewhat revived by her ride up the stairs, was also exhaling audibly, but she was doing it on purpose, as a joke, blowing her acrid, piney breath at Cora's cheek. "You like that, Cora?" she slurred, heavy-lidded. "That's gin is what that is. You should try it sometime. You know? Maybe you won't be such a wound-up pain in the ass."

Cora opened the door, moving through the kitchen to the bedroom. "Just put her on the bed," she said, yanking the chain for the bedroom light. He did, not too gently, and stepped away, still breathing hard and red in the face. Cora noticed he no longer appeared contrite. He actually appeared put-upon. She hoped he didn't feel in any way absolved, just because he got Louise upstairs. That was the least he could do.

"Nothing happened," he said. "Nothing. I just wanted to get her home."

She stared at him, trying to see any sign of real honesty. She wanted to believe him. She was desperate to. But he might say anything now, to get himself out of danger. The flush of his skin made him look younger than he was, boyish. Maybe he wasn't lying. But that was just it — there was no way to know.

Cora gave him a withering look. "Why are you still here?"

He held up his palms, turned, and made quick strides out of the room. The door to the hallway slammed behind him. Louise started laughing again, lying on one side, her bare knees curled up under her chin. But she stopped suddenly, the thin black brows going low. Her hand went to her belly, and she looked utterly somber, almost afraid.

"Oh. Oh-oh. I think I might upchuck."

Cora frowned. This, she supposed, was as close as the girl would come to remorse. She felt no sympathy at all. "Well, for God's sake, get to the bathroom. And don't think I'm going to carry you. If you can't walk, crawl."

To her surprise, that was what Louise did. She rolled over so she was belly-down on the bed and stretched both hands toward the floor. As she tried to slide the rest of her body to the floor, she lost her grip on the floor and fell forward, the hem of the gown hitching up around her thighs. But she recovered. Groaning quietly, she crawled like a toddler toward the dark bathroom. She was wearing underwear, to Cora's relief.

Cora followed her to the bathroom, pulling the chain on the light. Two shiny roaches scurried into the drain of the sink, and Louise crooked her elbow over her eyes. She was lying on her side by the toilet. Cora, feeling faint and closed in by the bathroom's red walls, braced herself against the edge of the sink. She wanted to go back to bed, to go back to sleep, but if she wanted answers, truthful answers, she would have to get them now.

"Where did you get the liquor? Where did Floyd get it?"

Louise smiled, her eyes still hidden by her pale arm. "I dunno. I just followed him." Her "him" came out like "em," all the new, clear diction gone. "It was the darnedest little place, Cora. You go in like you're going into a phone booth, but if you knock on the wall the right way, a door opens, and you're inside a room. Isn't that smart?"

"A speakeasy, then."

"Listen to you. So worldly. I'm impressed."

Cora wanted to kick her. She was mad enough to lean down and pull the girl up for a quick, hard shake that might have sobered her enough to understand that the matter at hand was very serious, and that none of her usual belligerence would be tolerated. She'd been out with a boy, unchaperoned and falling-down drunk. Cora would have to call her parents. And what would she tell them? That their daughter may have been violated? Would they want Cora to take her to a doctor? Perhaps Floyd hadn't been lying. Perhaps he hadn't touched her, and a doctor could assure them all that there had been no real violation at all. Cora would swear silence. She would. But Louise had to stop smirking, to stop acting as if this was all some hilarious joke.

Louise sat up with her hand over her mouth. Cora, who had little experience with drunks, but who had nursed her husband and sons through countless bouts of the flu, positioned Louise's head over the toilet just before she spewed out a stream of clear liquid that smelled more of bile than pine. Cora had to turn away so she wouldn't retch herself, but she kept her hands on the girl's narrow shoulders. With every additional shudder, Cora patted her back.

"Better to get it out," she said. "Keep going. Get it all out."

She waited until Louise sat back from the toilet, nothing left in her stomach to expel. The girl's nose and cheeks were pink, and her eyes were dull, unseeing. She scooted back until she was against the edge of the tub, and there she sat, bare legs splayed, one strap of the gown hanging off her shoulder. Cora flushed the toilet and lowered herself to the floor as well, her back against the wall.

"That was amazing," Louise whispered. "I feel so much better."

Cora shook her head. She'd been wrong to pat the girl's shoulders, to offer comfort and aid. There was no remorse, no understanding. "Louise. This is a very serious situation. I have to ask you, and you have to answer me honestly. Did he take advantage of you?"

The dark eyes focused on Cora's, and unbelievably, even now, with her chin still shiny with drool, there was the condescension, the smugness in her gaze. She snickered, but she shook her head.

"Louise? You understand what I'm asking? You're certain? He didn't take advan-

376

tage of you? You understand what I'm asking? You haven't been . . . compromised, Louise? This is what I'm asking."

Louise held up her hand as if taking a pledge. "He did not compromise me. I remain uncompromised."

Cora closed her eyes. "Thank God."

Louise laughed again, lowering her hand to wipe her cheek. "Thank me, why don't you. Floyd just isn't my type. I think I'd be a little much for him." She paused, moving her tongue beneath her lower lip. "Other fellows had more money for drinks."

"Oh, Louise." Cora shook her head.

"Oh, Cora." Louise shook her head as well. "Don't you be so worried about my virginity, me losing it here in New York. I didn't even pack it, for your information. It's back in Kansas somewhere." She stretched her pale arms up, arching her back away from the tub. "Sorry to tell you now, when you've been so passionate about your duties. It's been adorable, really." She crossed her arms and made a pouty face. "Poor Cora. Poor, dumb Cora, assigned to protect my virginity. You've been sent on a fool's errand, I'm afraid. I lost it long ago."

Cora watched the girl's face, her sleepy eyes. She might be lying, just trying to unnerve her. But if anything, Louise seemed

377

less guarded, and much less strategic, than she usually did. She was sloppy, but honest, with drink.

"You look surprised." She tugged a strand of black hair toward her mouth, but it wouldn't reach. "I guess you ladies in Wichita really don't know so much about all my rides to church after all."

Cora shook her head. She didn't understand.

Louise rolled her eyes. "Eddie Vincent?"

It took Cora a moment to recognize the name. "Mr. Vincent? He was your Sunday school teacher, Louise. You said he gave you rides to church."

"Yes. And so much more."

Cora swallowed, taking in the girl's mocking expression, the nonchalance in her voice. As if she weren't ashamed by what she'd implied. It was terrible, what she was suggesting.

"What are you saying? Do you mean to tell me that . . . Louise. Be clear."

"I'm saying we had an affair, dummy." She lifted the hem of the nightgown, then let it fall back to her knees. "He got me this pretty thing. Isn't it the berries? Took photographs of me in it, really beautiful. He has a good eye. He could have been an artist, but his wife got pregnant."

Cora was aware of the hard tile beneath her, the bathroom's warm and muggy air. "Louise. Edward Vincent is a respected man in Wichita. This is a serious allegation."

"I'm not alleging anything." She examined the back of her hand. "I'm telling you we had an affair. I was his lover."

Cora watched the girl's eyes for any sign of fear or regret, any flinch that might suggest she was lying, or at least exaggerating. But there was no such sign. She looked confident, even proud.

"Oh, Louise." Cora felt nauseous. "If this is true, if this horrible thing you're telling me is true, it wasn't an affair. You weren't his lover. Edward Vincent is older than I am. He teaches Sunday school. I have to tell your mother."

Louise yawned, a soprano trill escaping from the back of her throat. "Oh, I think she knows. She knew he was taking pictures of me, that I was posing for him. She thought I might be able to use the pictures for my career. We didn't get into the specifics." She looked at Cora reproachfully. "I don't think she'll want to talk with you about it. She probably won't appreciate you being so . . . familiar."

Cora put her hand to her throat. It was as if sour vomit and gin had somehow found its way to her own belly. Edward Vincent, with his combed hair and his smug smiles in church, always sitting in a front pew next to his wife. And Myra? What kind of mother let her daughter pose for those kinds of pictures? What was wrong with that woman?

"Louise," she said quietly. "Are you sure she knows . . . the extent of what happened? I find it hard to believe any mother would do nothing if she knew a middle-aged, married man had . . . compromised her fourteen-year-old daughter."

"He didn't compromise me. Why do you keep using that word, Cora? We fucked, okay?" She smiled wolfishly, then laughed. "I like to fuck. Maybe you don't, but I do."

Cora looked away. If the girl meant to shock with her language, her casual vulgarity, she'd succeeded. And she was clearly enjoying herself, playing the liberated little flapper, leaving Cora, and all her generation, dumbstruck and aghast. But when Cora turned back and looked hard into the girl's face, she didn't see liberation so much as posturing and bravado, real uncertainty underneath.

"No, Louise. No. If what you're telling me is true, Edward Vincent took advantage of you. You were a child. You still are."

"You don't know what you're talking

about. I said I enjoyed myself, and I did. I liked fucking him, Cora. You're just so old and dead you can't understand that."

Cora sucked her lips, so hard they hurt. Even drunk and flailing, Louise knew just where and how to strike. But that didn't matter. Not now.

"The minister needs to know."

"No! No. Don't get Eddie in trouble. Jesus."

"He's still teaching Sunday school."

"So?"

"So what about other girls?"

The dark eyes moved to the ceiling. "What about them? It's not like he's some kind of sex fiend. He liked me in particular. I don't see what's wrong with that. And if some other girl does get him next, bully for her. I'm in New York. What do I care?"

She was convincing, Cora thought. Perhaps it wasn't just bravado. Perhaps she was really so sophisticated, so nonchalant, her thinking so unlike Cora's that they couldn't understand each other. But she felt unable to just give up.

"He did a terrible thing, Louise. If what you're telling me is true, he did a terrible thing. He abused his position. And when did all this happen? Last year? When you were fourteen? Thirteen?"

"Oh, God. Hold the fire alarm. If you really want to know, he wasn't even my first." She laughed again, rubbing her nose. "Okay? How's that, Cora? Now you'll really lose your mind. I was compromised before we even moved to Wichita. Okay? Since long before Eddie. How do you like that?"

Another roach scurried out from behind the toilet to a crack under the opposite wall. Cora watched it with dazed eyes. It was a nightmare maybe, this middle-of-the-night misery, no more real than her drinking beer out of teacups with Alan and Raymond Walker. But the roach seemed real. And the tiles on the floor were smooth and hard beneath her. The red paint on the walls looked as garish as it did in daylight. And Louise still had real spittle on her chin.

"What are you talking about, Louise? Your family has been in Wichita for years."

"Just four."

"Are you telling me you had another affair when you were eleven?"

Louise looked up at her so blankly that Cora regretted the sarcasm. But she couldn't imagine. She just couldn't imagine. She'd never in her life had a conversation like this.

"Not an affair," Louise said dully, her toes pointing up on either side of the toilet. "But we were friendly. He was nice to all the kids. But nicest to me. And I was the one who went to his house."

"Whose house? What are you talking about?"

"Mr. Flowers. He lived by us in Cherry-vale. He was nice to all the kids, nice to my brothers. June was too little to play with us. He said he had popcorn at his house. He'd leave candy on his porch. So I went over. I was the only one who went over." She puckered her mouth. "Odd, isn't it? I lost my cherry in Cherryvale. I was deflowered by Mr. Flowers. Kind of funny."

Cora put her hands over her eyes. Everything in her wanted to believe that Louise was toying with her, making up some hideous story to distract her from the problem at hand. But this was a different Louise, this drunk Louise, slumped unglamorously against the tub with the black hair pushed behind her ears, her nose still red at the tip. Cora's very body believed her, her breathing fast and shallow. She wasn't even wearing her corset, and she couldn't get enough air.

"When you were a child?" Her voice came out as a whisper. "Louise? You were eleven?"

"No. That was a couple of years before we moved." She frowned at the tile floor. "I came home and told my mother, and she was mad, so mad at me."

Cora stared. Nine, then. Nine years old.

"She said I must have led him on. Really, though, when I remember it, I just wanted the popcorn."

A grown man, Cora thought. A grown man luring a child with popcorn. For what? What kind of craving? It had never occurred to her. She'd never heard of such a thing.

"Did she tell the police? Did she tell your father?"

The question seemed to perplex Louise, as if she hadn't considered it before. "She might have told him. But she told me not to tell anyone else, because people would say things about me. And not to go over there again. And to think more about the way I conducted myself."

"You were a child."

She shook her head, the black brows lowered, as if Cora were pestering her with unintelligent comments. "That didn't matter. Even then, there was something about me, something he saw. That's what she meant."

Cora, silencing a moan, remembered their first day in the city. What had she said to Louise? What idiotic thing had she said about the low-cut blouse? *Do you want to be raped?* And more. She leaned forward and tried to touch the girl's knee. Louise turned it away, out of reach.

"Louise. Your mother was wrong. You were a child. An innocent child." And wasn't she still? Cora wanted so much to reach out, to console, to smooth down the black hair.

"When I went in, maybe. But not when I came out." She looked at Cora coolly. "Don't be hard on Mother. She was right. People would have said things about me." She narrowed her eyes. "You would have. You would have been the first to. Because my candy got unwrapped, right?"

Cora felt it like a slap, the recognition of her own words. She held up her palms. "Forget I said that about the candy. Please. That has nothing to do with what you're telling me. Please forget I said that."

"I won't forget anything."

They looked at each other, and Cora, for the first time, had the miserable experience of seeing herself, truly seeing herself, the way Louise saw her. A confused, hypocritical old biddy. A fool on a fool's errand, indeed. She'd been a fool all summer, an unhappy woman spouting hurtful, stupid maxims about candy and virtue, telling lies to an injured child. And weren't they lies? Didn't she know that already? For what had been the real value of her own virginity, her own ignorance, at seventeen? Why had she been so very eager to teach this girl to be as delusional of its worth as she'd been? Why? What was in it for her?

Louise turned around and used the rim of the bathtub to pull herself to her knees. She had red marks on the backs of her legs, impressions from the tiles.

"I want to brush my teeth," she muttered, rising to her feet.

Cora nodded. She thought of extending a hand, wordlessly asking the girl to pull her up, but she was fairly certain she'd be turned down. She reached for the edge of the sink and hoisted herself up, feeling achy and older than she was.

"Could I have some privacy?" Louise asked, not looking at her now. "I have to pee."

Cora walked stiffly out into the bedroom. *Innocent when I went in, not when I came out.* The curtain was still pulled back from the window where, just fifteen or twenty minutes earlier, she'd kept her angry vigil. She went to close the curtain and saw the streetlights were still on, though the traffic on the street and the sidewalks had thinned. Was it four? Past four? She lay down on her side of the bed and pulled the thin sheet up to her chin. She would listen to make sure Louise came to bed and got at least a little sleep. But she understood the girl wanted privacy, or at least the illusion of privacy, even for the few remaining days they had to share this room. So Cora turned toward the wall and closed her eyes, though she already knew she wouldn't sleep.

SIXTEEN

The hook-nosed Russian at the corner grocery told Cora she was his first customer of the morning, continuing with friendly chatter until he noticed her blank, exhausted stare. Without having to make further conversation, she purchased a *New York Times,* a loaf of bread, strawberry jelly, a stick of butter, a tin of black tea, and six oranges. Out in the street, it was still early enough that the air was comfortable, almost cool, the sun only starting to brighten the sky.

The entry of their building looked as it always did, with no sign of the drama just a few hours before. On her way up the stairs, she saw Louise's shoe, the heel wedged between the rails near the second landing.

She was quiet as she let herself into the apartment, setting Louise's shoe on the floor and her purchases on the writing desk. She put water on for the tea, slipped off her shoes, and walked back to the bedroom. Louise was sleeping on her side, her arms and legs pulled close. Her hands obscured most of her face, but with every exhale, she made a soft whistling sound. Cora, reassured, moved silently out of the room.

The paper had an article about the boy killed on the stoop. It happened just as Louise had said: a police raid on a reported still, bootleggers with guns, the boy walking out to the stoop at the exact wrong time. There was a quote from the police chief saying he regretted an innocent person, a thirteen-year-old boy, had lost his life to violent criminals. Suspects had been arrested and charged with voluntary manslaughter as well as the illegal brewing of alcohol, for several barrels of gin had been discovered and destroyed. There was a quote from the victim's mother saying her son had, in fact, been a good boy who never once looked for trouble, and there was a picture of the stoop being mopped by a grim-faced man, identified in the caption as the victim's uncle.

Cora rested her palm on the picture, lightly, then with pressure, as if trying to blot it.

She needed something to keep her occupied, something quiet to do while Louise slept, so she read the whole paper, front to back. She regularly read the paper back home, and since she'd come to New York, she'd been reading the *Times*. But on this particular morning, she was struck by the hodgepodge placement of light stories alongside the disturbing. Babe Ruth had hit three home runs in one day for the second time. A twenty-one-year-old nurse in Rochester had leaped to her death because, according to her roommates, she didn't know how to tell her fiancé they couldn't marry: one of her parents was half-Negro. A movie star's divorce was upheld in Las Vegas. In Germany, the foreign minister, a Jew, had been shot outside his home, and a radical but committed group was threatening to kill more Jews in important positions. Brooklyn planned to create two thousand parking places for Coney Island. Armenians were suffering, starving. President Harding expressed commitment to ending the coal crisis. Textile workers were striking. There'd been another lynching in Georgia, this time of a fifteen-year-old boy. On a happier note, skirts that showed the knees were becoming passé, hemlines having dropped again, and so all across the country, parents, clergy, and educators were breathing a collective sigh of relief, as morality was back in vogue.

Cora sat back in her chair and stared up

at the front room's pale yellow walls, now bright with sunlight, and the painting of the Siamese cat. Her jaw was clenched. Her hands were balled in fists. There was no use pretending she was still just sad or disappointed. Twice, she had to get up and pace the room.

At a quarter to nine, she went into the bedroom and slowly pulled open the curtain, wincing at the screech of the hooks as they slid along the rod. Louise turned away from the window, pulling the sheet up over her head.

"Louise?" Cora walked to Louise's side of the bed. "It's time. If you want to go to class, you need to get up now. You need to get up and get dressed. And pack for Philadelphia."

There was no sound. But the black brows moved low.

"I have tea and breakfast in the other room." She waited. "Louise? If you want to sleep, sleep. I'll leave it up to you. But if you're late for class, you won't get to go to Philadelphia. And you might not get to join the troupe."

The sheet lowered a few inches. Louise stared dumbly at Cora, her eyes watery, pink-rimmed. But she was awake now, able to decide. Satisfied, Cora went into the kitchen. She poured two glasses of the cooled tea she'd brewed earlier. She put four pieces of bread in the oven and started to peel an orange. After a while, she heard Louise moving around the bathroom, running water, spitting. Cora carried their plates and glasses to the front room and set them on the table. She folded the newspaper and put it away. She didn't want a distraction now.

Alone at the table, Cora ate her orange, though it was difficult to chew and swallow, her dread a knot at her throat. Perhaps she shouldn't say anything. She could pretend last night's conversation had never happened, and neither of them would ever bring up Edward Vincent or Mr. Flowers again. In some ways, that seemed the best solution. She was just a chaperone. Perhaps it wasn't her place to meddle in such a private, awful matter. Still, she didn't think she could pretend that she knew nothing, not now, when she had an image of Louise, a little girl, invited into a house for popcorn, not when she thought of Edward Vincent teaching Sunday school.

Louise walked out of the kitchen with her hands pressed against her temples. She'd put on a loose cotton dress, and she appeared to have splashed water on her face and combed her hair. But she moved across the front room carefully as if it were the deck of a rocking ship. To Cora, already seated at the table, it did not seem possible that a person in her condition could be ready for rigorous dance practice in less than an hour. Even if she somehow suffered through it, she wouldn't be any good.

"Maybe you should stay here and rest," she said. "I can walk down by myself and tell Miss Ruth you're sick. You might only lose Philadelphia."

Louise slumped into the opposite chair, looking down at her plate of toast, her peeled orange.

"It's not a lie." Cora buttered her toast. "You are sick."

"What else will you tell her?" Her voice was gravelly, low.

"Nothing." Cora pressed too hard with the knife, tearing a hole in the toast. She looked at it, and after quick consideration gave up the whole pretense, her knife clanging to her plate. Louise looked up, startled.

"Louise, I'm not interested in ruining your chance with Denishawn. If you want to go to Philadelphia, go." Cora smoothed the edge of the oilcloth. "I want to talk about what you told me last night." She hoped her face communicated all her sleepless regret, and her outrage, too. But in case it didn't, she cleared her throat. "I'm sorry," she said. "I'm so sorry . . . to hear what happened. In Cherryvale, I mean."

Louise wiped her mouth with the back of her hand. She seemed embarrassed. Cora hadn't thought it was possible. But the look only lasted a few seconds before the more familiar, collected gaze returned.

"I don't know what you're talking about."

"Louise."

"I really don't."

"Flowers? That was his name?"

"Oh, God." She pressed her hair against her temples. "I should have kept my mouth shut." She wasn't even talking to Cora, just muttering to herself. "I'll learn. This is why I shouldn't drink."

"Someone should be told, Louise. He could still be luring girls, little girls, to his house."

"No." She held up a hand, waving weakly. "I never heard about any other girl going over there."

Of course not, Cora thought. If there had been other girls, their mothers would have told them to keep quiet, too. There was no way to know.

"And he left town anyway. Moved away before we did."

"Do you know where?"

"No idea. Cora, I'm not even sure that was his name. Maybe I just remembered Flowers. Come to think of it, it might have been Mr. Feathers, not Mr. Flowers." She smiled. "Maybe I was de-feathered."

"This isn't funny, Louise."

"Isn't that for me to decide?" The smile was gone. "Please drop it, okay? It's just something that happened. I'm fine. I don't want you to make a big production out of it."

"I'm not out to embarrass you, if that's what you're thinking."

"But you would embarrass me." Her stare was hard, unblinking. "So really. Understand. You bring up Eddie, or Cherryvale, and I don't know what you're talking about. Mother won't, either, just so you know. You'll just make yourself look crazy."

Cora looked at her torn toast. Myra. A sorry excuse for a mother. And Leonard, a blind and preoccupied father. Louise was the real orphan at the table. Cora had had the Kaufmanns.

Louise put her knife on the table, idly spinning it like a dial. "Did you mean what you said? You really aren't going to tell Miss Ruth about last night?"

"I meant it."

Louise stared down at her plate, her uneaten toast. She looked too confused to be grateful. "Good," she said finally. "Then I'll go to class. I'll pack now." She nudged her plate toward Cora. "I can't eat this. Sorry."

"You should try to eat something. Even just the orange. You'll be in class for five hours. And you'll be traveling after that."

"I won't keep it down." She scooted her chair back and stood.

Cora held up her palm. Louise stared down at her, bleary-eyed. She leaned to one side and steadied herself, her hand on the back of the chair. "What?"

"I'm worried about you," Cora said.

"I'm not hungry."

"Not that, Louise. I'm worried about you."

She didn't say it to get the last word, but it was the one time she got it. Louise only managed a low laugh before she turned and retreated from the room.

They were mostly quiet on the way to class. Louise walked with surprising competence, even in heels, her overnight bag swinging from her shoulder. But she did yield to Cora's suggestion that they stop and buy a bottle of aspirin, as well as an apple to put in her bag. By the time they descended the staircase to the studio, she gave no sign that she was feeling the effects of anything but a good night's sleep. She smiled at Ted Shawn and gave St. Denis a cheerful good morning as she came out of the changing room. Still, Cora lingered for a while, watching the warm-up from the metal chair in the corner. Any worries she had quickly disappeared: Louise's movements were as elegant and precise as ever, and when she finally glanced over at Cora's reflection in the big mirror, it was with a look of annoyance, or perhaps something harsher. Cora, seeing her vigil was unwelcome, made her way to the door.

The walk back to the apartment felt particularly long and hot. As soon as she got upstairs, she ran a bath. Her hair didn't need washing, but once she was in the tub, she let her head slip under the lukewarm water, her curls fanning out around her head, weightless. Finally alone, she let herself cry. Her hand moved up to the back of her neck, her fingers tracing her hairline. She would be going home soon, in just a few days, returning to her real life. And what had she accomplished? Nothing with Louise. And nothing with herself. She'd come here with the hope that finding her mother or father, or just finding out about them, would somehow make her more content, or show her how she might strive to be. She'd always assumed that this first, unremembered loss, even before she was sent out on the train, was the root of her unhappiness. But perhaps she was no different from anyone who'd grown up with their real parents, with brothers and sisters and a shared last name. Perhaps her orphan status was just an excuse. For now she knew her mother's name and her father's name, knew all she needed to know, and she didn't feel any different.

She'd been so envious of Louise.

Out of the tub, her hair still dripping wet, she closed the bedroom curtain and turned on the electric fan, not just for its coolness but for its drone that would quiet the sounds coming in through the open window, the gunning motors and backfires in the street. She lay down, water-cooled and naked under the sheet, and tried in earnest to calm her mind. She needed to sleep, to make up for all the hours she'd missed that morning, and so she tried to think of her wraparound porch in Wichita. In just one week, she would be sitting in the front porch swing with Alan, drinking lemonade and looking at the big oak in the yard, and waving to neighbors walking or driving by. She would do as she had always done, and go back to the life she knew. But even as she tried to keep Wichita in her mind, even as she pretended the breeze from the fan was a cool autumn wind moving through her own front yard, her eyes, for some time, remained open, staring up at the low ceiling with the expression of someone still stunned.

When she finally slept, she slept long. She woke with hair dry as yarn, most of it matted between her head and her pillow. And she was hungry. Very hungry. She squinted at her watch and gasped, jumping out of bed. She was half dressed before she realized she wasn't late for anything. Louise was on her way to Philadelphia, accounted for until tomorrow afternoon.

She sat back on the bed, pulling her fingers through the tangles at the back of her neck. She had this night to herself, to do whatever she liked. For now, she would need to eat.

A half hour later, she was sitting at the counter of the luncheonette, waiting for Floyd Smithers to acknowledge her presence. She knew he was just pretending not to see her there; it wasn't yet the dinner hour, and only three other diners, an older couple and a businessman, were seated at the counter. Floyd moved back and forth between them, offering refills on coffee and clean ashtrays. Cora waited, patient, looking down at the menu, though by now she was more than hungry; she was so ravenous she couldn't think.

"May I help you?" he finally asked, standing in front of her. His face held no trace of a smile.

"Floyd." She put down her menu and leaned a little over the counter.

He looked over her head, scanning the restaurant. "Look," he whispered, only glancing at her. "Please don't make trouble for me here. I'm sorry, okay? Believe me, I'm sorry. And I know you're sore. I know."

She saw then how tired he was, the skin beneath his eyes lavender. It had been a long night for him as well.

"I don't want to make trouble," she said quietly. "I just want to tell you." She glanced over each shoulder. The older couple was laughing about something between them, something private. No one was listening. No one cared. "I just want to tell you," she tried again, "that Louise told me you didn't . . . that nothing happened." She could feel her cheeks heating up. "I was too hard on you. A little. I mean, you knew she was young. You shouldn't have had her sneak out and meet you like that." She met his gaze, taking in his long lashes, the faint sprinkle of freckles across his nose. "But thank you for getting her home."

She'd surprised him. That was all she could tell, looking up at his face, his young forehead creased as he took her in. The bell from the window to the kitchen rang, and he turned to pick up the order. Cora again looked down at the menu, her gaze lingering on a detailed description of something called *The Mega-Sandwich.* Thin slices of roast beef. Swiss cheese. Special blend of herbs and spices. Freshly baked bread.

Floyd reappeared before her, his expression somewhat softened.

"Just so you know," he whispered, "I didn't want the night to go like that." He tapped his writing pad on the edge of the counter, exhaling through his teeth. "I thought I would take her someplace grown-up, you know? Impress her? Well, I played the dope. I sure did. Second I get her in, she treats me like a kid brother. She's going off and talking to other guys, some of them, you know, pretty rough-looking. Way older than me, for your information, and I couldn't get her to leave. I couldn't get her to listen to me. I put my hand on her arm and she about bites it off. I didn't know what to do." He blinked slowly, tiredly. "I've never seen a girl drink like that."

Cora wanted to reach up and pat his head, the way she might do with one of her own boys after they had confided some heartbreak. She could imagine the scene at the speakeasy, the change in Louise once she'd gained entry, and Floyd's rising panic as he realized what he'd gotten himself into. He was older than Louise, but just all of nineteen, maybe twenty. An appealing and decent young man. Louise was, in her words, a little much for him. And yet he'd waited, maybe for hours, to make sure that she got home.

"I just wanted to get to know her." He frowned, rubbing a dishcloth along the counter. "And you weren't going to let that happen. You weren't going to let me take her out. I knew that. She's the prettiest girl I've ever seen. I've been standing here waiting for you two to come in every day, thinking about her all the time. I didn't know what else to do."

Cora nodded. He was right. She wouldn't have ever let him take Louise out. So he'd gone and managed it the only way he could.

"I'm sorry," she said. "I'm sorry about everything, the whole mess. And I'm grateful that you're a nice young man." She paused as long as she could. "And I'd like a Mega-Sandwich, please."

His dishtowel went still. "What?"

"A Mega-Sandwich." She pointed to the description on the menu. "And a glass of milk, please."

He looked at her oddly. She didn't care. She'd said she was sorry and she was sorry, but now she was so hungry she wanted to walk over to the older couple and pick the buttered dinner roll right off the man's plate.

She drank the milk down as soon as she got it, its coolness filling her stomach. Right away, she felt the corset squeezing in on her. But that was wrong, of course. The corset didn't squeeze. It didn't move. It was always the same. It was her belly that was getting bigger, expanding from just the glass of milk. She set her glass down and shifted on her bar stool, trying to take a full breath. She hadn't even eaten yet. She had, it seemed, two options: continued hunger, or, if she ate a full meal, the corset's further reprimand. The gnaw from the inside or the squeeze from the outside. Which was worse? She knew she was tired of hunger. That was what she knew.

■ ■ ■ ■

It was late afternoon when she stepped back outside, the Mega-Sandwich — which had been delicious — heavy inside of her, her breathing shallow to compensate for the tightness at her waist. As full as she was, she wasn't tired, and given the length of her earlier nap, she knew she wouldn't be for some time. The sun was low, obscured by buildings, but heat radiated out from the sidewalk and brick walls. She could go back up to the apartment, but she'd finished her book. She would have nothing to do. She could buy a magazine, she supposed. She thought she would be glad for the night off, the peace of it, but really, a night without Louise was the same as a night with Louise, and not so different from so many nights in her life — hours to endure, hours to just get through. How much of her life had she thought of this way?

She decided she would see a movie. She understood that almost any movie she could see would likely play in Wichita in a few weeks, and that she wouldn't be taking full advantage of her diminishing time in New York. But she only wanted to occupy herself, to sit in the dark and relative cool, staring up at a screen so large and close that whatever it displayed would seem like the totality of her own vision, another world made real. She walked down to a film house and chose a Buster Keaton series, hoping she would laugh or at least not think for a few hours. That was what she needed. Something light. And time to not do, to not think.

The theater didn't have a full orchestra, just a pianist and an oboist playing side by side on the far right of the stage. When the first reel began, both musicians smiled up at the screen, and their music was jaunty, upbeat. Keaton, playing the hero, found a wallet, returned it to the owner, and was accused of trying to steal it. He tried to buy furniture secondhand and was accused of stealing that as well. The oboe twittered. The piano bounced along. Cora heard people around her laughing, everyone getting the joke — Keaton was doomed to appear a criminal, no matter what he did. The pianist switched to more dramatic chords as Keaton, just lighting a cigarette, accidentally threw an anarchist's bomb into a police parade. The oboist came in with a spirited melody as the entire police force gave chase. Cora was still and quiet. She understood the movie was funny, simple, and that on another night, she might have laughed.

She was taking it too seriously, her dark mood infiltrating everything, even what was supposed to be easy and fun.

At the end of the short, Keaton somehow managed to herd the entire police force into the jail, locking them inside and leaving himself out, the free man he deserved to be. It was a good ending, Cora thought. But it wasn't to be. A pretty girl gave him a disapproving look, and that was all it took for him to unlock the door, releasing his mistaken pursuers. The freed police pushed Keaton into the jail, locking him in for good. "The End" was carved on a tombstone. People laughed, clapped, and hooted for more as Cora, glad for the surrounding dark, stared somberly at the screen.

It took her over two hours to walk. She could have taken the subway, but at first, when she started out, she told herself she was just going for a stroll. It wasn't that crazy of a notion. There was still plenty of light in the sky, and by the time she crossed Fifty-seventh Street, the air was cool enough for a mosquito to whine near her ear and then sting the back of her neck. By then, she was aware that she only walked in one direction, and that she had a destination in

406

mind. She walked quickly, keeping up with the traffic on the sidewalks, the deliberate walkers of New York. She passed block after block, building after building, street after honking, roaring street, aware of the gathering darkness of the summer evening, the hot and breezeless air, the blisters forming at the back of her heels, and most of all, the way she kept moving forward, her jaw finally unclenched, compelled only by a clarity so new and sharp it felt like joy.

She aimed the pebbles at the second-floor window, next to the door where he'd pointed. It was all she could think to do. She threw one after the other over the iron rails of the gate, but the window was over twenty feet away, and most of her throws missed the outbuilding completely. She did hit the metal stairway twice, and she worried about the sound it made, and whether the nuns were asleep. The street was quiet, with a car sputtering by just every now and then, the sidewalks almost deserted. Whenever someone did pass by, she would face the street, holding the remaining pebbles behind her back. She nodded briefly at women and ignored all men, repeatedly glancing down the street as if waiting for a taxi. But who knew what passersby thought when they saw her — a middle-aged woman with no ring and no escort, holding no purse, just standing on the street? She felt herself growing anxious. But it didn't matter what they thought. This was what she understood now. There was no rational reason to care.

The window was curtained, but she could see the glow of a lamp. She waited, watching for movement.

She took off her right glove for better aim. The next pebble hit his door. There was a light by the door, a single bulb in a lantern secured to the wooden frame. Winged insects wandered in its glow, undisturbed by her pebble. Her next shot glanced off the sloping roof. It was the corset, limiting the range of her arm. She remembered playing graces in the barn with Mother Kaufmann, how it sometimes seemed as if she'd willed the ring to sail up just right.

The next pebble hit the door.

He opened it. She held her breath. It occurred to her that even though he was balding, and not so tall, he would not generally be thought of as an unhandsome man, and there was a possibility that he would not be alone, and that she could be in for humiliation. He stepped onto the tiny landing and peered across the dark courtyard, half his face illuminated by the single bulb. She smiled, even then, even before he saw her. He held a book in one hand, his fingers sandwiched in the pages, marking his place. He waved his other hand through the cloud of insects. He tilted his head.

She waved.

"Cora?"

He held up his finger, asking her to wait, and disappeared behind the door. A moment later, he reemerged without the book. He trotted down the stairs, keys jingling, jumping over the last three steps.

"What good surprise," he said. Again, he looked so happy to see her. He was already searching through his ring of keys.

She leaned against the gate, each hand holding an iron rail, still warm from the sun. "I was just . . . I was just in the neighborhood . . ." She stopped. The lie was ridiculous. It was nearly dark. What would she be doing down here? No. She had no excuse this time. There was no radio to purchase, no favor to ask. The truth was this: she'd walked over sixty blocks for no other reason but that she'd wanted to see him. It didn't matter that she was leaving in a week. It was precisely because she knew she was leaving that she didn't have time to be coy.

"I'm free tonight," she stammered. "I

wondered if you were free, too."

That was enough. He nodded, unlocking the gate.

SEVENTEEN

He asked about the impressions around her waist, on her shoulders.

"This is from what you wear?" His fingers, rough against her skin, traced a curve from just under her breast to her navel. "It is so tight? This must hurt."

She was embarrassed. He'd never turned off the lamp on the table. It was just a reading lamp, but the dim halo of light reached the bed. Despite her best efforts to relax, to concentrate on what she herself was feeling and seeing, she'd been so aware that she was visible to him, not covered in darkness as she'd been with Alan. And now, after, it seemed her fear was founded: there was something strange about her naked body, something she hadn't known was strange. Did other women have marks from corsets? Cora guessed, just from his reaction, that his wife hadn't had marks. Immigrant women didn't always wear corsets, especially if they worked. But did other women like her have marks? There was no way to know. Even while giving birth to the twins, she'd had a sheet over her, draped to her knees. No one had seen her bare belly since Mother Kaufmann stopped giving her baths.

"You get used to it," she said.

He frowned, lying back on the pillow. But he kept his warm hand on the curve of her hip, and her embarrassment quieted, quieted more, and finally fell silent. This, she thought. This, more than any shame or worry, was what she would feel for some time, what she wouldn't get used to or forget: his shin scratchy under the back of her knee, only a glaze of sweat between. She lay perfectly still. The back of her knee could sweat and itch or catch on fire, but she wouldn't move it away, not while she was still willing her skin to soak up the feeling, so that she might not waste it all now, when it was almost too much, and in less than a week, never again.

And to think he'd apologized. For finishing fast, he said. He hoped she would give him another chance. He'd smiled, so she smiled, too, though she didn't really understand — nothing had seemed fast in comparison to what she remembered from those few, lightless evenings with Alan. And Joseph had kept his hands on her, his mouth on her, his gaze on her. She was annoyed with herself. In comparison, she'd been a rag doll, too shy, too uncertain, to do more than put her hands on his shoulders, to even glance at his eyes, and even that had taken such will.

She would need another chance, too.

His room was spare and neat and small. From the bed, she could almost reach out and touch a clean white sink with a water pump. On the other side of the sink, a small icebox sat on what looked like a nightstand. The unpainted walls were bare except for two pairs of overalls and two white shirts, each garment hanging from its own nail. He'd converted the closet to a bathroom, he explained — no tub, just a toilet. He put it in himself, having learned about plumbing when he helped install toilets for the nuns and the girls. The plumber appreciated his help and told him where he could find used pipes and a stool.

"The first time, I make mistake," he said. "Not enough insulation. I didn't know. The pipe was outside, and in January, it froze, burst. Ruined. So I do it again, this time right."

When she'd first come in, feeling as if she were about to jump from a great height, he'd offered her one of the two chairs at the little table by the window. He'd offered her peanuts, too, apologizing, saying peanuts were all he had. She assured him she wasn't hungry, that a glass of water would be fine. A shelf above the sink held two mismatched glasses, two plates, and just one sharp knife. His daughter came over on Sundays, he said. They both liked sandwiches. He bought cheese and cold cuts at the deli. Through the week, the nuns fed him, whatever the girls didn't finish. It wasn't so bad. Oatmeal for breakfast. Peanuts. Bread. They got donations from the Hudson Guild. Sometimes fruit, vegetables. Most of the grocers in the neighborhood were Catholic, generous with the nuns.

He asked if she ever got the letter from Massachusetts, if she'd found out anything else about her mother. She told him briefly about the meeting at Grand Central, the family in Haverhill she would never know. He asked questions, and he made it clear he was ready to listen to an expanded account, but she kept trailing off, distracted. Just the other day, she'd wanted so much to talk with him about Mary O'Dell, to have someone to confide in, but now that she was here, she was only thinking about how he was looking at her, the slant of gold in his right eye. And being alone with him in a small room. On the wall above the table was a bookshelf, or really, a row of books resting on a long board supported by metal brackets screwed into the wall, with two bricks serving as bookends. Sipping her water, she'd scanned the dustless spines. *Principles of Wireless Telegraphy. Electric Oscillations and Electric Waves. Essentials of English. Automobile Engineering, Vol. III. Roosevelt's Letters to His Children.* Some of the titles were in German.

She asked him if he missed Germany or being with people who were like him. It would be easier, she imagined, living where the language was his own.

"I miss it sometimes." He set his water on the table.

"You miss your family? Do you have siblings? Are your parents alive?"

He scratched the back of his neck. "That was not so good. My older brother was a difficult person. He and my father were the same. My mother died." He shrugged. "Greta is my family."

Cora nodded. "I'm glad you have her."

He laughed, sadly. "Me, too."

"But do you ever feel . . ." She tried to pin down what she wanted to know. "Do you ever worry that you're supposed to be

in Germany? You were born there. I understand your family was difficult. But they're
yours, your blood relations. I know your
daughter is, but all of your other relatives
are there."

He shook his head.

She'd thought that he didn't understand
her question, that her English was too
Midwestern, too slanted or too quick. She
tried again. "But you've had such terrible
luck in this country. You don't ever wonder
if it was all a mistake? If you were supposed
to stay there, with people who are your relations? Where your history is?"

He shook his head again, more decidedly
this time. "Germany is where I was born,"
he said. "Only that. I am supposed to be
where I go."

Not long after that, they were on his narrow bed, and she was helping him tug at
the buttons of her blouse. Even then, she
was full of dread, knowing what she had to
say, the words she had to actually speak.

"I can't get pregnant." She'd breathed it
out, her eyes closed. Really, this was the bigger leap, the harder one, even more than
just coming to his door. "I mean, I can. It's
possible, but I shouldn't. The doctor said.
Also, I don't want to."

She opened her eyes. He pulled his face

416

back from hers, looking alarmed, his spectacles askew. She heard the low horn of a ship.

"Okay. Sorry." He rolled off of her, facing the ceiling, his hands behind his head.

She sat up. He'd misunderstood. She had no time for misunderstandings. "I don't want to get pregnant, I mean. That's what I don't want."

He looked up at her, surprised again, and all at once she was falling, terrified of what he might be thinking. This was why Margaret Sanger and her talk of birth control was called obscene. It changed everything, what Cora had just admitted, to Joseph as well as herself: she had not come to his bed in a trance. She had not been seduced in a moment of weakness. No. She was lying here with him because she wanted to be, and wide awake enough to stop and think beyond the moment and know what she didn't want, as well.

He might think she was crazed, unwomanly. There were names for women, the kind of women, who said the kinds of things that she'd just said. She moved her arm across her chest, her unbuttoned buttons.

But there was no contempt in his eyes, no judgment. In fact, he looked as abashed as she did. "I have nothing." He held up his

417

palms as if to show this were true. "I'm sorry. I have been alone."

She waited. She couldn't say anything else. She'd already said more than she thought she could.

He cleared his throat. "I can . . . you want me to get something?"

She managed a nod. He laughed, and unbelievably, she did, too.

"You will wait here?"

She nodded again. What did he think she would do — go with him? No. No one would pay attention to him, whatever he bought, wherever he could buy it. She, on the other hand, would be treated differently.

"Fifteen minutes. Okay?" He stood, tucking in his shirt, and she understood he hadn't been asking her to come with him. He was only asking if she was willing to wait.

It was after he left that she let herself get a closer look at the framed picture propped up on top of the icebox. She'd noticed it when she first came in, but she'd thought it best not to inquire about it or even look at it too long, given the circumstances, and how unfair it might be to him. He hadn't known she was coming here tonight. As he'd said, he'd been alone in this room. Now that he was gone, she moved closer and saw the photograph was what she'd suspected: Joseph with a full head of hair, wearing a good suit, his hand on the shoulder of a seated woman who held a baby in a baptism gown. It was a formal portrait, and the two adult faces were somber, but the baby, not knowing the rules, seemed to be caught mid-laugh.

Right away, Cora felt the pressure of tears. Greta. A happy baby who couldn't know what was coming. Influenza. Her mother's death. Her father's long absence in Georgia. Loneliness. Probably hunger. The New York Home for Friendless Girls, even after her father's return. The next years would be cruel to all three of them. Cora didn't dare touch the frame itself, but she leaned forward to study Joseph's younger, unlined face and also, to look more closely at the wife and mother, who was fair-haired and a little stout, and even prettier than Cora had imagined. But she felt no jealousy, no selfish resentment or need to turn the picture away. She felt only a pained sorrow for this luckless mother with the serious eyes. If anything, the dead woman's youth and beauty seemed a reprimand, not because Cora was here now, the first woman in this little room, but because she'd waited so long to come here at all. She'd lived too much of her life so stupidly, following nonsensical rules, as if she and he, as if anyone, had all the time in the world.

They had to leave well before dawn, he said, before the nuns were up. He would see her home. Cora suggested going to breakfast. When he hesitated, she felt a punch of fear. Was it true, then, what she'd been told about men? Did they soon tire of what came too easily? She was being presumptuous and naive, perhaps, assuming he felt the same urgency. But in a few days, she would be gone.

"Breakfast would be good," he said, though he looked anxious, and only then did it occur to her that he likely hesitated because of money. Of course. She was a dolt. How insensitive could she be? He lived on oatmeal, peanuts, donated fruit. Since Cora had come to New York, she and Louise had gone to restaurants every day without giving much thought to the bill. She had money from Leonard Brooks, money from Alan. She could easily pay for breakfast for both of them, but she knew that even suggesting this would likely be a mistake.

"I have toast and jam at my apartment," she said. "And oranges."

He held her hand on the subway. Even

when they got off at her stop, the street-lights were still on. Only the eastern sky showed a faint streak of rose, and the streets were quiet enough that she could hear the first twitters of birds. They passed a burdened paperboy and a limping woman in a garish gown. But they were often alone on the sidewalk, which at that hour seemed so expansive and uncluttered, as if laid out just for them.

He left before noon. He had to see if the nuns needed anything, and he had his daily tasks. But if he worked late, he said, he could get ahead, and he would be free to come see her tomorrow morning. No, he said, his hand on her cheek. No, he wouldn't be tired.

Tomorrow then, Cora agreed, her fingers moving through the light hair on his forearm. She was already thinking of a meal she could make him, or buy prepared, something casual that she could pretend to just have on hand. He could come as early as ten-thirty, she said. Louise would be in class.

After he left, she went to work. She took a quick bath, drained the tub and filled it again to wash the sheets, holding a bar of soap under the faucet until it lathered. She wrung the sheets as best she could before hanging them from the curtain rod in the bedroom. She tidied the rest of the apartment, washing the dishes and cups, shaking the pillows free of indentations. Still, when it was time to leave for the studio, she was certain Louise would know everything, just by looking at her face: her cheeks and neck were still sore from his stubble, and as anxious as she was, she couldn't stop smiling. She was dazed, distracted by memory. On Broadway, the sun blazing above her, she walked right into the pole of a streetlight. "Watch yerself," said a passing man, unhelpfully, and two little boys moved in a wide arc around her, as if she were dangerous, or a drunk.

By the time Cora reached the studio, Louise had already changed into her street clothes, and she looked surprisingly alert for having just endured a dance class on the heels of a bus ride from Pennsylvania. But she barely glanced at Cora, and it seemed she truly had no memory of the difficult morning before she'd left.

"My God, it's good to be home," she announced as they climbed the stairs back up to street level. "I mean, Philadelphia is fine. It's certainly a step up from Wichita. A big step, God knows. The audience was wonderful, very sophisticated. You could tell they thought we were amazing. But it was so strange: I felt absolutely *bereft* not to be in New York, even for one night. I just feel so at home here." When they stepped out onto the sidewalk, she inhaled deeply, her dark eyes taking in Broadway, the windowed towers all around. "Isn't that something? That I could feel so attached to a place that's still new to me? It's not even where I'm from."

She didn't seem truly interested in Cora's answer, as she gave her no time to respond. As they walked, she talked about what a marvelous partner Ted Shawn had made, and the flesh-colored paint all the dancers had to wear so they wouldn't technically be half naked, how the paint smelled like witch hazel and how silly the whole idea seemed to her. Cora half listened, silently considering Louise's question about being so attached to a place. If it was strange, then Cora herself was guilty of strangeness — for now, even with all that had happened, she still wanted to go back to Wichita. She already knew that she would think back on these remaining days with Joseph for the rest of her life, with longing, with real grief. But she missed her home. She missed the quiet streets she knew so well, the unobstructed sky. She missed hearing her name called out by friends she'd known for almost twenty years. After the loss of the Kaufmanns, the town had taken her in and made her feel a part of it. She wasn't an outsider there, and even now, that meant so much.

In any case, she had to go back. Of course she did. Her boys would be back for college breaks, and their home would need to be as it always was — with her in it, making them hotcakes and asking about their lessons and games and plans. And even without the boys, it wasn't as if she could just leave Alan. He was her family, every bit as much as her sons were. He'd lied to her, yes, but he'd also taken care of her, and he'd been a devoted father. If she left him now, there would be a scandal and then, perhaps, suspicion. He would have to marry again, and hope for his life, his very life, that his new bride would be as naive as Cora had once been, or as loyal as she was now.

They weren't far from the apartment when she realized Louise was looking at her, taking her in. Cora's glove went to her stubble-scrubbed cheek. The dark eyes felt penetrating.

"What?" Cora asked, glancing away.

"How long have you not been listening? My God. I guess I've just been talking to myself."

"I'm sorry, dear. What is it?"

"I *said*, Miss Ruth said I could move in the day after tomorrow. I thought you would like to know."

"Thank you." Cora feigned a smile. Friday. Her last day. There would be no reason she could give to stay longer. She could tell the Brookses she wanted to leave in the morning. Saturday, then. She would have three more nights in New York. She imagined herself on the train, looking out the window and seeing the same fields and towns and rivers she'd passed coming east with Louise, uncrossing every bridge she'd crossed. She could buy a new book for the journey, something light and distracting. By Sunday night, she would be home.

Louise was quiet as they walked past the luncheonette. Cora watched her glance through the big windows to the counter in the back. She did look somewhat remorseful, or at least put out that a friend had been lost.

"You might go talk to him," Cora said gently. "Try to patch things up."

Louise kept walking. "He hates me, I imagine." She moved her bag to her other shoulder. "And I told you. He's not my type."

Cora, still looking ahead, cleared her throat. "But you let him think he was, Louise. You hurt him. And still, he saw you home. You might thank him. And apologize. Or at least say goodbye."

Louise stopped walking. Cora did, too. An old woman grumbled and moved around them.

"What do you care?"

Cora sighed, fanning away a fly. A ridiculous question. Of course she cared. She cared about Floyd, but more than that, she knew it would do Louise good to consider someone's feelings besides her own, and not to fear real kindness and caring. All these weeks they had spent together, she'd known Louise needed mothering, someone to fill in where Myra, apparently, had left off long ago. Still, Cora saw now that the whole time they'd been in New York, she'd focused on all the wrong things — what the girl wore, if she went out alone, whether or not she could wear rouge. Nothing that mattered, not in comparison with what Louise truly needed by way of instruction and example. Louise was already capable of kindness — it was she, after all, not Cora, who'd given those men water that first night in the city. And even now, it was clear that Louise wasn't glad to have wounded Floyd, and that although she didn't love him, and probably couldn't, she at least missed him a little and perhaps understood she'd done him a wrong. It was a last opportunity, Cora thought. Now that they were about to go their separate ways, even now that she understood how much Louise had been wronged in her own life, Cora wished she would have spent more time on the essentials: when to say thank you and sorry.

"I think you feel bad." Cora tilted the brim of her hat. She was aware of people moving around them, as if they were rocks in a quick-moving stream. "I can see it, looking at your face. You know you should go talk to him. You know it's the right thing to do."

Louise looked at the sidewalk, pushing her hair behind her ears. The pout seemed real, not for show.

"Right now? I'm all sweaty from class."

"You look fine. You smell fine. You know you do."

"You'll let me go alone?"

"For one hour." Cora rubbed the edge of her glove against the mosquito bite on her neck. "You'll come back to the apartment in one hour. And you'll go nowhere else. Do I have your word?"

Louise looked at her dumbly.

"Your word, Louise. Your promise. I'm trusting you. One hour?"

"Fine."

"Your word?" Cora wanted to drill the concept home. "I have your word?"

"Yes. Yes, okay?" She seemed more flustered than annoyed. "Yes. You have my word."

Cora nodded. "Good luck then." She turned and walked on alone.

The apartment wasn't much cooler than the blazing street. Cora walked back to the bedroom, turning on the fan and immediately taking off her blouse and skirt and corset. She started to put on her tea gown but changed her mind — just her thin robe would be cooler. And she was tired. The sheets were dry, swaying in the breeze from the open window. She took them down from the curtain rod and made up the bed neatly, smoothing out wrinkles with the flat of her hand. Tomorrow. Tomorrow she and Joseph would lie in this bed, in these very sheets still warm from the sun. How long would they have? Three hours? Four? There might be time, as well, to talk, to go out to the front room and eat with him, or to just lie in bed with him as she had this morning, skin against skin. The feast before the famine. She put the folded blanket at the foot of the bed, unpinned her hair and lay down, her eyes still open. The water stain on the ceiling no longer looked like a rabbit's head. She couldn't imagine why she'd thought it ever had.

Two knocks. Then four.

She stood up, annoyed, tying the sash of her robe. She'd hoped Louise would take advantage of her full hour of freedom, if only so she herself could have a full hour as well. But she made herself pause before she opened the door. She should show appreciation and approval: Louise had kept her word.

Her expression quickly changed to surprise, however, for Joseph, not Louise, stood before her in the entry, his face grave. He was unshaven, but wearing a clean shirt and overalls, his cap stuffed into a side pocket. A large canvas bag was strapped to one shoulder, and someone small stood behind him. Cora couldn't see this other person, just a thin arm wrapped around his thigh. At the end of this arm, a hand clutched a wad of overalls above his knee.

"We have left the home," he said. "This morning. We move out." His voice was friendly, casual, but his eyes were locked on hers, with the look of an adult speaking in code for the sake of a child. "I need to say this to you. I worried you would go to the home."

Cora stared, silent. He'd been caught. They hadn't left early enough this morning. A nun had seen them. Or one of the girls had seen them and told.

"Please come in." She stepped aside and gestured into the apartment. She, too, was communicating with her eyes. He had to come in, she was saying, and bring in the small person who she knew must be his scared little girl. She was so sorry. It was her fault. It had all been her idea. Her lark, her freedom in a different city. And now he'd lost his job. Their home.

"It is all right," he said. "I have a friend in Queens." The arm around his leg went tight, and he spread his feet to keep his balance. "He works now, but we go there at five. He is a good friend. It is all right."

"Please come in," she whispered. "Please."

He limped in as if he had a wooden leg, the child still clinging to him. "Come on now, Greta," he whispered. He tried to free himself, using his fingers to unclench her hands.

Cora, behind them, could see the child now. The top of her blond head reached his belt. She wore a mustard-colored dress patched under the arms, her hair cut to her

430

chin. Her face was still pressed against his hip.

"Sorry," he said, turning back to look at Cora. "She is not always so shy."

"It's fine." Cora closed the door gently. Even as she moved past them, she wasn't able to see the girl's face. She wasn't sure she could bear to. "Are you hungry? Is she hungry? I have toast and jam."

The head popped out from behind him, so suddenly that Cora smiled. The child, however, did not. She had a pretty face, like her dead mother's. Cora continued to smile, though her heart lurched inside her. *I have been you,* she wanted to say. *It's all right. I have been as scared and as small.* She had to work to keep her face and voice composed. "I have strawberry jam. Do you like strawberry jam?"

Greta looked up at her father.

"You will like it," he said.

Cora moved to the kitchen and put six pieces of bread in the oven. She wished she had something better to offer, something more substantial. Had they gotten to eat that morning? Had the nuns just thrown them out? She peeked out of the kitchen. "Do you like oranges?"

Greta nodded. She was still standing close to Joseph, staring at the picture of the

431

Siamese cat. She would remember this, Cora thought. She would remember this day of upheaval, the strange details, the visit to the unknown lady's house, the unknown lady wearing a robe and loosed hair in the middle of the day. The child would never see Cora again, but Cora would be part of the day's painful memory, the unknowing and the fear.

She brought out two peeled oranges on a plate, setting them on the table. She went back to the kitchen to get glasses of water, and by the time she returned, Greta had already stuffed half the orange into her mouth. She was chewing as fast as she could, her little cheeks full, her lids aflutter over her pale eyes. When Cora set her water glass down, Greta grabbed what was left of the orange and put it in her lap.

"Slow down," Joseph cautioned. "You do not want to choke."

"And there's plenty," Cora added. She held on to the edge of the table, crouching low. "We have more oranges. And you can have all the toast you like. No need to rush." She smiled, but looking at the girl, the sharp bones of her face, Cora felt the sting of tears. What did she think — that a pathetic meal of toast and oranges would make up for the harm she'd done? All of this was her

432

fault. She'd gone to Joseph's on her own, without being invited. All because of what she'd wanted. Now she could go back to her easy life, and they would have to pay the price.

Joseph touched her arm. "Really. It is all right," he whispered. "We can go to Queens. I just did not want you to think —"

She nodded, wanting to believe him. Maybe it would be fine. Maybe he would find another job and be able to keep his daughter with him. He had savings. She could try to give him money. She already knew he wouldn't take it.

When the toast was ready, Greta, who had already eaten two oranges, devoured a piece slathered with jam.

"I tell you you like jam," Joseph said, and he and the girl exchanged smiles, which were similar, Cora noticed, with matching overbites. He looked at Cora. "We talk?" He tilted his head toward the kitchen.

As Cora stood, she leaned down toward Greta. "You can take the jam with you," she said. "The whole jar." She almost touched the girl's thin arm, but thought better of it. It would do no one any good if she lost her composure.

She led Joseph through the kitchen to the bedroom. She saw the made bed, the clean sheets she'd just been lying on, dreaming of tomorrow, the meeting that wouldn't come. She continued into the bathroom, wanting to be out of Greta's vision, out of her hearing. By the time she turned around, she was crying outright, cool tears on her cheeks.

"The nuns saw me leave?" she whispered. "Is that why?"

He moved toward her. "I only tell you so you will know. I did not come to make you cry." His hand moved to her cheek and then down her hair.

"It's my fault."

"No."

"Why did the nuns make Greta leave? She didn't do anything."

"They did not. They want to keep her, but I say no. I want to keep her with me."

She nodded, suddenly exhausted, depleted. Yes. He was right to insist. If they put her on a train, she'd be gone.

"You can stay with this friend in Queens? You can go there? You're certain?"

"Ya. He is good friend."

"For how long? How long can you stay there?"

He shrugged. He was putting up a front, she thought. He was scared. He must be.

"Where will you work? Who will look after her when you work?"

434

He looked down, his thumb and forefinger kneading the skin above his eyebrows. Even with the window open, cars moving by in the street, the apartment was quiet. From the bathroom, two rooms away, she could hear the clink of the knife against glass, Greta helping herself to more jam. Cora listened, as pained as she'd been as a young mother, distraught by the wails of one of her boys in another room. This was just a different kind of wail: quiet, cunning. Greta didn't believe the unknown lady would really let her take the whole jar with her, so she would eat all she could now, even if she was stuffed. Cora understood. She'd done the same during her first meals with the Kaufmanns. She'd eaten mashed potatoes until her stomach ached; she'd hidden entire biscuits in the folds of her skirt, sneaking them off to her room.

The knife again scraped against the jelly jar, and it was then, at that very moment, that the answer came to her, a ringing bell in her head. She drew in a deep breath and held it. Of course. She heard the engine of a truck, the cooing of pigeons, yet the world felt still, silent. She put her hand on Joseph's shoulder. She was already certain, every part of her. It was him she would need to convince.

"Come with me," she said.

He frowned. "Where?"

"Wichita. Bring her. We have a big house. Empty rooms." She watched his eyes. She would have to speak before he did, to lay out the reasons before he sealed off his mind.

"It's how you could stay with her. How else can you? We have an entire floor, unused. She could go to school."

He was already shaking his head. "Stop this. I will not take charity from you."

But it wasn't charity. Not at all. How could she make him see what she was just now seeing so clearly? What did she have in Wichita, now that the boys were gone? Lunches at the club? Dinner parties? No. She was meant to help this child. She'd learned nothing at Grand Central, nothing of who she was supposed to be from poor Mary O'Dell. And why should she? All this time she'd had the Kaufmanns. She had them even now, as if they were in the very room with her, pushing her on. *We'd like you to come live with us and be our little girl.* She remembered Mother Kaufmann wearing her bonnet, crouching low. *We have a room all set up. Your room. With a window, and a bed. And a little dresser.*

"Of course you would earn your own living, Joseph. You could get a job there, a good one." She heard the desperation, the pleading, in her voice. She was pleading for herself. She wanted to help this child as she'd been helped, but she also wanted more time with him, just to see, just to see. At least some part of her believed she deserved that.

"My husband has influence. He could help you find a job, and when you're working, I'll look after her."

He looked at her as if she were crazy, as if nothing she was saying made sense. "Why would your husband help me?"

"Because he owes me." She understood the truth of this as she said it. "And because he's kind." She put her hand to her mouth. She understood how outlandish the idea must sound. She was asking him to take a blind leap, his daughter in tow. He didn't know Wichita. He didn't know Alan. And really, he didn't know her, certainly not well enough to put his fate, his daughter's fate, in her hands. And she didn't know him any better. Then again, how well had she known Alan when she'd taken her leap with him? And they had done everything according to custom, with the long courtship and the engagement party, the approval of his family and the Lindquists. With all that carefulness, all that custom, she'd been soundly duped. Didn't she already know more about Joseph, really? Or at least as much as anyone could?

"You can always come back. If Greta isn't happy, if you aren't happy, you can just come back." She kept her hands at her sides. She wouldn't touch him now — she didn't want him to misunderstand. "I'll give you return train fare. For you and for her. I'll give it to you before we go, so you'll have it. You could come back, and you'd be no worse off than you are now."

She looked at him, waiting. She couldn't think of what else to say, how else to persuade him. It was arrogant, perhaps, presuming she was what Greta needed. But she thought she could be. And what had the Kaufmanns known? What had they presumed with her? She just wanted a chance to try. If she had to, she would get on her knees and beg.

She heard steps out in the hallway, then the rattle of a doorknob. Her hand went to her throat; the front door wasn't locked. Louise. She had kept her word. Cora tightened the sash of her robe as she moved quickly around Joseph. She had to get to the front door. She worried that Louise, startled, would scream and scare Greta.

That was her only thought.

When she reached the front room, Louise was standing in the open doorway, giving the table a puzzled look.

"Cora." She was impressively calm. "Who is the little girl under the table?"

When she turned, her eyes went wide, and Cora knew Joseph must have followed her through the kitchen, that Louise was taking them in together, as well as Cora's robe and undone hair. She looked at Louise and opened her mouth, thinking a helpful phrase would come to her, but nothing was right.

"Cora?" The black brows moved high.

Cora lifted her chin, her only answer. There was too much to be careful of, too much to complicate just for the sake of her pride. If Joseph said yes, if he and Greta came to Wichita, she would need to come up with a plan, some idea of what she would tell neighbors and friends. She didn't yet have an exact plan, so it was best to say nothing, to not give any story just yet, even if it meant she had to stand there dumbly while Louise's expression slowly changed from utter shock to thrilled amusement, the beginning of a howling, ridiculing laugh. That was fine, Cora thought. She could endure it. Withstanding it would be the beginning of her penance, fair punishment for her blindness and all the stupid things she'd said. She would bear the mortification and recover. There might be so much good to come. For now, she at least owed Louise this moment of cackling delight.

■ ■ ■ ■

PART THREE

■ ■ ■ ■

"Is it your idea, then, that I should live with you as your mistress — since I can't be your wife?" she asked.

The crudeness of the question startled him: the word was one that women of his class fought shy of, even when their talk flitted closest about the topic. He noticed that Madame Olenska pronounced it as if it had a recognised place in her vocabulary, and he wondered if it had been used familiarly in her presence in the horrible life she had fled from. Her question pulled him up with a jerk, and he floundered.

"I want — I want somehow to get away with you into a world where words like that — categories like that — won't exist. Where we shall be simply two human beings who love each other, who are the whole of life to each other; and nothing else on earth will matter."

She drew a deep sigh that ended in another laugh. "Oh, my dear — where is that country? Have you ever been there?"

— EDITH WHARTON,
The Age of Innocence

I'm not intimidated by anyone. Everyone is made with two arms, two legs, a stomach and a head. Just think about that.

— JOSEPHINE BAKER

EIGHTEEN

Home. Their train got in just before noon. At the station, Alan kissed Cora on the cheek, looking at her just long enough for her to see the anxiousness in his eyes. But he was friendly, welcoming Joseph with a handshake and pulling a lollipop out of his vest pocket for Greta. On the way to the car, he asked about the train ride and apologized for the misery of Wichita's latest heat wave, glancing at the cloudless, expansive sky. "Della has a fan going in every room," he assured them, as if he were perfectly used to his wife giving him three days' notice, via telegram, that she would be coming home with guests: in this case, her long-lost brother from New York, as well as his motherless daughter. When they got to the car, Greta was scared to get in — she'd never ridden in one before — so Joseph sat close to her in the back and quietly answered her questions: Yes, this was

Wichita; they would soon be at Aunt Cora's house. Yes, she would have a bed there. The tall man who was driving? That was Aunt Cora's husband, Uncle Alan. Cora, sitting in the passenger seat, turned to give Joseph what she hoped was a reassuring look — which he appeared to need — before she stole a glance at Alan. Before they left New York, she'd received his terse reply, which said only that he would have Della prepare the boys' rooms as she requested. Now, as he drove, he continued to make conversation, pointing out the library and city hall to Joseph and Greta, joking that Wichita's modest skyline probably wasn't what they were used to. When Joseph spoke, saying it looked like a good town, Alan made no remark about his accent. But Cora had no idea what he was thinking — he had always been so polite. Perhaps he was happy for her, or bewildered. Perhaps he believed the lie.

It was only later, after the luggage was carried into the house and Joseph and Greta were offered food and then shown to their rooms to rest, that Alan asked Cora if he might have a word with her in his study. There was no way to tell by his voice or expression if he was angry or not. She said she would be there in a moment — she needed a glass of water, and did he need one, too? No, he said. But thank you. Even after he shut the heavy door to the hallway and they were seated in the leather chairs on either side of his big desk, he was quiet, clearly waiting for her to speak. She sipped her water and looked at his shelves of law books, the ink blotter on his desk. She didn't know how to begin. She knew him well, and he knew her. But in regard to so much, they had not had an honest conversation in years.

"So," he said finally. "A lot happened on this trip."

She nodded. Upstairs, she could hear footsteps, Greta's excited voice. Cora guessed she was discovering the little balcony off her room — it was Earle's old room, his *National Geographic* magazines still stacked on the desk, the pennants of various football teams hanging on the walls. If Joseph and Greta stayed, Cora decided, she would move them up to the third floor, so the boys could have their old rooms when they came home for holidays.

"You're certain this man is your brother?" Alan asked. "How did you find out?" He frowned. "You don't look anything alike."

She turned to the window. Despite the bright afternoon, heavy curtains, almost pulled closed, gave the air the feel of dusk. Years ago, she'd often sneaked into this very room when Alan was away, rummaging through his drawers and papers to find proof of her dark suspicions, proof of Raymond, proof of all she already knew. After so many successful hunts, after she'd found the engraved watch, the poems, she finally stopped coming in here at all, as it made no difference what she found or what she didn't. They would go on aching with love.

"He's not my brother," she told Alan now. "But that's what we'll tell everyone." She said this plainly, with no threat in her voice. But she'd said it as she'd planned, as a statement, not a question. She would not pretend he could tell her no.

Alan stared.

She smiled.

"Oh God, Cora." He did not smile back.

Clearly, she'd surprised him. As if it were so hard to believe.

"You're . . . involved with him?"

She shook her head. "Not now. I was, but not now."

She did her best to explain. She and Joseph had decided they would be friends, only friends, at least until he got on his feet, until he and Greta weren't so desperate. Cora had made this stipulation — she had

446

no interest in being, once again, the recipient of a man's feigned desire, a necessary tool for his survival to be flattered and placated. So she would help without expectation, and without any intimacy that might make their arrangement unseemly, or a humiliation to them both. Once he had a job and savings, he could go, maybe back to New York, and she would wish him well, knowing she'd helped to keep him and his daughter together. That was her first concern.

In any case — she had insisted, and he had agreed — they could only decide what they might be to each other when they were on equal footing. And so on the train home, even while Greta was sleeping, they'd been careful not to touch, not to graze arms or even look at each other for too long. She'd meant what she'd said, and his agreement was real. But even just sitting next to him, she'd felt as if the hairs on her arms were standing up straight, as if reaching for him in spite of her.

"Cora." Alan's voice, strained and angry, jarred her thoughts. "What did you tell him?"

When she didn't answer, he slapped his hand on the desk. She flinched, her smile gone.

"This is your lover? Are you mad? What have you told him about me?"

She was disappointed that he only thought of himself, that he couldn't think of her at all. But she saw the fear in his eyes.

"Alan. He doesn't care."

He shook his head. Even in the dim light, she could actually see the color leave his face, starting with his broad forehead, then his clean-shaven cheeks, his cleft chin.

"He doesn't, Alan. And he's got nothing over you. If he . . . told anyone, which he wouldn't, we would be exposed. He's not my brother. We would be charged with lewd cohabitation. We'd all be arrested."

"Your punishments would hardly equal mine."

She put her hand on the desk, leaning forward. "He could lose his daughter. And he won't put you in jeopardy. He understands, Alan. Don't worry. It'll be all right. I just want to give them a chance here. Maybe they won't be happy. But we want to see. It's the only way we can know."

She sat back in her chair. Perhaps she shouldn't have told him the truth, if only to save him the worry. After all, she would have to lie to Howard and Earle. She would need to keep lying to Greta. But she needed Alan's support, or at least his complicity.

Without it, her lie would be more suspicious — no one in Wichita, save Alan, even knew she had come to Kansas as an orphan, or that she'd been born in New York. But if Alan stood by her, if he were the one to tell people the story of her hard beginning and her joy at finding her brother at last, fewer questions would be asked.

"What's he going to do here? Does he have any money? You expect me to support him?"

"I want you to help him find a job. It might be difficult because of his accent. But you know so many people. You could help him. He'll take any job. And he's good with wiring, machinery."

"What about the girl?"

"I'll look after her." Again, she smiled. On the train, Greta had continued to literally cling to her father, but there was a long stretch in Missouri where she and Cora had sat together, counting barns, and after a while, Greta fell asleep with her little blond head on Cora's lap. She'd swallowed the story whole. Aunt Cora. Her long-lost Aunt Cora who would take them to Kansas and keep her and her papa together.

Alan shook his head. "You're going to let her keep thinking she's your niece? You're going to keep lying to that child?"

"We have to. There's too much risk if we don't."

"How long do you plan to keep this up? What about when Howard and Earle come home? You're going to lie to them? Your own sons? You're going to tell them this man is their uncle? Uncle Joseph from Dusseldorf?"

"He's from Hamburg." She met his gaze. "And we've been lying to our sons for some time. Being truthful now would just confuse them about our marriage, about so many things."

He looked away. She felt no triumph. There was no pleasure in shaming him. But he had no right to shame her. Didn't she deserve some kind of happiness? Even if she had to lie? Surely he saw the logic in this. She would make him see.

"I need your help," she said quietly. "You owe me that. You know you do."

He frowned. She understood his distress. Even if she could convince him that Joseph would do him no harm, he was certainly considering how their lives, their home, would change. For years now, he'd kept up his charade, requiring her assistance and discretion, and he'd repaid her with caring, with the boys, with pretty clothes, and with the stature of his name. He must have hoped that would always be enough.

"It might be nice to have more people in the house." She looked down and rubbed her neck, still sore from the long ride on the train. "I was thinking, perhaps we could entertain more." She waited. "Perhaps . . . Raymond could come to dinner sometime."

He stared at her. She stared back. She wasn't negotiating. She didn't need to negotiate, and they both knew it. She still had him over a barrel. But she wanted him to understand that any happiness she might gain in this new arrangement would only work in his favor. Really, if she could have this chance, what did she care if Raymond Walker came to dinner? For twenty years now, she'd known he and Alan were still seeing each other, still risking everything for their secret visits. Their letters and gifts to each other had caused her so much pain. But now she felt decidedly neutral, unwilling to judge or impede. For wasn't she just as determined to risk disgrace, even arrest, to find out if she and Joseph could love each other? It only followed, then, that what she felt for Joseph was what Alan felt for Raymond, what he couldn't forget or ignore. What had once embittered her now filled her with sympathy, even admiration. She could only hope that if her risks were as great, she, too, would find a way.

Alan drummed his fingers on the ink blotter. "You're going to tell people you're German?" He squinted. "Are you German? Did you find that out? Did you learn anything about your parents?"

"Nothing that matters." She shrugged. "Let's say my father was German. My mother, too. She died in childbirth in New York. But they were married. I was legitimate." She looked at him evenly. If she was going to invent a story, why not invent one that would make things easier, not just for herself, but for Joseph and Greta, and keep things easy for Howard and Earle? "Let's say that when I was a baby, I was left in the care of a relative, and my father took my older brother back to Germany. Joseph immigrated back before the war, and I tracked him down in New York."

She watched Alan's face. She could see he was turning the story over, shaking it out. If there were any holes, he would find them first, as a good lawyer and a practiced liar.

"So how did you come to live with the Kaufmanns? What will you say?"

"The relative in New York died. I came to Kansas on an orphan train." She sighed. "I don't care if people know about that. It's the least of my concerns."

Alan blinked. "I'll say." He appeared dumbfounded, his lips parted, his gaze searching her face as if he wasn't quite sure who she was. She understood. Their life, his life, had required so much careful planning on his part, every decision calculated for secrecy and survival, every argument and justification rehearsed well in advance. And now she'd gone and ambushed him, coming at him with her own desires and plans. He would need some time to get his bearings, to comprehend that yes, this mutiny was real. But she couldn't help but feel they'd reached an understanding, or at least the beginning of one. She would force him to help her if she had to, but she would rather keep his love. She was quiet, but she looked back at him in such a way that he might know this for himself. She was careful not to smile. She didn't want him to hit the desk again. But really, she was just so happy to see him, so happy to finally be home.

Within the week, Joseph was working a press at Coleman Lanterns, where Alan had put in a good word to a former client. His shift started well before dawn, and so on a muggy morning in early September, it was Cora who walked Greta to school on her first day. Greta wore the pretty blue dress that Cora had bought for her at Innes Department Store, and her blond hair was clean and combed. Cora assured her that she would like school, that her teachers would be friendly, and that many of the other girls would be nice. "If anyone isn't, ignore them," she said. Greta looked up at her with somber eyes, and Cora worried she'd made the child nervous for no reason. After all, in her pretty new dress, Greta might simply blend in. She was shy and unsure, but she had no accent, and even if other parents had heard that her father was German and that she'd just come in from New York, there was a chance no one would care. People were more open-minded than they'd been when Cora was young, and Wichita was a good-sized town, with people coming and going all the time. Greta might make friends. Besides, even if she didn't, she would be all right. She'd survived her mother's death, after all, and her years at the orphanage. If the other children did isolate her, she would be able to bear it, just as Cora had.

Still, when they got to the school yard, which was already full of laughing, running children, and Cora caught sight of Greta's young teacher standing in the shade and waving to them, she felt her heart flutter. It was so strange — she didn't remember feeling so much worry with Howard and Earle, even when they were young. Perhaps she'd just known her own boys would do well, buoyed by each other and their comfortable years at home. Greta, still so thin, just seemed more vulnerable. She didn't know if this was how the Kaufmanns had felt, why they tried so hard.

"When will I see my papa?" Greta asked. "When will he come to get me?"

Cora, hearing the fear in the girl's voice, crouched as low as she could and smiled. "Your father works until five tonight, and you'll be home by then. We'll all have dinner together. Uncle Alan is picking up a special dessert, because you're being so brave. And I'll be standing here at three o'clock, right when you get out. If you like, we could get a pop on the way home. You can tell me all about your day."

She kissed the hot top of Greta's head and nudged her toward the gate. It was the best she could do. There was no sense in assuring her that she would have a good day, or, for that matter, a hard one; Cora didn't know what lay in store, for this day or any other. She could only promise to be there at three, to console, to celebrate, or to strategize, to help this child as best she could, to hold her hand and lead her home.

In late October, the first cool night, Joseph came to her room, knocking softly, saying nothing, only looking at her, waiting; but she'd been awake, turning in her bed, and when he reached for her hand, she pulled him to her. By then, he was paying rent to Alan and helping with groceries and household expenses. He didn't make anywhere near what Alan did, and his contributions would not have been missed. But he had not touched her, or even tried, until he had money of his own. So by the time he did, she was both comforted and thrilled, knowing that when he came to her, it was out of pure and genuine desire. Her want for him was as pure. They wanted nothing from each other but each other — no children, no security, no social approbation. What was between them mattered to no one else. No one else, besides Alan, and likely Raymond, even knew.

Still, it astounded her sometimes, the madness of what she'd done. She kept thinking they would all be found out, or that she and Joseph would become disenchanted with each other, or that Greta would decide not to love her, or that Alan would refuse to go on.

But none of these things happened. No one in town voiced suspicions. Viola Hammond only chided Cora for never mentioning her being born in New York, and she praised her for doing the Christian thing and taking in her niece. Alan's mood improved after Joseph tinkered with the car's engine until it no longer made a worrisome ticking sound, and it further improved when Raymond finally accepted one of Cora's many invitations to dinner. Raymond, who had by this time lost most of his red hair, was quiet at first, watchful — especially with Cora. But he got along well with Greta, and after a while, their evenings settled into an easy routine: Alan had, in fact, purchased a radio over the summer, and after dinner they would all go to the parlor to listen to a show or music. Cora noticed that Alan and Raymond rarely looked at each other or spoke to each other directly, and Cora perceived this as a well-honed strategy she and Joseph might borrow. When there was dancing, she danced with Alan. Never Joseph. (And never Raymond — that seemed a mutual understanding.) They kept up the act even in the house, so as not to confuse Greta. Still, it was enough just to have Joseph nearby, to hear his voice, even when she didn't look at him.

And they managed. The child slept soundly, and there was a lock on Cora's door. Even after Joseph had to get up and go back to his room, leaning over to kiss her good night, Cora would lie with her eyes open, content, and listen to the quiet house. In time, she would decide what she'd done wasn't madness at all. Was it mad to at least try to live as one wished, or as close to it as possible? *This life is mine,* she would think sometimes. *This life is mine because of good luck. And because I reached out and took it.*

Alan advised that there was little point in telling anyone what Louise had said about Edward Vincent. He agreed it was worrisome that Vincent was still teaching Sunday school, but if Louise refused to attach her name to the complaint, then Cora could only go to the church leaders with a vague accusation. Vincent wasn't likely to be let go over the matter, and if Cora confronted him directly, she would only succeed in making an angry enemy.

"Given our domestic arrangement," Alan added, "we might choose our enemies with care."

But Cora had to do something. Feeling

cowardly, she sent an anonymous letter to Vincent's office. She used plain stationery, and wrote the words with her left hand:

Stay away from the girls in your
Sunday school class.
We are watching you.

She didn't know what would come of this attempt, and it didn't seem like enough. But the following Sunday, the minister announced that Edward Vincent had decided to focus on business matters and spend more time with his family, and the church was looking for a volunteer to instruct young people on moral matters. For a moment, Cora considered raising her hand. Since her return from New York, she had been giving a great deal of thought to moral matters, and she would have liked the opportunity to share some of these thoughts, not to mention a few questions, with the young Presbyterians of Wichita. But she knew this wasn't the kind of instruction the minister expected. She doubted she could do as he wished. Given how she was living, if she taught the hard rules and fearful stories that she herself had been taught as a child, she would be as big a hypocrite as Edward Vincent. So when the minister looked down at her, sitting in the pew between Alan and Joseph, she politely averted her eyes.

In 1926, a nineteen-year-old Louise Brooks, still a relatively unknown actress, was cast as the leading lady in *A Social Celebrity,* opposite the well-loved Adolphe Menjou. When the film opened in Wichita, Cora and Joseph went to see it, and they brought along Greta, who at ten was almost as tall as Cora's shoulders, her hair even blonder from so many summers in the Kansas sun. But she insisted, to both her father and Cora, that she had a clear memory of the pretty black-haired girl she'd met briefly in New York when she was six. She'd been eating toast and jam, she said, and she'd hidden under a table when the pretty girl came in, and the girl had been laughing about something. As if those details weren't proof enough, in the theater, the moment Louise appeared on the screen, Greta breathed in, sharp and quick, clutching Cora's arm. "That's her!" she whispered. "Aunt Cora, I remember! She looks just the same!"

Joseph gently shushed her. Cora couldn't respond. She stared, openmouthed, up at the screen. There was Louise, the dark eyes flashing under the bangs, and then the bright, familiar smile. Cora was not at all surprised that Louise had found success, but it was still so thrilling, so startling, to see a person she knew in a real movie. But Greta was wrong — Louise didn't look exactly as she had that summer. Her hair was cut even shorter than it had been, and her face had grown slightly more angular, thinner, more like her mother's. Her eyes were heavily lined, and shadow darkened her lids. She played a flapper, a plucky girl who wanted to go to New York to become a dancer. That was hardly a stretch, of course, but her acting, in Cora's opinion, was solid. And no matter which way she turned, no matter what her expression, her luminous face beckoned to the eye. When she was in a scene, it was hard to look at anything else. She wore simple outfits at the beginning of the movie, and at the end, a low-cut beaded gown, her pale neck unadorned.

The next day, a gloating *Wichita Eagle* quoted a New York critic's review: "There is a girl in this picture by the name of Louise Brooks. Perhaps you've never heard of her. If not, don't worry. You will."

All at once, it seemed, her picture and her name were everywhere. Her posed portraits appeared in *Photoplay, Variety,* and *Motion*

Picture Classic. Sometimes she stared sultrily at the camera, and sometimes she smiled sweetly, her hair and pale skin always showing up so well in black and white. Even before her next film came out, the professional gossips started to track her. There were reports of her dining at expensive restaurants, dancing in clubs, and then there were rumors of her being seen around New York with Charlie Chaplin, who, the articles frequently noted, was not only married, but twice her age. The magazines also reported that just a few years earlier, Louise had been a Denishawn dancer until she was kicked out because of a bad attitude. She'd quickly become a Ziegfeld girl, still underage but living high and free at the Algonquin Hotel until the Algonquin kicked her out for lewd behavior. Of all the bob-haired, knee-showing flappers on the screen that year, it seemed Louise Brooks was the one, in real life at least, who was truly wild and rebellious. Howard wrote to Cora that he'd impressed his new classmates at law school by telling them he'd not only gone to school with Louise Brooks — his dear mother had chaperoned her for an entire summer. "The fellows were all jealous of me," he added. "But none could say they envied you!"

As well they shouldn't, Cora thought. She

saw it even more clearly now — that summer in New York, she may as well have been charged with trying to hold back the wind, or time itself. Even then, Louise had been a force. But when they were sharing that hot little apartment and Cora had made Louise scrub the paint from her face, she'd truly believed she was not just doing the right thing, but the only thing she could do. And like a well-trained parrot, over and over, she'd warned Louise of the dire consequences of a sullied reputation. Just a few years later, Louise's reputation had been soundly sullied by the popular press, yet the only consequence, as far as Cora could tell, was more movie roles and greater fame.

Still, she couldn't shake a feeling of worry, that same hesitant concern that had nagged her that summer in New York. Had Louise been happy to leave Denishawn? If not, what had she done to get herself kicked out? Had she gone out drinking? Was Louise satisfied being Chaplin's newest young mistress, or did she hope for something more? She was being silly, she told herself. Louise didn't need her concern, and likely wouldn't want it. In every magazine photograph, she appeared confident, with a savvy glint in her eyes. Cora supposed it was just as likely that Mr. Chaplin would be left feeling used — or that they would leave each other, unharmed. As young as Louise was, she was a grown woman, a modern woman, smart and fearless of judgment, a lovely sparkle on the blade of her generation as it slashed at the old conventions.

Within a few years, the movie house by Alan's office had a bold-lettered sign that read *Starring Wichita's own Louise Brooks!* which they added to the marquee whenever one of her films came to town. On the screen, Cora noticed, Louise often moved like a child, skipping, twirling. She perched in older men's laps, eyes wide, and she still regularly employed her pout. The gossip in the magazines, which portrayed a very different Louise, must have perplexed her fans. Cora wasn't surprised when she read that Louise was bringing a lawsuit against a photographer for circulating a picture in which she wore only a draped scarf, an entire nude hip on display. Louise defended her position to reporters, explaining that she had posed for the pictures when she was a chorus girl, but now her profession was very different. *"I have embarked on a serious career as a motion-picture actress,"* she explained, *"and I fear it will injure my chances of success in my new profession to have those draped photographs of myself scattered about the country. In my new profession I am called upon to play many innocent heroines, girls who are models of modesty and respect for all the time-honored conventions. In fact, my directors tell me that these are the roles for which I am preeminently suited. It would be too great a shock, I fear, for moviegoers who had admired me in one of these roles to come across a photograph of me as I looked when I posed before Mr. De Mirjian's camera wearing only a carelessly flung scarf, and sometimes a pair of sandals. The contrast would be certain to destroy or weaken some of the illusions of innocence and unsophistication my acting had created."*

She went on to clarify that she felt no shame for having posed for the pictures, which she believed were artistic and tasteful, and appropriate for a chorus girl. She pointed out that a low-cut gown might be perfectly acceptable for evening, but the same gown would be indecent in the afternoon. The gown was simply inappropriate for a given situation, not fundamentally incorrect.

"She could practice law," Alan chuckled. "She would do very well, I imagine."

Cora had to agree. Louise's argument seemed right for the times. Lately, it was hard to know what would be considered ap-

465

propriate or out of bounds from one day to the next. Two years earlier, hemlines had fallen again, almost to the ankles, but now they were back at the knee. And that summer in Wichita, the Ku Klux Klan's baseball team challenged the Negro League's Monrovians to a game, umpired by white Catholics, who wouldn't have an allegiance to either side. Cora, who feared violence, didn't attend, and she didn't let Greta go, either. But Joseph and Raymond and Alan went, and there wasn't any violence. For years, the three men would be able to brag that they were there watching the night the Monrovians beat the Klan, 10 to 8.

Even more surprising, at least to Cora, was the news that Myra Brooks had left her husband, as well as her two younger children still living at home. There were rumors of another man, but that could have been just rumor. What was known was that Myra was working in Chicago, writing a weekly column on health and beauty and psychology for a magazine no one had heard of. The women in Cora's circle were horrified, to say the least. One autumn afternoon, when Viola and Cora were addressing envelopes for the League of Woman Voters, Cora made the mistake of mentioning Myra's name.

"What that woman has done is despicable," Viola hissed, every other syllable marked with the tap of the pen on the table. "If she was unhappy with her husband, that's one thing, but I can't understand a woman leaving her children. Theo is being sent off to military school. Some relative is taking care of little June." She paused, making a weak attempt to lick an envelope. "And Zana Henderson is actually defending her! 'Giving her side,' is what she said. Apparently, Madame Brooks never wanted to be a mother. She wanted to be a writer, an *artiste,* and she felt she'd denied herself long enough." Viola shook her head, then stopped, reaching up to fix a pin that had slipped from her bun. "Well, I disagree. Maybe Myra didn't want to be a mother, but that's what she is, and she needs to act like one. I know Zana and Myra were great friends, but a *crime* has been committed against those children."

Cora was silent. Viola was angry, and right to be angry. But again, Cora knew what she knew. She finished addressing an envelope, aware that Viola was watching her, waiting for her to speak.

"It's true," she finally said. "What Zana said, I mean. At least that's what Louise told me once. Myra didn't want children, and she wasn't happy with Leonard." She met Viola's offended gaze and looked away. "But I don't disagree that it's very sad. I feel awful for Theo and June."

"I'll say it's sad. And I'm sorry, but I don't understand all this sympathy for that woman. I don't see what could be so wrong with Leonard Brooks that she would have to leave him. He's seemed decent enough whenever I've met him. And he certainly makes a good living. Zana said that Myra complained he was 'demanding and inconsiderate,' but I never got that impression from him. Everyone I've talked to thinks he seems a perfectly nice man. But even if it's true, she should have discovered that about him before she married him. If he's really such an ogre, she might have noticed."

"Do you think she meant sex?"

Viola was silent. But it was clear from her expression that Cora should not have wondered the question aloud.

"I just mean that perhaps that's what Myra meant." Cora stacked her envelopes neatly. "Maybe not. But if that's the case, she wouldn't have known what she was getting into, not in that respect. She was young when she married. That's all I meant."

Viola picked up her pen, her eyes still on

Cora. Her hollow cheeks had turned pink. "Goodness, Cora. I can't believe you just said that."

Cora made no reply. It would be unwise to continue, to join Zana Henderson's losing battle to defend, or at least understand, Myra's leaving. Cora wasn't sure why she'd bothered as much as she had — she didn't even like Myra Brooks. But then, she, too, had been a very young bride, with no understanding of what she was getting into, what the marriage, and the relations, would and would not be about. Cora had managed her escape in secret, but Myra hadn't had the luxury. She couldn't judge, now that she had Joseph. If Myra had meant sex, "demanding and inconsiderate" seemed a miserable combination, perhaps worse than nothing at all.

But no one could defend Myra once Ethel Montgomery's cousin in Michigan mailed her a handbill with Myra's picture that advertised: *Myra Brooks, youthful looking mother of film star Louise Brooks, to speak on beauty and health this evening.* It was soon discovered that Myra, riding the tide of Louise's swelling fame, had landed a spot on the Redpath Chautauqua circuit, giving lectures on how she had nurtured her famous daughter's poise and beauty — and how she managed to keep her own. The women of Wichita wondered aloud if Myra, when lecturing on her maternal wisdom, ever mentioned that she'd abandoned Louise's younger brother and sister, or if, because only Louise's name was lucrative, she didn't mention her other children at all.

They could only guess what Louise herself thought about any of this. By then, she was truly famous and unreachable. Her name was on the screen with W. C. Fields's, and the magazines were reporting that she was to marry her newest film's young and handsome director. Soon, the magazines were describing the newlyweds' beautiful new home in California, and lavish parties with caviar, and picnics with famous friends at the Hearst castle. Louise was photographed with her new husband in evening gowns and, when she visited New York, various fur coats.

That May, Greta came home from school and, after taking a bite of the apple that Cora had just handed her, announced that no girl she knew felt sorry for June Brooks, even if her mother did leave her.

"She gets to go to Hollywood," Greta explained, still chomping the apple. "She gets to live with Louise for the whole summer. I told June I met her sister in New York, and that I'd like to come visit, too. She said she would see. Her brother Theo gets to go there, too. Everybody says they'll be living in a mansion, probably with a pool and servants, and that Louise's husband is so rich he has six cars, and there'll probably be all kinds of movie stars just lounging around the house."

Here, Greta sat in one of the dining room chairs, her scraped knees crossed, her chin raised, as if she were an elegant woman posing poolside. Cora smiled. Greta was still shy at school and at social events, but in private, she had a theatrical streak.

"What happens at the end of the summer?" Cora asked. "Is June going to come back?"

Greta shook her head. "She's going to school in Paris. I forget the name, but when our teacher heard it, she said, 'My my, it must be nice to have a movie star for a sister.' And Louise is going to visit her in Paris all the time because she's so rich she can go back and forth across the ocean the way most people cross the street."

Cora was impressed, not with the money, but with the decency of the gesture. If someone would have told her, back in the summer of 1922, that her surly and scheming fifteen-year-old charge would soon be rich and famous, she would not have been so astounded. But she would never have guessed that in just a few years, Louise would not only be happily married, but also stepping in to care for her younger siblings, taking up where her mother left off. Cora admitted that she'd perhaps been wrong to worry. Louise, with all her boldness and blitheness, really was doing just fine.

But then everyone seemed to be faring well in those last, easy years. Earle got married in St. Louis, and though he was still in medical school and didn't have much money, the bride's parents splurged on a wedding with over three hundred guests, complete with a small orchestra and prime rib at the reception. Howard was Earle's best man, and Greta was the flower girl. Toasts were made to the couple's future, and though the police commissioner and the mayor were in attendance, no one seemed to care that one of the punch bowls was spiked with gin.

Joseph managed to get himself hired at one of the airplane factories — this was back when Clyde Cessna and Walter Beech were just men you might see on Douglas Avenue, and few understood what they, and the young industry, would become. Joseph started as a janitor and held that position for a year before someone let him start tinkering with an engine. He made an impression quickly. When the University of Wichita announced a new degree in something called aeronautical engineering, the company paid for him to go to school. He started to earn a good salary, and Ethel Montgomery asked Cora if her brother was "in the market," as she had a widowed sister in Derby. Cora explained that unfortunately, her brother's dying wife asked him to promise never to marry another, and Joseph, bless his heart, had agreed.

"That's so romantic," Ethel said.

"Yes," Cora said, "it is."

That afternoon, she told Joseph about her lie. "Women love to feel sorry for a man," she warned. "Now they'll all be after you." He thought this was very funny. They were alone in the house, so he kissed her.

It seemed good fortune was all around, like air you breathed but didn't notice. Stocks were high, rain fell as needed, and the future seemed bright and clear as the summer sky. It was 1929. All across the nation, bright young flappers danced to jazz, and every little breeze still whispered Lou-

ise in magazines and movie houses.
Of course, the wind was about to change.

NINETEEN

During the worst storms, they sealed the windows with tape and stuffed rags soaked with paraffin under every door. Still, the dust got in. Cora could taste it on her lips when she woke. She'd give the house a good sweep first thing in the morning, and three hours later, there'd be a new layer on the floor, so thick she could see her own footprints. Dust coated the dials on the radio, the papers on Alan's desk, and the dishes in the cupboards. Joseph would rinse off the lenses of his spectacles, and a few minutes later, he'd have to do it again. They couldn't leave food out. Della did her best with the wash, but on bad days, when the wind was so thick with it you couldn't see across the street, the buses would stop running and she couldn't come. When the schools closed, Greta stayed home, and she and Cora worked together, armed with wet rags and brooms. As the weather turned warm, they swept out not just dust, but spiders and centipedes. And that was in the home, their sanctuary. Outside, the wind stung the skin and eyes and chipped paint off fences.

They were far better off than most. Alan continued to make a good salary, and as he'd always been cautious with investments, they didn't lose much in the crash. Joseph took a deep cut in pay at Stearman, but by 1934, there were military contracts for training planes, and his pay went back up a bit. It was the farmers and their families who kept suffering, dry year after dry year. Sometimes, Cora would consider that she was likely sweeping some Oklahoman's home and livelihood off her living room floor. Cattle were starving, or suffocating, and people had no choice but to abandon their homes and make their way to the city. There were men selling pencils or Salvation Army apples on every corner of Douglas Avenue, and more than once, travelers with hunger-dulled children had come to Cora's back door, asking for food. She and Della would go to work, making sandwiches with whatever they had on hand.

Even some of Cora's friends and neighbors were having trouble, albeit of a milder sort. Viola Hammond and her husband, having lost so much in stocks, took in two boarders to help with their mortgage. The Montgomerys sold their Cadillac and bought a Buick Standard. The gardening club disbanded entirely, as by then, everyone had given up their flower beds to the dust. But many people didn't seem affected at all, even as the rain didn't come and the stocks didn't climb and a Democrat was sworn in as president. Cora still went to lunches and teas, where she and the women she knew wore white gloves and Florentine hats and the new, shin-skimming dresses with belted waists and bolero jackets. By then, even the older women were no longer wearing corsets, and it was easier to eat and breathe and move, but even the more-forgiving girdles were miserable in the heat. One broiling summer morning, after more than eleven straight days of hundred-degree temperatures, Winnifred Fitch, whose husband came from a prominent meat-packing family, rented out a theater and had the manager set up lamps and a long table on the stage so she and seven other ladies could eat a catered brunch in air-conditioned comfort. The cool air awakened Cora's appetite, and she ate five slices of fresh honeydew melon, savoring every bite.

After the caterers cleared the plates, Winnifred, seated at the head of the table, cleared her throat and stood. She was in her early fifties, just a little older than Cora. But they didn't know each other well, as the Fitches had only recently moved to town from western Kansas because — unbelievably — the air in Wichita was better.

"Thank you so much for coming today." Winnifred smoothed the front of her dress. "I know I invited you ladies here under the vague premise of social aid, and I promise you that if, on your way out, you can spare a few quarters for the mason jar by the stairs, I'll see that they get to the soup kitchen at First Methodist. But I should tell you I didn't call you all here today to collect a few quarters." Here she paused, pulling back her padded shoulders. "Ladies, I organized this brunch in the hope that we might band together against an enemy that all the soup kitchens in the world can't conquer, an enemy that preys on all of us, rich and poor alike."

Cora dabbed at the corners of her mouth, looking up with anticipation. If Winnifred Fitch had a solution to the dust, she certainly wanted to hear it.

But Winnifred looked grave. "As a newcomer to this community, I have been shocked to see . . . obscene items displayed where the general public, including innocent children, can see them. Contraceptive devices, I mean. It's my impression that in these difficult times, druggists have become so desperate for revenue that they've let their moral standards slide. I have a feeling even you more urban ladies aren't pleased it's become so difficult to protect your children and grandchildren from the vulgar implications of these displays." Her gaze moved around the table. "Virginia. Cora. I believe you both have teenage daughters?"

Virginia nodded. "I have three girls still at home," she said. "And I couldn't agree more with your concerns."

Winnifred, and everyone else, looked at Cora.

"Greta's my niece," Cora said.

She didn't elaborate. She understood she had not answered Winnifred's real question, but it hardly seemed wise for her to tell these women that she had no problem with condoms on display in the drugstores. In fact, just a few weeks earlier, Cora had actually mentioned these new displays to Greta, casually saying that if a girl and boy *did* find themselves in need of "birth control," to borrow Margaret Sanger's phrase, they would likely do well to avail themselves of a druggist's regulated merchandise, rather than take their chances with something purchased under the table in a pool hall or a gas station. Greta, usually so voluble, had gone mute with shock and then embarrassment. ("Aunt Cora! What kind of a girl do you think I am?" she asked. "The kind I love," Cora replied.) But Cora thought the conversation necessary, as Greta was now eighteen, and she had a serious boyfriend.

"Ladies," Winnifred continued, "I've invited you here today because I've been told that each of you is well connected and respected in the community. It's my hope that you'll each sign your name to a petition against these sorts of displays and advertisements, and that you'll work with me to create a decency code for downtown."

Up and down the table, there were murmurs of agreement and nodding heads. Cora fidgeted with her napkin, unsure what to do. She'd just enjoyed all that fresh melon and a glass of tea at Winnifred Fitch's expense; she couldn't very well excuse herself now. But she hadn't dreamed this brunch would be a call to arms against condoms. Really, Cora thought, the druggist's displays weren't so very startling. For years, *McCall's* had been advertising Lysol as a "feminine hygiene aid for nervous wives," and everyone knew what they were really promising: no pregnancy and no disease. Cora's doctor warned that it was all non-sense: Lysol wouldn't stop a baby and could likely do serious damage to a woman. That warning was fine for Cora, who, as a married woman, had the alternative of a prescription diaphragm — once she worked up the nerve to ask for it. But what about someone like Greta? Cora was actually relieved that these days a girl, or at least her beau, could walk into a drugstore and find what was needed. It wasn't that she wanted Greta to have intimate relations at seventeen — Cora didn't think much of the boyfriend. But young people would be young people, whether the druggists got rid of the displays or not. Just the week before, Cora received a solicitation letter from two Wichita doctors hoping to start a charity home for unwed mothers. The doctors wrote that some of the girls they wanted to help were very young, and that they came from good homes and bad.

So during Winnifred's speech, Cora was quiet. She listened to the ticking of her watch and focused on the feel of the theater's cool air against her skin. There was no point in arguing with a table full of women who seemed as certain of what was acceptable and what was not as Cora herself had once been. Cora wouldn't be able to change their minds, certainly not over brunch. She would only be ostracized. All she could hope was to manage her escape without actually signing anything.

Ethel Montgomery cleared her throat. "We might do better to stand against all types of immorality," she offered. "Did you know there's a current movement to legalize beer in Kansas so long as it's of a certain weakness? They aim to do away with Prohibition here, too. Winnifred, I'm certainly sympathetic with your concerns, but I think we could work to uphold temperance as well. It seems to me these two issues are two sides of the same leaf."

Cora worked not to sigh. The rest of the country had already deemed Prohibition a failed experiment. But Kansas hadn't yet budged. Still, the *Wichita Eagle* estimated that the city's inhabitants drank two hundred gallons of illegal alcohol a day. So much for enforced temperance. Two sides of the same leaf indeed.

The caterers were quietly filling glasses with water, and Cora recognized one of them as Della's youngest son, who was around the same age as Howard and Earle. She smiled, but he either didn't see it or pretended not to.

"I like your thinking," Winnifred said. She took her seat, whispering a thank you as her own glass was filled. "But that's a more expensive fight. The wets are well funded and well organized. I know most of us are hard pressed right now." She paused with a wry little smile. "If we want to take on alcohol, we'll have to get creative. Is anyone here related to a millionaire? A shipping magnate, perhaps?"

There was polite laughter. Viola, sitting at Cora's right, gave her a friendly nudge. "Cora knows Louise Brooks."

Cora turned and stared at her blankly.

Ethel Montgomery rolled her eyes. "Somehow I doubt she would support a ban on obscenity."

"She doesn't have any money anyway," added Virginia. "She declared bankruptcy, I thought. She told the papers she had nothing left but her wearing apparel."

Someone else clucked her tongue. "All those furs. Poor thing."

Cora looked at the ceiling, the sandbags and ropes, the dark stage lights. When Louise was still living in Wichita, when she was just a pretty black-haired girl performing anywhere her mother could book her, she may have twirled and jumped across this very stage for applauding classmates and neighbors. Cora looked over her shoulder, at the rows of empty seats.

"How could she be bankrupt?" Viola shook her head. "I knew she'd divorced, but she got married again, didn't she? Some millionaire in Chicago?"

"She left him," said the woman who'd clucked her tongue. "That marriage was even shorter than her first."

"If she's bankrupt again, she might go back to him. That's what her mother did."

Cora lowered her eyes. Myra was back in town. Her children were all grown, but she was living with Leonard again — just the two of them in that big house on North Topeka. Cora heard she'd simply run out of money, and that her health wasn't good. Everyone thought it was generous of Leonard to have taken her back.

"Louise Brooks won't have to go back to anyone," Virginia said. "If she divorced another millionaire, she should be set up nicely."

"I hope so for her sake. What is she now, thirty? Already twice divorced. That would make a man think twice. And Hollywood seems to have tired of her. She hasn't been in anything in years."

Winnifred smiled faintly. "Perhaps even Hollywood doesn't want to hold up as an example a woman who takes marriage so lightly. Now regarding the fundraising —"

"It was the talkies," Virginia said. "That's what I heard. She didn't have the voice for them. A lot of the people who were big in the silents just looked good. Now you've got to sound good, too. It's a whole different style of acting. That's why she had to make those films in Germany, to try to get a little more mileage out of her face. She didn't have a voice for sound."

"She has a fine voice," Cora said. "There's nothing wrong with her voice."

Every face turned toward her. Viola raised her brows.

"And she's been in talkies," Cora added. "*It Pays to Advertise* was a talkie."

"I forgot she was even in that," said Viola. "That was the last one she was in, wasn't it? And that was four years ago."

"Which one was that?" Ethel asked. "I don't know that I saw it."

"Carole Lombard was in it. She was the lead. Louise Brooks just had a side part." Viola turned back to Cora. "So what was it? If it wasn't her voice, why did she go bankrupt? Used to be you couldn't go to the theater without seeing her face, and now you don't. Where'd she go?"

"I don't know," Cora said. "I'm not in

contact with her." She looked at the center of the table and raised her voice. "Sorry. I only know she has a good voice. I don't know anything else."

No one replied. Cora realized she'd perhaps spoken more forcefully than she'd planned. She didn't want to keep sitting at this table. She scooted back her chair.

"Cora?" Viola touched her knee. "You're not leaving? Don't. We were just asking. Are you upset?"

Cora shook her head, tight-lipped. She was upset, but she wasn't yet sure she had a right to be. They weren't asking her anything about Louise that she hadn't wondered herself. But then, she had been wondering without any glee, while these women were clearly pleased that Louise, once so high above them, seemed to have fallen so fast. Now they wanted the story, details. Cora had none to give.

"I just need to be on my way," Cora said, rising to her feet. "Thank you for the brunch, Winnifred. What a treat to dine in this cool air." She forced a smile, pushed in her chair, and started toward the stairs to the right of the stage.

"Before you go, you should sign the petition." It was Winnifred, calling after her.

Cora moved down the steps, watching her

feet in the dim light. So much for her quiet escape. But maybe a little honesty was called for.

"No. I think the drugstore displays are fine." She paused, pulling on her gloves. "But thank you for brunch, anyway."

Without looking up, she opened her purse, took out six quarters, and dropped them into the mason jar at the edge of the stage. There was no sound but coins against glass, echoing through the theater, and then her clutch snapping shut. A little dramatic, maybe, but that was fine. This was, after all, a theater. As she made her way up the carpeted aisle, the women behind her were quiet, waiting. She breathed deeply, taking in all the cool, clean air that she could, knowing she'd soon be outside.

She might have left the brunch early anyway. It was a Friday, and Joseph would be home by noon. He'd long ago arranged to get to work early every morning so he could have Monday and Friday afternoons off. He'd told the lead engineer he was an early riser, and that he liked those solitary hours, just before and after dawn, when he could tinker with the engines and wings and landing gear in silence. He was good enough at his job that this preference was indulged without much inquiry. No one put together or cared that Della only came to the house on Tuesdays and Thursdays. If a widower wanted to get off work early twice a week so he could relax at home while his married sister kept house, that was no one's concern.

When she walked in, the house was silent and, with the fans running and the curtains in the parlor closed, almost comfortable.

"Hello?" She stood in the entry, brushing off her skirt. "Joseph?"

"I am here." He appeared in the front room's doorway, wearing trousers and a clean T-shirt. His hair was still wet from the shower, which he'd built onto the bathtub earlier that year — he didn't like the dust in the bathwater. Now everyone in the house took showers instead of baths, mostly to save on water, though Cora didn't miss scrubbing the beige waterline from the tub.

"How was the ice-cold brunch?" He moved toward her and leaned in to kiss her, smelling of mint. "Did your tea freeze in your cups?"

Instead of answering, she stepped away, glancing into the parlor and then the dining room.

"No one is here," he said. But he didn't move toward her again.

"I'll just go round to make certain." She

unpinned her hat and smiled. "Have you eaten?"

She wasn't always the cautious one. Sometimes it was Joseph who had to remind her that their privacy was never certain. A friend could stop by. A neighbor might glance through a window. And there was always the possibility of their greatest fear — Greta coming home early. But the high school was far enough away that if Greta ever fell ill in the middle of the day, she would need to call for a ride home. And for the last two summers, she'd worked part-time in Alan's office, filing and answering the phone. Cora had asked Alan to call at once if Greta ever left the office early, especially on a Monday or Friday. Alan, always the gentleman, had agreed without question or comment.

Over the years, Cora and Joseph had spent a good portion of their limited private moments anguishing over whether or not to tell Greta the truth. But it always felt too dangerous. When Greta was twelve, she and her friend Betty Ann Wills had a terrible row after Betty Ann, left alone in Greta's room while Greta finished chores downstairs, read enough of Greta's diary to become upset with the way she'd been described. The girls exchanged angry words, and after Betty Ann left, Greta was inconsolable, tearfully insisting to Cora that her diary was for her private thoughts, and that what she'd written hadn't been meant for Betty Ann's eyes. Even as Cora agreed and comforted her, she was relieved Greta hadn't been able to write anything far more damaging in her diary. Joseph and Alan agreed it was proof they had to keep lying to the girl they all loved. Betty Ann Mills might have held all their lives in her grubby, ten-year-old hands.

But the longer they waited, the less likely it seemed they would ever be able to tell her the truth. Now she was almost an adult, and she'd grown up believing Cora was her blood relation, her aunt. Greta didn't look anything like Cora; she was blond and tall and still so thin, which caused her great distress, as curves were back in fashion. But she once pointed out, quite happily, that she and Cora had similar noses and hands. "I know from pictures I look like my mother, at least in the face," she told Cora. "But it's nice that I look like you, too. And your mother died when you were a baby. You and Papa both know how I feel."

There was no telling what the news would do to her, or what she would do with the news. Every other member of the household mistrusted Greta's boyfriend, Vern, as he had made a long but as yet unsuccessful campaign to convince Greta to abandon her plans to go to university after graduation. Joseph had made the strategic decision not to get into a tug-of-war with the young man, and so no one overtly voiced his or her dislike for Vern. Greta still considered herself very much in love, so it seemed likely that if and when she learned the truth about her aunt Cora, she might confide in Vern, even if they asked her not to. Vern seemed to Cora capable of great spite, and they would all be in that much more danger.

And so they'd kept on with their secret, even at home. They knew they might be making a terrible mistake, and that if Greta discovered them by accident, she might be irreparably wounded. Then again, as of now, she appeared happy, and it seemed reasonable to suppose that if they didn't tell her, she might very well stay that way. After all, Howard and Earle had grown up with a lie.

But it was fair to say that year after year, Joseph and Cora's happiness was compromised, keeping their secret not just from Greta, but from almost everyone. They could go on walks or to movies or to the theater together, anything a brother and sister might do. But they couldn't hold hands, or use each other's names too often.

They might have gotten away with dancing, but they didn't try. She once complained to Alan how wearying it all was.

I'm sorry, Alan had said. I'm so sorry.

It wasn't what she'd wanted or what she'd meant. Alan was still her great friend, and now, her only confidant. She didn't blame him. On the contrary. She meant to say she understood.

"You are upset? The brunch was not good?"

Joseph reached over and touched her cheek with the back of his fingers. They were sitting on the couch in the parlor, the heavy curtains shutting out the sunlight. There was a time when these afternoons alone always began with a rush upstairs, to his room or hers. Sometimes they still began that way. But more often than not, they just wanted to spend their time sitting close and talking, his hand free to rest on her leg, her head free to lean on his shoulder.

She turned to him and smiled. She was upset, but she'd tried to hide it. They only had a few hours together, and she didn't want to waste them complaining about Winnifred Fitch's brunch. But she was still thinking of Louise. In truth, she was worrying, which seemed as silly as it always did. Louise was likely fine. She could be moving on to another marriage to another millionaire. And perhaps she'd grown tired of Hollywood, and not the other way around. That seemed entirely possible.

In any case, Cora hoped she was fine. It occurred to her, just then, sitting next to Joseph on the sofa, that this hope for Louise was something to be proud of, proof she hadn't belonged at that brunch. A thought came to her. It was just an idea, a wild thought. But already, the annoyance and confusion she'd felt that morning shifted into a restlessness that didn't feel bad. A grasshopper, undistressed by their presence, moved slowly up the opposite wall.

She lifted her head. "I got a letter from some doctors the other day." She saw the worry on Joseph's face and took his hand. "No no. Nothing about me. I'm fine. I just know one of them from the club. He and another doctor, and a donor who wasn't named . . . They're starting a home for girls in Wichita who are . . . well, who are pregnant and not married. They're trying to get a board of directors together." She watched the ceiling fan spin, Joseph's hand warm in hers. He was a patient listener, which was so helpful at a time like this, when even she didn't know where she was headed. "They'd like to have a woman on the board. Mostly fundraising." She smiled. "They said they wanted a woman of good repute, which was why they contacted me."

He reached down and squeezed the flesh of her hip. "Good repute," he said.

She pretended to fluff her bobbed curls with the flat of her palm.

"They only write you?"

"I don't know. No one mentioned it at the brunch this morning. But then, unwed mothers aren't a popular cause."

He drummed his fingers on her leg. As clean as he was, as hard as he scrubbed when he came home from work, his nails were usually lined in black. Oil from the engines.

"You are wanting to do this?" he asked.

"I don't know." She stared up at the fan. It would be taking on so much. But then, Greta would leave for college next year. Already, Cora spent most of her days reading. Howard and his wife had a new baby, but they lived in Houston. Earle and his wife had no children yet, and in any case, they were in St. Louis. "I'm forty-nine years old," she said. "I'm not sure I should be starting up with something I don't know anything about."

He smiled. "I have felt this way."

She pressed her forehead against his

shoulder. Of course. She'd forgotten. She rarely thought of all he'd lost, how he'd had to start over, following her out here with nothing but his daughter. He'd not only climbed back up — he'd climbed higher. Prohibition was still alive and well in the state of Kansas, but he was free to go back to New York, or just about anywhere, and start brewing again. But now he loved working on the planes, the constant puzzles and challenges each plan presented. He didn't want to go back to brewing, he said. If Kansas legalized alcohol tomorrow — they both knew this was unlikely, but if it did happen — he might stop at a bar and have a beer now and then. Otherwise, his life wouldn't change.

She lifted her head and looked at him. His head dropped to the back cushion of the sofa, and wisps of dust rose up.

"All right," she said, fanning the air above his face.

The doctors, good men that they were, wanted to call the home Charity House. They thought it was vague enough to appeal to potential donors, with no specific reference to the clientele. And they already had a house — from a woman who had willed it to the doctors, knowing their intent. It was a gigantic Victorian, all gables and porches, sitting on two acres just out of town.

"Charity House sounds like Dickens," Cora said. Like *The New York Home for Friendless Girls,* she thought. *A Home for Fallen Women.*

"How about Monica House?" asked the younger doctor. "Saint Monica? She was a mother."

"Too Catholic," the older doctor said. "Sorry."

The younger doctor was Catholic.

"How about Kindness House?" Cora asked.

The doctors frowned at each other.

"It's a bit . . ." The older doctor shook his head. "Sorry. It's a bit twee."

"Kindness isn't twee," Cora said. "Sweetness is twee. Not kindness."

She looked from one man to the other. Both were kind. Neither was twee. "I'm just thinking that idea should be the cornerstone of our mission. Our guide."

"What idea?"

They both looked at her, waiting. She tried to think. There was just one way to say it. "Well, that . . . compassion is the basis of all morality."

The younger doctor smiled. "You read

Schopenhauer, Cora?"

"A little." She smiled back. "He's often right, isn't he? But I don't know about Compassion House."

The older doctor shook his head. "If we say 'compassion,' people will hear 'passion.' That's not what we want with this population. No. That's no good."

It was difficult work, raising funds for Kindness House, especially in those early, lean years. Lots of people had a hand out for good causes, and, as some of Cora's rejecters plainly told her, she was competing with charities that served completely innocent children, who'd done nothing to deserve their suffering. Unwed mothers, one woman at the club told Cora, had sealed their own fates. "I feel sorry for the babies," she told Cora. "But the girls chose to uncross their knees."

"Some of them, certainly," was all Cora said. She would gain nothing with impoliteness. But it hurt her to hear the mothers talked about this way, especially after she got to know a few of them. She and the doctors had hired a house manager, along with a teacher and a live-in nurse, and Cora didn't help with the day-to-day running of the home. But she often stopped by just to

see what was needed, and though some of
the residents saw only a middle-aged woman
in hat and gloves whom they didn't want to
talk to, others seemed pleased to have
someone smile and ask how they were.
There were girls as young as thirteen, as
well as two women in their thirties. Clearly,
some were from good homes. A few sounded
more educated than Cora, though the girl
who seemed the brightest — a former college student — admitted being duped by
the claims of Lysol. Some of the home's
residents were from Wichita. A few were
from smaller, drought-ridden towns, and
one came from Oklahoma City. Whether
they were locals or not, they couldn't go
into town, certainly not once they were
showing. Cora would take requests for little
luxuries — chocolates, hairbrushes, books.
One girl, six months along, asked for a
teddy bear.

But Cora's main duty was to raise money,
and it turned out that she was good at it.
She'd raised money for many causes over
the years, but now, perhaps because of the
unpopularity of her cause, she felt more
inspired, more determined. She learned to
apply for aid, both state and federal. She
held well-planned lunches and teas. She
went to parties with Alan and worked on

his colleagues, and she did the same when she visited each of her sons. She was smooth. She could be both polite and persuasive. She learned to talk more about the babies than the mothers. Yes, she answered, again and again, most of the mothers would choose to give their babies up for adoption. Either way, she always emphasized, it would serve the babies' interests if the mothers were treated well.

Raymond gave her one of her largest donations. There was no fanfare, and there didn't seem to be a hidden meaning or message. He just came out of Alan's study one evening and handed her the check. He thought her project worthwhile, he said. And what else was he going to do with it? It wasn't as if he had children.

"Thank you," she said, or tried to say — she temporarily lost her voice. They were both surprised by the reddening of her face, and then Cora was compelled to put her arms around his wide shoulders and pull him close, to breathe in his clean, soapy smell. He was clearly startled, and for a few moments, he kept his back straight, his arms at his sides. She didn't let go. Under her hands, under the layers of Raymond's fine suit and shirtwaist, were the same freckled shoulders she had seen that awful day she thought her life was over — and when she was sure this decent, beloved man was her enemy.

She was grateful life could be long.

On a mild winter day in 1937, Cora went downtown to Innes Department Store to do some Christmas shopping, and Greta, home from college on break, came with her. Cora was glad for the help, as she still needed to get presents not just for Howard and Earle, but for their wives and for Howard's two small children, who would all be at the house by Christmas Eve. For the last week, Cora had been making up beds and beating curtains and even baking mis-shapen and slightly burned gingerbread men. She'd also purchased two pairs of warm, soft socks for every resident of Kindness House, and she'd bought Greta a tube of the lipstick she liked and a good-sized bottle of Chanel No. 5. She got Joseph a nice suit, having realized he would never buy one for himself, and she bought Alan and Raymond matching neckties, hoping they would find the inside joke inside enough to be funny.

"Greta? Do you think Howard's boys would like a pull toy?" Cora rolled a tiny wagon across a shelf, causing Mickey

Mouse, the only passenger, to wildly thump a drum. "Walter's four now. Is that too old for something like this?"

When Greta didn't answer, Cora looked up, and just then, the bell of the front door clanged and Myra Brooks walked in. She wore a black beret and a long black coat, the neck lined with fur. She looked very pale, perhaps because of her brick-red lipstick. But it was her. Their eyes met, then Myra's darted away. As she moved down the center aisle, Cora was silent. There was a chance Myra just didn't register who she was — so many years had passed, Cora's hair was now streaked with gray. But it seemed as likely that Myra just didn't want to talk — to Cora, maybe to anyone. In any case, Cora, still holding the pull toy, was resigned to let her pass.

But just as Myra was beyond the toy section, she stopped, facing the opposite direction. Even in heels, she seemed small, shrunken. Her shoulders rose and fell twice before she turned around.

"Hello, Cora."

"Hello, Myra." Cora tried to hide her surprise with a smile. "How are you?"

Myra appeared to find the question amusing. "Well," she said finally, "I'm here."

Cora wasn't sure what to say. Myra's voice

and expression were both so resigned that a cheerful response would seem doltish. And now that she was close, Cora could see she really was unwell, her beautiful face now gaunt, her neck thin under the fur collar. She stared at Cora as if waiting for something, until Cora, uncomfortable, glanced away. Greta was over in women's accessories, smiling at Cora and pointing to the red knit hat she'd tried on. Cora gave an appreciative nod.

Myra seemed irritated.

"Sorry," Cora said. "That's my niece over there. She's home from school. I don't know that you ever met her?"

"Hmm." Myra, clearly uninterested, didn't bother to turn around. She continued to stare. If she was going to be rude, Cora thought, Cora might as well ask what she really wanted to know.

"How's Louise?"

"Hmm." Myra didn't smile, but the lines around her eyes deepened. "I somehow guessed you would get to that quickly."

Cora put the pull toy back on the shelf.

"I'm not trying to pry," she said. "I assumed she must be doing well. I saw her new movie last year."

"Ah, yes. The western. You endured it, did you? I heard it was awful."

Cora looked at the black buttons on Myra's coat. Again, she didn't know what to say. She'd gone to see the movie because it was the first one Louise had been in in years. It had clearly been made on a low budget, with silly special effects and men jumping off horses to fight one another. Howard and his family had been in town, so Cora took her two young grandsons to see it. The boys loved the film, with all its rough riding and gunshots, but Cora had found it both inane and depressing, as Louise seemed bored and dull in her simple role as a love interest. Her hair was different — the back reaching almost to her shoulders, her bangs swept back from her forehead. Cora couldn't discern if it was really just the hair that had changed. Louise still looked young, and she was still pretty, though in a more common way. And even as she'd smiled and preened for the camera, her eyes appeared exhausted.

"I think she has to take what she can get these days." Myra pulled the fur collar close. "But in my opinion, she should let Hollywood just take her out and shoot her, get it over with, rather than dragging out her death like this."

Cora let her voice go cold. "Myra. What a thing to say."

She shrugged. "I'll say what I mean. It's true. She's already thrown everything away."

Cora moved close and lowered her voice. "I don't understand."

"I don't, either. I only know Louise is an idiot. And an ingrate. She could have been Hollywood royalty by now. Instead she's fast on her way to being nothing. And it was her own fault. She had every chance, but she was consistently stupid and difficult. You know she was offered the lead in *Public Enemy?* She didn't take the part because she was running around with some man who never planned to marry her. Jean Harlow was the second choice, but she was smart enough to take on the career Louise threw away."

"Is she still in Hollywood?"

"Oh, I'm not sure." Myra waved her gloved hand as if clearing the air of the question. "Do you know what I would have given to have her chances?" She stared, as if waiting for Cora to give her the opportunity to actually list what she would have given. "I poured everything into that girl, everything." She pushed back the sleeve of her coat and showed Cora a thin, blue-veined arm. "They sucked everything right out of me. I have nothing left. Nothing."

"But is she all right, Myra? Is she all right?

That's what I'm asking."

Myra seemed annoyed again. "Yes. She's all right, to use your word. That's all she is, it seems."

Stupid woman, Cora thought. She was the ingrate. But any anger she felt was quickly subdued by pity. It was hard to feel much else, looking down on this frail, small woman spewing so much bitterness and rage because fate wouldn't let her live her dreams, even vicariously. Even now that she was sick, Cora could see how beautiful she'd once been, certainly as lovely as Louise. And as talented. With the same love for music and books. It was hard to know what Myra might have been had she not married at seventeen, if she hadn't been the unhappy mother of four. Would she now be a famous musician? A nicer person? Happy? An inspiration?

"I'm sorry," Cora said, surprised by the sincerity she felt. "I don't know what else to say."

Myra, too, seemed taken aback. She nodded, gazing at Cora. "Thank you," she said. "I appreciate that."

"But if you do speak to Louise, please give her my best. Tell her I hope she's doing well."

Myra made no reply, though the red lips

almost curved into a smile. Cora would later wonder if even then, Myra knew her daughter better than anyone. For it was Myra — even with all her failings as a mother — who seemed to know, before anyone else, that Cora's good wishes would be in vain.

TWENTY

The reasons Wichita got the war contracts were clear: several of its companies had already been producing aircraft for years, and it was nestled in the middle of the country, safe from enemy attacks. Coincidentally, as continually noted by its promoters, the city had one of the highest percentages of American citizens of any metropolitan area in the nation. The census of 1940 counted 115,000 people living in the city limits, and over ninety-nine percent of them were American citizens. Wichita's entire foreign population consisted of 123 Syrians, 170 Russians, 173 Canadians, 272 Mexicans, and 317 Germans — not including Joseph, who'd been naturalized long before he was interned in Georgia during World War I. He fared much better in this next war, as his salary doubled when Wichita's Stearman got the contracts for B-17's. In 1941, Stearman became Boeing-Wichita and started hiring fifty people a day. The company would soon begin work on the new B-29's, though Joseph would honor his confidentiality contract and tell no one about the new bomber, not even Cora, until the new weapon against Japan was formally announced to the press.

By then, Wichita would be a different city, having doubled in size in just two years, the population swollen with newly trained aircraft workers and the masses needed to feed, clothe, and house them. The city had to change the timing of the stop lights so the larger crowds on the sidewalks could cross. There were traffic jams, and long lines at the post office, and even when Cora had the necessary ration cards, trips to the market took twice as long as they'd taken before. Garbage blew about on the street, as the city's services were overwhelmed, and it was nearly impossible to get a phone call through in the middle of the day. Still, there was energy in the air, a feeling of grand purpose. Everyone understood that the city and its newcomers were united in one endeavor: at any hour, day or night, the sky might be loud with Boeing's new bombers racing overhead in neat formations of four.

Cora stayed busy. The number of unwed mothers boomed right along with the general population, but there was once again plenty of money in town, and she was determined to put some of it to good use. She raised enough funds for a new wing for Kindness House, and within a week of its completion, every room in the new wing was full. Most of the girls and women had sad stories about fiancés gone to war and killed. Cora guessed some of them were lying, having calculated that there would be less judgment against premarital sex that was at least patriotic. Either way, she nodded and listened, and let them tell the stories they wanted to, reassuring them all the same. She knew some could be telling the truth. She'd seen flags in windows with blue stars, and some with the devastating gold ones. Trudy Thomas's son had been killed in North Africa, and Winnifred Fitch's nephew was still missing in the Philippines. Not a day went by when Cora didn't think about how fortunate she was — Howard still practiced law in Houston, and Earle was a physician in St. Louis. They had just turned thirty-eight. She was the mother of sons who'd been young men during a brief window of peace.

So she didn't have any suspicions when, in October of 1942, Earle announced that he'd cleared a few days from his schedule at the hospital so he could come to Wichita for a spontaneous visit. He only explained that he wanted to spend some time with his parents, as well as Uncle Joseph and Greta, now grown up and a mother herself. He would maybe see some of his old friends and teachers while he was in town. He didn't want to wait for the holidays. He would come alone, he wrote, as the children would be in school and their mother would of course need to be there for them in the evenings.

Cora and Alan were happy to welcome Earle home, even with the attending complications. They — along with Joseph and Raymond — had gotten used to having more privacy in the house since Greta had left for college. Greta had since returned to Wichita, but she'd married a schoolteacher and given birth to a baby girl, and she and her new family lived in a bungalow five blocks away. Greta rarely called before she came by, so there was still a need for caution. But Cora and Joseph weren't as vigilant as they'd been when she lived in the house. Late at night, when the front and back doors were locked, they moved freely between their rooms. Raymond came over more often, though he still left before ten o'clock so as not to arouse the suspicion of neighbors. A few had made good-natured remarks to Cora about their bachelor family friend, and how good Cora was to open her home and give him some sense of family life.

It was certainly worth the adjustment, those few days of having Earle at home. He did spend time going out and about in town, playing poker with friends from high school and visiting his and Howard's old haunts. But he had breakfast at the house every morning, much to Cora's pleasure, and he was as friendly as ever to Joseph and Greta, getting Greta's baby to laugh as he bounced her on his knee. He was perhaps more quiet than usual, but Cora didn't think much of it. One evening, he asked his father to take a walk to the river with him, and Cora was pleased by the sight of them headed down the street side by side, father and son looking so much alike.

It wasn't until Earle's last afternoon that she learned the real reason for his visit. Alan and Joseph were at work, and they were alone in the house together. She was out on the porch reading, and he came out and sat beside her on the creaking swing. It occurred to her, just then, how perfect the day was, bright with a gentle breeze, the leaves on the big oak just starting to turn red.

There'd been plenty of rain in the last year, and the sunflowers along the gate had come in nicely.

She closed her book, smiling at Earle. He wouldn't be home much longer, and she could read anytime. He didn't smile back. That was her first hint something bad was coming. She watched his eyes, his gaze soft and thoughtful, so much like Alan's, as he told her, in words that sounded firm and practiced, that there was a great need for doctors overseas, and he could no longer stand being a mere spectator at a time like this, especially as a surgeon. When she started to shake her head, he ignored her. He and Beth had already discussed the matter at length, he said. He'd signed up as a medical support to the infantry. He would leave in a month.

"What about your children?" Cora pressed her shoes to the porch so the swing would stop, her heels literally digging in. "Earle, think. You're a father."

He looked at her calmly, as if he knew everything she might say, every argument that would rise up out of her, as if they'd already had this conversation a hundred times. "I've talked with my family, Beth as well as the children. They understand."

"Do they understand that you could be

killed? Be reasonable." Even as she said this, she heard the tremble in her voice. She didn't want a flag with a star. Still, she worked to calm herself. She would be reasonable, too. "It's good that you want to help," she said. "It is. But you can help in St. Louis. We need doctors in this country. And what about the injured soldiers coming back? Why can't you help them? How noble is it to leave your wife and children?"

He shrugged. "Why should I get to stay when so many others have gone? Plenty of fathers, you can be sure."

They stared at each other. She had no answer. He was her child, still her child. That was her only answer.

"This is something I have to do," he said. "Mother, you're not going to change my mind."

Cora closed her eyes. He didn't need to tell her that. She knew exactly how stubborn he could be. Compared to charming Howard, Earle could seem passive and uncertain, but she'd long ago learned that really, he was the one with the ferocious will. When he was a boy, she'd been unable — despite threats, cajoling, and promises — to ever get him to wear a hat or mittens in winter, and when he was ten, he once jumped from the roof of the porch into a pile of leaves, though she was standing right there in the yard and shrieking at him not to. He'd always been a good boy, generally compliant, but once he made up his mind about something, that was that. Cora once shared this observation with Alan, who'd looked at her with amused affection and said, "Hmm, I wonder where he got that."

She didn't want Earle to be like her now.

"You've already talked to your father?"

He nodded. "I guessed he would go easier on me."

"What did he say?"

"That he respected me. That for this war, he'd do the same if he were younger. Mostly that he understood. It meant everything that he said that. I wish you would do the same."

She slapped her knee, angry. Alan. He always had to be so understanding.

"Mother, come on now. Please. You're as bad as Howard. Listen, I'm just going as a surgeon. It's very likely I'll never see any fighting."

"Where will you be?"

"I don't know yet."

"You don't know what country?" The flaming top of the oak blurred before her.

"Well, the Pacific. I know that. I told them about you being German. And about Uncle Joseph. I know he supports the war, but they still thought it might be better if I went to the Pacific."

She couldn't breathe. She could only see it all horribly unfolding. Earle would be killed, killed in the Pacific, and it would be her fault. Her self-serving lie. She would be responsible for her own child's death. But then, would he be any safer in Europe? In North Africa? She didn't know.

"Did you tell your father this? What you just told me? About why you'd go to the Pacific?"

He nodded.

"What did he say?"

"He thought the Pacific made sense. He thought both fronts looked equally dang— . . . equally safe, I mean." He sighed. "Do you have some secret information about the war, Mother? What have you got against the Pacific? I hear the Nazis are fairly tough, too."

She shook her head. If Earle would be any safer in Europe or Africa, Alan would have told him the truth. She knew that. But soldiers were dying everywhere. Going to the Pacific might doom Earle, but it might just as easily save him. And he might have been sent to the Pacific anyway, even without her lie.

They sat on the swing, Cora holding tight

to his arm with both hands. They watched leaves shudder in the breeze, a few letting go and drifting off into the neighbor's wide yard.

Earle leaned away and looked down at her. "On a different note, did you know Louise Brooks is back in town?"

She was at first annoyed, as he was clearly trying to distract her, trying to get her mind on a different subject so that he might eventually wrest his arm from her grip. But then she considered his actual words, and she turned to him, sitting up straight.

"Moved back? What are you talking about?"

"Just that." He waved a fly away from her face. "She's been back for a couple of years, apparently. I guess she opened a dance studio on Douglas, behind the Dockum Building, but it didn't go."

She watched his eyes. Earle — unlike Howard — had never been one to tease, but she simply couldn't believe what he was saying. How would she not have heard about this? She understood that Wichita was a real city now and that there was a war on and people had more to talk about than a movie star, or former movie star, moving back to town. But she thought she would have heard something. It was true she'd been busy with

Kindness House. And Viola Hammond, who'd once kept her apprised of the goings-on about town, had fallen sick with cancer at the start of the war. Cora went to visit her at least once a week, but Viola was often tired, and she'd lost her zest for gossip.

Earle, the circulation likely returned to his arm, stretched it out in front of him. "Nuts, isn't it? Louise Brooks — Wichita dance teacher. I guess she and her partner also performed, doing the tango and the waltz, that kind of thing. One of my old buddies said he booked them for a Young Republicans party."

Cora tried not to look startled. She didn't want to convey judgment, even to her own son. There was nothing wrong with Louise teaching dance, making an honest living. But a Young Republicans meeting? In Wichita? It was hard to imagine Louise had come down to that.

"What's she doing now?"

He raised his brows. "Making a fool of herself, if you listen to talk. One of my pals knows the fellow she opened the studio with. He's just a kid, a college boy who could dance. I guess things went sour between them even before they went under."

"How does that make Louise a fool?"

"How she's been acting. Even in school, people said she was a speed, but . . ."

"But what?"

"Nothing."

Cora crossed her arms. He was being careful, trying not to say anything that would shock her maternal ears. Despite her work for Kindness House, both of her sons seemed to frequently confuse her with Queen Victoria.

"Earle, tell me."

"Fine. She . . . threw herself at him, to put it mildly. This college boy. And she couldn't believe it when he turned her down. It could be just him talking, but my friend said her looks are gone. She drinks, and it shows in her face. He said she's been arrested for drunkenness." He grimaced. "And for lewd cohabitation."

Cora looked at the front steps, where Joseph had left a pair of muddy shoes. Even now, one could still be arrested for living in sin, for living as they did in this house. Louise had just been more open about it, not bothering to hide or deceive.

"Is she still with him?"

"Who?"

"The man she was living with?"

Earle looked at her as if she were hopeless. "Oh, Mother, I don't think that's likely.

It didn't sound like a great romance. From what I understand of how she lives, marriage isn't in the cards."

"Where does she live now?"

"With her parents. She doesn't have any money." He looked at her quizzically. "Now you look horrified. I would have thought you would be more disturbed by her behavior."

Cora frowned. It was hard to imagine Louise and Myra living easily under one roof, especially in their broken states. There was a chance, she supposed, that Myra would rise to the occasion and offer Louise sympathy and understanding. But from what Cora had seen, Myra had never loved Louise as a daughter, or even as a separate person. If she'd ever loved Louise, it was as another limb of her own body, a mindless extension employed to make one last grasp at her own dreams. Now Louise had failed her, truly failed her, as badly as Myra herself had failed.

Earle gently nudged her side. "I don't think you need to feel sorry for her. From what I hear, Louise is enjoying herself. She doesn't work. My friend says all she does is run around at night with that Danny Aikman. I understand they're quite a duo."

"Is that her . . . is that the man she was

living with?"

He smiled. "No, Mother. You don't re-member Danny Aikman from the club? He's Wichita's most famous . . ." Here, Earle paused and made a fluttering movement with his hand.

Cora shook her head, confused.

"He's an Ethel." His cheeks reddened a bit. "He's one of those. A poof." He looked up, exasperated. "Mother, he prefers men. To women."

"Oh." And he was looking at her as if she were thick. He really had no idea. His own father. Sometimes she wondered if one or both of the boys suspected or knew. But it was clear that Earle still knew nothing. It was likely that Howard knew nothing as well.

"Sorry, Mother. I don't mean to be vul-gar."

Cora shook her head, impatient. "You know this about him? This is common knowledge?" She was always trying to gauge what people would think about Alan, about Raymond, if they knew. Even in Wichita, perhaps, times were changing, with young people looking at everything so differently. This Danny person suffered insults, but he was known and apparently tolerated. That in itself was surprising.

"Well, I don't *know* that he prefers men. But I know he once got himself arrested for dressing like a woman on Douglas Avenue."

Cora's eyes widened. "He wore a dress?"

"No. His shirt had flowers on it."

"They arrested him for that?"

"Well, yes. It's clear what he's about. They get him on what they can."

She had to look away — Earle was snickering, and she could barely keep the dread from her eyes. Alan would never in his life wear a flowered shirt, but clearly, if he and Raymond were ever exposed, even now, they would pay a great price. She liked to think that Howard and Earle would stand by him, but what leaps their hearts would have to make. She could only hope Alan had never heard either of their sons joking about poofs and Ethels. If he had, he'd endured it in silence.

And now he'd told their son he could go off to war, that he respected his decision.

Earle turned to her, somber again, no longer trying to distract.

"I know you aren't happy with my decision." He took her hand again. "I know you'll worry, and I can't stop you from worrying. But this is something I have to do. And it's because of the way you and Father brought me up that I feel a responsibility. It would mean so much if I could go knowing I had your support. Your understanding. Father already gave me his, and so have Beth and the children. But I'd like it from you, too." Half of his mouth curled upward. "I don't want to be dramatic, but I suppose I'd like your blessing."

She nodded. At first, it was all she could do. She still didn't think he should go. He was a father, a husband, and her son. But she knew what was even more true, what Alan had understood from the start. She squeezed his hand until she could speak. "You already have that." Her eyes blurred again, but she tried to look at him, her son. "You've always had it, Earle. And you always will. It doesn't matter what you do."

The Brooks home was still the largest on its block, and from a distance, it seemed to be in good repair, a fresh pale yellow painted over the gray, and every window gleaming clean and clear in the sun. The lilac bushes near the gate were trimmed, and only a few golden leaves dotted the lawn. But as Cora approached, she remembered what Myra had said, all those years ago, about the weight of her husband's books actually sinking the foundation. When Cora stood directly in front of the house, she saw the forecast of damage was correct: even with the fresh paint, the house resembled a listing ship, with one side of the limestone porch clearly sitting higher than the other.

Cora was going up the front steps when she heard a friendly voice greet her by name. She looked to the sunken side of the shaded porch to see Zana Henderson, plump and pretty in a skirt and buttoned-up cardigan, sitting on a peacock-blue upholstered sofa. Next to her sat Myra, who looked as small as a child in comparison, wearing a flowered housecoat in the middle of the afternoon, her dark hair thinned and hanging to her shoulders. Cora said hello to both of them. Only Zana smiled.

"To what do we owe this pleasure?" Zana asked. "Did you come to join our little party?" She gestured at the table in front of the sofa, on which sat some sort of pie, a bowl of whipped cream with a serving spoon, and two pie-stained forks and plates. "It's such a perfect autumn day," Zana continued, "and I thought there was no better way to spend it than having dessert on Myra's front porch." She gestured grandly around her. "We even dragged the sofa out so we'd be comfortable."

"You dragged it," Myra muttered. Her voice was raspy, weak. "I didn't help at all."

"Well, you inspired me. And you trusted me not to hurt it."

Cora smiled politely. What a friend Zana was. She'd defended Myra when no one else would, and now that Myra was back and unwell, her abandoned children grown and gone, Zana was still here to cheer her. Cora was perplexed as to how someone like Myra had managed to make and keep such a friend.

"Would you like a piece?" Zana looked at Cora, pointing at the pie. "There's plenty, and you'll save me from finishing it myself."

"Oh, thank you, but no," Cora said. "I was actually hoping to see Louise."

Now Zana seemed perplexed. She raised her eyebrows and turned to Myra, who gave her a knowing look.

"Hmm." Zana's disapproval was evident. "Well, good luck to you."

Myra started to cough, each gasp for breath short and wheezing. She closed her eyes and covered her mouth, her small body curling in on itself, her feet lifting from the floor. It was terrible to just stand there and wait as she struggled, hiding her face.

"I'll get you some water," Zana said, standing.

"I can get it." Cora was already moving toward the door.

"Don't," Myra gasped. "It doesn't help." She gave Cora an inexplicably hateful look as she gripped the edge of the table. "And I'm fine." She coughed again. "Go on in. Third floor. I don't know which room. You'll have to knock."

The third-floor hallway was dark, windowless, with only a small sconce to light the way, one of its two bulbs burned out. Cora, a little breathless from two flights of stairs, leaned against the wood-paneled wall. It made sense, she supposed, that Myra didn't frequent this floor. The climb would likely kill her.

"Louise?" She stood in the center of the hall. There were three doors, all closed. "Louise?"

She heard movement, a clink of glass. Then nothing.

"It's Cora Carlisle. Your old chaperone. I've just come to say hello."

Silence. Cora leaned against the wall again. Perhaps it was stupid of her to come. They had no real connection to each other, no blood relation. It was just that one summer, and even then, Louise had never even feigned affection for her. Yet she had done so much for Cora, without even meaning to, without even knowing that she had.

"I imagine you hear me. And I'm sure I can't make you feel too guilty about turning away a fifty-six-year-old woman who just climbed two flights of stairs to see you."

She looked at her shoes, listening.

"You would loathe my shoes if you could see them. They're very comfortable, but they're wide in the toe, and they hardly have any heel. I recall you didn't think much of my style twenty years ago. You should see me now. My shoes get funny looks from women my age. I promise you'll feel instantly superior if you would just open your door."

Nothing.

"I'm not leaving. I don't have anywhere I have to be. I'll stand out here as long as it takes and talk and talk and —"

The door at the end of the hall opened. Louise appeared, her arms crossed in front of her chest. She was dressed in a black turtleneck sweater and black slacks. Cora tried not to look too surprised. She'd seen slacks on Katharine Hepburn, but never on a woman in real life.

"You're right." Her voice was lower, and her words slower, than Cora remembered. "Those are horrific shoes."

Cora didn't know what Earle's friend had meant about Louise losing her looks. Even dressed like Katharine Hepburn, she was still so striking with her dark eyes and pale skin. Her hair, black as her turtleneck, almost reached her shoulders, and she had her bangs again.

"Are you going to invite me in?"

"What do you want?"

"I . . . I want to see how you are." Cora opened her purse and took out a wrapped package. "I brought you chocolates. I remember you like chocolate." She held out the package to Louise, who looked at it with skepticism. Cora started to regret her visit. Perhaps Louise was perfectly happy, living in her childhood home, going out at night and getting arrested. Who was to say she didn't prefer this life? If she'd wanted to keep her life in Hollywood with her director husband and her pool and her furs, it seems she would have. Louise, as far as Cora remembered, usually did just as she liked.

She took the chocolates without a thank you, tucking them under one arm. "How's your German, Cora?"

Cora swallowed. Even in the weak light, she could see Louise's wry little smile. She was the first person they'd lied to all those years ago, when they were still panicked and unpracticed, and Cora was never certain if Louise had really believed that Joseph was her brother. At the time, Louise only reacted to the story with slight disappointment, quickly followed by disinterest. But the way she was looking at Cora now implied she'd known all along.

"My brother? He's fine, thank you."

Louise rolled her eyes. "I mean the language. I wondered if you were familiar with the term *schadenfreude.* Pleasure in the misfortunes of others? We don't really have a similar word in our language, and it seems to me we should. Especially in fair Wichita."

Cora shook her head. It was hard not to feel hurt. She hoped Louise knew her better than that. "I haven't come here to gloat," she said. "I've just come to see how you are. And I'll speak of this visit to no one."

"If you did, I wouldn't care." She gave Cora a guarded look that suggested otherwise.

"Well, I won't." Now Cora looked at the ceiling. She wanted to sit down. "Look, I'd like fifteen minutes. I'm sorry to have ambushed you like this. But if you give me fifteen minutes, I swear, I won't bother you again."

She stared at Cora. It was impossible to know what she was thinking. When Louise was famous and making films, Cora had read a review by a critic who'd thought her untalented as an actress. He admitted she might be the most beautiful woman ever seen on screen, but he complained that beauty was all she brought to the table. People were so swept away by her dark eyes and the perfect symmetry of her features that they didn't realize her face was inscrutable, and that really, there was no telling what feelings, if any, existed behind the eyes. The critic believed that if it weren't for the title cards that spelled out what she was supposed to be thinking, no one would ever know how to interpret her lovely gaze. He was in the minority; most critics just considered her a subtle actor, especially for her era of over-the-top expressions. But now, in the hallway, with Louise-in-the-flesh regarding her from just a few feet away, Cora could have used a title card that might have hinted at Louise's thoughts.

Louise glanced at her watch. "Starting now?"

"Starting when you offer me a seat."

Her room had a slanted ceiling, with one side meeting the floor, giving it the shape of an upright triangle. The single bed took up most of the limited space where an adult might hope to stand upright. And it was almost as dark as the hallway, the shades of both windows pulled down, the windows closed to the pleasant afternoon. There was a table lamp, but a scarf had been draped over the shade, weakening the bulb's light. And it was, to say the least, uncluttered. There was the bed, an oriental rug, a chest of drawers, and a nightstand on which the lamp sat. A bowl of red apples sat atop a stack of books next to the bed, and a pair of black heels sat under the dresser. Cora saw no other possessions. If this had been Louise's room when she was a child, she'd certainly purged it of all its girlish paraphernalia.

There was nowhere to sit but the bed, which was unmade, with a good number of pillows stacked at the head and a book facedown on the rumpled blanket. Clearly, the bed was Louise's seat. But the rug looked soft and reasonably thick, so Cora took hold of the bed's foot rail and lowered herself to the floor. Louise seemed mildly startled — either that Cora would do such a thing, or that she even could. But then, she'd only known Cora in her corset-wearing days, when getting down on the floor would have required both assistance and time. Today, Cora wore a belted cotton dress, with only a slip and underwear underneath. Although she was twenty years older, she likely appeared surprisingly lithe.

Louise looked at her watch again. "Starting now," she said. She set the chocolates on the nightstand and got in bed, sitting upright against the pillows, her black-slacked legs stretched out over the blankets, her bare, pale ankles crossed. Now that she was sitting by the lamp, Cora could see her face clearly, and she understood what Earle's friend had meant. Louise looked older than she should have, with lines around her eyes and mouth. The tip of her nose was a little pink, and a blood vessel had burst on one of her cheeks. But the eyes were the same, large and captivating. She stared at Cora, impatient.

Cora stretched out and crossed her own legs. She did not expect Louise to make polite inquiries, to ask about Joseph, about Greta, about the boys or Alan. She would not burden Louise with her worries about Earle. She was clearly on the defensive, unable to consider more than her own pain. This would be a one-way conversation, the kind Cora often had at Kindness House.

"Your mother doesn't look well," Cora said. It was probably the wrong place to start, but she didn't have much time.

"She isn't." Louise examined one of her hands. "She's dying, I think. Emphysema. She didn't even smoke — she has the hereditary kind. Which means I'll get it, too." She looked at Cora, annoyed. "Are you going to tell me I should be caring for her? Is that your mission today?"

"No," Cora said. It was another unfair accusation, but Cora guessed she shouldn't take it personally. Louise had been drinking. She wasn't drunk, but she was lisping a little, and Cora detected the same piney odor she'd smelled on her breath when she came home with Floyd Smithers all those years ago. Gin. Cora could recognize it now. It was what they'd poured in the punch at Earle's wedding.

"Well, good." Louise lifted her chin. "I assure you dear Mother already has plenty of friends ready to see to her every need."

"Yes," Cora said. "I just saw her with Zana downstairs."

"Ah, her fastest friend." Louise glared at the door. "Zana. Every time she sees me she makes sure to tell me what a horrible daughter I am, and how I should be taking better care of poor, poor Myra." She turned back to Cora. "But Poor Myra doesn't want me waiting on her. She doesn't want to look at me in my current, disappointing state."

Cora sighed. That seemed likely. "Did she tell you that?" she asked.

"In her way. Did you know that my mother

532

once held the largest collection on Louise Brooks in the world?" She paused to give Cora a smile, as wide as it was fake. "People would write me and say they were my biggest fans, but I knew my biggest fan was right here in Wichita. Mother saved every letter I wrote, every magazine I was in, every movie poster I graced. But that was in 1927." She frowned, the black eyebrows lowered. "She's a fair-weather fan, it turns out. When I first got home, she put every letter and photograph in two cardboard boxes, and she asked, 'Louise, do you want these? Or shall I throw them away?' "

"I'm sorry," Cora said.

Louise shrugged.

"How's your father?" It was the only hopeful question Cora could think of.

"Hmm." Louise tilted her head to one side. "Well, I'm not sure he knows I'm up here. But he's a busy man, and it's only been two years."

"Then why are you here?" Cora kept her voice soft. She wasn't trying to badger. She really didn't understand. Louise wasn't caring for her mother, and Myra, now that Louise held little promise, seemed unable to care for her daughter. And Leonard Brooks wasn't the reason.

"Because I'm broke." She said this as if

the idea of it was very funny. "Go ahead and tell your chattering friends. Let it be known. I have zilch! Nothing! I thought I was broke when I left California." She looked at the slanted ceiling of the room. "But then I had two dimes to rub together. Now I don't even have that."

"How is that possible?" Cora leaned forward, tucking her knees to one side. "Don't you get alimony?"

"I didn't ask for it. Both times I just wanted out. And I thought I would keep making more." She held her flattened palms up. "I could have been a fantastic prostitute. But I just never thought long term."

Cora winced. "Why did you stop making films?"

She didn't answer right away. Instead, she looked at Cora carefully. It was as if she were a stray cat, trying to decide if she should come closer or if she would run away. Finally, still watching Cora's eyes, she shrugged. "I was disgusted with Hollywood. They don't even read there. They just watch." Vertical lines deepened between her eyes. "They only know what they see, and they see you and think they know you, and then you think they do, too. The outside gets on the inside. It's no good."

Cora nodded as if she understood. But

this story didn't fit what she knew. It wasn't as if Louise had left Hollywood in her prime, her dignity intact. She'd gone out with desperation, lowering herself to one silly western and then another. Cora had heard she was supposed to be in one last film, but every scene she was in was cut. Perhaps, in her mind, she'd walked away from it all, but it seemed more likely she'd been pushed. Why? Myra had said she couldn't get along with people. That she threw everything away. She may have been drinking, even then. But maybe the drinking had nothing to do with the fall. Maybe she'd fallen first and started drinking as a result. It was hard to know what, exactly, had led her back to this sad little room. Maybe all the rage and grief could be traced back to Cherryvale and Mr. Flowers. But it was as likely her current sadness was planted before that by her own unhappy mother. Cora would never know. There was a chance that neither Myra nor Mr. Flowers had altered Louise in any real way. Maybe even before them, even without them, she was destined to be what she would be, driven by yearning and fury that were as much a part of who she was as her beautiful face.

Cora looked at the stack of books by the bed. One had no writing on the spine. One was by Nietzsche. The bottom book was by Schopenhauer, one that Cora hadn't read. For the first time, she wondered what might have become of Louise if she'd had a slightly different face — an imperfect nose, smaller, asymmetrical eyes, a jutting chin. She might have been a spinster librarian or a scholar, happily surrounded by books.

"Why here, Louise? Why come here of all places? You can be broke anywhere."

Louise looked at her blankly.

Cora leaned forward. "You have no love for this house. No love for this town. You never did. Why come back? What? Are you a homing pigeon for misery?"

Louise looked away, then back at Cora. She seemed both startled and annoyed. "It's my home. It's where I belong."

"Horse feathers!" Cora slapped her hand against the side of the mattress, truly angry, but the action made Louise smile in her old, condescending way. Cora supposed she should have said "bullshit" or something else that would have sounded hard, but she still hated vulgar language. Louise could smile all she wanted. She knew what Cora meant.

"You don't belong here if you're un-happy," she continued. "Your mother makes you hateful, and you make her hateful. It doesn't matter if she's your mother. It's an accident of birth. It doesn't have to mean so much." She looked down at the rug, the intricate patterns and swirls. "You belong where you have the best chance of being happy, Louise. You don't like Hollywood? Fine. Don't go back there. But don't stay here. Go somewhere else, even if she's dying. Go where you think you have the best chance to be happy. Get on the train and go."

Cora looked away, a little breathless. She was so outraged. She wanted to stand up and shake Louise by the shoulders. But she'd already done all she could. She'd felt this feckless many times before, working at Kindness House. No matter how she pleaded, she couldn't climb in someone's head and start steering. People did what they would do.

"I'm too old," Louise whispered. "I'm all used up. I'm not even me anymore."

"What?" Cora looked up at her, disbelieving. "Louise, how old are you?"

"Thirty-six."

Cora tried not to laugh. It seemed so young, so impossibly young. But then, she'd been thirty-six exactly the summer they went to New York, and hadn't she felt old before they left, almost broken, almost

537

hopeless? She'd had no idea how much living was in store for her — Joseph, Greta, her grandchildren, her new love for Alan, for Raymond. The hands she'd held at Kindness House.

"You're not used up, Louise. I know you. I remember you. I'm certain there's still quite a bit of you left."

Louise stared at her dully. She could be thinking anything. Downstairs, Zana was laughing, and the screen door slammed shut. Louise glanced at her watch.

Cora took hold of the foot rail and pulled herself to her feet. A contract was a contract, and she was out of arguments. But before she left, on an unchecked impulse, she leaned down and kissed the top of Louise's head, just as she'd done for her boys, and then for Greta, when telling them good night.

She resigned herself to not knowing what effect — if any — her visit to Louise had had. She knew she could start checking the paper every morning, searching the arrest log for Louise's name. Then, at least, she would know that she'd tried and failed. But it would make her so sad to see Louise's name there, and she decided she might be better off not checking.

She wished she could have been as disciplined when it came to news of the war. Every morning that spring, she searched each page for word on the Pacific front and then for any mention of a hospital or medical team. She only knew Earle was on a ship somewhere — his two letters had been purposefully vague, in keeping with censors' requirements. So when any battle and casualties were reported, Cora waited in quiet terror. She knew that if bad news came, it would go to Beth first, so her stomach dropped with every ring of the phone. She checked the mail with obsessive anticipation, though Earle's letters took weeks to reach Wichita and were no guarantee that he was fine. She wondered if her mother's intuition would somehow tell her, at the very moment, if he was harmed. She'd read stories of people who'd sensed the passing of loved ones long before they heard the news.

Some part of her also thought she might feel Mary O'Dell's death in Massachusetts. Cora, as her blood daughter, would somehow feel her go and have her own private moment of grief, far from her half brothers and half sisters in Haverhill. But Cora never felt any moment like that. Either Mary O'Dell was enjoying a long life or there was no special conduit between them.

One hot Saturday in June, she was at Kindness House all morning, and by the time she parked outside the house, Joseph was already checking the mail. She ran across the lawn as best she could, but he shook his head.

"Nothing from him. Sorry." He looked at her with sympathy, but that was all. Anyone could be looking, and though any brother might embrace a worried sister, they were so used to caution they didn't risk it. "But you have this," he said, handing her a postcard. The picture was a black-and-white still life, a shadowed iris in a vase. On the back, Cora's address was written on one half, and *Thanks* was written on the other. Still, Cora might have recognized the hand-writing, unchanged after all these years, even if *LB* wasn't written below.

The postmark read NYC, stamped just a few days before.

TWENTY-ONE

Earle wasn't killed in the war. The ship he was on engaged in battle three times, but he would only tell Cora and Alan this after the war was over and he was back in St. Louis, his life with his wife and children and his shifts at the hospital resumed. There was no way to know if he would have survived Europe just as well — Cora was only relieved he was home and safe. And then Greta had another baby, a girl she named after her mother, and she would bring both Donna and baby Andrea by almost every week. Cora was aware of her good fortunes, all the grief she'd been spared. Not every mother had been so lucky, and she was still trying to comprehend the new reports coming in about the suffering in the concentration camps, as well as in Dresden and Hiroshima and Nagasaki. It scared her to think how much her life's ease and happiness had been granted by chance. Earle could have been killed of course — but even more than that, she could have been born anywhere in the world, and to anyone, she and her loved ones suffering in ways she could barely fathom when she listened to the international news. This idea seemed a revelation, something that it had taken her years to really understand. But it was not so different from the way she'd felt as a child, grateful for the Kaufmanns, but anxious to know how easily the train might have left her with someone else. Everything would have been different.

They had their minor troubles. In the winter of 1946, Joseph slipped on a patch of ice and broke his right wrist. His cast turned his hand into a giant, immobile claw, so that he resembled the irritable crab he became during the twelve weeks he couldn't work. And a rough spring storm knocked over one of the neighbor's sycamores, which fell away from their neighbor's house and right onto their own. But the third floor took most of the damage, and no one was hurt. Even as Cora had heavy rain and opportunistic squirrels ruining the upper floor of the house, she knew she should count her blessings.

And then, Alan got sick. At first he was just more tired than usual, only going to the office in the mornings. Then he started sleeping through dinner, and though Cora would save a plate for him, he only picked at it. She told him she was worried, but he assured her he was fine, just needing to rest. It was Raymond who made him go to the doctor. They had a terrific fight about it, which Cora heard from up in her room. The fact that Alan put up such resistance was itself cause for concern. Later, both Cora and Raymond understood that he must have guessed he was truly ill. Pancreatic cancer, already progressed. There was no time to be astounded, to disbelieve. The doctor said two months, and warned none of it would be pleasant.

Within just a few weeks, he couldn't manage the stairs. Cora carried meals up to his room, soup she could spoon up to his lips. She brought up meals for Raymond, too. He'd retired from his practice the year before, so his days were free, and he posted himself in the green upholstered chair by Alan's bed, reading aloud in his still-commanding voice whenever Alan felt up for listening. He administered the morphine, and he helped Alan to the bathroom at the end of the hall. Raymond was seventy, just one year younger than Alan, but he was still wide in the shoulders and strong enough to easily lift him into the bath.

The whole while Alan was sick, Greta was pregnant with her third child. But she came over every afternoon at two, when Donna was in kindergarten and Andrea could be counted on to stay quiet and asleep in her buggy. If Greta thought anything of Raymond's constant presence, she said nothing. She may or may not have understood that he was there all day, every day. In any case, Raymond still left by ten every night. Even then, they had to think about the neighbors, what they could and couldn't explain. But Joseph was home at night, and he could manage any lifting until Raymond returned in the morning.

Alan wasn't always in his mind. The doctor said it was the morphine. More than once, he confused Cora with his grandmother, asking if he'd been a good boy and if he could still go sledding with Harriet; an hour later, he would be calling her Cora again. He told her he loved her more than he ever planned to. He told her how sorry he was. She didn't know if he was apologizing for his illness or for leaving her, or if he was still feeling guilty for marrying her, for her unhappy years.

"It's all right," she would say. "Don't worry. Please don't worry yourself."

"Don't tell the boys," he whispered once, looking at her with such burning focus that she knew he wasn't delirious. Spittle clung to his pale lips until she dabbed it away.

"Promise me, Cora. Promise me. Don't ever tell the boys."

"I promise," she said, taking his hand. "I understand."

When he was clearly nearing the end, Howard and Earle came home. They dragged a mattress from Howard's old room into their father's room, and they took turns sleeping at the foot of his bed in case he woke in the night. One of them was always with him, sitting in Raymond's chair. Raymond himself had disappeared the day Howard and Earle arrived. He might have gotten away with a few visits, as they knew him as their father's oldest friend. But his bedside vigil, had it continued, would have seemed strange to them, and Cora understood that Alan had made his wishes known to Raymond, too. They'd likely said their goodbyes on the last day they could.

She worried about Raymond. At the funeral, everyone was kind to her, solicitous, so many people embracing her and telling her how sorry they were. She appreciated their sympathy, and she listened with longing to the good things they had to say about Alan. But the whole time, even with the ache in her own chest, she was aware of Raymond standing off by himself. Joseph went over and tried to have a quiet word, but Raymond shook his head and turned away. Maybe he knew what he could manage. When he left, he left alone.

She kept inviting him to dinner. He said no the first few times, but after a while, he started saying yes. She didn't know how hard it was for him to sit at the table with her and Joseph and the empty chair. But he kept coming, and he certainly didn't come for her cooking. She assumed it meant something for him to spend time with the two people in the world who knew and recognized his grief. Fifty years he'd been with Alan, including the years when they had tried to cease. Now, he seemed grateful to be with Cora and Joseph, at the table where one of them could point at Alan's empty chair and say "he" or "his," and the other two would understand.

"I am not so much younger than Alan was," Joseph told her one night. It was just the two of them doing dishes. Raymond, especially quiet that night, had left just after dinner.

Cora offered him a plate to dry. "You're twelve years younger," she said. "And I'm the same age as you."

Joseph moved a towel around the plate's brim. Watching his face, she understood that he wasn't just being morbid. He was thinking about something. She waited. He wore thicker spectacles now, and the gold streak in his right eye appeared wider and brighter.

"I do not know if we should tell Greta," he said. "I could die. We could die. And she will not ever know."

Cora frowned. They had not had this discussion for years. She'd made up her mind long ago, and she thought he had, too. She looked at her hands, her familiar hands, wrinkled with age in the soapy water. What was it Schopenhauer wrote? *The closing years of life are like the end of a masquerade party, when the masks are dropped.* But they might not be in their closing years, and their masks, as far as she could tell, weren't doing anyone harm.

His cloth squeaked against the plate. "You know what she said to me the other day? She said with each pregnancy, she wondered if she would have twins. Since it runs in the family. Cora, she believes you are her aunt."

None of this was news.

"It's not a good time," she said, handing

him another plate. "She's about to have a baby, and we just lost Alan. She doesn't need the shock." She could feel him watching her, waiting.

He turned off the faucet, not angry, just wanting her focus. "You do not think we should tell her," he said. "Not now. Not ever."

She dried her hands on her apron. She shouldn't be afraid. Whatever she said, he wouldn't judge her. He was who he had always been. He would take in the information she offered as if she were a pilot offering a suggestion for one of his engines or wings. He was a careful, listening person, a thoughtful chooser. She loved him still.

"I don't," she said. "If you think we should, I'll listen to you. I'll hear what you have to say. But no, on my own, I don't think we should tell her. Ever. I don't see what good it could do, and it could do so much harm. To her. To Raymond. What if she tells her husband? What if he tells someone?"

"But it is the truth."

Cora shrugged. She'd once thought truth important. She'd gone all the way to New York in search of it, what she believed she needed to know. And what had it gotten her? Mary O'Dell. Even then, in her pain and confusion, Cora had known better than to go up to Haverhill and tear into that woman's life. And now she had no desire to tear into Greta's — not over something as trifling as a bloodline.

"I'll think on this," Joseph said, turning the water back on.

She nodded. She'd said what she needed.

Aunt Cora, who loved her niece.

In the winter of 1953, Cora heard sad tidings about Louise. Someone at a fundraiser had a friend with a nephew living in New York City, and the nephew reported seeing Louise Brooks, the old silent-film star, at a bar on Third Avenue, alone and drunk and mumbling in the middle of the afternoon. Cora knew she'd heard the story at least twice removed, and she didn't know how many details had been made up or embellished. Allegedly, the nephew, who remembered seeing the beautiful Louise Brooks in films as a little boy, almost didn't recognize her, as she'd grown her hair down to her waist, and it was stringy and threaded with gray. She'd grown out the bangs, too. The nephew reported that Louise was practically falling off her bar stool, and when he approached her and very politely asked if she was who he thought she was, she'd turned hostile, screeching at him to leave her alone.

Cora didn't know if any of this was true, but she understood that it could be. There was no reason to expect that just being in New York, the city she loved, could save Louise entirely, that it could rescue her from whatever had made her love gin. As far as the hairstyle, Cora presumed the neglect was purposeful. If Louise truly wanted to be left alone, what better way to divorce her fame than to let her hair go gray and let it grow long, especially the bangs? It didn't seem accidental that she'd gone to the other extreme.

Still, Cora hoped the story was embellished, or even completely untrue. Louise would be in her mid-forties now, and if she was truly spending her afternoons falling off bar stools, that might be the end of her story. Cora wondered if there was anything else she might have said to her that day up in her darkened room on North Topeka Street, something that might have done more for Louise than just getting her out of that house. But she doubted there was. Even then, Louise had a momentum, just as she'd had that summer in New York. It didn't matter if she was headed up or down. Really, it was amazing that Cora, even with so much effort and insistence, had altered her path at all.

But as it turned out, Louise's story wasn't yet over — not at all. The next time Cora heard anything about her, it was from an unexpected source: Walter, Howard's eldest son. Cora didn't know Walter as well as she would have liked. He and his sisters had grown up in Houston, and though Howard brought them up to Wichita for holidays when he could, it got harder for him when they reached adolescence, and Cora never felt she got to know them the way she knew Greta's children. When Walter was in his early twenties, he became Walt, and Cora knew he was scholarly and interested in film, and that he was doing something purposeful in Paris, albeit on his father's dime. But she usually only heard from Walt when he wrote his perfunctory thank-you notes after cashing the checks she mailed every birthday and Christmas. So she was very surprised when, in late 1958, she received an actual letter from him, sent airmail from France.

Dear Grandmother,
    Dad said that you knew Louise Brooks better than anyone in the family, and I

thought you might be interested to know I just saw her here in Paris. She's still very admired here, and the Cinématheque Française organized a retrospective of her films. I actually talked with her at one of the parties, and I asked her if she remembered you, but honestly, she was too pickled to have a real conversation. I hear she was quite the guest of honor. Apparently, she would order room service, charge it to the CF, and then throw most of her meal out the hotel window. Some of her fans picked up what she threw, I guess so they could have a piece of Louise Brooks's coq au vin, saved for posterity! So she's a bit off, but I have to say, she's a first-rate writer. She's had articles in Objectif and Sight and Sound, and they were both very good. But she's mostly famous for who she was. In any case, I thought you might like to know all this. When I come home, maybe I can get up to Wichita, and you could tell me some stories. As it is now, when I tell people my grandmother in Kansas was Louise Brooks's chaperone, no one believes me. Hope you and Uncle Joseph are doing well.

Love, Walt

Cora was happy to feel reproached. While she'd imagined Louise falling off bar stools until she died a lonely death, the real Louise was actually the toast of Paris. Life could be long, indeed. Clearly, Louise was still drinking, and now she was throwing chickens out windows, but what was this about the articles in film journals? Either she was sober some of the time, or she could write very well when drunk.

Even after Cora turned seventy-five, she felt neither old nor frail. She continued driving herself to fundraisers and meetings at Kindness House. Joseph's continued health seemed unsurprising, as aside from that terrible slip on the ice, he rarely suffered so much as a cold. But Cora had never thought of herself as a particularly hearty person, and when she started to notice the number of people listed in the local obituaries with birth dates more recent than her own, she was aware of the possibility that she might be nearing her own end. But year after year, she didn't get sick, and her appetite stayed strong, and though she was terrified of falling and breaking her hip, as that seemed to be what happened to every old woman she knew, it didn't happen to her. Despite her worries and resignation, she kept getting out of bed every morning, feeling, more or less, herself.

Her physician, who looked like he might have been born around the time she'd turned fifty, asked if she had longevity in her bloodlines. "Did your mother or father live a long time? You're still in very good health."

"I don't know," Cora said. "I was adopted."

"Hmm." He was writing in her chart. "Well, whoever they were, they gave you good genes. You're ticking like a watch."

She was seventy-nine when Senator Frank Hodge introduced a bill in the Kansas Senate that would require the Health Department to furnish information on contraception upon request to any Kansas resident. Hodge wasn't a particular favorite of Cora's, as he'd made it clear he was more interested in trimming the welfare rolls of dependent children than safeguarding the health and dignity of women, but whatever his motivation, she thought the bill was a good one, and she threw in her support, financial and otherwise. She offered to testify on the extent of grief she'd witnessed at Kindness House and the rampant and damaging use of Lysol as a prophylactic. However, her testimony was never sought. She thought at first that she perhaps wasn't the best face for the campaign, as a white-haired widow of means. As it turned out, during the hearings, no women testified at all.

She did what she could. She met with representatives who'd known Alan, and she wrote letters, and she asked old friends to do the same. Many flatly refused, including women who were younger than she was. It was 1965, and birth control was still a radical cause. A spokesman for the Catholic Bishop of Kansas told the papers that the bill was essentially "state-financed adultery, state-financed promiscuity, and state-financed venereal disease." Raymond warned Cora that she might be wasting her efforts, as the bill was unlikely to pass. The *Wichita Eagle* threw in its support, but the *Advance Register* threatened to print the name of every senator who voted for it, and warned that careers would be ruined. In the end, the bill did pass, though without the governor's signature, and only after the supporters agreed to change the wording of the bill to only include married citizens. The unmarried of Kansas would have to wait another year before a federal law mandated that health departments provide information on birth control to every adult, married or not.

Raymond bought her a cake — Cora's favorite, white with lemon icing — delivering it with both his congratulations and his apologies: he said he hadn't meant to be discouraging — he really thought the bill wouldn't pass. Greta and her husband came over to celebrate. Joseph got out some champagne, and Cora found herself the subject of a toast. She was embarrassed, and a little tired, but she did her best to soak up the goodwill. "How nice to have cake and a party without having to get any older," she managed, thinking how good it was to see the faces of people she loved around her, smiling at her little joke.

Later that night, when they were standing by the sink and brushing their teeth, just the two of them in the house, Joseph nudged her arm. "You can take a rest now," he said. "You can retire."

She rolled her eyes. "You're one to talk," she mumbled, leaning over to spit. Joseph had retired from Boeing years ago, but he spent much of his time going around and fixing people's cars. People were always coming by or leaving notes, saying they'd heard he could help. "I'm like you," she said. "I like to stay busy."

He cocked his head, watching her in the mirror. "It's more than that. You do not do needlepoint."

She was quiet. She thought of the cemetery in McPherson, how light the rain had been the last time she drove out to pull weeds and put out flowers for the Kaufmanns. The farm was gone now, the property divided up into small tracts of land for little houses with built-in garages. The Kaufmann children must have sold.

"You're right." She put her toothbrush back in the holder. "I suppose I want to do some good in the world."

"You have." He looked at her in the mirror, unblinking, until she understood.

Maybe he knew. Maybe he didn't. But he gave her that before he died. A month later, he was out in front of the house, looking at the engine of someone's car, when a blood vessel burst in his brain. It was the middle of the day on their quiet street, and no one saw him fall. Cora was inside, taking a nap. The little neighbor boy, maybe seven years old, saw him on the pavement, already blue, and ran home crying to his young mother, who was crying herself by the time she knocked on the front door, waking Cora from her dreams.

At this funeral, too, people were kind to her. It was a hard thing to lose a brother, they said, even a brother she didn't grow up with, whom she'd only met as an adult. Family was family, and they were sorry for her loss. But how amazing they had found each other in the first place, people said, and Cora knew they were trying to say something good because she looked the way she felt — scared, aching. But yes, she said, it was amazing that they'd found each other. Such wonderful luck, even so late in life, and she was grateful for the years they'd had. Greta held her hand, and Howard and Earle each stood up to say good things about their uncle.

But she held on to Raymond the longest, reaching over his walker, her face pressed into his hunched shoulder, his dark lapel smooth against her cheek. She closed her eyes like a child hiding in plain sight, just the two of them knowing and known.

Later, when Cora became something of a marvel to people, the eighty-five- and then ninety-year-old woman with the sharp mind and the steady gait who still got up in the morning and made her own coffee, who still read the paper every day, she would try to explain that there was a downside to all her genetic good fortune, her indefatigable health. The problem, she sometimes explained, was that she outlived so many people she loved. At ninety-three, she was healthy enough to fly with Greta down to Houston for Howard's funeral, to reach out with steady hands and touch his grand-child's — her great-grandchild's — soft cheek. Howard died at seventy-six, an old man with a fortunate life. From the eulogy, it was clear the minister saw his death as sad, but hardly tragic. And yet it still seemed so wrong, so backward, for Cora to live to see her funny and lively son's casket, to stand beside Earle, her remaining, gray-haired son — scared that she would outlive him, too.

Oh, but there were great rewards for inhabiting the world for so long. She was aware of that, too. She could remember riding in the Kaufmanns' wagon, a black horse trotting in front, yet she'd seen the topsides of clouds from the window of an airplane. No generation before hers had seen the earth from so far above. She'd lived for years without indoor plumbing, without feeling too deprived, and some ninety years later, she let Greta help her into a Jacuzzi tub at a hotel in Houston. She got to vote for Della's grandson when he ran for the state senate. And though she would outlive Raymond, and reel from that loss as well, he was still alive in 1970, and the two of them were watching the news together when the first gay pride marches in New York and Los Angeles were reported; after the news cut to a commercial, the two of them stared at each other in disbelief, their TV dinners going cold.

And she got to be with those she loved for so long. Cora remembered Greta as a little girl hiding under a table, and she remembered her as a young mother, and now Greta herself had two grandchildren. Little Donna, whom Earle had once bounced on his knee, turned into the adolescent who told her parents and her great-aunt Cora to quit calling people "colored," and who once stood up in church to ask, with a trembling voice, a room full of white Presbyterians to support the sit-in at Dockum Drugs. Greta's youngest, Alan, who grew up to be as handsome as his namesake, became a science teacher in Derby with two boys of his own.

And to Cora's surprise, one day in 1982, Howard's son Walt really did come to Wichita to talk to Cora about the summer she spent in New York as a chaperone to Louise Brooks. By then, Walt was in his fifties, a portly college professor of film studies, and Cora was living in the retirement home not far from Greta's new house. Walt brought with him a little box he called a VCR, and he plugged it into the television in Cora's room, explaining he'd brought along a few Louise Brooks movies — he had them right in his bag. They could watch one if she was feeling up to it. Yes, he said, right on her television. And if she got tired, he could just push a button, the film would stop, and she could resume it again whenever she liked. Yes, he agreed, yes. It really was a marvelous little machine.

He wanted to talk with her about Louise. He was writing a book about Hollywood's Golden Age, he said, and anything she could remember about Louise Brooks, any particular story, would help. Cora told him what she could, avoiding what she'd promised not to tell anyone. She said nothing of Mr. Flowers, and she said nothing of how she'd found Louise in 1942, drunk and broke and raging at her mother in her attic room. Cora wouldn't betray her, even now. But as it turned out, Walt already knew about Mr. Flowers and Edward Vincent and about Louise's miserable return home during the war. He knew everything. He'd read her memoir, he said.

He was apologetic for Cora's confusion. Sorry, he said. Did she not know Louise Brooks had just published a book? Yes, he said. A book. Just last year. *Lulu in Hollywood.* It got quite a bit of press, all good. Yes, he said, she was still alive. She was seventy-six, living in Rochester. He heard she'd stopped drinking, but still, her health wasn't good. Emphysema. But her book was sterling. It wasn't just a memoir, but a collection of essays, some about her own life, some about the film industry and the famous people she'd known. She'd gotten rave reviews from *Esquire* and the *New York Times.* Everyone was so impressed with the writing, the sharp observations and wit.

"I'll get you a copy," he told Cora. "You would enjoy it, I'm sure."

Cora thanked him. She couldn't read anymore, but Greta read to her when she came to visit, pausing like Walt's amazing little VCR every time Cora drifted off. And really, she was just so happy to know that this book existed, that Louise, hardly down for the count, had bloomed again. And at seventy-six! Perhaps she'd needed that long to discover that she was more than youth and beauty, more than her mother's ambitions, more than circumstance. Her beloved Schopenhauer was perhaps right: old age did drop the masks.

Greta was never able to read Louise's book

to her. Not long after her grandson's visit, Cora suffered a stroke, and she spent her last days in bed, moving in and out of memory, the past and the present as one. She couldn't see anything but gray and shadows, but she knew that Greta and Earle were there with her, her children, one on each side.

"Aunt Cora?" Greta said. "Can you hear me? Cora?"

She couldn't talk, couldn't form the words, but she could hear — she could hear her name. And the low rumbling of a train. She was not in her room, but at a hospital, lying on a bed with scratchy sheets, and there were beeps and unfamiliar voices. And more and more, she heard the train. There were tracks near the hospital, perhaps, and every time a train rumbled by, she could feel a slight vibration, not enough to rattle the window, but just enough for her to recall the feeling of being on board, rocked gently but relentlessly forward.

"Yes," she said. "I hear."

An unfamiliar woman's voice, friendly. "What's your name?" A hand on her shoulder. "Can you tell me your name?"

She knew it. She was Cora, of course. She was every Cora she'd ever been: Cora X, Cora Kaufmann, Cora Carlisle. She was an

563

orphan on a roof, a lucky girl on a train, a dearly loved daughter by chance. She was a blushing bride of seventeen, a sad and stoic wife, a loving mother, an embittered chaperone, and a daughter pushed away. She was a lover and a lewd cohabitator, a liar and a cherished friend, an aunt and a kindly grandmother, a champion of the fallen, and a late-in-coming fighter for reason over fear. Even in those final hours, quiet and rocking, arriving and departing, she knew who she was.

ACKNOWLEDGMENTS

I'm indebted to the people who helped me do research for this book. Al Jenkins was kind enough to answer my questions about cars in 1922. Tracy Floreani helped me with the Italian spoken by the woman in the drugstore. Eric Cale and Jami Frazier Tracy of the Wichita-Sedgwick County Historical Museum helped me imagine the interior of Wichita's Union Station. Kathryn Olden, a longtime resident of Wichita and wonderful conversationalist, met with me to talk about her memories. Alice Lieberman put me in touch with Ann Kuckelman Cobb, who answered questions about the hazards of childbirth in the early 1900's.

Here are some of the books and documents I read while writing this book:

Lulu in Hollywood by Louise Brooks
Louise Brooks: A Biography by Barry Paris
Louise Brooks: Lulu Forever by Peter Cowie

Wichita: The Magic City by Craig Miner
The Damned and the Beautiful: American Youth in the 1920's by Paula S. Fass
Only Yesterday: An Informal History of the 1920's by Frederick Lewis Allen
1920's Fashions from B. Altman & Company (Dover Publications)
The Historical Atlas of New York City: A Visual Celebration of 400 Years of New York City's History by Eric Homberger
We Rode the Orphan Trains by Andrea Warren
Tears on Paper: The History and Life Stories of the Orphan Train Riders compiled by Patricia J. Young and Frances E. Marks
Orphan Trains: The Story of Charles Loring Brace and the Children He Saved and Failed by Stephen O'Connor
You Must Remember This: An Oral History of Manhattan from the 1890's to WWII by Jeff Kisseloff
Lost Broadway Theatres by Nicholas van Hoogstraten; with additional photography by Jock Pottle and Maggie Hopp
Denishawn: The Enduring Influence by Jane Sherman
Etiquette in Society, in Business, in Politics, and at Home by Emily Post, 1922
"Unspeakable Jazz Must Go!" by John R. McMahon, *The Ladies' Home Journal,*

December 1921

New York Times articles from July 1922

Darkness and Daylight; or Lights and Shadows of New York Life, a Pictorial Record of Personal Experiences in the Great Metropolis by Helen Campbell

"The War Department: Keeper of Our Nation's Enemy Aliens During World War I" by Mitchell Yockelson

The Irish in Haverhill Massachusetts by Patricia Trainor O'Malley

Erin's Daughters in America: Irish Immigrant Women in the 19th Century by Haisa R. Diner

The History of Family Planning Delivery Systems in Wichita, Kansas 1965–1975 by Jane Weilert

Plains Woman: The Diary of Martha Farnsworth, 1882–1922, edited by Marlene Springer and Haskell Springer

The Tihen Notes by Dr. Edward N. Tihen, Wichita State University Libraries' Department of Special Collections

Yesterday's Stories: Popular Women's Novels of the Twenties and Thirties by Patricia Raub

The Daily Routine of a Kansas Farm Wife in the Nineteenth Century by Georgie L. Steifer

The Purity Myth by Jessica Valenti

I will be forever grateful for the help I received from my writing group: Lucia Orth, Mary Wharff, Judy Bauer, and Mary O'Connell. Each read drafts and gave feedback that was both sharp and encouraging. I would also like to thank my wonderful editor at Riverhead, Sarah McGrath, for her insight and careful reading, as well as my agent, Jennifer Rudolph Walsh, for her continued encouragement and discernment. I'm very lucky to work with these talented women.

I would like to thank the College of Liberal Arts and Sciences at the University of Kansas for giving me a semester off of teaching to focus on this project.

On the home front, several good friends stepped in to entertain Viv on days when I felt particularly frantic to finish a chapter. Anna Neill, Margaret Marco, Jason Slote, Barb Willis, Jill Cannon, Michelle Ward, Ken Jansen, and Gretchen Goodman-Jansen always returned Viv healthy and happy. Ben Eggleston, despite his own busy schedule, hung out with Viv *and* read drafts and always seemed happy to do so. Viv and I continue to benefit from his patience, his wit, and his thoughtfulness.

ABOUT THE AUTHOR

Laura Moriarty earned a degree in social work before returning for her M.A. in Creative Writing at the University of Kansas. She was the recipient of the George Bennett Fellowship for Creative Writing at Phillips Exeter Academy in New Hampshire, and is now a professor of Creative Writing at the University of Kansas. Her previous novels are *The Center of Everything, The Rest of Her Life,* and *While I'm Falling.* She lives in Lawrence, Kansas, and is at work on her next novel.

CPSIA information can be obtained
at www.ICGtesting.com
Printed in the USA
FFOW020700010713
1326FF